A THOUSAND BENJAMINS

A novel by Michael Kun

A THOUSAND BENJAMINS

A novel by Michael Kun

Lawson

Lawson Library

A division of MacAdam/Cage Publishing

155 Sansome Street, Suite 550

San Francisco, CA 94104

Library of Congress Cataloging-in-Publication Data

Kun, Michael.
  A thousand Benjamins : a novel / by Michael Kun.
    p. cm.
  ISBN-13: 978-1-59692-103-0 (trade pbk. : alk. paper)
  ISBN-10: 1-59692-103-X (trade pbk. : alk. paper)
  I. Title.
PS3561.U446T48 2007
813'.54—dc22

                                                            2006029649

Manufactured in the United States of America.
10 9 8 7 6 5 4 3 2 1

Book and jacket design by Dorothy Carico Smith.

Hardcover edition published by The Atlantic Monthly Press, 1990.

Publisher's Note: This is a work of fiction. Names, characters, places, and incidents either are the product of the author's imagination or are used fictitiously. Any resemblance to actual events, locales, or persons, living or dead, is entirely coincidental.

Dedicated to the Class of 1988 of the University of Virginia School of Law

Yes, the entire class

PREFACE

I'M SORRY, but I don't remember writing this book.

I'm not saying that I *didn't* write it. I'm sure that I did. I just don't *remember* writing it, that's all.

I wrote *A Thousand Benjamins* during my third year of law school, between (and, occasionally, during) classes. I don't remember those classes, either. According to the registrar of the University of Virginia School of Law, I passed all of those classes, which explains the diploma on my wall. I'm looking at it right now. It is impressively large and austere, which ought to scare the bejesus out of any lawyer who dares to walk into my office.

I was a very young man when I wrote this book (or when I must have written it because, again, I don't remember doing so). I was twenty-four years old, which is far too young for anyone to be allowed to put anything into print, at least not anything with a hard cover and a fairly hefty price tag. After some delay and a change of publishing houses, the book was published when I was twenty-seven. When I meet twenty-seven-year-olds now, my first thought is, "I wasn't that naïve and full of myself when I was twenty-seven, was I?" I'm sure I was.

The book had an excellent editor (hello, Anne, wherever you may be now), and, as you may know, the book received some very generous reviews, some of which I'm certain my publisher has slapped on the back of this edition. You can take a moment to look now, if you would like. The book sales were moderate—not a bestseller, but enough to make everyone involved pleased.

A bizarre series of events involving the film rights ensued. Someone was shopping a movie script based on the book to Hollywood studios. In fact, I had never heard of the woman. And while I make every effort to be a generous man and am well known for leaving my extra pennies in the "extra penny" tray at the convenience store, I assure you that I had not given the film rights to this book to a complete stranger.

In any event, time passed. Imagine the pages of a calendar flying as they used to do in old movies. Imagine me getting older, heavier, less hirsute. Unbeknownst to me, the book had gathered a small following. And, as I would learn from a concerned friend, customers on amazon.com were speculating that I had died. I had not. I was merely practicing law. I will leave it to you to fill in an appropriate punchline here.

When I finally published my second novel, *The Locklear Letters*, thirteen years later in 2003, my editor and I discussed re-releasing this book. As you no doubt concluded, we decided to do so.

My editor did not want me to edit the book at all. His reasoning, if I recall, was that the book was complete long ago, and nothing good could come of changing it now. Because my editor is frequently wrong, and terribly so, I insisted on editing it to try to make it a better book.

Reading it for the first time in nearly fifteen years, I did not recognize a single sentence other than the one that provides the book with its title. Ultimately, I could not get myself to revise the book, other than to make a few minor changes here or there to tidy up matters that appeared glaring. The reason I did not revise the book has nothing to do with its quality: of course it could be improved upon, perhaps substantially so. No, the problem is that the book was written by someone far more interesting than I am now. The book he wrote was complete long ago, and nothing good can come of changing it now. So, on that subject, my editor is correct.

Michael Kun
December 2006

A THOUSAND BENJAMINS

CHAPTER 1
THE PINKISH CREEK

THE COWS AREN'T COWS, they're more like lambs the way they follow the sweeps of her arms, unafraid and bemused.

"Come here. Go there. Come with us to St. Louis," she orders. The mother sheep. The cowherd. "No, wait," she says. "I think we're already past St. Louis."

They're well past St. Louis, almost two hundred miles west now. St. Louis is where they had lunch yesterday.

"Ben," she calls. "Sweetheart, are we past St. Louis?"

"Mm hmm," Benjamin says, and he nods. "Remember, that's where we had frozen custard."

"That's right," she says. "Thanks." She turns back to the cows. "We're past St. Louis, ladies," she tells them, "although if you're ever passing through yourselves, I have a frozen custard stand I'd like to recommend."

Kim is gentle, thin at the waist and hips, but solid still, orchestrating the movements of a field full of cows with a confidence that belies her city upbringing. She was born and reared in Baltimore. Benjamin was born there, too, a full eighteen years before her. Bluefield is where he grew up, though, fifty miles out and farther from the water.

A truck passes by, and it startles Kim. She shakes. She's standing on the bottom rail of the fence, leaning onto it, her body a bow as she rummages through her shoulder bag until she finds a candy bar among her tissues and makeup.

"Come here, C18," she says, calling the closest by the heavy yellow tag clipped to its ear, "and have some chocolate."

Soon the bar is gone, and Kim is laughing. She puts the wrapper in her shoulder bag, and she rubs C18's head and picks dirt from its marbled hide in the same way she pulls lint from her skirts, pinching it, then rubbing her thumb and index finger together to drop the tiny specks to the ground.

"Do we have anything else for her?" Kim calls.

Benjamin is sitting on the hood of his car, a red Mustang parked in the gravel fifteen feet off. He's watching her in a detached sort of way. At home, she looks less at home. Now he's rediscovered her, this Kim perched on the rail, some country girl in a red-and-white Coca-Cola T-shirt and khaki shorts.

In western Maryland, this same Kim had thrown a baseball with him in a field beside the highway, slinging the ball faster and more accurately than he did, making his mitt pop like a drum, keeping time like a slow heartbeat. "Look," she beamed. "I'm Frank Robinson. I'm Johnny Bench. I'm Tom Seaver."

This Kim, in Ohio, waved at truck drivers and, later, pointing first to her flat stomach and then thumping Benjamin's chest, told the cashier at a fast-food restaurant, "I'm carrying his baby. At least I think it's his. I mean, how can a girl be *certain* these days?" Benjamin blushed and shook his head, *no, no, no*. She wasn't carrying his baby.

This Kim. The new Kim isn't new at all. The new Kim is the old Kim, really, and Benjamin understands that. This is the Kim who'd worked at Yumi's restaurant, waiting tables in a black kimono, her hair pulled back in a short ponytail, her face painted. This is the Kim who baked him chocolate-chip cookies and took pictures of him while he slept, the comforter twisted around him like a toga. This is the Kim who surprises him. She's funny, but he never expects her to be. This Kim. This is the Kim he missed. Or this is the Kim he remembers. Missing and remembering, Benjamin's always had a problem telling the difference between the two. Sometime he missed Mary Jude, sometimes he remembers her, and sometimes he can't tell what it is he's doing. He just knows that he's in Baltimore, with Kim, and Mary Jude is in New York with her new husband.

From where he sits, Benjamin can see Kim and the cows, numbered as high as L22 and separated into groups of threes and fours like guests at a cocktail party. A small brown farmhouse squats between waves of hills as if hiding. A breeze hits him, and he feels omniscient and young.

Benjamin hops off the car and climbs into the passenger seat. He holds the cooler on his lap and pushes his way through what's left of lunch: a spoonful or two of potato salad in an orange plastic bowl, half a container of blueberry yogurt—Kim's—his second hero sandwich, which he hadn't the appetite to start, a package of Fig Newtons, two diet sodas and a banana. He's still worried about Kim. She won't take her shirt off, but he's happy nonetheless. He isn't sure he wants her to remove her shirt. He isn't sure how he'd react. He's resolved to think less about the scar today, to put it out of his mind.

"Benjamin?"

Benjamin closes the lid of the cooler and walks to the fence. "How do you think she feels about yogurt?" he asks, and he hands Kim the container and a white plastic spoon from the glove compartment, hesitating before putting a hand on her waist to help her keep her balance.

"I haven't met a woman yet who doesn't like yogurt. It's something peculiar to our gender," she says, "like Fig Newtons are to yours." Kim pulls the cap off and stirs the yogurt with the spoon, bringing pieces of blueberry to the top. "Don't look at me that way. I wasn't going to cheat you out of the blueberries."

Her voice floats.

And Benjamin grins absently. It's a good sign, Kim joking. He watches as she cups C18's chin in one hand and carries the spoon to its mouth as if she were feeding a baby. The cow won't open her mouth this time. Kim tries to encourage it by cooing and whistling. Nothing. Finally she sets the open container on top of one of the posts and climbs down. She wipes her palms on her shorts as she walks to the car.

"She'll have it when she's hungry," she says. Then she surprises Benjamin. She throws her arms around his waist and kisses his neck. Her bag slips and catches in the crook of her arm. She jerks it back to her shoulder.

"You're getting a rash." She frowns, running a hand over his jaw with its two days' growth of beard. "Poor Benjamin, all sad and cracking up. Maybe you should shave. Shave the stupid thing right off."

Benjamin nods. "Maybe so." He follows her to the car, a patch of his skin still cool from her lips. The air strikes him differently here. It preserves the kiss, while in Baltimore her kisses evaporate quickly.

Benjamin closes the door for her, then walks around to the driver's side, drumming his fingers on the hood, then the vinyl roof.

The gas gauge in the car is broken. It has been for years—it always says full. Benjamin and Kim have been stopping every two hundred miles for gas. The air-conditioning is broken, too, and they've been driving with their windows half-opened to catch the breeze. "It's a million degrees in here," Kim had said somewhere in Ohio, "Celsius, not Fahrenheit," and all Benjamin could do was shrug.

Now, he rolls his window down to the bottom before he starts the car and says, "Want to open yours?" He makes a fist in the air and turns his wrist in small circles, pantomiming the motion.

"It is open." The window on her side is halfway down.

"I mean all the way."

She looks at him suspiciously. "Why?"

"Well," he says, "because one of us smells like a farm right now. I won't say which one."

Kim pokes his shoulder with a finger then rolls down the window. Several miles along, she brings her hands to her nose, as she would to catch a sneeze, and says, "Oh, God, do you think it'll come off?"

"Maybe with gasoline." He cracks a smile to let Kim know he's kidding. "No, it'll come off," he reassures her. "Everything washes off."

His mind wanders as he drives. He thinks about goodness. Everything good he can think of.

Steak sandwiches.

He thinks of the smell of his mother's bureau, all perfumes and powders.

The Orioles.

His wedding day, with Mary Jude in ivory satin, pearls and bubble beads on the bodice.

The Charles Theatre.

The elephant ride at the fair, he and Phinney sitting on their father's knees.

Fig Newtons.

Trips to Ocean City.

Chief Thunderthud on "Howdy Doody," calling out, "Kowabunga, Buffalo Bob!"

Kim, in a T-shirt, pulling on her kimono before going to the restaurant.

Phinney reading books in the tree behind the garage.

Truman Capote, especially *Breakfast at Tiffany's*.

The last of these occurs to Benjamin as he looks at Kim. She's reading his paperback copy of the book as he drives, her knees pulled up to her chest, her head tipped toward Benjamin and away from the open window. She puts two fingers to her forehead at one point, and Benjamin thinks she must have reached Holly Golightly's description of her relationship with Sally Tomato.

It's the first book Benjamin's seen her read since his birthday. She had been reading his copy of *Franny and Zooey* then and, as far as he knew, had never finished it. She just left her bookmark in there and the book on top of the nightstand in the bedroom, each time he turned off the lamp a reminder of how much she wasn't in the room.

It was his birthday, and it was as wide as his thumbnail. It was smooth like plastic and pinkish-gray, a scar running from the notch of her throat, between her breasts like a fat creek, coming to a pointed halt just above her ribs, turning back into perfect flesh there, and Benjamin ran his fingers along it, and pressed it and forgot it was a part of her until she woke.

"Jesus Christ!" she shouted, finding her T-shirt rolled to her armpits and Benjamin applying pressure to the crooked line on her chest. She tried to speak. At first, she couldn't. Then speech came like a flood, the words pouring into the room and over him. "I told you not to do that. I mean, I *asked* you not to do that. How many times did I *ask*?"

Benjamin didn't try to count them. There had been too many to count. As she hadn't stopped talking, he didn't think really she wanted an answer. In nine months he'd never seen her with her shirt off, not once, though he'd tugged at her shirts like a baby and pouted, curling a lip—she always wore those T-shirts of hers—but now he had, and Kim was out of bed quickly, her shirt back down, the shirt that read THE PEP BOYS across the front, three men with oversized heads dancing among the letters.

Standing beside the bed, the light from the liquor store sign across the street slipping through the curtains as it always did, Kim looked small and pale, her skin the color of cooked fish. She started toward Benjamin, to strike him. *On his birthday,* his forty-first one. Then she fell back on her heels, her forearms tight, her face, too, and when she cursed him something small fell out of her mouth. A piece of food, a drop of saliva, Benjamin didn't know, but it fell to the sheet, and he studied it as it lay there, a piece of her on the bed, the rest of her standing barelegged on the carpet, clutching a pillow to her chest, hollering like a bad neighbor and just as indecipherable.

The words came and went.

"When we first started dating, I said, 'Benjamin, there's something I have to ask you,' and you were such…you don't know what it's like…trying out for the softball team…what else is…a hole the size of a marble…"

He didn't want to look at her, and he was barely listening. He watched the piece on the sheet and ignored the rest, feeling neither good nor bad, but puzzled. His birthday had revealed a fat, pinkish creek. A creek that started and stopped. A creek that ran nowhere.

"Bathing suits and light," Kim was saying now. "What could've happened…a doctor from Towson said it was the only way. Dr. Plessy…or maybe…the heart is something…why is it that for men it's a sign of strength, but for women it's…heaven…like having a window inside me big enough for people to pass through…a sailor fell from his lookout, and he was dead when he landed…my father didn't…they gave it to me, and the doctors wouldn't give me…like it's a movie or something…whatever happens, there's always a chance…circulation…Yumi was right about men…a happy child isn't always…Kevin Purcell never came to see me, not…if you were a man…beauty isn't…Benjamin…"

It went on and on, Kim's shouting, until she finally spun and went into the living room. She slept there on the couch, chair cushions for pillows, for the three weeks before the trip, touching nothing of his laundry, including the bed linen. She moved her books into the living room, too, and stood them on end on a card table, she hung her blouses and dresses in the coat closet and folded the rest of her clothing in stacks about the room, beside the recliner and the couch and beneath the tables, and she kept a separate set of silverware and dishes in the bathroom in the hallway, in the medicine chest. He was alone in that bed, again.

She couldn't go anywhere. Benjamin knew that. She couldn't move back in with her parents in Druid Hill. Moving back would be failure for her. Her parents had stayed in their bedroom, their door closed, while Benjamin and Kim carried boxes from her bedroom out to Benjamin's car. They'd rarely spoken with her since. Her mother wrote letters once a week, as if Kim had moved across the country and not just downtown.

Kim couldn't move in with her sister Christie in Charles Village. Benjamin had been there. There wasn't enough room. She couldn't get an apartment of her own, either. She didn't work, not since she left Yumi's, not since Yumi had to let her and two other waitresses go for the summer, when business was slow. As it stood, Kim was keeping track of her groceries so she could pay Benjamin back. "I'm a modern woman," she'd told him, "out on my own." She'd taken root in his home.

As for Benjamin, for three weeks he had been thinking of the scar that looked like a creek. He thought of it at the office, looking out the window onto St. Paul Street, with his pen in his mouth and shipping orders piled as high on his desk as the stacks of Kim's T-shirts beside the recliner. He thought of it when he talked to Babisch. He thought of it while he dressed and undressed, quiet in order not to wake Kim out in the living room, quiet because what would he say if she were up when he had to pass through the room? He thought of it when she went out for a run, when he watched the clock, afraid that she might collapse in the street but knowing she was too strong for that, that she was stronger than he was. He thought of it while he ate breakfast at Dunkin' Donuts and dinner at P.J.'s Pub; the same meals every day. Even when he spoke of something else, he was thinking of the creek. It didn't go anywhere. He was thinking of himself, bobbing in it, hopeless.

Benjamin was in bed, watching the Channel 2 news, when his brother called. Kim answered the phone, and Benjamin could hear the hum of her voice as she told Phinney a story, laughter but no words, then she knocked on the bedroom door. When he opened it, he expected her to be there, but she'd left the receiver face up on the carpet and gone back to the couch. He could see her turning beneath her covers.

"Come out to Nebraska for a couple of days," Phinney said. Benjamin was happy to hear his voice. "A vacation, Ben. I have a house—"

"You have a *house*?"

"Just for the summer. I'm watching someone's house—my boss's house. So, come out. And bring Kim." Always he sounded as if he were winking when he mentioned her, pleased at Benjamin's good fortune in sharing the apartment with such a young woman. Benjamin wanted to tell him that he didn't know the whole story. He didn't know the half of it, but Kim might have heard him if he'd said that.

"God, Phinney," he said. "I need to talk to you." He thought of Phinney's hands on his head when they were boys.

"Can you talk about it now?"

"No," Benjamin said, "it'll keep," and he agreed to the trip. Nebraska was somewhere. It was somewhere to go, and he taped a note to the refrigerator the next morning, asking Kim to go with him.

Not until the afternoon he was to leave, as he was walking home from work, did Benjamin learn that Kim would drive with him to Phinney's. For three days she'd acted as if he hadn't left the note, still sleeping in the living room, not turning on the lights, as quiet as a housekeeper, and Benjamin had packed only for himself.

He turned the corner, the top button of his shirt undone and his tie loose about his neck, the *Sun* folded under his arm. He didn't recognize her on the stoop. She was sitting in front of the apartment building, her knees together, bony and browned, wearing a flowered kerchief in her hair, a green T-shirt and a blue-jean skirt. There were suitcases at her sides and a cherry popsicle in one hand. She clutched her shoulder bag to her with the other. Benjamin thought she was someone's niece or cousin or sister come to visit. As he started up the steps and her eyes, cast downward, glanced up to his own, he realized it was Kim. He realized he hadn't looked into her eyes for weeks.

"Oh, God," Benjamin said. He put his hand over his heart, and the *Sun* fell to the sidewalk. He squatted to retrieve it. "I didn't know that was you." He stood again.

"Well, it is," Kim said. She was still seated. "It's me, the woman who sleeps on your couch." Her lips were a brilliant red from the popsicle.

"So, you're coming?"

"Mm hmm. If it's okay." She studied Benjamin's face. Awkwardly, he climbed two of the steps, then stood there.

"It's great," he said. "It's great. I wouldn't have asked you to come if it wasn't okay. But you know that I wouldn't have asked if it wasn't okay."

"Really?" Kim stretched her legs out and moved the shoulder bag to her lap. Her T-shirt said BEN & JERRY'S ICE CREAM. There was a cartoon cow on the front. He hadn't seen it before. It must be a new one, he thought, from the past three weeks.

"Really."

"Well, I called Phinney to let him know that I was coming, too."

"You didn't have to do that. I told him I was going to ask you to come along."

"I just wanted him to know. You know, make sure he had room and everything." She paused. "Look, if you don't want me to go, then I won't but I sort of thought it would be a good idea if we went together. But if you don't want me to go, don't think I won't understand, because I will. I'll understand."

The look in her eyes, thought Benjamin. Look at what I've done to them. He looked elsewhere rather than think of it. He looked at her chest.

"I'll just run up and get my suitcase," he said, "and we can go," but Kim grabbed the cuff of his pants leg as he was about to pass.

"Ben?"

"Yes?"

"I've got it. Your suitcase, I've got it." His suitcase was beside her, their baseball mitts folded on top. "It was on your bed, and I just closed it up and brought it down with my stuff."

"Good." Benjamin hesitated, trying to remember if he'd packed every-thing. He thought about washing up and changing his clothes. In a moment he was looking at Kim again and forgetting about washing and changing. "Then, well, let me just go get the car. Stay here. I'll be right back."

Benjamin backed down the steps, and they exchanged brief smiles. When he returned with the car, she was standing, surrounded by the suit-cases, the thin legs beneath her skirt seemingly too tiny to support all that her expression held, the weight she carried with her.

Kim handed Benjamin the luggage, and, piece by piece, he arranged it in the trunk. Then he opened the passenger door for her. He started the car toward Charles Street.

It was five minutes before she said, "Benjamin, are we allowed to talk to each other?" and an hour or more on the interstate before he turned his head from the road to look at her. She was looking right back at him, and he knew she'd been watching him since he'd started the engine, since he'd turned the key in the ignition. She'd been watching him since Baltimore.

Occasionally Benjamin turns his eyes from the highway to watch Kim and catches her mouthing the words to a song on the radio. It happened with a Neil Diamond song. It happens every time a love song comes on. She knows the words to all of the love songs, and she turns the dial from station to station to find them.

"I *like this song.*" She defends herself when she sees that he's watching, and, gently, he presses her wrist with his fingertips as if he were taking her pulse.

"Go on," he says, "sing all you want. Sing until the cows come home."

Kim straightens in her seat. "Did you see the way they listened to me back there?" she asks. Her finger marks her place in the book, near the end. The radio is still going strong.

"Sure did."

She laughs a hiccup of a laugh. "Ben, I was watching where they were going, then making it look like I was directing them to go that way. 'Come here. Go way over there. Hey, you—go talk to the pretty brown one over there.' I still felt in control though. Know what I mean? I still felt happy even though they knew where they were going and I didn't."

Benjamin smiles weakly. He's pretty sure he doesn't know what she means. He thinks of her standing before the apartment on Friday afternoon, waiting for his car, the kerchief knotted in her hair, looking lost despite all their luggage.

"Good, I'm glad," he says, and when he says nothing more Kim returns to *Breakfast at Tiffany's*.

Soon she's done. "Fantastic book," she says and drops it to the floor where it lies with her running shoes, the atlas, four soda cans, empty and rattling, and their baseball mitts. She sinks into her seat, tapping her feet against the dashboard, and folds open Friday's *Sun* to the half-finished crossword puzzle.

"I like it that Holly's husband came to find her toward the end," she adds.

"Me, too." Benjamin can't remember the end of the book. He'd forgotten that Holly had a husband. He just remembers that he'd enjoyed the book when he'd read it. He isn't even sure when that was.

"Not that it's realistic or anything."

"I don't know what you mean."

"Not that it's realistic that someone could have a husband and not mention it to anyone for almost a whole book, not even her closest friends," Kim says.

"Well, sometimes things happen. You know, things that you don't want to talk about."

Kim didn't hear him. "Like you and Mary Jane, for instance."

"Mary Jude," Benjamin says. Kim always refers to her as Mary Jane or Mary Jean or Mary Ann, never by her right name. She's only teasing, but it bothers Benjamin nonetheless.

"Right, Mary Jude. I mean, you hardly ever talk about her, but I know she's out there. So if she showed up at the door, it wouldn't be any great surprise."

"It would be for me." And it would. It would be a great surprise.

"I mean, I wouldn't be too thrilled about it, but it wouldn't be a surprise, if you know what I mean."

Benjamin keeps his eyes on the road, intent. "I wouldn't be too thrilled either, if that's any comfort." That's why he says so, to comfort her.

Kim rocks her head from side to side. When she rocks it toward the open window, the wind catches her hair and sweeps it behind her.

"Did I ever tell you about Tug Macy?" Kim says.

"*Tug?*"

"Uh huh. Like the boat. You know," she says, "tugboat."

"Like the boat," Benjamin repeats.

"You know, I would've married Tug Macy," she says, "in a heartbeat."

Again, Benjamin doesn't turn. "Why? Did he ask you?" Sometimes she says things just to sound adequate. She acts as if she has a past, to make up for Mary Jude. She compensates, he thinks.

"No. I'm just saying I would've married him if he had."

"Is that right? You would've married the Tugboat?"

Kim pretends to be lost in thought. "Tug," she says, "not Tugboat. I only said it was like the boat so you'd get the picture. We went to Poly High together. I'm sure I've mentioned him before. As a matter of fact, I think we ran into him at Schaefer's Pub about a month ago. Who knows, maybe it's been longer than that." She writes TUG in the margin of the newspaper, alongside the crossword-puzzle clues, the letters large enough for Benjamin to read when he glances, then surrounds the name with hearts and flowers. Her half-smile is meant to bait him.

"Sandy hair," she continues, flicking her hands about her ears, "brown eyes the size of half-dollars, a huge chest that was as hard as cement, but a teeny waist. I mean, his waist was almost as small as mine, if you can believe it."

"Great," Benjamin answers, "maybe you two could've swapped clothing. 'Hello, Kim? It's me, Tug. I was thinking, if you're not planning to wear your beige jumpsuit to school tomorrow…'"

Kim ignores him. "He asked me to go with him to Hopkins once to watch a lacrosse game, but that was the weekend my mother took me and Christie to Philadelphia. We went shopping for dresses, for Easter, I think. Not that it matters."

Benjamin snaps his fingers and shakes his head sadly. "Darn. One weekend in Philly, and you miss your chance forever to be with the great Tugboat Macy."

She sinks her chin into her chest. "Who knows about forever," she says and runs her pen over the letters of Tug's name. TUG becomes fatter and fatter.

"That's right. Keep your hopes up. He could show up on our doorstep tomorrow, asking to borrow one of your skirts."

Kim slips further in her seat. "Dean Winwood, too."

Three or four seconds later Benjamin says, "What about Dean Winwood?"

"Would've married him, too. Quicker than you can say Ronald Reagan."

"But you'd have nothing to wear," Benjamin says, "not that Tug's got half your wardrobe."

Kim turns to face him and arches her eyebrows. "Guess I'd have to wear nothing, huh?"

Benjamin sees that she doesn't realize what she's said. Kim wearing nothing, and there it is: the scar. Kim with her T-shirt off. The creek.

"I guess so."

He tries to send the vision from his mind, but the more he tries, the more he thinks only of himself, floating in the creek like a log yet headed nowhere certain. "Anyone else I should know about before we stop for dinner?"

"It could take until breakfast."

The first night of the trip Benjamin slept flat on the floor of the motel room and covered himself with the bedspread, letting Kim have the bed to herself. In the night, he heard something jostling about the room, and he woke, though he lay still. Kim stood before the mirror in the near dark wearing only her shorts, and Benjamin could only see the smooth, wing-like blades of her back as she dabbed Maybelline on the scar to dim it. When he realized what she was doing, Benjamin closed his eyes and bobbed, going under and then coming back to the surface in time to take another drink of air, closer and closer to drowning, feeling all of his forty-one years, too old to swim ashore, yet too vibrant to be dragged down. Not moving, he thought of how he'd registered at the front desk, as Mr. and Mrs. B. Sacks, without hesitation. It was the only time he'd signed that way and not meant Mary Jude.

"Well," he says, "could we maybe take a break for dinner then? You could pick up where you left off."

"Fine with me." She puts the newspaper on the floor. "Did I ever tell you about Mark Greerson? He played the guitar, and he had a very sweet voice. You had to hear him sing to believe it. Our mothers were very close. They used to bake together. Now, *they* thought we were going to get married." She toys with her hair as she speaks, twisting it like noodles. "I don't know if I would've married him, but there are plenty of other things I would've done," she says. Then she shouts, "There!"

Benjamin jumps in his seat, as if she'd caught him dozing. "What?"

The only other traffic on the highway is half a mile ahead and moving fast. There's nothing in the rearview mirror but where they've been.

"That's where we're going to eat," and she raps her knuckles against the windshield, gesturing toward the orange roof of a Howard Johnson's. "Then we can play catch over there." She points past the motor lodge to nowhere in particular, the land flat and dry as far as Benjamin can see, and bends to put on her running shoes.

Benjamin pulls the car into the right lane, then onto the exit ramp. He parks in the lot beside the Howard Johnson's. Kim laces her shoes, and Benjamin steps out of the car and stretches his arms above his head, growling.

"Steffan Boone. Soccer player. Six feet tall, maybe. He had very muscular legs, but they all do." Kim gets out and stretches too, reaching to touch her toes, then putting her hands on her waist and twisting sharply. "Peter Glancy. He was a lacrosse player at Gilman High. He was a year older than me. No, make that two years. Anyway, I met him at a party at Debbie Valentine's my sophomore year at Poly. He ended up playing lacrosse at Syracuse," she says. "The university."

She rises and smiles at Benjamin over the roof of the car. "Come to think of it," she adds, "you're the only guy I've ever been with who wasn't, you know, big."

They walk toward the restaurant. Benjamin, his fingers braided in hers, feels heavy and weak. He feels weighed down, and his reflection in the restaurant door, he thinks, doesn't look much like him. Awkward in the blue jeans Kim had bought for his birthday—501s, she called them, and they had *buttons*, no zipper—he looks more and more like one of those men who dye their hair too black and wear warm-up suits in an effort to look younger; she, a tomboy still, but on the brink of being too old to work that sort of charm. She's twenty-three.

There's nowhere to go, he thinks, without doing so ridiculously.

And yet, a good man would stay with her and go nowhere. He holds the door open, and Kim slips past, clipping his shoulder with her own. Leaving her would be like running from a car wreck with someone still trapped inside.

Kim slides into one of the booths near the counter, and Benjamin heads toward the men's room.

"I'll be right back," he says. "Order spaghetti for me if our waitress comes."

He stops suddenly at the door, turns on his heels, and calls to Kim, "Are you going to wash your hands, or what?"

"What?" Kim mouths, and Benjamin holds both his hands up to his nose. Embarrassed, she nods. "Oh, yeah." She rises from the table.

Benjamin turns the faucet of the sink on full. The noise wooshwoosh-woosh fills the room, and he looks in the mirror. His hair seems to be getting light on the side, and his eyes look like those of an alligator, a thousand years old.

Benjamin pulls his medication from his left pants pocket and flips off the lid of the vial. He'd had the prescription refilled before the trip, and the pills nearly reach the rim of the vial, a hundred of them. He tips the vial slightly until a single pill drops onto his palm, then places it on his tongue and returns the vial to his pocket. The pill tastes like strawberry jam.

Benjamin flicks off the lights in the men's room. He enters one of the stalls and closes the latch, then leans against the partition, slumping. It's as

dark as being underwater, and he feels himself go under, sinking. Please, God, don't let me cry, he thinks. Please don't let me cry, and he doesn't. The taste of marmalade fills his mouth like air.

Kim is back at the table when he returns, and she holds her hands up for inspection.

"Want to smell?" she says. "No more farm."

Benjamin shakes his head. Soon the waitress brings his spaghetti and Kim's cheeseburger. He feigns interest in Kim's conversation, hoping he can keep his food down.

After Kim finishes a sundae, she leads Benjamin to the car to get their mitts, then down the road to a schoolyard. The mother sheep. The cowherd. She leads him to a baseball diamond, the grass dried and brown like wood bark.

They stand twenty yards apart and throw the ball back and forth, softly at first.

"Look," she calls, "I'm Brooks Robinson," and Benjamin lofts the ball high, bending. It lands in her mitt without a sound. "Ben? Can you call Phinney and tell him we'll be late, that we hit some traffic or something and won't be there until tomorrow?"

"We could make it tonight," he says. That's what he wants to do. Phinney's the only one who can help. "We're not even a hundred fifty miles away."

"I know," she says. "Please?"

Benjamin's eyelids fall, and he sniffs and rolls the ball in his palm. "Sure," he answers, "we don't have to go anywhere tonight. We can get a room right here."

When he opens his eyes again and throws the ball back, he notices how worn Kim's T-shirt is. He can barely make out the red script COCA-COLA across her chest. It looks more like CO A-COL, and Benjamin remembers seeing T-shirts behind the cash register at Howard Johnson's, orange and blue ones. He decides to pick one up for her before they leave tomorrow morning.

The ball passes between them with an odd regularity, the air striking Benjamin's skin more coolly as the evening arrives. Kim's throws become brisker and brisker until Benjamin's thumb begins to grow sore from catching the ball the wrong way. He catches her throws in the palm of his mitt, and each smack of the ball feels like a deep, sad kiss.

CHAPTER 2
YOU-ME

SHE WASN'T JAPANESE AT ALL, Benjamin could tell. She was just pretending to be, with all that orange rouge and the heavy eye shadow, the ponytail and the kimono. She walked on the balls of her feet, her steps clipped. No, she wasn't Japanese, she was just waiting tables, and all the other waitresses at Yumi's were Japanese.

It was the Monday after Thanksgiving. He'd spent the holiday in Bluefield, and Mrs. Van Devere had sent him home with what was left of the turkey wrapped in tinfoil. "Eat it," she'd said. "Turkey's good for your blood." The package had leaked gravy on the passenger seat of the car. By Monday night, he'd picked the bones clean. After work, Benjamin had gone home to change his clothes and take a nap before thinking about dinner. The first three restaurants he'd tried were too crowded. He hadn't ended up at Yumi's intentionally. He didn't much care for Japanese food, it was just that there had been room there, no waiting. He'd sat alone at a table for four, his overcoat folded over the back of the chair opposite his, and from there he could hear the woman at the hostess stand call "Sachiko, table fourteen." The waitress moved to his table. She bowed briefly and pulled her head up to look him squarely in the eyes.

"Can I get you a drink, sir?" she said. Benjamin hesitated, then shook his head no. He was confused. "Let me show you a menu then," and she handed him one. It was burgundy with gold Japanese letters across the front, and Benjamin opened it without looking.

She said she'd give him a minute, but before she could leave, before she had turned fully, Benjamin said, "Is your name really Sachiko? You don't look Japanese."

She heard him and moved closer. "I'm not," she said, her voice hushed, speaking conspiratorially, "I'm American." When Benjamin didn't say anything, she went on, "My real name's Kimberly Cassella. They just call me Sachiko here." Her eyes were green, the color of summer grapes. It was a marvelous and unforgettable color. "I needed a job. You know how it is."

"Does that mean something? Sachiko?"

"Uh huh," she said. "It's Japanese for 'happy child.' Well, actually it depends on the characters you use to spell it. You know, the characters. It means 'happy child' or 'intelligent child,' but they mean the one that means 'happy child.' They all think I'm happy."

"Why is that?"

"I don't know. Because I'm always smiling, I guess," and she was, smiling, her pencil-thin lips pulled taut. When she smiled, her eyes widened, two perfect grapes.

"Well, are you happy?"

"It depends on how the tips are going," she said, then she smiled to let him know that she wasn't to be taken seriously. "I'm just kidding. God, they'd kill me if they heard me say that. I mean, sure, I'm happy. Who isn't?"

"Beats me."

He wanted to say that he wasn't, that he hadn't been happy for close to a year, since Mary Jude had moved out, and for some time before that, though he wasn't sure when the unhappiness had taken him over, just that it had kept him pinned to the recliner in the living room late at night, until he was sure Mary Jude was asleep in bed, and then he would sneak under the covers like a burglar. He wanted to tell her that the divorce papers were sitting in his living room like a new magazine, documenting his unhappiness. He wanted to say no, he wasn't happy, but he didn't. He had never

told anyone that, not Phinney, not Mary Jude, not Frank Babisch. Instead, he turned his eyes to the menu.

With short steps, Kim made her way through the restaurant, from the kitchen to a small table in the rear of the restaurant to the bar. Benjamin looked over the top of the menu to follow her. He traced her movements with his eyes, this happy child dressed like a Japanese doll, with green eyes that betrayed her. He read through the menu, and when she returned, he handed it to her.

"Made up your mind?"

"The usagi."

She asked, "Do you know what that is," as she wrote on her pad. She shook her pen.

"Sure," he said. "Eel." He'd seen the menu taped to the front window of the restaurant. On it, someone had described the dishes in English using a red felt-tip pen. USAGI = EEL, it'd read.

Kim apologized and smiled in an exaggerated way. Her lips stretched. "I'm just in the habit of asking people that. I mean, so many people come in here and don't know what they're ordering, and if they think they're getting swordfish and you give them eel, well, you know, they might get upset."

"Sure, I understand," Benjamin said. "I guess it's not that often that a man of the world like me comes in." This time he was the one smiling to let her know he was kidding.

Kim clicked her tongue. "Hmm, I'll have to remember that. Man of the world at table fourteen." She pretended to write it on her pad. "Got it," she said when she was done, and Benjamin watched her throughout his meal, as she bowed and smiled at each table and bent to point to the menus. A woman without care, he thought, without anything to weigh her down the way he felt weighed down. After he put his napkin beside his dish and paid, he returned to the table to leave a tip, and he did something unusual for him. On the back of one of the slips from his bank machine, one he'd found in his wallet, he wrote: I'LL BE AT J. C. MARTIN'S, HAPPY CHILD, GETTING A

DRINK. I'D LOVE IT IF YOU STOPPED BY. BY THE WAY, MY NAME IS BEN. BEN-
JAMIN SACKS. Then he pulled on his overcoat and left in a hurry, his pace
brisk so he would be out of Yumi's when Kim found the note.

The bar was two doors down from Yumi's. It hadn't always been called
J. C. Martin's. When Benjamin used to go there with Mary Jude, it had been
know as the Blue Cloud. There'd been an elderly black piano player—Duke
Monroe was his name—and he'd played exuberantly, singing hundreds of
songs each night, though his fingers refused to accompany him with anything but "Blueberry Hill," the Fats Domino song, in different tempos.
Mary Jude and Benjamin had danced like crazy cats between the tables.

Benjamin had no idea when the Blue Cloud had become J. C. Martin's,
or where Duke had gone. There were too many tables for dancing and a
video jukebox in the corner. Benjamin watched the screen while he waited
for Kim to show, doubtful she would. And why should she, he thought. He
ordered a drink. She didn't know him, she'd just served him dinner. Still,
he hoped something would pull her into J. C. Martin's, that something
about him had appealed to her. It would be nice to have a date.

Denise and Francine at the office didn't count. With them, it was just
someone to eat with after work. They usually ended up talking business.
"How big of an order did you get from Macy's?" or "Is Hecht's your
account, or is that Babisch's?" Francine had asked him up to her apartment
after dinner, and Benjamin had kept talking when she sat next to him on
the couch. "You have such big eyes," she'd said, "tell me more and more,"
and he'd only been talking about work. She'd guided his hand to her breast
and put her own on his belt buckle before he'd excused himself.

Those hadn't been dates. Those had been company. Benjamin hadn't
been on a date since Mary Jude left, since she packed her things in boxes
and left with the good car, the Volvo. Sometimes she'd call to ask if she
could come by and pick up something she'd forgotten, and then Benjamin
would shower and shave and wait for her. But she hadn't come by for
months. Still, Benjamin couldn't get himself to consider other women, to
imagine another woman in his arms or in his home. And he felt guilty,

remembering the nights on the recliner, remembering how sad he'd made her, so sad that she left him.

Mary Jude had known that there was something going on in Benjamin's mind, always, something about his parents and about Phinney that kept him on the recliner for weeks at a time, in the recliner and not in bed. Something that kept him earnest.

"I'll stick with you through thick and thin," she'd said, kissing him on the cheek before she went off to bed, alone, leaving him to his chair and his thoughts. But it had become too thick, thick as a milkshake, Benjamin had thought. Too thick to get out of. He sat in the recliner, thinking of how he carried a constant reminder of the summer that his parents died, one after the other, carrying this reminder with him like a birthmark: Mary Jude. With her, he couldn't separate love from sadness, not entirely. One had brought the other.

Benjamin drank some of his scotch and soda while he waited for Kim. He took a pack of cigarettes from his pocket and smoked one. "I'm glad you could make it," he was going to say if she showed. That or, "You really are very pretty." Whichever felt right.

But when she came in, still in her kimono, he didn't say anything but her name, twice, as nervous as he'd been the first time Mary Jude had pulled him onto the lifeguard stand with her. For an instant, he wondered where Mary Jude was, what she was doing at that moment.

"Hi," Kim said. "Sorry, I'm late, but we had to split up tips." Benjamin rose halfway from his seat as she took hers. She put the bank-machine slip on the table and said, "Thanks, now I know how much money you have in your account. They don't pay men of the world too much these days, do they?" She winked, poorly, her nose wrinkling. One of her grape-green eyes disappeared for a moment, then reemerged like it'd been lost. She raked her hair with her fingers.

Benjamin picked up the bank slip. Printed on the slip were the date, the time, the amount he'd withdrawn and his account balance.

"You weren't supposed to read that side. You were supposed to read the other side," and he turned the note toward her.

"I figured that out." She winked again, just as poorly as the first time. "So, how have you been?" she asked.

Benjamin smiled, then looked at the base of his glass. He fiddled with the cocktail napkin while he spoke. "Since dinner? Fine, I think. How was work?"

"Oh, God, it was so busy." She started, and it was as if she hadn't spoken in days, as if she were bursting with things to tell someone, even someone she'd just met. She had seen something in the restaurant, Benjamin thought: my loneliness.

"First there were the ladies who came in. There were these two heavyset women. What am I saying? There were these two fat women. I only call them heavyset because they were so nice. I don't want you to think I'm the kind of person who calls people fat." She spoke in an animated way, her words racing, girlish and pleasant. "Well, anyway, these two women come in, and you can tell that it's a big treat for them to eat Japanese food. The first thing they do is call me over to their table, and they whisper, 'Excuse me, miss, but we've never had Japanese food before, and we only have fifty dollars. Is that going to be enough?' It was so sweet. You had to be there. So I give them their menus, and they have no idea what anything is. So they call me back over, and I have to tell them what everything is, that tako is octopus, that maguro is tuna, that futo-maki is thick rolled sushi. I have to tell them everything, and they keep saying, 'Oooh, that sounds good,' and 'Ugghh, that doesn't.'" She made faces when she spoke, faces like in horror movies and cartoons. "Finally they end up ordering the futo-maki, the tempura, the usagi—that's eel."

"I know," Benjamin interrupted, but he said it softly, not rudely, just as he'd intended. "That's what I had."

"Oh, that's right, sorry. Usagi, did you have usagi? That's right, you did. I forgot. So they order the futo-maki, the tempura, and the usagi, and then they call me over again, and one of the ladies says, 'Honey, we don't know how to use these,' meaning the chopsticks, so I show them how to do it."

Kim held her right hand out in front of her, pantomiming the movement of chopsticks. "They don't do too well, and they have these sad looks on their faces, so I go get them forks and say, 'We wouldn't make you eat with your fingers.' And one of them says, 'But we wanted to be *real* Japanese tonight,' so they end up using the chopsticks anyway. They really had fun. It was so cute."

"It sounds like it," Benjamin watched her eyes. She had a look that he had only seen in children, a look of amazement and wonder, the look children get when they stare into a candle flame.

"Well, it was, it really was. That's what I like about waitressing. Every once in a while you meet some people who really, you know, touch you." She touched her fingertips to her chest. "I mean, usually you just get people who want to eat, and you don't remember them at all, like they're just a bunch of mouths that come in to get food put in them. But sometimes you meet people who are real people. So, anyway, when the ladies are finished and I give them the check, they call me over again and say, 'We don't eat out very much. How much of a tip are we supposed to leave?' So I tell them that most people leave ten or fifteen percent, which works out to be about six dollars for their check, and one of them says, 'But you were so nice, we wanted to give you *more*.' As if she wasn't allowed to give me more. Is that adorable, or what?"

Benjamin chuckled and leaned back in his chair. He couldn't think of being anywhere but here. "So, did they? Did they leave you a bigger tip?"

"No, but that's not the point. They were so sweet." Then she repeated what the women said, shaking her head from side to side, 'We wanted to give you more.' Isn't that sweet, Ben? That's what you said your name was, wasn't it?"

Benjamin nodded and wiped his cheek. "Ben," he said, "Sacks."

"Well, Ben, next there was a group of men who came in, five or six of them. I think they were lawyers. They all looked the same. But I had to get another waitress to wait on them because they said they wanted a 'real Oriental.' What a bunch of jerks. The funny thing is that sometimes people really believe that I'm Japanese. I'm not kidding. I even had one guy the other night who said he thought I have a very Western way of thinking. I almost said, 'Well, that's not much of a surprise since I was born half an hour from here.' Know what I mean? But I didn't. I almost did, though."

The waiter stood next to their table, and Kim ordered a Diet Pepsi. "I don't drink," she said to Benjamin, "sorry." Benjamin asked for another scotch and soda, and when the waiter left, Kim said, "I'll bet you don't know what Pepsi means in Japanese. It means, 'raising your ancestors from the dead.' Really, it does, so don't ever order a Pepsi at a Japanese restaurant, okay?"

"I won't," Benjamin said, and they sat quietly, just looking at each other. "I don't know how to say this," Benjamin said, "but I'm divorced."

"Oh, I'm sorry," Kim said. "I had a feeling it was something like that because you were eating alone. I mean, I couldn't figure out why someone like you would be eating alone because, well, forget it. Anyway, I'm sorry you're divorced."

"It's okay."

Kim hurried to explain herself. She leaned forward in her seat. "Well, I don't mean I'm sorry you're divorced, because I'd feel funny if you weren't. I mean, if you were married, I would. I don't know what I'm saying. I mean I wouldn't want to be alone in a bar with a married man." She shook her head. "I'm not very eloquent sometimes. What I mean is I'm sorry that you're divorced if you're sorry that you are."

"I just wanted you to know."

"Thanks, I guess. Anyway," Kim said, regaining herself, "that's not all that happened tonight. There was this family that came in, just a father and a mother and their son. He was probably seven or eight years old, and the first thing he said to me was, 'Where are the pineapples?' His mother said, 'That's Chinese, dear, this is Japanese,' and he frowned," and Kim frowned, imitating the boy, her face instantly dismal and cherubic, "and said, 'But you said there'd be pineapples.' He looked so disappointed, but he ended up loving it. Really. He had the toro, and he told me about how when his father took him fishing they caught a fish, and when they cut it open they found a watch in its stomach, and it was still ticking. He was wearing the watch right there in the restaurant. Isn't that funny?"

Benjamin nodded again. "I work for a watch company," he said, "Lomax Timepieces," and Kim bobbed her head in recognition.

"Sure," she said, "because everyone needs time, right?"

"Mm hmm." LOMAX TIMEPIECES...BECAUSE EVERYONE NEEDS TIME was what the billboards said. It's what the blond woman sang in the television commercials, and it was what they—Benjamin, Babisch, everyone in sales—said at work, trying to talk the department stores into increasing their orders. Everyone needs time.

"So," she said, "what do you do? I mean, what do you do for Lomax?"

"I'm a salesman."

"Really?"

"Uh huh. For close to twenty years."

"Wow."

"Well," he said, "I haven't always been a salesman. I taught school for a year a long time ago."

"Here?"

"No. Back in Bluefield. That's where I'm from."

"You didn't like it?"

"Bluefield or teaching?"

"Teaching."

"No." He waited. "I worked in a bookstore once, too." His voice trailed off.

"Oh, that sounds very, you know, interesting."

Benjamin couldn't think of anything to say, and he didn't want to say anything, he just wanted to watch Kim and listen to her talk, listen to her voice.

The waiter brought their drinks, and Benjamin held his glass out for Kim to clink hers against. He tried to think of a toast to her, but he was afraid he might scare her. He was afraid she'd excuse herself and leave if she knew that already she was making his life better. "To Yumi's," Benjamin said instead, pronouncing the name as "yummy."

Tapping her glass against his, Kim corrected him. "You-me," she said. "It's Japanese. It's pronounced 'you-me.'"

Benjamin didn't miss the double meaning.

"That's right. You-me," he said, "you-me."

Kim took a sip of her soda. She pressed her front teeth against her lower lip. "You know, she was there tonight," she said.

"Who?"

"Yumi. Could you see her?"

"There's really a Yumi?"

"Sure, Yumi Saguro. She owns the restaurant. Her and her husband. She saw you, you know."

"Really?"

"Uh huh," Kim nodded, "she thought you were very handsome." Embarrassed, she said, "She has a message for you, but I don't know if I should tell you."

"What is it?"

"I can't. I'd feel silly."

"Come on. I can take it. I'm a man of the world."

"Okay," and Kim closed her eyes. "She said to tell you—God, I don't know why I'm telling you this—she said to tell you that you're a dirty old American man, and if you touch me your hair will turn gray."

Benjamin smiled uneasily.

"Don't worry," Kim reassured him. "She always says things like that."

"Well, I'm sorry I didn't get a chance to see her."

Kim slid in her seat and crossed her legs at the knee. "She's very small, even for a Japanese woman. Four and a half feet, tops. She only comes in a couple of nights a week in the winter because she travels. Anyway, I don't think she comes by to check up, I think she just comes by for the shabby talk."

Before he could ask what that meant, Kim said, "Have I told you what shabby talk is?" He shook his head no—how could she have told him what shibby talk was, and, at the same time, why did he feel as if she could have already told him that and a hundred other things? Kim swallowed more of her soda and said, "I just learned myself. Shibby talk is Japanese, well, sort of Japanese, for nasty talk. All of the Japanese women—and me, of course— we all get together after work and split up the tips, and everyone talks about their husbands and boyfriends and, you know, sex and stuff. It's very nasty, but it's funny. Yumi says the funniest things, and she says them in a way that's very strange so that they sound profound or something. Like Confucius."

Kim paused. "No, wait," she said, "Confucius is Chinese. Why can't I remember that? You know what I mean, though. Like Yumi will say, 'It isn't good to make love all night then come to work. That's how you get corns on your feet.'" Kim sipped from her drink. "As if you could get corns on your feet from having sex with your boyfriend."

Benjamin asked without considering the consequences. "Do you have a boyfriend?" he said. "If you don't mind me prying."

"No," she said, and Benjamin felt flushed and relieved, "not since Kevin Purcell, and that's a long story. Long, long, long, long, *long*. Anyway, the funny thing about Yumi is that sometimes I think the other women believe the things she says. Sometimes I do, too. It's like here she is, Yumi the Great, here to spread her wisdom. It's like she's Yoda in *Star Wars* or something.

"She sounds like quite a character."

"Well, she is," Kim said. "Did I tell you that she had three miscarriages when she was younger?"

Benjamin shook his head, and Kim held up three fingers on her left hand, her thumb and pinky turned down.

"Three of them. And she had another one die of crib death at eight months, and another was killed by a school bus when he was only six. It's all very sad. She's quite a woman, Yumi. I don't know her husband at all." The animation was gone from Kim's speech now. In an instant she was serious, as if she were about to cry just thinking about Yumi, childless.

Benjamin studied her face, her eyelids shut like nutshells now, her grape-green eyes covered, her cheeks sharp as a mannequin's, the rouge set in them like half-moons. The tip of her nose turned pink, and he realized why he'd asked her to meet him. Looking at her now, it was as if he could see inside her, through the makeup. He could see that she had it in her to be happy, and she had it in her to be sad and weak just as well. Kim. Her beauty tugged at her. It was as if it held her down, all that was inside her; too much beauty for someone so small. She was weighed down to the earth, like he was, but he didn't know what it was that weighed her down. Her grape eyes didn't betray her. No, it was the opposite: the rest of her betrayed her grape eyes.

Benjamin reached across the table and placed his hand to her cheek. Not for a moment did he consider that she might pull away from his touch, and she didn't, she let her head rest there.

"I'm sorry," she said, rubbing her nose with the flat of her hand, "I was just thinking, and sometimes that's not good." Benjamin told her that it was okay, there wasn't a thing to apologize for. He told her to just close her eyes.

She closed her eyes for nearly a minute.

When she was finished with her soda she said she would call her father to pick her up, but Benjamin offered to give her a ride. She walked with him toward his apartment, to his car, with Benjamin's overcoat on her shoulders like a cape. Like Supergirl, he thought. He drove her to her parents' house in Druid Hill with the radio turned up the whole way, Kim singing along. She shoved the door to the Mustang shut, then tapped on the window, crouching to mouth, "Thanks for listening, Benjamin."

He watched her walk to the door, untying her kimono when she reached it, and the next song on the radio was one he'd heard on television, one that he'd heard at the Van Devere's house. It was one a marching band had played in the Macy's Thanksgiving Day Parade.

Benjamin didn't remember its name, but that was the song he thought of when he stripped down to his shorts and T-shirt back at his apartment. He hummed the song and started toward the living room to sleep in the recliner. He decided on the bed instead. He pulled down the comforter and slid beneath it. The sheets were as cool as lemonade. They'd been untouched for eleven months, part of a ghost house. Benjamin lay flat on his back, his arms folded across his chest. He studied a single long, gray string of a spider web in a corner of the ceiling. When he turned on his side, his leg scraped something. A piece of paper, a tear in the sheets. He reached under the covers to retrieve it. The note read GO TO SLEEP, BENJAMIN, and he folded it and slid it into the drawer of the nightstand with the rest of Mary Jude's notes.

He didn't want to overreact, but he couldn't help it. Twice in the middle of the night, Benjamin got out of bed to call Babisch and Julie and tell them about Kim, but he thought better of it. When he woke, he showered and shaved and raced to work without eating to wait outside Babisch's office.

"Can I get you some coffee or something, Mr. Sacks?" Babisch's secretary asked, but Benjamin said, "No thanks, Margaret." He knew the smile on his face was big and silly.

He paced, and while he did he remembered a conversation he'd had with Babisch not long after Mary Jude had left.

"Let me tell you how I maintain my sanity," Babisch had said. He'd been on his back in his bathroom, squirming like a fish on the tiles as he toyed with the pipes under the sink, *Mechanix Illustrated* opened on the toilet. "I maintain my sanity by forgetting all my problems once they're in the past. Keep trouble around until it stops being amusing, and then toss it out on its ass. Don't let it stay any longer than it should, and then don't let it back in. And I suggest you do yourself a service and do the same thing." Babisch had groaned beneath the sink. "I'm looking at life more philosophically these days. Life's too short, so you've got to fix your own plumbing. Do you see what I mean? Do you see the philosophy?"

"Sort of."

"Listen, Ben. I know you've been in the dumps for—what's it been—

ten, twenty years?"

Benjamin had laughed. "Twenty."

"Why? What's wrong with you that can't be fixed?"

"What do you mean, what's wrong with me?"

"What's wrong? What's the matter?"

"Everything. So much has happened."

"Ben," Babisch had said, "things happen to everyone. If they didn't, the world would be pretty dull. We wouldn't have newspapers. What's happened to you that doesn't happen to people in newspapers?"

"My parents."

"Benjamin, that didn't happen to you. That happened to them. There's a big difference. Besides, everyone loses their parents. I've lost mine. Julie's lost hers. Everyone does."

"Phinney, then."

"Same story. That happened to Phinney, it didn't happen to you."

"Mary Jude."

"Aha," Babisch had said, and his voice had rung off the pipes. "Aha, I was waiting for you to say that."

"So?"

"So, why are you so serious all the time? You brood more than anyone I know."

"What does that have to do with Mary Jude?"

"Just tell me why you're so serious all the time."

Benjamin hadn't answered at first. He read the *Mechanix Illustrated* instead.

"I want to be my best all the time."

"Only idiots are at their best all the time." Babisch was quick like that. He always had a snappy answer. "Everyone else has to take the ups with the downs," he'd said.

Everything's different now, Benjamin thought, and when Babisch stepped off the elevator, his briefcase in one hand, Benjamin hustled to meet him.

"How are you, Babisch?"

"It's too early to tell."

"Get in your office," Benjamin demanded, "and quick."

"I tried to call you last night. Julie and I wanted to see if you were busy for dinner."

"Is that right? Well, thanks, but I was out. Now, will you get in your office already?"

"This isn't business, is it?"

"Unh uh, now get in there."

Benjamin and Babisch stepped into the office, and Benjamin pushed the door closed after them. Babisch pulled off his coat and sat behind his desk, and Benjamin circled the room. There were photographs of Babisch and Julie, his arm around her shoulder, on the credenza catty-corner to the desk and pictures of Babisch with Benjamin, both of them in swimming trunks and sucking in their stomachs. Babisch had stuck the photographs that included Mary Jude in the drawer or the closet.

"Well?" Babisch grinned. "Is this about a woman?"

Benjamin arched his eyebrows.

Babisch clasped his hands over his head like a prizefighter and tipped his head back. "Aha, I knew it."

Benjamin took nearly half an hour to describe Kim. For once, Babisch was a silent listener. When Benjamin was through, Babisch said, "God, I'm happy for you. It's about time. Everyone needs time, that's what we say, right? What have I been telling you for *months*?"

"I know, I know."

"What have I been telling you for *months*?"

Like a schoolboy, Benjamin answered, "You've been telling me to start dating other women."

"See, I've been telling you that for months. For months I've been telling you that, and I was right. Was I right, or was I right?" He shook a finger at Benjamin. "When are you going out with her again?"

"Kim?"

"No, Elizabeth Taylor. Yes, *Kim*. Who've we been talking about? When are you going to see her again?"

"Tomorrow. The next day. Who knows? You know what she said, Babisch? She said, 'I couldn't understand why someone like you would be eating alone.' I think she thinks I'm *handsome*, Babisch. Can you believe it?"

"Jesus, Ben. Marry her or have her committed, one or the other," Babisch teased.

Finally, Benjamin took a seat across from Babisch, pulling the chair to the lip of the desk. He was out of breath, and he rested his arms on Babisch's desk. His legs felt light beneath him. "You know what I was thinking before I went to bed last night, Babisch? I was thinking how, when you're a boy, you want to be a man. But when you're a man, you want more than anything to be a boy again. So there has to be some time in there"— he moved his hands as he would if he were weighing a pair of basketballs, one in each palm—"there has to be some time in between being a boy and a man, an instant even, when you're happy being *exactly* who you are. It's like a mathematical equation or something. It's like a graph, and there are these two lines that cross, and it's just a matter of figuring out where they cross to figure out where you'll be happy, exquisitely. See what I'm saying?"

Babisch cocked his head. "Sort of."

"You think I'm crazy, I can tell. Your eyes do that whenever you think I'm crazy."

"My eyes didn't do anything."

"Yes they did. What I mean is, maybe I haven't grown up yet. I'm forty years old, and maybe I'm still a kid, and maybe last night was that moment when I was happy being exactly, *precisely* who I am. I don't want to be any older, and I don't want to be any younger. See?"

"I thought you were happy with Mary Jude, for a while. I know you were. Don't forget, I was there for some of it. Don't go off the deep end here. I'm happy for you, about meeting this woman and all, but don't go off the deep end."

Benjamin was too excited to discuss Mary Jude. "I know, I was happy with Mary Jude. So maybe I'm one of those people who's lucky enough to be happy about who he is twice in the same lifetime. First Mary Jude saved me, and now this woman is going to do it. I can *feel* it. I get to be happy *twice*. You're getting jealous, aren't you? You poor soul, you only get to be happy once."

"Whatever you say, Benjamin. Now go do some work, and don't—are you listening?—don't scare this woman off. That's my only advice. I just don't want to see it, and I certainly don't want to have to deal with it."

"I couldn't scare her off if I tried," Benjamin said. "I'm too handsome to do something like that," and he left Babisch's office and jogged to his own. He closed his door and sat at his desk, looking out onto St. Paul Street, toward the harbor and the giant orange Domino Sugar sign sitting above the water. He lifted his feet from the floor and swirled the seat of his chair round and round on its swivel until he became a little dizzy.

Kim was going to save him, she was going to pull him from the recliner. Life was going to start again, he knew it, and at lunchtime he left a note at Yumi's.

> KIM, IT'S ME, BENJAMIN. JUST FOUR QUICK QUESTIONS.
> 1. DO YOU LIKE ITALIAN FOOD?
> 2. HAVE YOU EVER BEEN TO CAPRICCIO'S IN LITTLE ITALY?
> 3. DO YOU HAVE ANY INTEREST IN GOING TO CAPRICCIO'S SOME TIME IN THE NEAR FUTURE?
> 4. IF YOU ARE INTERESTED IN GOING TO CAPRICCIO'S SOME TIME IN THE NEAR FUTURE, CAN I COME, TOO?

He waited for Kim to call through the afternoon, staying off the phone to leave his line free, jumping every time his secretary's phone rang. When she called at four-twenty, Kim was laughing. Her laughs skipped like hiccups.

"You're a strange guy, Benjamin Sacks," she said. "I mean, oh, don't be offended. I'm glad you got in touch. I meant strange in a funny way. Not strange-peculiar. Strange-funny. Does that make any sense? Do you see the difference? Sure you do, what am I saying?"

"So, yes or no to dinner?"

"Do you mean dinner, or do you mean"—her voice dropped—"Dinner?"

"What?"

"There's a small d dinner, and there's a capital D dinner."

"What's the difference?"

"The capital D dinner's more of an event. It means I have to wear a dress, mostly."

"You don't have to wear a dress if you don't want to."

"Well, I don't want to. I hate dresses. They make me look chesty, if you know what I mean. Is that a word, chesty? Not that any of this matters because I couldn't go to dinner, small d or capital D, even if I wanted to. I work nights, remember?"

"Lunch, then? Tomorrow?"

"Sounds great," she said. "I'll meet you in front of the restaurant. That is, I'll meet you in front of Capriccio's not I'll meet you in front of Yumi's."

Benjamin smiled.

"I've got to get back to work. Yumi will kill me if she sees me on the phone," Kim said. "Women aren't supposed to call men, you know. It'll give you a cold."

She said good-bye.

Something weighed her down to the earth, too. Benjamin could tell.

Benjamin tried to figure it out at lunch at Capriccio's, and he tried to figure it out on their other dates, and he tried to figure it out while he waited for her at Yumi's, and he tried to figure it out when she moved in that February. All he knew was that it had something to do with the T-shirts. There were dozens of them.

CHAPTER 3
I'D HATE TO BE YOU IN THE RAIN

AFTER CARRYING THEIR SUITCASES from the car to the motel room, Benjamin dials the operator. The room is decorated in an odd combination of brown and blue, and there's a seascape over the headboard of the bed. The way it's painted, blurred, Benjamin can't tell where the beach ends and the ocean begins.

He sits on the edge of the bed, atop the flowered bedspread, and tells the operator Phinney's number. Kim's in the bathroom with the water running. The baseball mitts are on the floor in front of the television, the keys to the room on the nightstand. Phinney's phone rings distantly in Benjamin's ear.

Soon, Phinney says hello.

"Phinney?"

"Ben, where are you?"

"Did I wake you, Phinney?"

"No. What time is it, eight? Where are you?"

"Missouri."

"Missouri isn't Nebraska," Phinney says, disappointed.

"I know, I know. We're in Missouri. Outside Independence, I think. I don't know. Kim's the one with the map."

"Is everything okay? If everything's not okay, let me know."

"Everything's okay. It's just that we'll be here tonight, if that's all right with you. We checked into a motel."

"Sure, it's all right with me. But, you know, is everything okay?"

"Mm hmm," Benjamin says. "Stop asking that. Everything really is fine," and he raises his head to look at the closed bathroom door.

Kim steps out of the bathroom, wearing a gold and burgundy Washington Redskins T-shirt, and kneels beside Benjamin on the bed. She tugs the receiver from his ear and says, "Hi, Phinney," into the mouthpiece, then releases her grip.

"That was Kim."

"I know that," Phinney says. "Say hi to her for me."

"I will," Benjamin says. "Night." It occurs to him that that's one of the few times he's said that to Phinney since they were boys sharing the same bed. Then he could sleep.

He hangs up the receiver, and Kim turns the television on. She sits before it with the phone book on her knees, using that as a desk as she fills out postcards. Benjamin takes a book from his suitcase—*Iacocca*—and puts his back to the headboard. A playing card marks his place, and Benjamin places the card faceup on the nightstand.

"Listen to this one," Kim says, and she reads the back of one of her postcards. "Golden grain of harvest. Keeping the beliefs and customs of their forefathers, the Amish use horse-drawn equipment on their farms. Fields of neatly stacked sheaves of grain dot the countryside at harvest time in northern Indiana."

She holds the postcard up so Benjamin can see the photograph. She bought it at a gas station, off a carousel rack. "Isn't that pretty?" she asks.

"I can't tell what it is."

Kim looks at the photograph, acting as if she's amazed. "Are you kidding? They're fields of neatly stacked sheaves of grain dotting the countryside at harvest time in northern Indiana, what's it look like?" She laughs.

"Thanks," Benjamin answers. "Who are you sending that one to?"

"Frank and Julie."

"Good. Say hello to them for me, too."

"I already did."

"Did you tell Babisch that we stopped at that place he told us about, for frozen custard?"

"Yup," Kim says. "It's right here," and she points to the ink on the back of the card. "I've got one for your friends, Mr. and Mrs. Van Devere. You'll have to address that one yourself. I haven't got the faintest idea where they live. I'm sending one to Yumi, too." She holds up another. "It's the Indianapolis 500."

Benjamin just nods.

"I miss Yumi, you know."

"I know you do. Say hello for me. Tell her my hair's just fine, thank you." He goes back to his book.

"Okay."

Later, when Kim climbs into bed beside him, Benjamin closes *Iacocca*, keeping his place with the playing card. He gets up and pulls the bedspread off.

"You don't—" she says, but he's out of bed as quickly as she's into it. She sets one of the pillows on the floor with the bedspread.

Kim is sitting stiffly on the bed, her legs together.

Benjamin pulls off his jeans and shirt and folds them on top of his suitcase, then he lies down and rolls the bedspread around his body like a sleeping bag.

Kim turns off the lamp and sighs, "Night, darling," and Benjamin can hear her punching the covers down with her leg.

"Night." Benjamin doesn't sleep well at all, though. He shuts his eyes and dreams of Mary Jude. She appears, over and over, and when he can't sleep, he counts the flowers on the bedspread like sheep, and they remind him of the night in January that Kim first stayed at his apartment, in his bed, the one that had been his and Mary Jude's. He and Kim hadn't even kissed, they'd just undressed and fallen into bed after a late dinner, and there she was when he woke that next morning, lying there on top of the sheets in her T-shirt and underpants, her kimono a black heap on the floor. He dressed and went to the florist. He returned with a bouquet of flowers, and he spread them around her, dropping them lightly so that she'd wake in a field, the scent surrounding her like a blanket.

Benjamin celebrated the mornings. That first morning Kim had found him in the bathroom, shaving. She tucked a carnation into the waistband of his shorts. With her arms looped lazily around his waist, her head on his back, she said, "You're the greatest, Benjamin Sacks." Then "I'd better call my mom," and he was alone in the bathroom.

As he shaved, he listened to her talk to her mother. Her tone was fretful. "Mom, it's me, Kim. I just wanted to call to see…no, I don't want to talk about it …you, I should have called, but I just wasn't thinking …will you please let me get a word in sideways. You make me feel like I'm an idiot. I do have a mind of my own …I said …please, Mom …you called the police? I can't believe you called the police, like I'm a lost dog or something. You didn't call the police, you're just saying so to make me feel guilty, and I won't …I'm reconciled …well, I'm sorry I worried you, but I just stayed at a friend's house …no, you don't know her. We were out late …" When he came out of the bathroom, Kim was back in the bed.

Now, in the middle of the night, when she hears him tossing, counting the flowers, mumbling, Kim reaches down and grabs his hand, rubbing it in her own.

"You can come on up here," she says, "in the bed," but Benjamin refuses.

He remains on the floor, afraid that Kim will think it's because he doesn't want to touch her, and just as afraid that that's what it is.

It's the creek, he thinks.

And it's me, the way I am. Soon he's asleep, uncomfortable.

He wakes, hours later, because Kim is stepping over him as he lies on the motel floor. He pulls the bedspread up over his eyes and turns his face to the carpet so the sunlight won't sting him when she opens the door to go for her run.

She's run for more than an hour each day of the trip, leaving him time to himself, which is both good and bad. It's more time to read the books he's packed away—*Sophie's Choice* and *Iacocca*—but it's also given him more time to think.

"Are you up?" Kim asks. She shakes him roughly. "Hello, is there anyone in there?"

Benjamin makes a noise, a harrumph, and Kim squeezes his ankles through the bedspread, turning his feet.

"God, you're like a mummy in there," she laughs. "It's like you've been mummified in that bedspread for time eternal." Benjamin folds his hands over his face, wrapped in a flowered bedspread, all posies and daffodils above him.

She says, "I'm only going to run six or seven today." The absence of anger in her voice relieves Benjamin. Either she doesn't remember that I didn't get into bed last night, he thinks, or she doesn't think anything of it.

He speaks through the bedspread. "Good. What's that in time? An hour? An hour and a half?"

"God, I don't know. I'll be back in a while, okay, darling?" she says.

"When?" he asks, but she closes the door without answering. "When?"

When she first moved into his apartment, her runs only lasted thirty or forty minutes. Since then, they've become longer. Now, depending on the weather and her mood, they can be as long as two hours. Benjamin can't translate that into miles the way Kim does. She keeps track of the distance she runs. For Benjamin, it's the time.

"I have to run," Kim explained, "or do aerobics or stuff like that." She was under the comforter, her head on Benjamin's chest. The room was dark, except for the light from the liquor store across the street. "See, I've always had bad circulation, even when I was little. My fingers and toes can get pretty cold."

"I've never noticed them being cold," Benjamin said.

"That's because they're not. If I run, they stay warm. Feel." She pressed her fingertips against his forearm. "Warm, see? Now, if I didn't run, believe me, you'd tell the difference. If you had a soda, say, and it got warm, all I'd have to do is stick a finger in to get it all cold again."

Benjamin smiled. "You're exaggerating."

"Yeah, but not by much. Really, they get pretty cold if I don't run."

She took Benjamin running with her a couple of Saturday mornings, even bought him new shoes to encourage him—gray ones with a blue Nike flourish on the sides. She tried to convince him that it was good for his circulation, but he started gasping early, the sweat slipping down his neck like molasses.

"Good," she'd said the first day, "you did three-quarters of a mile. Three-quarters of a mile is very good for a beginner." Benjamin had looked at his watch as he lay on the living-room floor, panting and groaning, his arms and legs stretched to form an enormous X.

"Fifteen minutes," he said, then he fell asleep in his damp clothes.

Kim had been running when Mary Jude called. It was April. It was two years after Mary Jude had moved out and only two months after Kim had moved in, taking Mary Jude's half of the closet and her half of the bed.

It was the first time Benjamin had heard Mary Jude's voice since she had moved to New York.

He'd been in bed when the phone rang in the living room. He'd been lying on his side, a Sunday morning watching television and eating Fig Newtons. Kim had brought them from the kitchen before leaving the apartment in a T-shirt and running shorts.

"Benjamin?"

"Yes?"

"It's me, Benjamin. Mary Jude," but he knew that already. The same voice had said good morning to him for more than twenty years. Throaty and plaintive. Good morning, a whisper in his ear.

Carrying the phone, he returned to the bedroom.

"Benjamin?"

"Yes."

"It's me, Mary Jude."

"Yes, I know." He got into bed again. He pulled the box of cookies onto his lap, setting one on his tongue, chewing while he spoke to sound casual, though her voice had suddenly made him feel a hundred years old. "So, how are you?" He couldn't think of another thing to say.

"Fine, Benjamin. I have something to tell you, Benjamin."

He chewed. "What's that?" He swallowed and pulled another Fig Newton from the box, pinching it before biting it in half.

"Benjamin, I'm getting married again."

There was a pause, a silence where Benjamin should have spoken, where he should have congratulated her, and he continued chewing noisily, smacking his tongue so she would think that he wasn't speaking because his mouth was full, not because a feeling of loneliness had hit him in the chest like a ball he couldn't quite catch.

It was Hallyday. Hallyday, who had lived two doors down from them in the very building where Benjamin was sitting. Hallyday, who lived in New York now.

"Benjamin?"

"Yes."

"Benjamin, I know you heard me. I just thought I should call you before you heard about it from Phinney or someone else." Her voice sounded sad and wise at once.

"You talked to Phinney?" He wondered if Phinney had told her about Kim. He hoped not. "You already told Phinney?"

"This morning. I didn't know how to handle telling you, so I called to see what he thought."

"To see how to tell me so I wouldn't kill myself?"

She whispered his name, gently. "Have you been taking your pills?"

"Mm hmm," he hummed into the receiver. "What did Phinney have to say?" He put the Fig Newtons on the bed beside him, where Kim had slept, and folded the box shut, then pulled the blankets to his throat, though he wasn't cold.

"He said he thought I should call you and tell you and that you'd be happy for me. Benjamin, I hope you're happy for me. Please be happy for me."

He wasn't, though. There wasn't much to Hallyday. There wasn't enough to him for someone like Mary Jude. He was a lawyer, and Benjamin had never been able to tell when he was serious and when he was kidding, when he was frustrated or happy. Everything he said he said with equal feeling—or lack of it. He was a man without emotion, Benjamin had always thought. But it wasn't just that it was Hallyday. It was that it was someone else. Anyone else.

"Benjamin, please."

"Congratulations, I guess. Who is it? No, no, don't tell me, let me guess," he said, feigning happiness, trying to be playful. "Let me see if I can guess his first name." He knew it was Reggie Hallyday, but he wouldn't guess it.

She said, "Benjamin," trying to stop him.

"Give me three guesses, okay?"

"Benjamin."

Benjamin paused as if he were thinking. "Robert?"

"No, it's not Robert. I don't know a soul named Robert."

"Okay, that's one down. Steve?"

She blew into the receiver, impatient. "No." She sighed.

"All right. One left." Benjamin paused again. "Robert?"

Mary Jude laughed, a squeak of a laugh, and Benjamin smiled. "You already guessed Robert, silly," she said.

"Oh, yeah."

Mary Jude sniffed to stop her laughter. "You know it's Reggie, and I know what you're thinking, and you're wrong."

"I'm not thinking a thing."

"Benjamin, I know you. I know what you're thinking, and you're wrong. I loved you, Benjamin. You know that. I wouldn't have done a thing to hurt you."

Benjamin knew she was right. He rubbed his shoulders. He'd hurt her, not the other way around, though when he told people how she moved out, abruptly and noisily, thumping a suitcase against the elevator door, it always sounded the other way around. He could make himself sound very sympathetic, Benjamin could. Knew he could make it sound as if Mary Jude had been unfaithful with Hallyday, their *neighbor*.

"Benjamin, are you there?"

"I'm always here."

"Benjamin, what are you thinking?"

"Nothing."

"Please, Benjamin, what are you thinking?"

Somewhere he had learned that in ten years a mattress collects enough skin particles to cover a person from head to toe. That's what he was thinking: there are two of Mary Jude in this bed and two of me. There's something in here that's a part of each of us. That's why I can't get myself to throw the mattress out and buy a new one, a comfortable one without the caverns worn in it. It'd be like throwing away both of us, twice. Again.

And now that Kim has moved in, her skin particles are mixing with Mary Jude's and mine in there. Everything's getting mixed up, he thought. Kim's mixing with Mary Jude, and every day she becomes more a part of this mixture and Mary Jude less.

"Benjamin," Mary Jude said, "I know you're thinking something."

"I'm just sorry about everything. Thanks for putting up with me. I really am sorry."

"Oh, Benjamin, Benjamin, Benjamin," she said, repeating his name over and over like birdsong. "Oh, Benjamin, Benjamin, Benjamin," the same word she'd repeated when they'd first kissed, when he first thought that no one had ever said his name properly before. She repeated it now until Benjamin put another cookie in his mouth and said good-bye, chewing.

"Are you eating Fig Newtons?" she asked, amused.

"Yes."

"Have you been eating them the whole time we've been talking?"

"You know I have."

Mary Jude laughed. "God, Benjamin, promise me you won't ever change."

"I couldn't if I tried," he said, and he knew that was true. He put the phone down and finished off the cookies, sometimes putting two or three in his mouth at a time, nearly choking on them.

Phinney went to the wedding, but Benjamin and Kim didn't. Benjamin didn't even tell Kim it was happening. She went to Yumi's, and he stayed at home that day, working his way through the apartment like a cleaning woman gone berserk. He scrubbed the tiles in the bathroom, rubbed Pledge into the living-room furniture until it shone like china, pulled books from the shelves and wiped off the dust as if this were a normal thing to do on the day that his ex-wife was becoming someone else's wife, as if she weren't taking her vows again in an apartment two hundred miles north, as if all of this wouldn't have been happening if it weren't for him, for the way he'd been, trapped in the recliner, helpless with the past.

"What are you doing?" Kim asked when she returned from Yumi's. He'd forgotten to meet her, to walk her home, but she didn't mention that. She was still in her kimono, and she looked startled, her mouth open, at seeing Benjamin cleaning. There were rags tucked in the waistband of his shorts.

"Nothing," he said. "Cleaning." He ignored Kim, and she went to the bedroom to change.

Before she went to sleep, Kim came out in her T-shirt. "Oh, yeah," she said, "Yumi said to say hello. She says you're still a dirty old man, and your hair's still going to go gray for touching me, but she thinks you're okay."

"I'm glad," Benjamin said, and he pulled another book from the shelf.

When he took *To Kill a Mockingbird* down to wipe its jacket, he saw his own handwriting on it, a note he'd written at the beach one summer. He remembered the precise moment he'd written it. "This guy Hallyday," the note read, "Wears the slightest swimming trunks I've ever seen and can build up the appetite of a gorilla."

The writing was seven or eight years old, but the way the ink had dried it had an odd, historical look, as if it were on a scroll. He'd been sitting alone in a beach chair at Ocean City with a pitcher of lemonade beside him and coconut oil on his chest. It was the summer that Benjamin and Mary Jude had rented a beach house for a month, the year she'd given him *To Kill a Mockingbird* as a birthday present. Babisch and Julie had come for a weekend. Hallyday had come to visit for a week, sleeping on the porch and doing some of the cooking. "It'll be fine," Mary Jude had said when he arrived, to Benjamin. "Everything will be fine."

Benjamin wasn't much for swimming in the ocean. It was always too cold, even at the tail of the summer, so he usually pulled a chair onto the beach and read, leaving Mary Jude to Hallyday and the water. He hadn't given that summer much thought until he found the note, and he began imagining. Me on the beach, them in the water. Me at the grocery, them alone in the beach house. Me on the toilet, them God knows where. He imagined Hallyday, the gorilla, making love to Mary Jude then, and at the same time he knew that it hadn't happened.

Cleaning the apartment, he doubted what he was certain of. He sat in the recliner with *To Kill a Mockingbird*. He wouldn't stop the wedding, but he thought about it. But where would he get the children?

Mary Jude was a sucker for children. She'd wanted children and he'd said no, that he would never be a good father, but now he pictured children running down the aisle after Mary Jude had taken her place at the altar, running like they were attached to kites. Little blond-headed girls in white dresses and bows. Boys in navy suits, wiping their bangs from their eyes while they raced to stop her. They'd tug at her dress, and she'd turn around.

"Benjamin's sorry," one would say.

"Don't marry the gorilla," another would say.

"*Benjamin te quiere*," another would say. "Benjamin still loves you" in

Spanish.

And the last child wouldn't be lying.

Mary Jude wasn't getting married in a church, though. She was getting married in an apartment, Hallyday's. There was no aisle to run down, just a hallway, probably. And where would he get the children?

Benjamin sat in the recliner, imagining Mary Jude and Hallyday at Ocean City, holding their breath underwater and kissing like blowfish. He sat with the book, holding it like a talisman, waiting well past midnight before he called. Phinney had said they'd be at the Waldorf. First he called and asked for the room number of Mr. and Mrs. Reginald Hallyday, and the clerk gave it to him without a question. With that, he waited fifteen minutes and called the desk again.

"Front desk."

"Yes, I'm in room 312," Benjamin said, making his voice sound husky and disturbed.

"How can I help you?"

"I don't know if you know this or not, but there's a loud dog barking in the room next to us. It's making a racket, and my wife and I can't get any sleep."

"A dog?"

"Yes."

"Well, we don't allow pets."

"I didn't think you did. My wife and I haven't been able to sleep at all."

"Room 310?"

"Yes," Benjamin said, "room 310."

"We'll send someone up to check it out," the clerk said. "Please accept our apologies for the inconvenience."

The bedroom door opened when Benjamin hung up the phone. Kim stood in the doorway in a T-shirt, rubbing the sleep from her eyes with her fists.

"Were you on the phone?" she asked.

"Uh huh."

"Who were you talking to?"

He gave her the name of one of the men from the office.

Kim went back to bed, and Benjamin sat in the recliner throughout the night, the television on, thinking about Reggie Hallyday's enormous appetite. At one and three he called the Waldorf again, shouting, "Will you send someone up to Room 310 already and shut that dog up?"

At four-thirty in the morning, the clerk told him that the couple in 310 had become angry themselves and had checked out, both in bathrobes, the woman sobbing. Benjamin closed his eyes and held his breath when he heard this.

He sprang from the recliner. He ran to the bathroom holding his chest, wondering if he would get there in time. His heart knocked against the wall of his chest as if it were trying to find a way out. He ran, and he still couldn't get there. He was breathless, as if he'd just run a mile at full trot. It was as if the path from the recliner had gotten longer, as if it had been stretched out of shape, and when he finally reached the bathroom and pulled up the toilet seat, he coughed and coughed, but nothing came up. He coughed without control, and then Kim was at the door, slapping her hand against it with thumps as rapid as his heartbeat.

"Benjamin, are you okay?"

"Fine," he said through his coughing. He wondered if this was what it was like to have a heart attack, the throbbing, the tightness.

Kim turned the knob, but the door was locked.

"Benjamin?"

"I'm fine, really," he said, and soon the coughs subsided.

"Let me see you," Kim demanded, "let me see you." He opened the door after turning out the bathroom light.

"See," he said, "fine."

She kissed him on the cheek and put a hand on his waist. Benjamin kissed her cheek in return, then sent her back to bed. Once she'd gone, he closed the door again, locked it, and then turned on the light. He looked at himself briefly in the mirror of the medicine cabinet before he opened it.

His pills were on the top shelf. He put one on his tongue and turned the faucet on. He cupped water in his hands and drank in gulps, washing the pill down. He sat on the floor, his back against the cabinet, the water running, thinking about Mary Jude in a wedding gown, flowers falling on her.

Later, he colored his hair with the Lady Clairol Home Coloring Treatment Kit he'd hidden in the cabinet beneath the sink, among the sponges and Ajax. Behind the pipes, the note was still up, one that Mary Jude had left just before she moved out: DON'T LEAVE THE HAIR COLOR ON TOO LONG!

He scratched his scalp madly, working the color in, then pulled the plastic cap on. The cap was still there three hours later, when the sunlight had filled the apartment, and when he slid it off his forehead, his hair was as glossy and black as shoe polish, darker even than it'd been when he was a boy, blacker than burned wood, blacker than an ink stain, so black it almost wasn't black anymore. It was nearly something else.

Benjamin figures he has an hour before Kim will be back. He pulls himself up from the floor and tosses the bedspread onto the bed. It covers the indentation she'd left, and Benjamin moves slowly toward his suitcase. His head feels as if it's webbed with frayed wires; his mouth is dry and sour. It's as if he has a hangover, though he hasn't been drinking. It's the driving that's done it. It's the driving, and it's Kim, and it's the sleeping on the floor—or not sleeping.

He checks his watch. It's eight-fifteen, and he clicks open his suitcase and takes out all the shirts and shorts and underwear that he's packed into one side. He places them folded, on the dresser, piece by piece. Beneath them is a plastic bag he takes with him to the bathroom.

"I'd hate to be you in the rain," he says as he takes the haircoloring kit from the plastic bag. Before the bathroom mirror, he talks to himself in whispers, hunched over the basin, his hair up in his fingers. "I'd really hate to be you in the rain." He imagines himself caught in a sudden downpour, the black water pouring down his face, staining it and his shirt as well, forming a dark lake about his shoes, the gray spot on the side of his head appearing, the patch the size of an apricot above his ear that's been there since he was a boy, since Phinney hit him with a stone. They'd been playing in an empty lot, tossing stones and cans at each other, trying to make the other flinch, and when Benjamin did, when he flinched, the stone hit him on the side of the head, not the front. His father drove him to the hospital, along with Phinney, and Phinney had cradled Benjamin's head like a small animal in his arms and said, "Lord, please make Benjamin's head whole again." He needed eighteen stitches in his scalp to seal the cut. The hair never grew in the same color as the rest. It grew in gray, as if a small part of him had grown old. Without the Lady Clairol, it looks like a bull's-eye.

Benjamin doesn't read the directions on the box before he starts. He knows what to do. He'd started coloring his hair when he was twenty-five or twenty-six and Mary Jude would buy the haircoloring at the drugstore so he wouldn't be embarrassed. Sometimes she'd sit with him in the bathroom while he waited for the color to take. "Benjamin Sacks," she'd say, her voice deep and booming, mocking the television commercials, "husband, salesman, and Lady Clairol user. Benjamin, tell us, how long have you been using Lady Clairol?" She'd hold a hairbrush out in front of him as if it were a microphone, and Benjamin would say, "Keep it up, Mary Jude. Just keep it up."

In short, brisk strokes, Benjamin massages the black lotion into his hair, then wipes his forehead with the back of the plastic gloves. There are black smudges on his cheeks, zigzags like Indian warpaint. There are streaks on his neck and forehead.

Benjamin pulls the plastic cap out of the box and puts it on, tucking the loose strands of his hair beneath the elastic. The cap is tight across his forehead, and it usually leaves a mark. He takes off the gloves, raises the toilet seat with his foot, drops the gloves in, then flushes them down, watching the black whirlpool they leave. He hoists himself up onto the counter and sits there, his had bowed.

This is the part he likes least: the waiting, the fifteen minutes before he can step into the shower. He reads the ingredients on the side of the box over and over to pass the time, studying the photograph of the woman on the box, her hair full and buoyant, her smooth moon-white skin making her look too young to need haircoloring. Kim's hair is sleek and black, and the woman on the box couldn't be more than five years older than Kim.

Benjamin put the cap on at eight-thirty. He checks his watch every minute or so, turning his wrist. If he leaves it on less than fifteen minutes, the patch stays gray. If he leaves it on too long, he looks like a game-show host. He's also careful about the kit, careful about leaving nothing behind, about leaving no trace that he'd colored his hair. Kim doesn't know he does it. She didn't even seem to notice the day after Mary Jude's wedding, and she doesn't know anything at all about the spot. If she saw it, she might think Yumi was right about his hair turning.

At home Benjamin flushes the cap and gloves down the toilet, scrubs the sink and tub free of black streaks and fingerprints, and puts the empty tube and instructions in a plastic bag. Then when Kim goes out for a run, or when she's shopping, or when she's asleep in bed, or later on the couch, he walks across the street and puts it in the garbage bin next to the liquor store. Sometimes he whistles when he does this, to add to the casualness of it all.

Now, anxious, Benjamin whistles one of the songs he and Kim have heard on the radio over and over again this trip, a love song. "This one's my favorite," she's said whenever it comes on. He reads the box. He checks his watch. There are nine minutes to go, and the ingredients are exactly the same as they were two weeks ago.

Maybe I don't want to touch Kim, he thinks. Maybe it's like those men who act differently around their wives after their wives have mastectomies or hysterectomies. He scans the assortment of containers Kim left around the basin.

Eye shadow.

Vaseline.

Lip gloss.

Q-tips.

Makeup remover.

Nail polish.

Nail-polish remover.

The bottle of Maybelline cover-up.

If she'd gotten up in the middle of the night to spread Maybelline over the scar, he'd missed it, and since he'd slept so poorly Benjamin assumes that she hadn't.

He whistles and knows that there's no difference between what he does to his hair and what Kim does to her scar, the creek that winds through her, that hiding is hiding no matter where the hiding's done. He's tried to convince himself that all he's hiding is his hair, and not even all of his hair at that, that everyone does it, everyone colors his hair, that that's why the haircoloring section in the supermarket is as large as it is: three full shelves.

There are still two minutes left for the Lady Clairol, and Benjamin brushes his teeth while he waits. He spits out the toothpaste, then puts shaving cream on his face, running a blade slowly over his cheeks so he won't nick himself, pressing the blade firmly against his upper lip, where the hair is coarsest. When he's done he splashes cold water on his face. His skin looks fresh and pink, much different from the darkness he'd been carrying with him so far on the trip. He runs his palms over his face, pleased by its new texture.

When he's done shaving, he pulls off his cap and rolls it into a tight ball the size of a chestnut and drops that into the toilet. He flushes it down, then steps into the shower stall. The water keeps changing temperatures, cold to hot, then back again, making Benjamin wince. A pool of black water forms about his feet. A ring of black remains at each ankle when he steps out, as if her were wearing socks. He scrubs his feet until they're white, then towels off his hair and body. The towel turns damp and gray.

Benjamin moves back into the bedroom and pulls on a pair of long green shorts, the same shade as an army uniform, and a navy-blue polo shirt. Then he goes back into the bathroom and swishes the towel around until there's no evidence of Lady Clairol. He opens the towel and sets the box, the empty tube, and instructions inside and wraps them like a gift. He checks the mirror, and his hair is black, the color of tar, through and through.

It's nine-ten, and again Benjamin is in the bedroom, on the bed, the stained towel beside him. He puts on his socks and sneakers, then walks over to the hotel restaurant, leaving the door to the room unlocked so Kim will be able to get in when she returns. He drops the towel in the large metal dumpster in the parking lot, whistling when he does this. He whistles Kim's favorite song.

The woman behind the cash register smiles and holds a hand up while she finished chewing whatever it is she's eating. Her lips smack. "G'morning," she says when her mouth is empty. "Do you need a table?"

"No," Benjamin answers, "thank you, though. I just wanted to pick up one of those," and he gestures with a quick nod toward the orange-and-blue Howard Johnson's T-shirt tacked to the wood paneling directly behind the woman. The tacks run through the shirt at each shoulder, pulling the shoulders up high so that the shirt looks as if it would be uncomfortable.

"What size do you need?" the woman asks, and she reaches beneath the counter. Before Benjamin's said anything, she comes up with a shirt folded in plastic. "You look like a medium."

"It's not for me," Benjamin says. The woman behind the cash register is in her sixties perhaps, her face rangy and crinkled like Eleanor Roosevelt's, like Mrs. Van Devere's, and Benjamin doesn't want to let on that he's here, hundred of miles from home, with a woman he's not married to. He starts to whistle to himself, quietly, the same song as before. Finally, he says, "It's for my wife."

"And what size does she need?"

"A medium."

The woman hands Benjamin the same shirt. Embarrassed, he hands her his credit card.

"That's right," he says, "we're both mediums. Funny."

The woman slides the sales slip to him, and he signs it quickly and stuffs his copy in his wallet. He thanks her and tucks the T-shirt under his arm and walks back to the room.

Kim isn't back yet, and Benjamin drops the T-shirt onto her suitcase so she'll find it when she gets back. He presses the button on the remote control to turn on the television, leaving it on the station they'd been watching last night, then climbs onto the bed. He pulls the flowered bedspread on top of him, stacks both of the pillows up against the headboard and sits upright. It's the "Dating Game," and it doesn't hold his interest long.

"Bachelor Number One, say hello to Katy."

"It's my pleasure, Katy," the man says, "but it could be yours."

Benjamin snorts and picks up the phone to call Phinney for directions. He carries the phone to his lap and dials the hotel operator, giving her Phinney's number.

"Bachelor Number One," Katy says on the television, "if you had to design a negligee for me, what would it look like?"

"It'd be black, and skimpy, and on the panties it'd say 'I love you, Katy.'"

The audience applauds, and Phinney's phone rings, and the thought of Kim in a negligee is in Benjamin's head, but only for a moment. He makes himself think of Phinney.

"Bachelor Number Two, the same question."

"Well, I don't know how to design negligees, but I'll tell you this. There wouldn't be enough material to write 'I love you, Katy' on it."

This time the audience hoots, and Benjamin thinks of Phinney, desperately. There was a time when Phinney could have helped me, he thinks. He shuts off the set with the remote control. He thinks of Phinney. He thinks of Phinney making everything better. He does *not* think of Kim, and he does *not* think of Kim in a thin, black negligee, all the lights on, and he does *not* think of the scar, as plain through the negligee as it would be if she were wearing nothing.

He needs to hear Phinney's voice, but the phone's still ringing. The

Yellow Pages lie open on the floor. Kim's read the Yellow Pages at each of the hotels, turning the pages with elaborate interest. Benjamin hadn't thought that strange. At home, she kept the phone books by the couch.

Benjamin can't make out what page the book is turned to, but when he leans over, turning on his side, he can, and in the upper corners of both pages he reads PHYSICIANS—PLASTIC SURGEONS in bold, black type.

A plastic surgeon for the scar.

Kim in a negligee.

Benjamin hangs up the phone just as he hears his brother answer. He slides down onto the bed until he is flat upon it, pulls the pillows over his face as he had when he was a boy, when he didn't want to go to school or church or cut the lawn, and he throws his arms and legs open, forming a giant, vulnerable X on the wrinkled white sheets.

The scar won't go away. He can't wish it away. His hair leaves a smear on the pillowcase, a smear that will never be bleached out.

* * *

"A town called Benjamin," Kim had said, and she turned the atlas sideways on her lap and pressed her finger to a spot on the page marked INDIANA. Her red fingernails matched her Coca-Cola T-shirt.

"What?" Benjamin answered, watching the road.

"Right here in Indiana, a town called Benjamin. A town with your name."

When she wasn't reading *Breakfast at Tiffany's* or working the cross-word puzzle in the *Sun,* Kim had been studying the *Rand McNally Road Atlas.*

"Have you ever noticed that Atlanta is one of the few cities that's spelled the same backwards as it is forwards?"

Benjamin shook his head and said, "Unh uh." After a moment, he turned to her and said, "It is not."

"It is not what?"

"It isn't spelled the same backwards as it is forwards."

"Well," Kim answered, "it's awfully darn close." And she flipped the pages. She called out the names of towns she liked. Frankfurt, Rome, Versailles, London.

"Isn't it funny how you can see all of Europe right here in America," she'd said, and when they passed a radio relay tower she shouted, "Look, Benjamin, it's the Eiffel Tower. Let's take a picture."

There were towns named Fortune and Fish and Gooseneck, but the ones that made her smile were the ones called Eden and Hurt. Kim marked the twenty miles between the two with her fingers. They should have been a continent apart, she told Benjamin. He said they were just names, they didn't mean a thing.

Now Benjamin glanced at the atlas, tightening his grip on the steering wheel, but he couldn't tell where Kim was pointing. Her finger took up a good section of the northwestern part of the state. He turned his head back to the highway, running as straight as a seam into the distance.

"Let's go to Benjamin," she cried.

"Where is it?"

"C4." She answered, giving the square of the map where Benjamin fell.

"No, I mean where is it from where we are? Where is it from I-70?"

"North," she said. "Let's go, Benjamin. Let's go to Benjamin, Benjamin," she said. "Benjamin, Benjamin. Benjamin, Benjamin. Benjamin, Benjamin."

"I don't know if we have the time." But he was curious to see what the town was like. Already he imagined Kim buying a T-shirt with the town's name on it, his name: BENJAMIN, in block letters.

"Sure we have the time. We have plenty of time."

"No, we don't. We have to get to Phinney's."

"Oh, come on. Benjamin's nearby. It's not like it's another continent or something."

"How far is it?"

Kim put the index finger of her left hand on the blue line that marked the highway, I-70, and the same finger of her right hand on the light gray dot of Benjamin, then she held her fingers up, separated as they were.

"It's only eight inches away." She smiled, raising her eyebrows. "Eight inches to Benjamin, Benjamin."

"Is that two hundred miles?"

"Not even a hundred. Ninety, maybe. A hundred, tops."

He said, "Tell me how to get there," as though she'd talked him into it, and she pulled her legs up to kneel in her seat and gave him the directions.

As he drove, she called out figures she saw in the clouds, though the sky was almost clear.

"A duck," she called, pointing. "See it?"

"Mm hmm."

"The letter *d*."

"Uppercase or lowercase?"

"Lower."

He didn't see it. He thought of Phinney.

"A bag of marshmallows."

"Where?"

"There."

"Kim, they all look like marshmallows."

"I know," she said, "but that one looks like a whole bag."

She called them out as they approached Benjamin, too excited to read.

"Lucille Ball."

"Mm hmm."

"Lucille Ball eating Fig Newtons," she called, and when Benjamin looked, she said, "Aha, I knew that would get you."

She tapped her fingers against her thighs to the songs on the radio while she searched the sky, and when they arrived in Benjamin, she was the first one out of the car. There was only a small green sign on the side of the road to let them know that they were there, a sign that read, ENTERING THE TOWN OF BENJAMIN, INDIANA. Benjamin pulled the car beside it.

The land next to the road was dry as far as they could see. Dirt blew up into swirls like ghosts. The ground was cracked into a billion puzzle pieces that did not fit. Kim looked at the zippered ground, disappointed. She walked around to the driver's side of the car and put her hand on Benjamin's elbow.

"Poor Benjamin," she said, "all sad and cracking up." He couldn't tell which Benjamin she meant.

Benjamin and Kim got back into the car and drove farther into town. The land still wasn't green, not green the way farmland should be. The town seemed to be collapsing into itself. Benjamin could imagine how beautiful it would be when the rains came regularly, he could imagine fields of wheat and corn and yellow-orange tractors crawling through the fields like bugs. But it wasn't easy. It was like imagining another era.

The road led to a small shopping area. There were two traffic lights and a dozen stores or so. A bakery. A supermarket. A hardware store. A five-and-ten. People chugged along the streets carrying bags, people whose very posture revealed that their fortunes were tied to the land and to the water, to the rains that hadn't come this summer. It was a town full of people who walked as his father had in his last days.

That was it exactly: Benjamin could see his father in Benjamin, walking these streets. He didn't stop, not for gas, not for a soda, not to let Kim look for a T-shirt. He stopped the car at the traffic light only because he had to.

"Is this the main street?" Kim called to a woman on the sidewalk. The woman held a small girl's hand. Both were dressed in jeans, their hair pulled back off their faces.

"Yes," the woman answered, "this is it." She was sweet-faced and large. "It cuts right through the center of Benjamin. Where is it you're headed?"

"Nowhere in particular," Kim said, "we're just sightseeing," and she thanked the woman politely.

When the light changed, Benjamin turned the car around in the center of town and headed back toward I-70, an hour and a half away. Again, Kim was studying the atlas, a map of the United States.

"Geez," she said. "Did you know there's a town in Texas called Paradise?"

"Nope," Benjamin answered, watching the road before him, tow lanes, one in each direction. He'd thought the past was in a different state, in Maryland, and that they'd been driving away from it for two days, but, suddenly, here it was again.

"Well, there is." Kim paused. "Look how far Baltimore is from Paradise. God, we're closer to New Jersey than to Paradise. Can you believe it?"

She called out the names of towns, measuring the distances between them.

"It's twenty miles between Charade and Daffodil."

"Fifty miles between Folly and Reason."

"It's thirty-five miles between Rising Sun and Heaven."

When the road widened to two lanes, Benjamin speeded up, driving seventy miles per hour as calmly as if it were thirty, racing for the interstate and away from town. He was racing toward Phinney, recklessly, and he had the strange sensation that someday he would remember this moment differently. He would remember himself being stronger. He would remember Benjamin meaning nothing to him.

The pillow is over his face still. He listens to himself breathe.

When Kim returns to the hotel room, she's puffing, her hands at her hips.

"God," she says, "it's so humid here. It makes you wonder how places like this got settled. I mean, did someone say, 'Geez, this looks like miserable weather. Let's settle here.'"

She jostles the bed with her foot.

"Come on. Get up," she says, "sleepyhead," but again Benjamin pulls the bedspread over himself.

"Forget it," he answers. "I'm not moving."

"We've got to go. I'll take a quick shower, and then we'll go. Checkout's in less than an hour, isn't it?" She's breathless.

"An hour, two hours. Who knows. How was your run?"

"Fine." She stretches, pushing against the wall. One knee is bent, the one closest to the wall. The other is straight. Her T-shirt says Harborplace in black script on both front and back. "It's pretty around here, if you ignore the humidity. I mean, you run and you can't help but think that this is what the world looks like."

"How far did you go?"

"Seven miles, maybe seven and a half. It's hard to tell when you don't know the streets. You know, I saw a hamburger place with a giant red rooster in front of it. A plastic one. It must've been fifteen feet high, and it had a bib on." She shifts legs, still pushing against the wall. "Now, are you going to get up or am I going to have to drag you out of there?"

"Listen, Kim, why don't we stay here for the day?" Benjamin says from beneath the pillows. "We could just go shopping or something. You know, just relax, throw the baseball around for a while, sit by the pool, grab some lunch. That doesn't sound horrible, does it? What do you think? What's your opinion on this?"

Kim leaps onto the bed and slides on top of him. "Love to," she says. "But are you sure you want to? I mean, is it okay?"

"Positive," he says, though he isn't sure why. For some reason he wants to go nowhere with her today.

"We can go shopping, Benjamin. It'll be great." She hovers over him. Her hands are above his shoulders, by his neck, her knees at his hips. "We'll have to call Phinney again. Have you called him?"

"No, why don't you do it?"

"Isn't he going to be mad?"

Benjamin shakes his head.

Kim dials the hotel operator, and Benjamin tells her Phinney's number.

"This is going to be great," she says, "Benjamin, it'll be fun. Just you and me going shopping out here in the middle of wherever we are. Let's buy a car. No, let's buy diamond necklaces and earrings. Gold ones the size of almonds."

Benjamin's face is expressionless beneath the bedspread.

"Shhh," she says. "It's ringing. What should I say?"

Benjamin sits up in bed, and Kim falls against him, her head on his chest. She's as light as a pillow against his skin. A spot on his shirt becomes moist from her perspiration.

"Say we had problems with the carburetor," he sighs. "Say you're going through menopause. Say your aunt died. Say we lost our traveler's checks."

Tell him whatever you want, Benjamin thinks, just don't tell him my soul is too tired to be driving.

CHAPTER 4
A WOMAN IN HERE

MARY JUDE HAD A MARK, too, but that was different. There was a mark on her calf, her left one, the size of a coin and the color of chocolate, like coffee spilled, but Benjamin liked it. A beauty mark. He'd noticed it the first time he'd met her, at the YMCA in Bluefield when they were teenagers. It wasn't like the creek, it was more of a curiosity, like his gray spot. It didn't mean anything.

Early in the mornings, he would slide down on the bed and clutch Mary Jude's leg, considering the mark, and when she'd wake up, rubbing her eyes, one leg pinned to the bed, he'd press his lips against the stain and smack them loudly.

"Will you cut that out," she'd giggle. She was coy and romantic, Mary Jude.

"Why? I like it."

"It's my leg, not yours."

"It's part of the package, sweetheart," he'd said. "I got you, for better or worse, including the leg. The whole package. You can look it up. It's legally binding in every way."

"You're bananas."

"Call your lawyer."

"It's ugly, Benjamin. I can't stand it."

"Don't say that." He'd put his hand on his chest, over his heart. "I like it. Honestly. Truly. Sincerely. It's your mark, Mrs. Sacks. It makes you special."

Whenever he'd said that, she'd grab him by his shoulders and pull him up, then pull his mouth to her own. She'd kiss him as if she were drinking. The mornings were what Benjamin waited for.

Once, lying at the end of the bed, studying the mark, he'd laughed aloud and rolled onto his back. He'd put his hands on the top of his head.

"What's so funny?" Mary Jude had asked.

"Nothing." He'd tried to catch his laugh by tightening his jaw.

"Really, what's so funny?"

"I finally figured out what it looks like. I finally figured out what your beauty mark looks like."

"And what's that?"

"Nothing. Forget it." He was laughing hard now, a rumbling, chesty laugh.

"Forget nothing. Tell me, Benjamin."

"No. Some other time."

"Tell me now. I want to know now."

Benjamin had covered his face with his forearms to protect himself, like a boxer. He'd separated his arms enough to peek through. "It looks like the guy who hosts 'Soul Train,'" he'd said, "Don Cornelius," and Mary Jude had kicked her legs like pedaling a bicycle until he pulled himself up to the top of the bed.

"I love you," he'd said, hovering above her, and she'd said, "What? I can't hear you."

Though he'd suspected she'd heard him the first time, he'd repeated the words directly into her ear and pressed his palms flat against her own. Her hands were smaller than his, but only slightly. He'd pressed his hands to hers and kissed her. Even when they were teenagers, her hands were smaller than his, which was only odd because he had such small hands for a boy.

It was twenty-four years after they met, nearly twenty-five, when Mary Jude began packing, and that's what Benjamin thought of. He thought of how small her hands were. Mary Jude moved her bags to the living room, by the front door of the apartment. Benjamin had heard her packing, but he stayed in the recliner and let her continue, not sure how to stop her, or if he should. He shut his eyes and put his hands over his ears so he couldn't hear, and he sat and remembered.

His own hands had been a ten-year-old's hands on a boy of seventeen, he thought. His hands were narrow, his fingers, too, like beans, and the skin of his palms had been fleshy and white, as smooth as calfskin. Even digging the well in the backyard the summer he met her hadn't raised a blister on his hands, but Phinney's hands—and their father's and mother's— were relief maps of blisters from the digging.

Mary Jude's wrists were small, too, so thin that Benjamin could encircle them with his thumb and index finger. It was a snug fit, as if he held the future too tightly, and though Mary Jude and Benjamin grew in their years together, his small hands, hers and her thin wrists remained the same.

Benjamin didn't pull himself from the chair until she had her coat and scarf on and was standing at the door. She flipped her hair from her collar and said, "I don't know how to do this, Benjamin. I love you, though. Okay?"

Benjamin moved closer. The coat was tan wool. It'd been an anniversary present to her. The coat was long and masculine, but the way she walked and her scarves always disguised that.

Benjamin pulled the collar up around her neck so the wind wouldn't strike her when she got outside. He touched her hair, rubbed it between his fingers as though it were fine fabric. Mary Jude pursed her lips. He touched her wrists next, squeezing them gently as she held them at her sides.

"Look, I've left notes all over the place so you don't forget to do things. You know, take your pills, buy coffee, things like that. You'll find them. I'm going to stay with Frank and Julie for a couple weeks, so if you need me— I mean *need* me, Benjamin—if you really need me, call me there. I'll be back to get more of my things sometime soon. I'll come back with Julie while you and Frank are at work or something. And please don't be angry with them for letting me stay there. They care about both of us."

Benjamin stood before her, holding her wrists. He stood like a statue of himself.

"I," she said, stuttering, "I just don't, you know, I just don't know what to do anymore. I'm lonesome, and you're not with me. You're here physically, but God knows where you really are, and I don't know what to do anymore, and so leaving just seems like the thing to do."

He wasn't about to speak. "And don't tell me I'm running away from my problems because, first of all, I'm not. You're only running away from something if you can still fix it, if you can repair. And, second of all, even if I am running away from my problems, there's nothing wrong with that. But I'm not, so don't think I am. I've thought this all out. I've considered."

His fingers were around her wrists still, the fit snugger than ever. The tips of his index fingers made only the slightest contact with his thumbs, and he was afraid his grip was hurting her now.

Benjamin thought of telling her that he loved her.

Benjamin thought of telling her that he didn't want her to go.

Benjamin thought of telling her that he just needed more time, but nothing came out of his mouth.

"I can't be your psychologist or psychiatrist or whatever it is anymore. And don't tell me about how I used to say that no one really needs a psychologist or psychiatrist if they have someone who they can talk to who cares about them. I just—God, Benjamin—how can I help you if you stay in your chair all the time? How can I help you if you won't *talk*? Look what's becoming of me."

Her sadness was stunning.

"You just don't make me happy anymore, Benjamin. A thousand Benjamins couldn't make me happy anymore."

Delicately, he pulled her wrists together in front of her, the line of her shoulders a half circle. Mary Jude still wore his mother's engagement ring and wedding band.

"Please, Benjamin," she pleaded, softly, "you have to let me go," and she bent at the knee and tried to twist free, her elbows rising and falling and moving at odd angles. The fabric of her skirt bunched above her knees.

"Please?" she said. "I have to go. The past isn't what it used to be," she said, "at least not for me."

When he released her, she seized the handles of her suitcases and lifted them from the ground. They were so heavy she was thrown off balance as she walked. The suitcases banged against her legs and against the elevator doors.

Benjamin moved into the hallway. "Sweetheart," he said finally, "am I supposed to help you with those?" He pointed to the luggage. "I don't know what I'm supposed to do. I never know what I'm supposed to do."

She pitched her head to the side. "I can't hear you."

"Am I supposed to help you with your suitcases?"

"I'm already here," she said. "I'm already gone, Benjamin. Really, I hope everything gets better soon, it's just that"—a bell sounded, and she turned her head quickly back and forth—"it's here," and the elevator was there. She bent and pushed her suitcases on. The doors closed before her like theater curtains, and Benjamin returned to the apartment and walked directly to the recliner. Across the room, taped to the side of the television, was a note that read SHUT OFF THE TV BEFORE YOU FALL ASLEEP.

All of my experiences here, in Baltimore, Benjamin thought, have been similarly uninspiring. Nothing happens here. And when it does, when something does happen, it happens without event. I just bob along.

He bobbed along, and time passed with such speed that Benjamin barely noticed it washing by. A month, two months, six, and then a full year without Mary Jude, nearly. And each day felt like New Year's Day: cold and nothing to do. The days were indistinguishable. As Benjamin went to the office in the morning and came home at night, the change in clothes was his only reminder that time was passing. Coats in winter, short sleeves in summer.

Without Mary Jude, the apartment began to feel larger, and yet there was no place to get lost in it. Wherever Benjamin went, he was visible to himself. She was visible, too, and not just in the photographs on the bookshelf and in the bedroom. In the kitchen, cooking. In the bedroom, on top of him. In the bathroom, her fingers massaging his scalp. These images remained in the apartment like the ghosts of flashbulbs.

But they grew dimmer, and within weeks of her departure, the apartment had stopped smelling of her. Within a year, it smelled like any other place.

Benjamin's office faced east, and in the mornings the Venetian blinds cast long slanted shadows across the room. The divorce papers arrived at work with the mail one morning. Benjamin opened the manila envelope and held the papers on the palms of his hands like a scale, as though he were weighing the divorce itself.

The divorce agreement was longer than Benjamin had expected: thirty-nine pages, as fat as a deck of cards. Along the top of the front page was UNCONTESTED DIVORCE AND PROPERTY SETTLEMENT AGREEMENT. Hallyday had drawn up the papers with Benjamin's lawyer. Benjamin hadn't even had a lawyer at the time. He found one in the Yellow Pages and only after Babisch had insisted.

"I know she wouldn't take advantage of you," Babisch had said, "but everything has implications these days. Do you know what I mean, implications?" and Benjamin had nodded.

Benjamin closed the door to his office. "Cecily," he said, calling his secretary on the intercom, "Cecily, could you get me a cup of coffee?" He settled down in his chair to read the agreement.

THIS AGREEMENT is entered into this 17th day of October, 1986, by and between Benjamin Eugene Sacks (hereinafter referred to as "Husband") and Mary Jude Glover Sacks (hereinafter referred to as "Wife").

The date had been filled in in black ink.

EXPLANATORY STATEMENT

The parties were married by a religious ceremony on June 6, 1966, in Bluefield, Maryland. No children were born to the parties as a result of their marriage. Differences have arisen between the parties and they are now, and have been since December 19, 1985, living separate and apart from one another, voluntarily and by mutual consent, in separate places of abode, without cohabitation, with the purpose and intent of ending their marriage.

Benjamin's secretary buzzed his phone. Benjamin spoke briefly with one of his customers, then tried to find his place again.

No children were born to the parties as a result of their marriages. Differences

His secretary knocked at his door. Benjamin called, "Come in," and she set a cup of coffee on the desk.

"Are you all right?" she said. She was a thin blond woman, just out of college, and her Baltimore accent leaked out of the corner of her mouth.

"Fine. Don't I look all right?"

"No," she said, "you look the same as always."

Benjamin thanked her and she left, closing the door behind her.

Bluefield, Maryland. No children were born to the parties as a result of their marriage. Differences have arisen between the parties and they are now

Benjamin flipped the pages, reading sections at random.

The parties agree from the date of this Agreement to continue to live separate and apart, voluntarily and by mutual consent, in separate places of abode, without any cohabitation, in termination of their marriage. Neither of the parties shall interfere with or molest the other, nor endeavor in any way to exercise any marital control or right over the other, not to have any marital relations with the other, nor to gain entrance into the other's home without prior consent. Furthermore

In consideration of the provisions contained herein, Husband and Wife hereby waive and relinquish any claim or right which either of them have to temporary or permanent alimony, past, present, or future. Each party acknowledges that this provision

Benjamin took a sip of his coffee. It was still warm, and he set the cup down on the divorce agreement. He rang Babisch's office. When he answered, Benjamin said, "We didn't even talk about alimony."

"What?"

"The divorce papers just came, and there's something in here about alimony."

"What, she wants alimony?"

"No, she doesn't want alimony."

"So what's the problem?"

"It just seems like something we should've talked about."

Benjamin apologized for calling. He lifted his coffee cup from the papers. It left a brown stain on the page. He didn't try to wipe the mark off, he just returned to reading. By noon, he was tired. The document didn't tell him anything new, it just did it in different language, and he picked up the clock off his desk. It was an old-fashioned, round-faced, wind-up model, the kind Lomax used to make before the electric ones became popular, long before anyone had even heard of digitals. It was the first clock Benjamin had had in his office, and it still kept time closely enough for him.

He ran a tissue over the face of the clock, then threw the tissue in the trash basket behind his desk. The sun was almost directly overhead. His office could be facing anywhere, Benjamin thought. He always found that disorienting. He placed the clock face down on his desk and unscrewed the back of the clock with his thumbnail. He put the back piece and the tiny screws off to the side and cleaned the wheels and gears with a black brush from his top drawer. He blew the loose dirt free, replaced the back, and set the clock upright on his desk, then rose to get his overcoat to go to lunch.

He brought the divorce papers with him and read them again while he ate. When he returned, the sun had shifted to the opposite side of the building. He twisted the wand of his Venetian blinds to open them fully. He hung his coat on the back of the door and returned to his desk. Again, he looked at the papers, starting from the beginning, UNCONTESTED DIVORCE AND PROPERTY SETTLEMENT AGREEMENT, and when he looked at the clock it said one-forty. He checked his watch: twelve-fifty. He looked at the clock again: one-forty.

Benjamin depressed the talk button on the intercom. "Cecily?"

"Yes?"

"Do you have the time?"

"Twelve-fifty," she said.

Time was moving too quickly in his office.

By cleaning the clock, he'd made the wheels spin too fast. When Benjamin realized this, he removed the back again. He wasn't in the mood to call on customers. Instead, he wadded up small pieces of tissue and typing paper and dropped them into the clock casing. He sharpened a pencil over it, letting the scrapings fall in. He rummaged through the desk drawers and the trash basket for items to add. Paper clips and dust balls—things like that.

He wanted time to do everything. He wanted the clock to work backwards, to go back to before the time Mary Jude left, past when he'd started spending so much time in the recliner, past when they moved to Baltimore, past when everything happened with his parents and with Phinney. When his watch said one-oh-five, the clock said two.

At one-thirty, it said two-twenty-one.

At two, it said two-thirty-three. He went down the hall to the men's room and took one of his pills.

Finally, both the watch and the clock said two-fifty-two.

At three o'clock, the clock read two-fifty-eight.

The real time and the time in the office kept diverging.

Three-forty-five; three-oh-six.

Four o'clock; three-twelve.

He thought he'd stay until dawn, to see if the sun rose on the wrong side, west to east, dragging time backward. Then he'd go to the apartment and fiddle with all of the clocks there, the one in the shape of a teakettle in the kitchen, the miniature grandfather's clock on the mantelpiece.

There was a digital one in the bedroom, on Mary Jude's side of the bed, the side that had been hers.

As the office emptied, Benjamin continued watching the clock. His secretary poked her head into the office to say good night, and Benjamin said, "Leaving already?" and she nodded yes.

Time wasn't going anywhere, and he was ashamed.

He spent that weekend alone, in the apartment, not answering the door or the phone. He was in the recliner and Frank Babisch was thumping his fist against the apartment door. Benjamin ignored the knocks.

It was four o'clock.

The divorce papers were on the coffee table in the living room. There were brown rings from his coffee cup on nearly every page.

Benjamin sat in the recliner in his underwear and socks.

The rain tapped against the window like the keys of a typewriter clacking.

The thermostat read sixty-eight degrees, but to Benjamin the apartment seemed much cooler.

The bookshelves and closets were half-filled.

West Side Story was on the television, and Babisch was thumping his fist against the door.

"Benjamin?"

Benjamin wondered whether he should allow him in. He stood beside the door, careful not to make a noise. Babisch had been visiting Benjamin to check up on him since Mary Jude moved out. He and Julie had tried to keep Benjamin busy. Benjamin appreciated their motives, but Babisch was becoming a downright nuisance. It was the sympathy that he showed Benjamin. Benjamin didn't feel he deserved it, not an ounce. I *made* her leave, the way I was, the way I am.

Besides, Babisch was happy, Benjamin thought. He could never understand sadness.

"I know you're in there, Ben. What's wrong with you?"

"Is that you, Babisch?"

"Of course it's me. Now open the door already."

"I'm busy, Babisch. I'll give you a call later, okay?"

"Listen, Benjamin, open the door. You're making a fool of me out here."

Benjamin huffed, then answered, "Babisch, be a good friend and go away."

"What does that mean?"

"It means I'll give you a call later, that's all it means."

"What's wrong with you today? You're acting like a nut. Now open up already. I've got plans for us."

"Where's Julie today?"

"She's shopping," Babisch said. "She sent a cheesecake over for you. I'm holding it right now." Babisch addressed him as he would a stubborn child. "Can you smell it, Benjamin? Mmmm good. Cheesecake, Benjamin."

Benjamin said nothing.

"Now open up the lousy door already."

Babisch rapped his fists against it again and again. He wasn't about to leave, and Benjamin's mind raced, searching for a good explanation for the way he was behaving. Finally he pressed his face against the thick oak door. He whispered, "Babisch, please leave me alone. I've got a woman in here."

"What? I can't hear you."

Benjamin spoke up, his whisper nearly as loud as his normal speaking voice. He was sure Babisch had heard, but he repeated himself nonetheless. "I've got a woman in here, Babisch. She's coming out of the shower this very minute. Please, I'll call you later."

If anyone should have known better, it was Babisch. Still he replied, "Enough said, Benjamin. Enough said. I'll bring the cheesecake by later. But don't forget to call later."

"Promise."

He left, and Benjamin returned to his bedroom to finish dressing. Mary Jude's note remained on the closet door: GO TO THE DRY CLEANER'S TWICE A WEEK OR YOU'LL RUN OUT OF CLOTHES! The clock on her side of the bed was keeping perfect time: 4:08. He pulled on a light blue sports shirt, a navy sweater, and gray slacks, then moved back into the kitchen and made himself a pot of coffee. The note on the cupboard said BUY FOOD.

Once when he was a boy, Benjamin had asked his parents for a big brother. Many years later, there he was: Frank Babisch. Benjamin had known him for nearly fifteen years. When Benjamin and Mary Jude moved from Bluefield to Baltimore for his new job, and to be closer to Phinney, Babisch was in the office next to Benjamin's. It was Babisch who took him to lunch and introduced him around and taught him about watches. Ten years older than Benjamin, he was distinguished in appearance with his crown of gray curls. Benjamin found it easy to talk to Babisch. He always listened, and Benjamin admired him from the start, the way he seemed to keep his life in order. But he couldn't tell Babisch why Mary Jude had moved to New York.

Benjamin poured himself a cup of coffee and carried it to the living room, set it down on an end table, and let the coffee go cold before he brought it to his lips to wash down one of his pills. The divorce papers were unfolded atop the stack of *Baltimore* and *Life* magazines. Benjamin took a seat in his recliner and pushed the arms forward and turned up the volume on the television set with the remote control. Natalie Wood was singing in a dress shop. Benjamin touched the divorce papers, grazing them with his fingertips. Sometimes he believed that he'd imagined them but they were real all right. They were real, with brown coffee stains on nearly every page, rings that interlocked like chain links.

Wife shall retain ownership and title to the 1980 Volvo diesel automobile, which she presently operates and which is titled in the names of both Husband and Wife. Wife shall hereafter assume and pay in accordance with its terms any outstanding loan or indebtedness in connection with said automobile.

Wife shall deliver to Husband all necessary fully executed and acknowledged documents, which shall convey to Husband all of Wife's right, title, and interest in and to the 1978 Ford Mustang automobile, presently operated by Husband, to the end that Husband shall be the sole owner of good and merchantable title to the same. Husband shall hereafter execute all necessary documents to assume and pay in accordance with its terms any outstanding loan or indebtedness in connection with said automobile.

They'd bought both cars, used, from the same lot in Silver Spring, the Mustang first. Benjamin flipped pages with his thumb.

The parties have agreed to a division of their tangible personal property, including, but not limited to, artworks, antiques, furniture and household chattels presently located at the 4310 Burton Avenue residence, and each shall hold as his or her separate property such articles of tangible personal property as are set forth on Schedule A attached hereto and incorporated herein, free and clear of any interest of the other party.

Benjamin got up from the recliner and fixed himself a sandwich. He opened a package of bologna and laid two pieces on a slice of white bread. I have to make myself forget, he thought as he spread mustard on one of the slices of bread and cut the sandwich in half. I have to try to make myself forget Mary Jude, and forget my parents, and forget Phinney, or I'll be like this forever. He poured another cup of coffee and brought the cup and sandwich back into the living room. There was a commercial on, and he switched stations to a basketball game. The New York Knicks were racing across the screen in their unseasonable shorts, and Benjamin adjusted the color and sat back to watch, though he wasn't much of a basketball fan. He set the coffee cup down on top of the divorce papers.

The phone rang. It was Babisch.

"What do you want, Babisch?"

"I just called to see if that woman's still there."

"Why?"

"Well, if she's not, I though we might reserve one of those indoor tennis courts and hit around some. The courts up in Towson."

"Sorry, Babisch, but she's still here."

"Well, how long is she going to stay?"

"Geez, I don't know, Babisch. How should I know that?"

Babisch was still talking, but Benjamin stopped paying attention. The basketball game was being played in New York, and Benjamin didn't watch the players. He searched the crowd for Mary Jude. She never like basketball much either, but who knows what Hallyday had taught her.

He knew she was in New York with Hallyday, whether she told him so or not. It was too much of a coincidence that both of them should be in New York.

"Benjamin, are you still there?"

He scoured the crowd for the red-orange tangle of Mary Jude's hair.

"Yeah, I'm still here."

Benjamin lifted his coffee cup from the divorce agreement, wrapping his fingers around the rim, and took a drink, and the cup left a fresh stain on the page, a perfect brown circle.

"Will you call me as soon as your lady friend leaves?" Babisch asked.

"The second she leaves, Babisch."

CHAPTER 5
BIG SISTER

"GOD, PHINNEY, IT'S THE THINGAMABOB that begins with a C," Kim says. "I don't know. It's metal or something. Round."

Phinney's voice on the other end of the phone is a buzz sounding deep, dull notes. Benjamin sits up in bed and props the pillow against the headboard.

"That's it," Kim says, "the carburetor. I couldn't remember what it was." She winks at Benjamin conspiratorially. There are half-moons of sweat at three and nine o'clock on her T-shirt and a triangle at noon. Her legs gleam with perspiration. "They're trying to fix it now," and she sounds concerned and genuine, apologizing.

She's silent while Phinney speaks, just nodding her head and humming, "Mc hmm." When he's through, she tells Phinney about the woman they passed on the highway, drinking from a baby bottle while she drove. The bumper sticker on the back of her car read CAUTION: DRIVER APPLYING MAKEUP. She tells Phinney about how Benjamin had blushed when she told the woman at the cash register that she was carrying his baby. She tells Phinney about a sign above the grill in a diner in Ohio that read BONELESS CHICKEN DINNER ONLY 30 CENTS, and how she asked the cook what that was, and he'd explained that it was a hard-boiled egg. She tells Phinney everything she can remember about the trip, then she says, "We'll see you tomorrow, sweetie." Though she's never met him she calls him sweetie, but she calls everyone that. She hands the phone to Benjamin.

"Phinney, hi."

Phinney snorts. "Benjamin, is there really something wrong with the car or are you two just screwing around?"

"No," Benjamin protests, "it really is the carburetor. It nearly blew up. We've got the car over at the Mobil station." He gestures meaninglessly toward the door.

"All right, if you say so."

Kim stands at the foot of the bed, her back to it. She twists off her running shoes and slides her shorts and underwear to her feet, stepping out of them. They lie there on the floor, without shape. Listening to Phinney, Benjamin watches her the way he would watch a cheap magician, while Kim removes her brassiere without first removing her T-shirt, her arms twisted behind her like a half nelson, producing the brassiere like a rabbit from beneath the shirt. It's the same pink as her underpants.

She walks to the bathroom, drawing her arms above her head to loosen her muscles. Her T-shirt rises to uncover most of her bottom. The shower water begins running almost as soon as the bathroom door closes.

Phinney talks and Benjamin listens, listening to his breath as well, deep and evenly spaced, almost as loud as the shower water splashing. He is, he thinks, a man gasping for air. A man preparing to test his lungs underwater, holding his breath until he gets to Phinney and yet purposely postponing that. Phinney can help, he reassures himself. Maybe.

When Phinney pauses, Benjamin says, "Phinney?" He listens to the sound of the shower. It reminds Benjamin of the autumn rain, fat drops thumping against the windowpanes as eagerly as children. It reminds him of the rain against the Laundromat and against the windows of Earl Van Devere's apartment, the autumn after their parents died. Only the sound of the shower with Kim in it is fuller, musical, as if the sound of the water on the porcelain were mixing with the sound of the water against Kim, an orchestra of two instruments. Kim and the porcelain.

Benjamin listens to himself breathe in and out. He nearly asks Phinney how he is. Usually when he does, his brother puffs, "The same as always," as if he's forgotten that he used to be different, before that summer. We were just boys then, Benjamin thinks. Maybe Phinney would've changed anyway. Instead he says, "Sorry about this carburetor thing."

Phinney is silent.

"Look, I've got to run. We'll be there tomorrow. I really am sorry about this carburetor thing, okay?"

"It's okay. See you tomorrow."

"Tomorrow," Benjamin says, and he hangs up the phone. He breathes in and out, his chest expanding. Phinney's the only one who can help. Benjamin hears Kim turn off the shower. When he sits up in bed he spots the smeared pillowcase, the black streak of haircoloring, and he stuffs it under the bed, pillow and all.

The bathroom door clicks open, and Kim pops her head out, peeking, gripping the doorframe with her fingers. "Benjamin," she calls, "what are you doing?" Benjamin says that he's doing nothing. She says, "Well, honey, would you mind turning your back for a second? I forgot to bring a clean T-shirt into the bathroom."

Benjamin looks to the window, the drawn brown-and-blue drapes. "My back's turned. Oh, I picked up a T-shirt for you in the restaurant," he says just as she discovers it on top of her suitcase.

"Great." He hears the shuffling of cloth against her skin. The bed jumps, and Kim's sitting beside him, her legs folded beneath her. "Thanks," she says, kissing his ear. "You're wonderful." Her hair is wet and slick. It smells like strawberries from the shampoo.

Benjamin breathes the smell of strawberries, with her cheek pressed against his. Suddenly, she pulls away.

"Did you shave?" she says sternly.

"Mm hmm. I thought you wanted me to."

"Did you have shaving cream?" she asks.

"Yeah."

Kim pushes at his shoulder. "I didn't know you had shaving cream with you."

"Sure," Benjamin answers, "in my suitcase," and he flicks his hand toward the dresser.

"Jesus, Benjamin, I shaved my legs in the shower yesterday without shaving cream. I didn't think you had any."

"Well, I did," he says, and she sneers before pressing her cheek against his again.

"Your face feels better smooth," Kim says.

Benjamin breathes in more of the smell of strawberries, listening to himself. He sits unmoving. Finally, he slaps his palm lightly against Kim's thigh, then plucks at her knee. "Come on. Get dressed and we'll go get something to eat."

Kim hops off the bed, and it jumps again. She digs through the clothes in her suitcase. The pattern on the shorts she chooses is of leaves and pineapples, and she zips them up, her back to Benjamin, and sits on the edge of the bed to tie on her running shoes.

"Let's go," she says, and she takes Benjamin's hand. "Oh, hold on." She picks up her running shorts and underwear from the floor. When Benjamin unlocks the car, she hangs them from the suit hook behind her seat. Her brassiere hangs like a pink medallion, and Benjamin raises his eyebrows.

Kim responds, "So they'll dry out," and Benjamin gets in the car.

"Maybe you want to tie your bra to the antenna. Maybe I should hang my boxers from the rearview mirror," he says in mock frustration, and Kim whoops, falling back into her seat. "We can drive around town, and everyone will say, 'Look at those two people driving around in the…'" he pauses, searching for something to keep Kim laughing, "in the Underwearmobile.'"

And Kim does laugh.

"We could paint it on the side of the car," Benjamin continues.

Kim twists in her seat.

"In big green letters."

Kim laughs in coughs.

"Big green script letters."

Kim holds her hand over her chest. It bounces with her mad cough.

"The Underwearmobile. What do you think? Not a bid idea, huh?"

Kim slips further into her seat, her feet against the glove compartment now. "The Underwearmobile," she cheers. The strap of her brassiere, floating in the breeze, clanks against the rear window without rhythm, without tempo, without care.

The rooster in front of the restaurant is as tall as Kim had said, fifteen feet at least. It has a yellow beak and SAL'S BURGERS painted across its chest, also in yellow.

Benjamin only saw Kim turn Japanese on Saturdays, his day off. The rest of the week she was gone before he returned from work, and at eleven-fifteen he'd walk the four blocks to Yumi's to wait in the entranceway by the hostess stand to walk Kim home.

Saturdays, from the bedroom, he would watch as she stood in front of the bathroom mirror in her underwear and a T-shirt, bending at the waist and leaning over the counter and toward the mirror, making an O with her mouth to apply her lipstick, folding her lips to apply her rouge. He would watch her legs, thin and taut, and the tug of her breasts against the T-shirt.

In March, one Saturday months before his birthday, he walked in on her, into the bathroom, and stood behind her, running his hands along the silk of her panties and along the outside of her thighs. He rested his chin in the crook of her neck and soaked in her perfume.

"How are you, Sachiko?"

"Great."

"Why?" he whispered in her ear.

She laughed and swatted his hand from her rear end with the brush of her eye shadow. "You know, I was thinking how Yumi says you should always wear a bra and panties that match."

"Why is that?"

"That way, if you're having a bad day, you'll think, I'm wearing *matching underwear*, and the whole world will look brighter."

"Is that right?"

"Yeah," Kim said. "It's psychological, I think, but yeah."

Benjamin brought his lips to her earlobe. As coyly as he could he asked, "So, are you wearing matching underwear today?"

"Mm hmm."

The fingers of Benjamin's left hand grabbed the bottom of her T-shirt at the back, and he began to inch it up. She swatted at him as she had before, but he continued, kissing her earlobe. She shook him off, cocking her head to bring her ear to her shoulder, smiling.

"Cut it out," she said, "that tickles."

The shirt inched up her back. She couldn't feel it, Benjamin could tell, moving it deliberately, distracting her at the same time.

He kissed her again, on the back of the head, and she protested, "I have to go to work. Now, be a good boy."

When his fingers and the shirt reached the strap of her brassiere, she wheeled to face him, her features distorted, one hand pressing the shirt to her belly, the other behind her, holding it to the small of her back.

"What are you doing?" she shouted, and Benjamin ducked as if he could escape her anger that way. She smudged eye shadow over her left eye when she turned, leaving a line the width of a pencil from her eyelid to her cheek.

"What do you *think* I'm doing?" He was confused, still smiling devilishly, but she'd confused him before this way.

"I know what you're doing, and don't do it anymore. You're always pushing."

"God, you sound so mad."

"If I sound mad," she said, "it's because I am. I want to keep my shirt on. Is that such a big deal?"

"No," he answered timidly. Still he wanted to hold her, to feel her skin in his hands and against his own skin.

"Now, get out of the goddamn bathroom." She banged the door closed with her bare foot. The lock clicked, then she mumbled, "Goddamnit," but he didn't know if she said that because of what he'd done or because she'd noticed the stripe of eye shadow.

Benjamin went to the living room and turned on the television. He picked up the new issue of *Life*, the one with Reagan on the cover, then sat in his recliner and turned the pages. The bathroom door opened, and Kim went to the bedroom, locking that door. Benjamin stayed in the recliner. That's where he was when Kim emerged from the bedroom in her kimono, a ski jacket over it. She tugged the zipper of the jacket up. Then she put on a wool hat and mittens, yanking the mittens on with her teeth as she moved toward the chair.

"Listen," she said, "I'm sorry. You just don't understand. It's just, well, forget it. I'm sorry, okay?"

"Want me to come get you at eleven-thirty?"

"Mm hmm," she said, and she squeezed his fingers. He could feel her fingers through the mittens.

Benjamin read in his recliner until eleven o'clock, not stopping to eat, then went to the closet, pulled on a wool overcoat, and headed out to the street. The overcoat wasn't his own. It used to be Phinney's—he'd left it behind when he'd moved to Nebraska—and their father's before that. Two of the buttons were missing, the top one and the second one from the bottom. The top one was the more troublesome, and he held the coat closed at the collar with his left hand to keep from getting a chill. It was the first time he'd ever worn the coat. Why he'd plucked it from the closet instead of his London Fog he didn't know.

As he walked, he wondered how he was supposed to act when he saw Kim. He'd been dating her since the beginning of December, the week after Thanksgiving, in February she moved in, and here it was, the second week in March, and he still hadn't seen her with her shirt off. He hadn't seen her breasts, and he wanted to, and he wondered if he was selfish or sick for wanting that.

When he reached Yumi's, Benjamin undid the buttons of the coat and waited by the hostess stand, rubbing his hands together and pacing tiny circles while the waitresses sat around a table in the back, all dressed in black kimonos, all black-haired. Kim looked up and saw Benjamin, then tapped her watch with her fingertips, held up all five fingers, and mouthed, "Five minutes."

Benjamin bobbed his head. It didn't make any sense. Mary Jude had loved the way he kissed her breasts. This didn't make sense.

The other waitresses turned and looked. He recognized several of them. Kim had introduced him to Terri, who waved at him now when she saw him in the doorway, and to Debra, who nodded in recognition, and, of course, he knew Yumi, who sat at the end of the table and divided the night's tips into stacks. The women spoke while Yumi pushed the money on the tabletop, their voices blending as they interrupted one another, and they fell back in their chairs laughing.

It was the shibby talk Kim had told him about. All he could do was watch.

He backed up against the wall and buried his hands in the coat's huge side pockets while he waited. The world had always seemed two sizes too large to Benjamin, and now the way the coat hung from him, billowing, made him feel like a little boy in man's clothes. His father had been a large man, six four, and, though Phinney was younger than Benjamin, he was larger. Phinney had grown to be six three. He'd passed Benjamin in height when both were in grade school. Then Phinney had grown four inches when he was in the hospital.

Benjamin leaned against the wall, thinking of Kim wheeling around in the bathroom, shrieking at him, and he felt tiny. The women erupted in laughter now and then, and Benjamin examined the restaurant, red-and-black linen on each table, exotic paintings of bare trees and dragons on the walls. He wondered if they were laughing about him, the old man in the oversized coat, he wondered if Kim had told them what had happened in the bathroom that afternoon. He walked toward the men's room at the rear of the restaurant. The women stopped talking as he approached the table, like a tribe of Indians blood-sworn to keep their secrets from men, Benjamin included. They didn't start up again until he'd closed the door to the bathroom. Only Yumi hadn't turned to glare at him, and that had made him feel more the intruder.

Their talk washed into the men's room through the heating duct. Their voices were as clear as if they were on the radio. Benjamin took off the coat and draped it over the stall, them moved to the urinal. His pee drowned out their voices momentarily, but after he zipped his pants he sat against the front edge of the sink and listened to them. He couldn't tell who was who, and their voices drifted in and out. He could only hear the words.

One of the waitresses said, "You know, Stuart is so in love with himself, I think his greatest dream is to die in his own arms."

"What does that mean?"

"He loves to hear himself talk. He never shuts up. Always trying to teach me things, like philosophy or art or stuff. It drives me up a wall. Always talking. 'As Socrates explained …' or 'As Hobbes said in Something-Something-Something-Something…' Yap, yap, yap, yap, yap, like a little dog. You know, once—this is true—once I didn't talk to him for three days straight."

"Were you mad at him?" another asked.

"No, I just didn't want to interrupt."

The women laughed.

"Well, last week was it. I mean, I'd had it up to here with him being such a know-it-all, so I told him to get out. Get out. So, do you know what he said? He said, 'If the phone doesn't ring, you'll know it's me.' Fat chance. The guy couldn't shut up if you Krazy-glued his lips together. The phone rang the very next day, and he apologized for everything, and he's back now."

"Does he shut up now?" another asked.

"Be serious. This week he's telling me all about photosynthesis."

"Forget about him. No one needs to put up with that."

"A man like that isn't worth your trouble," another waitress said.

"A man like that will get a very bad ear infection." That one was Yumi.

"Let me tell you something about Doug. Doug loves cartoons." Another waitress.

"So what? Big deal."

"No, I mean he loves them. Like, the other day, I come home from shopping, and he's sitting in front of the TV in his underwear, and he says to me, 'Who do you think is the sexiest cartoon character, Veronica on "The Archie Show" or Daphne on "Scooby-Doo?"' and he's serious."

The women laughed again, a chorus.

"That's weird."

"Listen, I don't know much about psychology, but there's a psychological term for people like Doug: fruit loop. F-R-U-I-T L-O-O-P."

"I wouldn't worry about it." It was Kim talking. "You knew Doug was a little bit strange."

"Yeah, I'm just afraid that we'll be in bed one night and we'll be doing it and he'll start saying, 'Oh, Daphne, I *love* you, I *love* you.'"

The women hooted, and, their voices shrill, they repeated, "Oh, Daphne, I love you." And smacked their lips. Benjamin laughed, too, and tried to contain it. He washed his hands, then sat against the sink again.

"You weren't making babies before you were supposed to work, were you?" Yumi asked.

"Yes, Yumi, I was."

"I told you that's very bad for you," Yumi said.

"I know, Yumi, but what am I supposed to do when I'm going to lose my man to a cartoon character? I mean, can you believe it?"

"I lost mine to a beautician once. I guess that's pretty much the same thing." It was another of the waitresses. It might be Debra, Benjamin thought. She sounded familiar. "She had an ass the size of a Volkswagen. You'd have to see it. It was pretty scary, especially, in 3-D." There was a pause. "It was like she had her own gravitational pull."

"I lost mine to a guy once."

The women laughed.

"Really," the same waitress said. "Nothing makes you feel more like a piece of dirt than when your guy leaves you for another guy. It's like you turned him off women single-handedly."

"Maybe you did."

"Aren't you a card, little Miss Lock-Up-the-Chastity-Belt-and-Toss-the-Key-in-the-Ocean. What do you know? You haven't had a boyfriend in a year."

"I'm picky."

"This is Baltimore, sweetie. You can't live in Baltimore and be picky."

"She's right about that." There were speaking too quickly, their voices running together, and Benjamin couldn't tell who had said what.

"That's what it says on the billboard as you drive into town: 'Welcome to Baltimore. Ladies, please don't be picky.'"

"Hey, Kim, what's the story with what's-his-name?"

"Benjamin," Kim said. "Shhh, he'll hear you."

"Are you living in his place now, or what?"

"Yeah," Kim said. "It's been a couple weeks now."

"Sachiko, you don't make babies before you come to work, do you?" It was Yumi.

"No, Yumi, I'm a good girl. I don't make babies before I come to work," Kim answered. She hadn't told them about what had happened in the bathroom. "I'll get corns on my feet if I do."

"Good, it's bad enough that you date a dirty old man. Dirty old men will leave you every time, and then Sachiko will not be Sachiko anymore."

"I thought he was just going to go gray because he touched me," Benjamin heard Kim say.

"He will go gray, and then he will leave you. First one, then the other. Mark my words. Do I know men, or don't I?"

"Yes," several of the women said at once, resigned and obedient. Benjamin remembered what Kim had told him about Yumi.

"Can I ask you a personal question about your guy, what's-his-name?"

"Benjamin," Kim said. "Sure, I guess."

"Well, at home, does he always spend so much time in the bathroom?"

Again the women cried out with laughter.

"I mean, the guy's been in there for ten minutes already."

Benjamin lifted the overcoat from the stall and left the men's room. All of the women were sitting at the table, their money in front of them, all of their heads bowed, some with their fingers over their lips, trying not to look at Benjamin.

When Kim saw him, she said, "I'm ready, honey," and she, too, was trying not to laugh. She introduced him to all of the women.

Benjamin waved a hand and said, "Hi, it's nice to meet all of you."

"And you already know Terri and Debra."

Benjamin waved again. "Hi." He put his overcoat on, then helped Kim with hers. They began to walk toward the door, but Kim stopped and retreated, bending to talk to one of the other waitresses.

"I love you, Daphne," she teased, "kissy, kissy," and the waitresses frowned and gave Kim a shove. The others rocked in their seats.

Some of the sugar packets at their table have miniature pastel drawings of famous ships on them. They're the same packets that they have at P.J.'s Pub, in Baltimore, where Benjamin ate after his birthday, trying to stay out of the apartment to avoid Kim. The bar wasn't far from where Kim's sister lived, and though Benjamin thought of stopping to see Christie, to talk about Kim's scar, he never did. He stayed at the bar instead, eating, drinking scotch and smoking cigarettes, toying with the sugar packets. He had them all memorized.

The *Nina*.

The *Constitution*.

The *Merrimack*.

The *Mayflower*.

The *Queen Mary.*

The *Half Moon.*

The *Beagle.*

The *Monitor.*

Mixed in with these are pink packets with trivia questions on the backs, and Kim pulls these one at a time from the metal dispenser. She reads them haltingly, carefully enunciating each word, then stacks the packets in a pile beside the ashtray. The pile looks like a small pink office building.

"Who is pictured on the ten-dollar bill?" she reads.

Benjamin shrugs his shoulders. Kim says, "Alexander Hamilton," then holds the packet out so Benjamin can read the answer himself.

"Alexander Hamilton," he says. "I used to know that," and he stirs his coffee though he's added nothing to it.

"How many stomachs does a squid have?"

"Two," Benjamin says.

"Three," Kim says.

"How am I supposed to know that?"

"Hey, I'm just reading them. If you've got a complaint, take it up with the management."

Kim lifts the coffee cup from the saucer and brings it to her lips. She drinks it the same way Benjamin does, cold and black, and Benjamin notices that she even holds the cup the same way, not touching the handle, curling her fingers around the rim. "Not bad," she'd said the first time she'd tried her coffee cold. "Not half bad."

Kim takes another sugar packet from the dispenser, and Benjamin lifts his hamburger to his mouth.

"What is the capital of Connecticut?"

"Um um um," Benjamin says, chewing his hamburger.

"Hartford." She adds the packet to the stack.

"Who was the only president to be elected to two nonconsecutive terms in office?"

"Teddy Kennedy."

"Teddy Kennedy wasn't a president."

"Is that right?"

Kim starts to say yes, then catches Benjamin's sheepish expression. "You knew that." She tosses the pink packet at him, and it strikes his chest and drops to his lap. "Anyway, it was Grover Cleveland."

"Uh huh." He takes another drink of coffee and another bite of his hamburger.

"How many quarts in a gallon?"

Benjamin answers, "Four," then gives Kim a suspicious look. "Let me see that. Does it really say that?"

Kim clutches the packet to her chest. "Nope, I made that one up so you wouldn't feel stupid."

"Thanks. Thanks a lot. I was really beginning to feel like an idiot, but now I feel much better."

"Anytime, sweetheart," Kim responds.

She adds the packet to her stack and then picks up her coffee cup. While she drinks, she looks out the window across the highway, looking as if she were expecting something, though Benjamin doesn't know what it could be. They're in the middle of nowhere.

"I like this state, Benjamin," she says. "Which one is it?"

"Missouri," he answers.

"Well, I like Missouri. Remind me to send the governor a Christmas card."

Benjamin and Kim are sitting across from the jukebox. There's a painting of Jesus above it, in a gold frame. At the table beside them, a man in jeans and a gray T-shirt is eating with two children. The smallest is on his lap, the other across from him in a booster chair. Both boys have hair the color of sand, swept away from their eyes.

"Cute, aren't they," Kim asks, dipping her head toward the children, and Benjamin says, "Mm hmm," almost inaudibly.

"Can I ask you something?"

"Sure."

"Is Franny pregnant?"

Benjamin doesn't know what she means until she adds, "From Franny and Zooey."

Benjamin thinks for a moment, trying to remember the book. It's been sitting on the nightstand for nearly a month, a playing card tucked in for a bookmark, but he hasn't read it in years. "I don't remember. Why don't you finish the book and find out."

"I did finish the book," she says. Embarrassed, she curves her lips into a smile, and she says, "I kept reading it, I only put it back on the nightstand every day before you came home. Anyway, do you think she's pregnant? She never comes right out and tells anyone she's pregnant, but maybe she did before the book started or after it ended. You know, in the time before the book takes place or after it ends."

"Why do you think that?"

"I don't know. It just makes sense. I mean, why else would she get religious and contemplative? She's always thinking. Think, think, think, think, think. She thinks all the time. It just seems like the sort of thing you only do when something drastic is about to happen."

At the next table, the older of the boys reaches for one of the containers next to the napkins, and the man pushes his hand away. "No," he warns the child, shaking a finger, "don't touch. It's bad," then he breaks off a piece of his hamburger and holds it in front of the younger child. The boy opens his mouth like a tiny bird being fed.

"I like children," Kim says. "I used to be one, you know," and she makes her eyes large. "It's a joke, Benjamin. Come on. Laugh," she commands.

Benjamin smiles and the boy reaches for the container again. Again, his father swishes his hand away. "Bad. Bad," the man says.

"I'd like to have kids, only I don't want to have to go through labor." Kim picks a French fry from her plate. "I mean, I've seen that enough on TV to know that that hurts like a son of a bitch, excuse the language. When I have my children, it's going to be quick. I'm going to have them give me the Heimlich maneuver or something."

Benjamin thinks how much Kim is like Mary Jude that way, the way they both love children. Mary Jude left, he thinks, because he didn't want to have children. It reached a point where, before he climbed into bed, he would ask if she was still taking her birth-control pills. Sometimes they'd used condoms, but not often. Benjamin hated the way they felt, as if they were choking him down there, and Mary Jude didn't like the way they felt inside her. And Benjamin hated buying them, too. He was as ashamed of buying them as he was of buying the haircoloring. He was ashamed putting the thin plastic package on the counter for the teenaged cashier to pick up and inspect and drop into the paper bag like a dead mouse. So, when they did use them, it was Mary Jude who bought the condoms. And later, when she started taking the birth-control pills, he had his doubts. He didn't trust her with them. He was afraid that she'd try to trick him into being a father. After a time, when she'd put her hand between his legs, he'd get out of bed. He'd sleep on the recliner.

"I wonder what kind of mother I'll be, though," Kim says. "I come from a long line of mothers, so I ought to know what I'm doing."

When Benjamin doesn't respond, she huffs. "God, Benjamin, that was a joke, too. I'm being amusing today, and you're not even appreciating it."

Benjamin apologizes.

"Anyway," Kim says, "do you know what I mean about not knowing what kind of mother I'll be? It's like I have this feeling about kids, that they're so innocent and so cute and everything, and things just sort of happen to mess them up. So I want to be the kind of mother who makes everything okay again. Like if my babies—"

The waitress appears with a coffeepot, poised to fill their cups, and both Benjamin and Kim gesture to let her know that they don't want any more.

"—like if my babies get bad grades in school and they come home crying, I want to be the kind of mother who does something to cheer them up. You know, say, 'Come on, let's go paint the dog' just so my baby'll laugh. I mean, I want my kids to know that school's not everything, and sports aren't everything, and what the other kids say doesn't matter, and they should just be happy."

"'Let's go paint the dog'?" Benjamin is confused.

"You know what I mean, just say something so completely stupid that they won't be able to help themselves from laughing. Just something to keep things in perspective. The only problem is that it's easy to say that you're going to be the greatest mom in the world when you don't have any kids. Everyone probably thinks that, then you have kids, and—boom!—there you are yelling at them because they can't spell anything right. Things from when you were a kid stick with you, you know? Like, can I tell you something I've never told anyone before?"

"Sure," Benjamin says, "of course."

"It's stupid, but it's taken a real long time to deal with it, and I don't know why, just that it did. Anyway, this is back when I was in the second grade and we had a pageant."

"Second grade, huh?"

"Second grade. We have a Christmas pageant, and I won or was awarded or whatever the part of an angel." Kim's eyes were unfocused. She wags her hand beside her head. "I had to go up on a ladder above these kids who were crying—I guess they were supposed to be Mary and Joseph or something—and say, 'Why are you crying?' But when the day came that we had to do it, I had to go to the bathroom. You know how it is when you're a kid, how you can't control it. So I kept telling the teacher that I had to go, and she wouldn't let me. I peed all the way up the ladder, and you could hear it because of the linoleum. I ran to the bathroom crying, and the cherry on top was that I locked myself in the boys' bathroom."

Benjamin eats and doesn't know what to say.

"You think that's stupid," Kim says, and she scoops up her hamburger, "don't you?"

"No, not really. It sounds a lot like something that happened when I was teaching in Bluefield."

"God, I forgot that you used to teach."

"It was only a year. Sometimes I forget myself."

"What happened?"

"Nothing much. Just some girl, I can't remember her name, some girl from one of my classes forgot her lines in one of those things, and all the other children were laughing at her, and her mother looked really embarrassed."

For the first time in years, he feels guilty for having done nothing.

"You know, you never talk about when you were a kid. You hardly talk about it at all, like you didn't have parents."

"I did. It's just that they died. There's not much to talk about."

"Were they good? You know, were they good people, your parents?"

"Sure, they were," and Benjamin thinks of his father, writing out checks for a million dollars each then tossing them onto the fire in the fireplace. "I'm throwing away money," he'd say, and he'd ask the boys who he should make the checks out to. "Eisenhower," Benjamin said, and his father wrote President Eisenhower a check for a million dollars, then tossed it on the logs. "Tommy Dorsey," Phinney said, and they went on and on, naming names until their father was out of checks and their mother had to order new ones.

At the table next to them the boy finally grabs the condiment container and brings it to his lips. Almost immediately he's crying, howling like a small animal in the booster chair, and the man takes the container from his hands.

"I told you that was bad, didn't I?" he says. "That's barbecue sauce, not ketchup." With the other child still balanced on his lap, the man opens both arms in front of him, curling his fingers. The one who's crying turns on his stomach in the seat and lowers himself to the floor, his shirt coming untucked and his belly uncovered. The man hoists him up and sits both children on his lap.

"Bad," the man says, and lightly he slaps at the barbecue-sauce container. "Bad barbecue sauce."

The boy begins to smile, though his face remains ruddy and moist.

"Bad," the man repeats. "Bad, bad, bad." He moves the container closer to them, then takes the boy's hand in his own and guides it to the container. "Bad," the man says.

"Bad," the child repeats.

"Bad."

"Bad," and the child slaps at the container, and he knocks it over. He slaps at it while it lays on the table, and he laughs so hard that his words are unrecognizable. "Bab, bab, bab, bab, bab, bab, bab."

The man pays his check and walks out with both boys, the youngest tucked against his chest, the older one hopping beside him, slapping at chairs and tables and the waitresses' legs on the way to the door, yelling, "Bab," as he touches each.

Kim and Benjamin raise their eyebrows.

Kim says, "You know, I've been thinking. I've been thinking that you'd make a good father."

That's what Mary Jude used to tell him.

Benjamin is about to tell her no, that he wouldn't, when he realizes what she's up to. "Oh, geez," he says, "you're not going to tell the waitress that you're having my baby again, are you?"

Kim smiles, and when their waitress leaves the check, Kim calls her by name. "Dolores," she says, "come here. Want to hear a secret?"

The waitress congratulates them.

Mary Jude had wanted children so much that she adopted a Little Sister one year. Usually the Big Sisters were college women or women in their early twenties, but Mary Jude had signed up anyway. She came home from work one day and said, "Look, Benjamin, I'm a Big Sister," and pointed to her new T-shirt, with I'M A BIG SISTER in red block letters.

Mary Jude only wore the shirt the first time she drove to East Baltimore to pick up her Little Sister. Her Little Sister was an eight-year-old girl named Rosa. Rosa Hidalgo, with black hair and skin the color of dried cornhusks, and Mary Jude drove out to pick her up every Wednesday in time to have dinner with Benjamin.

When Rose first came to the apartment, she cringed at the sight of Benjamin, and she clung to Mary Jude's skirt with both fists. Benjamin was in the kitchen breading flounder. He left the flounder on the cutting board and walked into the living room.

"Rosa, honey, this is my husband, Mr. Sacks."

Rosa wouldn't let go of Mary Jude, and Benjamin didn't know what to do. He got on his knees and walked across the living room that way, until he was before her.

"Hello there, Rosa," he said. "That's a pretty name, Rosa is."

The girl still clung to Mary Jude.

"There's nothing to be afraid of," Mary Jude said.

"I'm not," Benjamin answered, but she was speaking to the girl.

"Rosa's a Spanish name, isn't it?" he said, and the girl nodded. "I took Spanish in high school, you know. What's Rosa Spanish for?"

"It's Spanish for Rosa," she answered, and when Benjamin laughed, so did she.

"Well, Rosa, I'm fixing us some dinner," he said, "in the kitchen. Do you like seafood?"

"Mm hmm."

"What's your favorite?"

"Saltwater taffy."

"Well, I made flounder. Is flounder okay with you?"

"Does it taste like saltwater taffy?"

"Vaguely."

That year they drank milk on Wednesdays. After they were done with their meal, Benjamin would clean the dishes while Mary Jude and Rosa read stories in the living room and played with Barbie dolls on the rug, laughing like tattletale sisters until Benjamin and Mary Jude drove Rosa home.

Sometimes Benjamin would call out to Rosa from the kitchen while he washed the dishes, using all the Spanish he could recall. *"Hola, mi amiga pequeña.*" (Hello, my little friend.)

"*Hola, Señor Sacks.*" (Hello, Mr. Sacks.)

"*¿Como estas hoy?*" (How are you today?)

"*Bueno. Yo te digo ya. ¿Recuerdas?*" (Good. I already told you that, remember?)

"*Si, pero me diga en inglés. El mundo total oiga diferente en español.*" (Yes, but you told me in English. The whole world sounds different in Spanish.) "*¿Piensas que mi esposa comprende cuando nosotros hablamos en español?*" (Do you think my wife understands when we speak in Spanish?)

"No."

"*Entonces, puedo decir a tu que mi esposa no puede cocinar, y sus pies no ollan bueno.*" (Then I can tell you that my wife can't cook, and her feet smell bad.)

The girl laughed, and Mary Jude just shook her head and said, "I hate it when you two do that. You're like two old hens."

"*Lo siento,*" Rosa said. "That means, 'I'm sorry.'"

"See," Mary Jude said, in bed one Wednesday after they'd returned to the apartment. "It wouldn't be that bad to have a child. You wouldn't make such a bad father."

"As long as I only had to do it on Wednesday nights," he answered. It wasn't that he didn't like children. She couldn't understand that. He did like children, he was afraid that he wouldn't do a good job as a father. He was afraid that he'd fail them, and her.

In December they drove to Hunt Valley Mall and shopped for presents for Rosa. Mary Jude was excited. She'd never bought presents for a child before, and she nearly ran from store to store in her high heels, accumulating bags. A Sit 'N' Spin. A Barbie van. A stuffed Winnie the Pooh. A pink party dress with a white bow on the back. Chocolate Santas and red, white and green striped candy canes.

Rosa hugged them both on the Wednesday before Christmas, after she opened her gifts. "Happy Christmas," Mary Jude said, and Benjamin said, "*Feliz Navidad,*" then Mary Jude walked her into the bathroom, pushing lightly at the girl's thin shoulders so she could try on the dress. When they came out, Mary Jude called, "Benjamin, come see a beautiful little girl."

Benjamin rose from his recliner. Rosa was standing in front of Mary Jude.

" ¡*Que bonita*!" How beautiful, he said, and she was.

Rosa thanked them when they drove her home, and so did her mother.

"You did a good thing," Benjamin told Mary Jude, but on Christmas day, without Rosa, Mary Jude cried as if she'd lost her own child. She didn't sign up for the program the following year.

CHAPTER 6
PARADISE

HE DOESN'T KNOW HER SIZE, but she's not much smaller than Mary Jude, just narrower in the shoulders. They're at the shopping mall in Independence. Benjamin tells the saleswoman that he wants the dress in the window, size four. It's a blue flowered sundress. He'd seen Kim looking at it in the shop window, and when Kim walked into the store that sold running shoes, three shops down, he said, "I'll be right back."

The saleswoman returns with one from the rack, and Benjamin pays for it with his credit card, then finds Kim trying on a pair of yellow-and-green running shoes. He pulls the dress out of the bag, and she hops out of her seat.

"It'll look great," she says, pecking him on the cheek, "with my Nike shirt underneath." She holds the dress in front of her and looks in the mirror, still wearing the yellow-and-green shoes. The laces are undone.

Kim sits again, the dress draped across her knees, and puts her own shoes on. They walk through the mall, Benjamin with his hands in his pockets, Kim with an arm crossed through his, and Benjamin suggests that they go back to the motel and sit by the pool.

"Will you go *in*," Kim asks.

"Maybe."

Five yards away, a teenaged girl argues with her parents. The girl has permed black hair, and she's wearing blue jeans tucked into short white boots. Her face is ruddy, and she stomps her foot and swings her purse. "Really," Benjamin hears her say, "let me go off by myself. You're embarrassing me. You're ruining my life."

"Why won't you go into the pool?" Kim asks.

"I might, I said," Benjamin answers. "I might. No promises."

Benjamin doesn't think of Kim in a bathing suit. When they're back in the motel room, Kim goes to the bathroom to change. The bed has been made. Kim emerges after two or three minutes. Over her bikini top she wears the Howard Johnson's T-shirt, and she keeps it on the entire time that she and Benjamin are in the lounge chairs, not even bunching it up to bare her stomach. She keeps it on as if it were nothing, as if the cotton were her own skin, and she doesn't complain about the heat.

Benjamin lies in his chair bare-chested, his flesh white and doughy about the waist, reading *Iacocca*. Kim sits in the chair beside him, with the newspaper, Friday's *Sun*. She works the crossword puzzle, and, having done all she can, she fills in the empty boxes with X's, the way she always does. "It gives me a sense of accomplishment," she'd told Benjamin, "to see all the little squares filled in."

There's an old couple across from them. There's a girl in a red bikini, lying on a towel and painting her fingernails, and there's a woman in the shallow end of the pool with a small boy. The boy has an orange bubble strapped around him to keep him afloat, and he holds the woman's fingertips in his own small hands while he kicks. The bursts of water at his feet make a noise like a Jacuzzi. Shoopshoopshoop.

Kim rustles her newspaper as she puts it down on the cement and rises from her chair, then walks to the shallow end of the pool, and Benjamin sits up when Kim steps into the water. Before she does, she tucks the T-shirt into her bikini bottoms, and she walks down the steps the same way she'd gone into the ocean at the beginning of the summer, when they'd gone to Ocean City: she walks in backwards. She doesn't look at the water.

"I don't know," she'd said at the beach, when Benjamin asked about it.

He'd taken her there to cheer her up after Yumi had to let her go for the summer. "I've always done it this way. I just can't go in forwards."

She closes her eyes, inhales deeply, and dives underwater, and when she pokes her head through the surface, she's at the other end of the pool, by the diving board.

"Are you coming in?" she calls to Benjamin, and he feels the other people at the pool gaze at him. "*Benjamin?*"

"No," he answers. "I'm reading." He points to the book.

Kim swims toward Benjamin and folds her arms across the ledge to hold herself up. She rests her chin on her forearms. "*Benjamin?*"

"What?" he says, and he doesn't look up from *Iacocca*.

A splash of cold pool water lands on his feet and soaks into the cement at the bottom of the lounge chair. Now he looks up, and Kim stares at him, mischievously.

"Come on in," she says. She jerks her head toward the pool.

"I'm reading," he protests. "I'm getting a tan."

"Come on, you sun god," she says. "Come on and get in the pool. The water's great," and she flicks some on his feet again with her fingertips.

Benjamin tells her to cut it out, and he checks to see the expressions of the other people at the pool. None of them seem to be listening. The girl in the red bikini is still painting her nails. The old couple both have their heads tilted back, and their eyes are covered by sunglasses. The child is still kicking up a storm. Shoopshoopshoop.

Kim pushes off the wall and goes under. A slosh of water strikes his feet and ankles, and he shakes them to dry them off.

He watches as Kim swims the length of the pool and back again, then makes her way over to the woman and the child.

"Hi," Kim says to the woman.

"Hi," the woman responds. She can't be much older than Kim, maybe twenty-seven or twenty-eight. Kim's back is turned, so Benjamin watches.

She squats in the water to say hello to the boy. "My name's Kim. What's yours?"

The boy huffs. "Tommy. I'm learning to swim." His voice is tired and dramatic.

"And you're doing a great job. I'll bet you'll be in the Olympics in no time."

The boy begins kicking again, and Kim stands straight. The water is as high as her hips.

"I'm Kim," she says, and she extends her hand to the woman. The woman lets go of the boy with one hand to shake Kim's, and when she does, the boy slips underwater for an instant. She jerks him back up and holds the boy with both hands.

"Sally," the woman says. "Sorry."

"Is this your son?"

"Uh huh. We're here on a business trip. His father's at a meeting now."

"He's a cutie," Kim says, and she bends again to run her hand across the boy's hair, hair the color of rust. "I mean Tommy, not your husband."

Kim and the woman continue talking, and Benjamin tries to read. The shoopshoopshoop of water at the boy's feet drowns out most of the conversation, though Benjamin can hear bits and pieces of sentences.

"That's my boyfriend over there," he hears Kim say.

Shoopshoopshoop.

"We've been married for six years and three months September," he hears the woman say.

Shoopshoopshoop.

"Benjamin," he hears Kim say.

"Tommy's six. He'll be in the first ..." he hears the woman say.

Shoopshoopshoop.

"...really is a cutie," he hears Kim say. "And he has an outie belly-button. Most people have innies. That makes you special."

"He sells electrical supplies throughout the mic..."

"I used to work in a Japanese restaurant but now..."

"Are you cold or..." he hears the woman say.

Shoopshoopshoop.

"Why?" he hears Kim say.

"…you're wearing a…" he hears the woman say.

Shoopshoopshoop.

"Yes, I'm cold," he hears Kim say.

Shoopshoopshoopshoopshoopshoop.

Benjamin settles down to his reading and ignores the women entirely. Later, ten minutes perhaps, when Kim comes out of the pool, squeezing the water from her hair as though she's wringing a towel, the T-shirt is pasted to her, HOWARD JOHNSON'S: 26 FLAVORS tattooed across her chest, and it's still tucked in. Though the T-shirt hugs her, the scar is invisible to Benjamin.

Kim waves good-bye to the boy and his mother as they pass through the gate and walk through the parking lot. She stands over Benjamin and shakes her hair violently, whipping it from side to side so drops of water fall upon Benjamin's chest.

Benjamin flinches. "You'll get it on the book." He wipes off the jacket with his palm.

"You should've come in," Kim says. "I met the nicest woman."

"I was reading," Benjamin says.

"Well, I told her we'd baby-sit for her tonight."

"What?"

"She and her husband haven't been alone the entire time they've been here, and she's such a nice woman, so I told her we'd baby-sit so they can go out to a movie or something."

"You got a baby-sitting job during our vacation?"

Kim laughs. "Yeah. She's not going to drop Tommy off until after dinner. It'll be fun. We'll have room service bring ice cream. Won't that be great?" She wipes a wet band of hair from her forehead.

"Ice cream. Yum, yum–" Benjamin teases, "my favorite. Besides, they don't have room service at Howard Johnson's."

"You'll have fun. You'll see," and Kim eases into the lounge chair to Benjamin's left. Immediately, a puddle begins to form beneath her. "Really," she says. "I promise."

Across from them the girl in the red bikini waves her hand in the air to dry her nails. Kim waves back.

"People are so friendly here. It's absolutely amazing. Perfect strangers just talking and waving. Isn't it amazing? This is what Paradise must be like. Paradise Paradise, I mean, not Paradise, Texas," and Benjamin just grins and doesn't explain about the nail polish.

Benjamin was out of his mind—Benjamin, Indiana—and Kim was twenty pages into *Breakfast at Tiffany's* when Benjamin saw the signs for East St. Louis, Illinois. He tried to remember what Babisch had told him about East St. Louis. There was somewhere he was supposed to stop, but now he couldn't remember it.

Babisch had said that there was some place in East St. Louis that sold frozen custard. "*Real* frozen custard, Benjamin," Babisch had said. "Do you know what I mean? The real stuff, not the fake kind they sell everywhere. Nope, it's real, honest-to-God frozen custard."

"If I remember, I'll stop," Benjamin had said. "What's the name of it?"

"It's world famous, Benjamin. It's called—" and that's all Benjamin could remember. He pulled off the interstate at the last exit in East St. Louis. The way the metal cages blocked the store windows, the way people sat against the buildings, going nowhere, reminded him of North Avenue in Baltimore.

Kim looked up from her book and said, "What are we doing here?"

"It's a surprise."

He drove aimlessly, circling the blocks, looking for the frozen-custard stand. Three times they passed the same row of stores—a pharmacy, a wig shop, a dry cleaner's.

"We're lost, aren't we?"

"Sort of. I'm looking for a place Babisch told me about."

"What's the name of it?"

"I don't remember."

"Well, did Frank tell you what kind of place it is?"

"Of course he told me what kind of place it is. I can't tell you, though. It wouldn't be much of a surprise then."

"Well, if it's a wig store, I think we just passed it," she said, twitching her thumb in the air, "three or four times."

"It's not a wig store."

When he saw a police car parked in a bank lot, Benjamin pulled his car behind it and stepped out to talk to the police officer. He was a black man in his fifties, alone.

Benjamin excused himself. "I was hoping you could give me a hand."

"With what?"

"We're not from around here, and a friend of mine told me about a place around here that sells frozen ice cream, I mean, custard." When the police officer didn't respond, Benjamin continued, "It's supposed to be world famous, or at least that's what I was told."

The police officer nodded once. "Ted Drewe's." Benjamin recognized the name immediately. "Sure, how's your memory?"

"Excuse me?"

"I mean for directions."

"Oh," Benjamin said, "fine."

"Okay. Ted Drewe's isn't in East St. Louis. It's in St. Louis, Missouri, only the east part of it," and he reeled off street names before pointing Benjamin back to the interstate. Seventy to 55, 55 South to Gasconade, Gasconade to Broadway, Broadway to Merrimack, Merrimack to Grand.

Benjamin thanked him, then returned to the car. Kim was humming to a song on the radio.

"It's not in East St. Louis," he said, "it's in the eastern part of St. Louis."

"Not that I know what you're talking about."

"Not that I know what I'm talking about," Benjamin said with a grin, and he guided the car back onto the interstate. Soon they were over the Mississippi River, and Kim held her head out the window to look down as they crossed the bridge.

"How deep do you figure that is?" she asked.

"I haven't got the slightest idea."

"It doesn't look too deep from here," she said. "I read about a couple who went swimming in there on their wedding night."

"Oh."

Benjamin followed the police officer's directions. They drove past the arch, dwarfed by it and by its shadow, and the interstate took them through downtown St. Louis. The traffic was heavy and slow.

"I don't understand traffic jams," Kim said. "Is there one car up there, up front"—she pointed through the windshield—"that's slowing down everyone else? It just doesn't seem fair," she said, "that people you don't even know can slow down your life." She stuck her head out the window. "Come on you slowpokes," she shouted, and Benjamin watched the road signs.

He was surprised at how well he'd remembered the officer's words. They passed the Anheuser-Busch brewery, and soon they were in a residential area of the city, passing churches and grocery stores. On the right, he spotted Ted Drewe's Frozen Custard and pulled the car into the parking space in front.

"There she is," he said, and Kim asked what. "Ted Drewe's. Babisch said it's the greatest custard in the world."

The building was a white A-frame with plastic icicles hanging from it.

"Come on," he said, and they walked to the service window. He asked the girl at the counter what they should order.

"Everyone orders concretes," she said. She was a brown-haired girl with thin cheeks and a small sharp nose. Like the other workers, she was wearing a gold T-shirt with the words SINCE 1929, TED DREWES'S around a drawing of an ice-cream cone. When Benjamin cocked his head slightly the girl explained, "Concretes are real thick milkshakes, sort of."

"Good," Kim said.

Benjamin looked at Kim, and she smiled at him. He asked the girl what the best flavors were.

"Frisco—that's like mixed fruit. I personally like that one the best, but a lot of people don't. Blueberry. Chocolate. Chocolate chip—that's our real most popular flavor."

Benjamin ordered chocolate chip and Kim blueberry, and Benjamin paid the girl and thanked her.

They walked while they ate their custard, down a side street and back again, and when she was done with hers, Kim said, "I'll be right back. I have to go to the bathroom."

Benjamin watched as she crossed the traffic to get to the gas station across the street. The sign above it said *Sinclair* in green letters, a little red dinosaur beneath it. He watched Kim talk to one of the attendants, he watched the attendant give her the key, he watched her run to the ladies' room.

He finished his custard while he waited, and she ran back across the street, her thin legs moving in an exaggerated way, as if they were being held back from moving as fluidly as they normally did. Always, her legs looked too thin to support her. They looked too thin to support anything.

They returned to the car and headed back to the highway, and it wasn't until they were at the Howard Johnson's in Missouri that it occurred to Benjamin that he should have bought her a Ted Drewe's T-shirt. He should've bought them for Babisch and Julie, too, but he'd been too busy trying not to think of the scar.

Kim throws the ball to Benjamin, and it snaps against the leather of his mitt. Her tosses are flat and sharp, and they make Benjamin's thumb sore again. His tosses are like wedding bouquets thrown by a bride.

It's nearly five o'clock, and they're in the Howard Johnson's parking lot, beside the swimming pool. Kim's still wearing her wet bathing suit, and her feet are bare, as are Benjamin's, though his suit is dry. He hadn't gone in the pool, he'd just read *Iacocco* in one of the lounge chairs, sunning himself and thinking about Kim's scar.

He tosses the ball to her, and he shakes his right arm over his head to loosen his muscles. His shoulder and neck still ache from sleeping on the floor, from being forty-one.

"Do you want to see a curve ball?" Kim asks, and she digs at the ball in her glove, her face pinched as she spreads her fingers around the seams. "Watch this. My dad taught me," and she swings her arm behind her. Her tongue hangs to one side, and the ball swoops like a glider into Benjamin's mitt.

"Not bad," and Benjamin returns the ball to her lightly. He had never been able to throw a curve ball. His fingers were too small to grip the ball properly. "Not bad at all."

"He wanted a boy," Kim says, laughing. "My dad." Her next throw is straight and flat, and Benjamin grabs it in front of his hip.

"I wasn't trying to make that one curve, in case you were wondering. That one was my fast ball." She brushes her hand against her T-shirt.

Behind her, a tan car pulls into a parking spot, and a woman with springy, blow-dried hair steps out. The woman's tight white shorts show the line of her underwear, and she jingles her keys as she walks into the restaurant.

"I used to play on his softball team at work," Kim says, "my dad's. I used to play right field, just like Frank Robinson. I pushed my hair up into my cap because I figured no one would know that I was a girl, but that was sort of stupid." She taps her chest. "I mean, it was probably pretty obvious."

Kim throws another curve ball, and Benjamin can't catch it. It bounces at his feet, then against his shin. He rubs his leg, then retrieves the ball.

"Oops," she says. "Sorry," and she crosses her arms in front of her. "Sometimes it's harder throwing a baseball than a softball."

Benjamin picks the ball up from where it rests against a car tire. "What position did you play in high school?" he asks. "Right field?"

"I didn't play on the high-school team."

Benjamin is confused. "I thought you did."

"Unh uh." Kim shakes her head. "I mean, I was going to, and I probably would've started, but then, well, I couldn't."

"Oh."

"I mean, well, forget it." Dipping her head, she wipes her lips against the shoulder of her T-shirt. "My lips are dry. Are yours?"

"Forget what?"

"Nothing. It's nothing you want to hear about."

He knows this has to do with her heart, with the creek. If he's stayed in the middle of nowhere with her today when he could be at Phinney's, he assumes that this must be why. He's stayed because he wants to learn, he needs to try to understand.

"No," she says, severely. "I've tried before, and I know you don't want to know about it."

"Please tell me."

"Benjamin," she says, "you won't love me anymore. You'll stop. Can't we just play catch? I like just playing catch with you."

"Please," he says, "sweetheart," and she holds the ball in her glove, fifteen yards away from him.

"I love it when you call me that," she says. "Can't we just drop it?"

"Sure. We'll drop it. We'll drop it like a hot rock."

She smiles.

"I saw the phone book this morning," he tells her. He jerks his shoulder toward their room.

Kim sniffs. "What about the phone book?"

"You know. Plastic surgeons."

There's a long pause. It occurs to Benjamin that she'd meant him to find the Yellow Pages.

"Yeah, well," she says. "I've got do to something. When you can't look at yourself, you have to do something."

Benjamin says nothing, he just catches the ball when she returns it to him. Again, his thumb is growing sore.

"Benjamin, I have to do something."

"Kim, you're alive and well. That's all that matters." He sounds trite, he can tell.

"I'm not well. I remember what it feels like to be well, and this isn't it."

"You just need time, sweetheart," Benjamin says.

"I really love it when you call me that." She waits a moment. "You just don't understand, though, and I don't want to talk about it. How can you understand things that you can't understand?"

On their first date—lunch at Capriccio's—Kim wore a black-and-blue sweater and spoke of her mother. The sweater was mostly black with irregular patches of blue splashed across it. It had a V neck, and she wore a bleached-out navy-blue T-shirt beneath it. Benjamin could only see the collar of the T-shirt.

"Are you going home to see your parents for Christmas?" Kim asked him.

"No, my parents aren't around anymore," and he didn't explain.

"Geez, I'm sorry," and she patted his hand.

"It's been a long time."

The waiter returned from the kitchen with their meals balanced on a huge platter. Each had ordered tortellini.

"Can I try some of yours?" Kim asked. Benjamin looked at his plate, then at her, then at his plate again.

"It's the same as yours."

"No, it's not. Yours is yours, mine is mine. So they're different," she said, "intrinsically speaking," and she poked at his plate with her fork, then brought a tortellini shell to her mouth. "Mmm," she said, "yours tastes good."

Benjamin had a scotch and Kim ordered a Diet Pepsi. Again, as she'd done at J. C. Martin's the night they'd met, she apologized. "I don't drink," she said.

"Do you mind if I ask why?"

"No, I mean, I don't know why I don't, really. Partly, I guess, it's because I'm not supposed to for health reasons."

Benjamin didn't ask what that meant.

"Mostly, I'm not a big fan of drinking. My mom drinks a lot. She drinks like a truck driver. Christie and I—Christie's my big sister, did I mention that?—Christie and I used to try to get her to stop, but it's hard to do. She's not a very happy person sometimes, my mom."

Kim buttered a slab of hot bread, then reached across the table to dip it into the tomato sauce on Benjamin's dish.

"Anyway, you're going to think this is funny, but I remember once when I stayed home sick from school because, well, it doesn't matter, just because. You had to bring a note in for the principal from your parents telling him why you'd stayed at home. So, in the morning, I went into my parents' bedroom to get one of them to write out a note. My dad had already gone to work—he works down on the docks, so he's history at about five-thirty in the morning—and my mom, she just stunk, if you know what I mean. She just reeked of bourbon or something. I don't know what it was, but I couldn't get her up, so I wrote the note myself. You know"—she pantomimed the movement of a pen—"'Dear Mr. Principal, Kimberly Cassella was absent on such-and-such a date because she wasn't feeling well.' Then I went back in her bedroom and told her that she had to sign it or else I couldn't go to school. So I gave her the pen, and she signed it without even sitting up, and I shut off the light and let her go back to sleep. But when I gave the note to the principal's secretary, she says, 'Is this supposed to be funny, Miss Cassella?' And I asked her what she was talking about, and she showed me the note."

Kim paused for effect. She picked up her soda glass. "My mom had signed Marilyn Monroe at the bottom. Can you believe it? My mother and Marilyn Monroe. Ha."

Kim was wearing the same sweater, the black-and-blue one, when she moved into Benjamin's apartment. Benjamin hadn't had to make much room. It was as if the apartment had already been arranged for her. Mary Jude's dresser drawers remained empty, so he hadn't needed to make space for Kim's clothes, and all along he'd kept her half of the closet empty as well. He'd already taken down Mary Jude's notes when Kim had started spending more time there. He'd taken them all down except for the ones she'd taped to the bottoms of his bureau drawers. One note said, YOU NEED TO DO YOUR LAUNDRY—YOU'RE OUT OF SOCKS. There had been similar ones in his underwear and shirt drawers.

He'd cleaned the apartment the weekend before Kim was to move in. He'd filled a grocery basket with cleaners and scrubbers.

"Just moving into town?" the woman at the cash register had asked, and Benjamin had nodded and said, "I guess you could say that."

He'd worked on the place for most of the afternoon, while Kim was at Yumi's. He'd changed the light bulbs. He'd put in hundred-watters. He'd never realized that the old ones were only sixties, and the only reason he'd bought the new ones was that they were next to the sponges on the shelf. He'd bought something to keep the toilet water blue. He'd cleaned the oven, though he'd hardly used it. He'd hung a new shower curtain in the tub, tan and gray plastic with seashells painted on it. He did all of this a week in advance, to give the apartment a chance to settle, the way a new haircut needs time to stop looking like it's been cut.

It was a Saturday morning when they brought her things downtown.

"She's messy," her mother said when she let Benjamin in. Her mother was only four or five years older than Benjamin, and she regarded him suspiciously. "I hope she doesn't drive you crazy like she did to us."

"Thank you, Mom. That's very generous of you," Kim said, and then her mother was gone. Benjamin followed Kim to her bedroom. The room was painted pink, and there was a white canopy bed in the center. There were dolls on the bookshelves and a small record player in the corner.

"She says what she thinks," Benjamin said, "doesn't she, your mother? Like you do."

"Well, there's a lot of heredity in our family," and Kim picked up a box from the floor and blew her hair off her forehead. "Let's get this junk out of here."

It didn't take much more than two hours, including the trips to and from her parents' house. She only had a dozen cardboard boxes from the supermarket. Her shoes were piled in a box with the word BRILLO on the side. Her blouses were in TIDE, her skirts and slacks in CHEERIOS, her T-shirts in WHEATIES, her books in CHARMIN…Everything else was in CASCADE, RONZONI, COLGATE, DR. PEPPER, and BUMBLE BEE.

It was only when she moved in that Benjamin realized just how differently she approached the world. She approached it as a mother approaches baby formula on the stove, testing drops of it on her wrist. She pronounced sandwich "samwich," and smiled whenever she did. "Samwich," like a small girl. She called the roaches "tamaretta bugs." "It doesn't mean anything," she said. "It just sounds prettier. Who's afraid of a tamaretta bug?" She ran every day, stretching in the living room first. She had too much energy to watch television for long. When she wasn't at work or running she was reading something from the bookshelves or cooking or working the crossword puzzle in the *Sun*. And she went through three or four T-shirts a day.

"Call me Ahab!" Kim shouts. She's standing on the double bed, rocking it up and down. The boy is standing beside her. The couple brought him by at eight o'clock, after dinner, and the first thing he did was run to the bathroom to play with the cosmetics and shaving cream. He came out and smacked his wet hands across his face. "What are you doing?" Kim asked, and the boy said, "I'm putting on aftershave."

"Why?"

"Because there's something about an Aqua Velva man."

Now both Kim and the boy have their hands at their waists, their elbows pointed out, as the bed bounces. They're pretending they're searching for Moby Dick on the high seas.

"Call me Ahab!" the boy repeats. He's wearing green GI Joe pajamas, and his feet are bare.

"You can't be Ahab," Kim tells him. "I'm Ahab."

"Call me Tommy!"

"That's better. These are some pretty big waves we're getting out in these parts, aren't they?"

"Uh huh." The boy laughs.

"Do you know what we're looking for?"

"Nope."

"Whales," she says. "There are whales in these parts."

The bedsprings creak.

"Do you know what a whale looks like?" Kim asks.

"Nope. We only have goldfish."

"Well, a whale is bigger than a goldfish, about a zillion times bigger."

"What's it look like?"

"They have black hair, and they eat Fig Newtons," Kim says, "so keep a lookout."

"I found one!" the boy calls.

"Where?"

"There!" He points to Benjamin, sitting in front of the television.

"Oh, my Lord!" Kim puts a hand over her mouth. "Not only did you find a whale, but you found the biggest, most ferocious whale ever. You found," she says, "the Benjamin-whale."

"What do we do now?"

"Shh," Kim says, and she stops rocking the bed, "he'll hear you."

"Shh," the boy says, and he kneels on the bed.

"There's only one way to catch the Benjamin-whale," she says. "Only one way, and if you fail, he'll eat you up. Chomp, chomp, chomp, like that."

"You go then."

"I can't. I'm too big. He'll catch me in a second."

"I could hit him with some dog-doo," the boy exclaims, and Kim laughs.

"No, that won't do it. There's only one way to capture the Benjamin-whale, you have to take his Fig Newtons away from him."

Benjamin tries not to laugh. He's been watching out of the corner of his eye, and he sees the boy sneak off the bed and move slowly, shoulders hunched, toward him. Benjamin lets go of the cookies, and the boy swipes them from the ground. Benjamin grabs him by the back of his pajamas.

"Come here, Captain Tommy," he says. "Why don't we watch some TV?"

"Okay," and the boy lies on his stomach at the end of the bed. Benjamin leans back, his head beside the boy's.

The television shows a man and a woman in a restaurant. "When have I ever lied to you," the man says, "that you know of?"

"Plenty of times," the woman answers and takes a sip of wine.

Kim pats the boy on the head and says, "Good job, Captain Tommy. You captured the Benjamin-whale." She sits cross-legged on the bed and pulls the Yellow Pages to her lap.

"How does Dr. B. Catwalliton sound?" Kim asks.

Benjamin doesn't move. "What?"

"I'm looking at doctors. You said you'd help." He had said that. He'd told her at dinner that he'd help her as much as he could, as much as she'd let him, but he wasn't sure that was much at all. He didn't want to think of the creek.

"Oh, yeah," he says.

"So, how does Dr. B. Catwalliton sound?"

"I don't know. Old guy. Sixty. Alcoholic. Hasn't operated in twenty years."

"He could be a woman. It says B. Catwalliton. It could be a woman."

"Could be." Benjamin holds three Fig Newtons in his palm and slips one into his mouth. Tommy taps him on the head, and Benjamin turns to look at him, then hands him a cookie.

"How about Dr. Allan Finkel?"

"All thumbs."

"Yeah," she says. "You're right. How about Dr. Robert Bump?"

"All *toes*."

"Benjamin?" she says, and when he turns his head, she touches her fingers to her lips, twice, tapping them. Benjamin flips a cookie onto the bed, and she picks it up from the blanket.

"Dr. Michael P. Gilchrist?"

"God, I think that was the name of our veterinarian."

Kim cracks a smile. "It was *not*."

"No, really. I think it was."

"We have a veterinarian," Tommy says.

"Do you know what a veterinarian is?" Kim asks, rubbing his back.

"Yeah, it's a doctor for dogs and cats and stuff."

Kim asks if he has a dog, and he shakes his head and says, "Unh uh. I told you. I got goldfish."

"Yeah, how many?"

"Three. I used to have more. I use to have six," and the boy holds up six fingers, "but the other ones got flushed down the pottie. I'm going to get them back."

"How?" Kim asks.

"I'm going to flush myself down the toilet and go into the sewer and get them," he says.

"Into the sewer? Yuck."

"Yuck!" the boy shouts, and soon he's lying down again.

Kim shifts on the bed. She props her head up with both pillows. She reads the names of plastic surgeons at random, and Benjamin tries to say something amusing about each of them. He's trying to forget they're talking about the scar. After a while, he stops listening and just says, "Fine" or "Good" to each name. They're all in Kansas, these doctors, and Kim would never go to any of them. If she's going to go, he thinks, she'll go to one in Baltimore.

"Dr. Sandra Halfits?"

"Good."

"Dr. Anthony P. Smith?"

"Fine."

"Dr. D. Belton?"

"Fine."

"Dr. Zhivago?"

"Good." Kim slaps him on the top of the head and says, "I knew you weren't paying attention."

Mary Jude would catch him not paying attention, too.

"Sorry."

Kim closes the book and drops it beside the bed. "Are you tired, Tommy?" she asks, and he says he isn't, but minutes later his eyes are closed and his mouth is open. Kim slides her arms under him and moves him to the center of the bed, then sits beside Benjamin on the floor. The boy looks as small as a pea in the bed.

"Hey, are you going to sleep on the floor again tonight?" Kim whispers.

"I think we both are if his parents don't come back to get him."

"They will. But, really, are you going to sleep on the floor again?"

"I don't know. I guess so." He opens the Fig Newton box and unfolds the plastic wrapper inside, then holds three cookies in his hand again. Kim pulls his fingers apart and takes one.

"You don't have to," she says.

Benjamin doesn't answer.

"Can I tell you something?"

Benjamin nods.

"I hate sleeping alone in Baltimore. I really hate it. I mean, until I was about fifteen or so, I always slept in the same bed with Christie. And then when our parents got us our own beds, it wasn't the same anymore. Do you know what I mean?"

He does. He slept in the same bed with Phinney until they moved into Mrs. Magruder's when their parents died, until Phinney went into the hospital. And he shared a bed with Mary Jude until he couldn't sleep in the same bed anymore and took to the recliner for good. He knows what Kim means.

"Wasn't it different for you trying to sleep at home after Mary Lou left?"

"Mary Jude," Benjamin answers, "and, yes, it was."

"Anyway," she continues, "it's been the same thing lately, the same think like with me and Christie when we got our own beds. The last couple weeks have been absolutely *killing* me. I can't tell you how many times I just wanted to climb into bed and have you hold me. I mean, I was mad at you, but every time I saw you I'd think about how much I like being in the same bed with you. It was like, there you were, but I was still missing you. God, it was murder being without you. I missed you *tons*."

"But," Benjamin hesitates, "we haven't been sleeping in the same bed so far, you know, since we've been driving."

"Yeah, I know," she says, "but that's different. Baltimore's home. You shouldn't have to be alone at home. You know?"

He nods and says, "Uh huh," then chews another Fig Newton.

Neither says anything for a while.

"Can I tell you something else?"

"Sure."

"I'm having the time of my life now."

And Benjamin realizes that he is, too, in an odd way. He is, when he isn't thinking of the creek.

"I feel like we're packing twenty-four hours into each day."

It's a minute or more before she says, "Can I ask you one more thing?"

"Mm hmm."

"Did you used to have as much fun with Mary Jo?"

"Mary *Jude*."

CHAPTER 7
BENJAMIN, BENJAMIN

A CLOUDLESS SUMMER is how Benjamin remembers it from a distance of nearly twenty-five years, the summer that he met Mary Jude. The summer that his parents died, that he met Mary Jude, that something happened to Phinney. In that order, he has to remind himself. That summer was cloudless, cloudless except for the rainstorm at the tail of the summer that trapped him in Earl Van Devere's apartment. Earl Van Devere, from the Texaco station.

Benjamin had wondered why such a perfect sky, the color of cornflowers, had to be accompanied by the heat, heat like an oven opened. He didn't understand the heat. He didn't understand how the heat could have such effect, and not only on the vegetable gardens and the dogs. The heat touched everything, and harshly.

It was the hottest summer in Bluefield since the turn of the century. At least that's what the *Bluefield Register* said. It was a hundred degrees practically every day, starting in late May. It was the summer the heat made the tar on the roof shingles soft like syrup, when the lawn was scorched brown and eventually burned away, when their mother soaked their bed sheets in cold water so Benjamin and Phinney might sleep more comfortably. When they woke, their skin was moist but cool.

One of the last days in June their father came home from work and bounded into the house, shouting, "Surprises! I've got surprises for everyone!" Their father was a large man. Not muscular, just large. He was six four, an inch or so taller than Phinney would eventually grow to be. Benjamin had stopped growing two years ago, at fifteen. He'd stopped short at five eight. "Five feet eight inches above sea level." His father would say.

His father was always so much bigger, with black hair and a thick, rounded chin. His eyes, too, were big, and the planes on his square face, like his hands, seemed to have been cut from some warm wood, soft but strong enough for furniture. Teak maybe, or oak.

Usually he came home and went straight to the dinner table, and when the meal was through he would kick off his shoes and stretch out on the couch.

"Baby?" their father would call in to the kitchen. "Baby?" as their mother washed the dishes.

"Yes?" she'd answer.

"Baby, do we have any cookies?"

"Now, Gene, you know we have cookies."

"Where?"

"The same place as always. The cabinet over the stove."

"What kind do we have?"

"Oreos," she'd say. "Fig Newtons. Chocolate chips."

"What was that third one again? Fig Knuckles?" He always called Fig Newtons Fig Knuckles and laughed at himself when he did.

"Chocolate chips. Do you want me to bring them in?"

"No, no, baby, I'll get them myself." He wouldn't leave the couch, and she'd bring them in to him.

"Surprises," he shouted again, still standing at the front door.

Phinney and Benjamin came down from their bedroom when they heard their father, and their mother walked out of the kitchen to greet him. Her hair was wrapped in a scarf. She never fixed her hair.

"What is it, Dad?" Phinney asked.

"What is it? I'll tell you what it is." Their father was nearly drunk with excitement. He swirled in place, a giant top, and gestured for them to follow him out to the driveway. "There," he said, "in the car. Take a look for yourselves."

Benjamin and Phinney peered through the rear window. Four new shovels lay across the back seat, their handles long bars of polished wood, their blades as spotless and shiny as the side of a toaster.

"So, what do you think? Are those the fanciest shovels you've ever seen, or are those the fanciest shovels you've ever seen?" their father asked, and their mother asked what they were for.

He said, "They're for the well, that's what they're for."

"What well?" Benjamin asked, and his father touched his fingers to his temple and said, "Aha! Precisely, Benjamin."

His father's eyes broadened, popping like buttons from beneath his caterpillar eyebrows, and he opened the back door of the car. He handed each a shovel.

"Phinney, tell your brother what well."

"I don't know what well."

"Am I the only one who knows what well? We'll have to correct that, won't we," and he led them to the backyard, marching them in single file to a patch near the rear of the property. He thrust the blade of his shovel six inches into the ground, and the shovel stood upright there, planted like a sapling. "This well."

"Gene, we don't need a well," their mother said. She pushed at her scarf and pointed to the house. "We've got water running right into the house, or haven't you noticed?"

"My foot, we don't need a well. Do you know how much money we'll save if we've got our own well?"

She shrugged, curling her shoulders, and he answered his own question. "Millions," he said, "that's how much. If we build a well ten feet across"—and he made a hoop with his arms before him—"and thirty feet down, we'll save millions."

"Millions? You're exaggerating. You're always exaggerating."

"Ah, darling, it makes life more interesting, doesn't it?"

And he always was exaggerating. He exaggerated about his work. He exaggerated about his athletic abilities—he'd told the boys once that he'd nearly played basketball for the Boston Celtics. They hadn't realized it was a story until he went to the schoolyard with them to shoot the ball. He dribbled with both hands. There were hundreds of stories. They did make life more interesting, Benjamin had thought.

Their mother grinned. "That may be so," she said, "but it's too hot to be out here digging. Digging in the heat isn't all that interesting."

"Don't worry, I've thought of that, too. I've *planned*. We've not going to dig during the day. No, no, no, my girl." Again he touched his temple and grinned. "No, no, no. We're going to dig," he said, "at *night*. We're going to dig the whole thing at night, by porchlight," and this he said triumphantly. "It's a vertical world. Everything good is either straight up or straight down. You've got to go up or down to meet it, see, and we're going to dig *down*. At night, when it's cool. Now let's hurry and eat so we can get a good start."

He left his shovel planted in the soil, and after dinner they returned to the spot.

"Now, let's get down to the meat and potatoes," their father said, "as we like to say in the meat-and-potato business," and he scooped out the first of the dirt. They started working, the four of them standing in a small circle, dumping the soil over their shoulders. Their father was still in his work clothes, shirt sleeves rolled to his elbows. Their mother was in a housedress and apron, wearing a pair of Benjamin's sneakers and his gym socks. Her feet were as small as Benjamin's. Size seven.

Next door, Mrs. Magruder stood on her porch. She'd come out to wash off her dinner dishes with the garden hose, then stayed to watch the digging, shaking her head dramatically. Cupcake, her beagle, lapped the wet scraps from the yard.

Phinney stopped shoveling to wave. He called, "Hi there, Mrs. Magruder. Nice night for digging, isn't it?"

She turned up the corners of her mouth slightly for him. Mrs. Magruder was fond of Phinney. Most everyone was. Adults, that is.

"Ignore her," their father grunted.

"What do you think she's doing?" Phinney asked. "She's just sort of standing there."

"She's being a busybody. She's got nothing better to do with her time."

"She probably thinks we're crazy," Benjamin said.

"Now, that's the horse calling the kettle black, isn't it?" their father said. "We'll see who's crazy when we've got ourselves an honest-to-God well thirty feet from our kitchen. She'll be coming over here fifty times a day saying, 'Oh, my, can I borrow another bucket of that delicious water from your beautiful well?' Mark my words."

"Beautiful," Phinney repeated. By ten o'clock they were all tired, their faces and arms as soiled as their clothes.

Their home was a brown-and-white two-story house in the northeast part of Bluefield. It was an odd neighborhood, separated from the rest of the town. The way the neighborhood was penned in by forest on three sides, as plush as a rug at times, reminded Benjamin of photographs he'd seen of New England. It was odd, too, in its noises. Always, dogs were barking.

Everyone in the neighborhood seemed to have a dog. Mrs. Duhaney had a German shepherd named Muffin. It stood four feet off the ground and had teeth the size of walnuts. When it broke loose from its chain, most of the neighbors locked themselves in their houses until Mrs. Duhaney called on the phone to tell everyone that it was safe to go outside again. Mrs. Kilkenny had a mixed breed named Napoleon. Mrs. Hardenbrook had a collie named Sugar. Mrs. Reaver had a cocker spaniel named Crumpet. Cupcake, Mrs. Magruder's beagle, was brown, black, and white.

The bedroom Benjamin and Phinney shared was over the kitchen. In the winter, their room smelled of pancakes and tomato sauce; in the summer, with the windows open, of the forest behind. The room was, at once, part of the small house and part of something much larger, somehow removed from the rest of the structure. Benjamin always knew that it was Phinney who made it feel that way.

Their bedroom window looked onto Mrs. Magruder's house. She was a widow, and Benjamin only remembered her husband vaguely. He was killed in Korea, and Mrs. Magruder worked at the luncheonette counter of Millhauser's, the five-and-ten. When she wasn't working, she was in the yard, sitting with Cupcake on her lap. She covered her legs with her dog the way people do with blankets.

Their bedroom had powder-blue walls, and the drapes and bedspreads were red, white, and blue, the same shades as the flag. There were magazine photographs of Baltimore Orioles players tacked to the walls.

Gus Triandos, the catcher, Benjamin's favorite.

Jerry Adair, the second baseman.

Jim Gentile, the first baseman and Phinney's favorite.

Ron Hansen, Walt Dropo, Arnie Portocarrero.

Books, most of them Phinney's squeezed so tightly in the shelves that they popped out like watermelon seeds through wet fingers.

Youngblood Hawke.

The Pictorial Encyclopedia of American History, in fourteen volumes.

Rough Road Home.

Preacher's Kids.

The Artist.

Give It Back to the Lemongrowers!

The Book of Knowledge, in nine volumes, not including the index.

The Last Angry Man.

King of Bright Water.

Phinney had also thumbtacked newspaper clippings to the walls. "This way, you can see the world happening," he'd told Benjamin. He swept his arms proudly. "It's like a chronology of life. The way things from the past shape our lives, see."

KENNEDY DEFEATS NIXON, a picture of John and Jackie, smiling and waving.

SOVIET UNION SENDS FIRST WOMAN INTO SPACE.

ORIOLES SWEEP DOUBLEHEADER, MOVE INTO FIFTH PLACE.

EDDIE LEAVES DEBBIE FOR LIZ, a photograph of Debbie Reynolds looking sad as a hound.

BLUEFIELD ELECTS NEW MAYOR: DONNER.

FATHER PULLS SON FROM HOPE SPRINGS.

COLTS WIN WORLD CHAMPIONSHIP!, a photograph of the parade in Baltimore, Bluefield's hook-and-ladder company in the background, a banner on the side of the truck reading TODAY, LET BLUEFIELD BURN! THE COLTS ARE CHAMPS!

ELVIS BIG AS EVER!

POPE JOHN XXIII DIES, his picture beneath the headline.

BLACK STUDENTS TO ATTEND UNIVERSITY OF ALABAMA.

GREGORY PECK WINS OSCAR FOR TO KILL A MOCKINGBIRD.

LOCAL GIRL SPOTS FIRST ROBIN OF SPRING 10 A.M. FRIDAY.

Phinney was usually in bed before Benjamin. He would pray before he crawled under the blankets, reciting a long list of names to be blessed, ending, "If I should fall from grace with God, please lift me up again."

Benjamin would read with only the desk lamp on. Sometimes, when his eyes ached, he would move down to the kitchen table, but normally he studied in the room, dark as it was, so he could talk to Phinney before he fell asleep.

When they were smaller, their father would climb the stairs to their bedroom and tell them wild stories, stories about trees that turned into people and birds that spoke in French. Still in his work clothes, he would tuck them into bed while their mother washed the dishes. With the lights out, he'd turn the desk chair toward the bed and talk.

"A baby wolf wandered into the city one day and happened upon a group of mechanics standing on the street corner, talking about the raffle." It was one of the stories he told often. Sometimes it was a baby wolf, sometimes a baby tiger.

"What raffle?" Phinney asked.

"It was a raffle that they were having for a toaster. Whoever won the raffle got a brand-new toaster. But the toaster isn't important. Come to think of it, neither is the raffle. What is important is the baby wolf."

"Oh."

"Well, the mechanics saw that he was lost, and they took him home to raise him as their own. Over the next several years they taught him everything they knew. They taught him about pistons and carburetors. They taught him how to push the buttons in the elevator."

"A *wolf*," Phinney asked. Benjamin never interrupted.

"A baby wolf," their father answered. "They taught him how to push the buttons in the elevator. They taught him how to make banana soup. They taught him how to clean the outside of the apartment windows from the inside. They taught him how to drink whiskey with a cigarette in his mouth. But, because the larynx of a wolf is like that of a human in very few respects, he was unable to reproduce their sounds—"

"Like Benjamin?"

"No, Benjamin's going to speak just fine. They were never able to teach the baby wolf to speak, though. As a result, he never really fit into society and couldn't answer the telephone. So, the wolf became very unhappy and wrote notes to the mechanics telling them so, and the mechanics howled at his poor penmanship. The wolf spent many hours devising methods to get even with them for their insensitivity, and he might have if he hadn't gotten his pilot's license."

"Is this a true story?"

"I'm sorry, Phinney. I really should stop here and apologize. I made all of this up, especially the part about the banana soup."

Then Benjamin and Phinney would go to sleep to the sound of dogs barking outside.

* * *

After work, Benjamin and Phinney came straight home to eat, and when the sun had dipped enough they would start up on the well with their father and mother. In three days, they were five feet from the surface. In ten, they'd dug past the water pipes. They dug a few hours each evening, and more and more of the neighbors watched from Mrs. Magruder's porch. But after three weeks of labor, they were far behind schedule. They were more than ten feet down, and they passed the earth to the surface in buckets, carrying them up a ladder.

"It's just going to be an ugly ditch right in the middle of our backyard," their father said, "unless we get to work on this, pronto." He began to dig until the early morning hours, and their mother started digging in the day-time, when the others were at work, doing as much as she could in that temperature.

Benjamin was working at Kitchener's Bookstore that summer, five days a week, eight hours a day, handling the register and stocking shelves, helping customers find their books. The store was normally empty and hot, despite the fans Mr. Kitchener had set up, the ones he'd bought at the Sears in Baltimore. Alone, Benjamin walked squares around the place, pacing from corner to corner to keep cool, from fan to fan, but the fans worked poorly, clanking, and the breezes only shot out in streams. Hardly anyone came in. The women from the church came in the mornings, after mass, to get out of the heat. They stood in front of the fans with their arms spread like wings and their eyes closed behind their thick glasses.

"Aah," they'd say, a choir when the cool air hit them.

"That's one of them," one of the women whispered to her friends, "one of the Sacks," and Benjamin behaved as if he hadn't heard.

Once, a boy from school stopped in, but he had only come to say, "Hey, Benjamin, some of the guys are talking about your family again. And I'm one of them." Then he walked out.

It was the digging. People were talking. The whispering wasn't any-thing new, nor were the looks they were getting. They were the same whis-pers and the same looks as when Benjamin's mother broke her foot. She broke it kicking a shopping cart in the market, and she wrapped the cast in tinfoil before they went to the beach. "So the sand won't get between my toes," she'd explained. They were the same as when his father sang in church, loud and off-key, and when he built a pitcher's mound in the front yard.

The looks were nothing new. This time it was just the well, and boys called out, "Hey, gravedigger," to Benjamin as he walked home at night.

Earl Van Devere stopped in the bookstore once or twice a week to look for books about cars. He was the only regular, but he never said anything to Benjamin. He never spoke to anyone. He'd just tuck his books under his arm and leave.

Sometimes Phinney came by to share lunch.

Those days Phinney worked at the bakery, the Bluefield Quality Bakery, sweeping and cleaning. They were at work when their mother fell in the well, when her heart gave out in the sun: Benjamin in the bookstore and Phinney in the bakery and her husband, their father, thirty miles away, in Elmira. She collapsed and fell in like a coin, and the firemen found a pitcher of lemonade at the lip of the well when they carried her out. The pitcher was nearly empty, not a glassful left.

The ambulance and the fire truck had passed by both the bakery and the bookstore at four o'clock and then back again, half an hour later, and neither of the boys knew it had gone to their house until they went home for supper. Mrs. Magruder was waiting on the porch, and she drove them to the hospital, both boys in the front seat of the car with her and the air vent on full the whole way, blowing like a tiny storm on their faces and chests.

Phinney said, "There's nothing to worry about," and Benjamin believed him. He always believed Phinney, as if Phinney were the older brother and not the younger one. Their father met them in the hospital, his tie undone and twisted like a noodle. It was July, almost August, and it was too hot for ties. It was too hot for anyone to be digging a well.

"Everything's going to be okay, Dad," Phinney said, and Phinney moved his lips, praying.

But little was okay that summer, the summer they slept on the cold sheets. There were two funerals, nearly indistinguishable, and Benjamin and Phinney moved in with Mrs. Magruder after the second, packing their clothes and carrying them across the yard to her house, to the guest room, sharing the same bed.

Something was happening to Phinney. Benjamin could see it. The first night they were there, at Mrs. Magruder's, Benjamin put his arms around Phinney as they slept, weighing his brother to the bed.

Don't leave, too, Benjamin thought, but he could feel his brother going.

"I'm sorry about what happened," Mary Jude said one day at the YMCA pool. She was a lifeguard there, but Benjamin had never seen her before. When she said she was sorry, she entered his consciousness for the first time, and in a bathing suit.

After everything quieted down some, after everything stopped happening, Mrs. Magruder said she didn't think it was a good summer for a boy to be working, and Benjamin listened. Mr. Kitchener said he understood, that Benjamin could come back to the bookstore whenever he was ready, and Benjamin spent the rest of that summer sitting by the pool.

Mary Jude knelt down beside Benjamin, pushing her hair behind her ears, and he closed the book Mr. Kitchener had given him on his last day, *The Naked and the Dead*, closing it without marking his place. He set it down beside his chair next to his box of Fig Newtons.

"I'm sorry about what happened," she said. She was tan and strong-shouldered.

"Thank you."

"Are you and your brother okay?"

"Phinney? Yeah, we're both fine, thanks," he lied. Phinney wasn't fine.

"I'm in Phinney's class," she said, "in school. It must be horrible for you two," and Benjamin didn't say anything, he looked at the cement and picked his book up, trying to find his place. "It must be horrible for him.

Everyone knows he's very"—Mary Jude seemed to search for the right word—"introspective. He's introspective, wouldn't you say?"

"I guess you could say that. Everyone thinks that's very funny, the way he is. You're not making fun of him, are you?"

"What?" she said. Her voice was wheaty, the way it seemed to tip with the wind, and she cocked her head when she spoke. "I have a little trouble hearing out of this ear." She tapped her right ear, like an old woman. "I didn't hear what you said."

"I asked if you were making fun of Phinney, is what I asked."

"No," Mary Jude protested. "Some people do, but I think he's sweet."

"Well, he's fine. We're both doing fine."

"I'm glad. Please give him a hug or something for me," Mary Jude said. "Tell him I'm sorry." She stood and returned to the lifeguard stand. Though Benjamin had intended to stay only a while, he stayed until three o'clock, when she was finished with her shift. A boy walked over and kissed her on the cheek—a boy he recognized from school, Steven Costello—and Benjamin watched Mary Jude put shorts and a blouse on over her bathing suit, a one-piece one with red-and-blue stripes, while she talked to the boy. When she was dressed, she and the boy walked to their bicycles and rode away. Then Benjamin rode home himself. The sun had turned his shoulders and cheeks red, but Mrs. Magruder said it made him look healthy.

Mary Jude swam often and well, with the grace of a dolphin, Benjamin thought. He liked to watch her, looking over the top of his book. She went back and forth across the pool, her head tipping every fourth stroke or so to bring in air, her mouth an O. Sometimes Benjamin pretended she was in the Olympics. Sometimes she was in the ocean. And sometimes he pretended he was with her, swimming side by side, but he hardly ever went in the water. He could swim a little, but the water was never warm enough. The water always made him shiver. And when he swam, he worried, not understanding science, always amazed that his weight didn't pull him down to the bottom of the pool and keep him there. It should have held him there, like a boulder.

"How did you know?" he asked her once. She'd just pulled herself out of the pool and was shaking her hair dry. The drops that fell stained the cement like fat polka dots, and Benjamin noticed a mark on her leg, the color of coffee.

"How did I know what?" She didn't seem surprised that Benjamin was speaking to her. Boys at the pool were always talking to her, Benjamin had noticed, and they were always clowning on the diving board to amuse her. And the same boy, Costello, came to get her at three o'clock every day.

She wrung her hair.

"You know, how did you know about everything? You must have heard everyone whispering about us."

She tapped her earlobe. "I don't hear whispers," and she smiled, awk-wardly. "It was in the papers," she said, "about your father." He'd forgotten it had been in the paper, the front page of the *Bluefield Register*. His father, the crazy man.

"But how did you know it was me?"

She smiled, and said throatily, like a movie actress, "Won't you come sit and talk with me, Benjamin? It gets pretty lonely sometimes sitting there by myself," and she pointed to the lifeguard stand at the deep end of the pool.

"Will your boyfriend mind?"

"No, and if he does, who cares?"

Benjamin picked up his towel and his shirt and walked with her to the stand. Mary Jude climbed up, then held out her hand to help him, pulling at him as he'd imagined a lifeguard would. Her arms were strong for a woman, he thought, stronger than his own.

From atop the lifeguard stand, Benjamin sat and scanned the pool area, the children bouncing a yellow beach ball in the shallow end, the women in lounge chairs with black glasses covering their eyes and the shine of lotion on their legs, girls from the junior high school doing flips off the diving board, applauding one another, Mary Jude beside him in a navy-blue bathing suit, her skin brown, freckles gracing the bridge of her nose, her long hair a mad, spaghetti mess, neither red nor orange, but red-orange, the same color as Ann-Margret's. Benjamin wasn't just observing, he was committing these facts to memory.

It was a minute or so before Mary Jude touched Benjamin's forearm. "Will you tell me what it was like?" she said. "Will you tell me what it was like with your father and your mother and everything? If you don't want to talk about it, I'll understand. If it were me, I wouldn't even be able to stand up straight, I'd be so sick. I'd be sick to my stomach."

Sickness never hit Benjamin, though. Missing them is what hit him, missing his parents. Missing or remembering. Something else entirely had hit Phinney, something Benjamin didn't understand, and he didn't tell Mary Jude about everything, not that day. He told her later that summer, about his parents, but not about Phinney. Phinney was different.

And three weeks later, when Mary Jude came over to Mrs. Magruder's for dinner for the first time, on Benjamin's birthday, his seventeenth one, and Benjamin opened the door and saw her there, in a pink sundress with a ribbon in her hair, he felt as he did at parades, the feeling that life was just beginning.

Benjamin didn't know who'd arranged the talks with the psychologists, just that Mrs. Magruder drove him and Phinney to Baltimore for the day and had them wear their Sunday clothes. Benjamin sat in the front seat with Mrs. Magruder, and Phinney held Cupcake on his lap in the back. Benjamin thought of Mary Jude. He imagined himself kissing her, closing his eyes and kissing her, while Mrs. Magruder whistled aimlessly through her teeth, looking at her dog in the rearview mirror.

The sessions were all the same, and Benjamin knew what they would ask. He knew it. The psychologists asked the same questions over and over again, the order nearly identical.

How are you, Benjamin?

Is there anything you want to talk about, Benjamin?

Do you have a girlfriend, Benjamin?

What do you talk to Mary Jude about, Benjamin?

Do you talk to her about your parents, Benjamin?

Do you miss your parents, Benjamin?

How do you feel about what your father did, Benjamin?

Do you think it was right what he did, Benjamin?

What are you going to do when you get out of high school, Benjamin?

Benjamin, Benjamin, Benjamin. The doctors ended every comment with his name, as if it were punctuation, and he was becoming sick of hearing it.

He waited on a couch for the next interview, for someone to take him to another little office to discuss everything, and when Phinney took a seat next to him, Benjamin was surprised. He thought the psychologists were planning to keep them apart for the whole day.

"So, how's it going?"

"Fine," Phinney said. He made a clicking noise with his tongue and considered the room. The couch and the drapes were yellow, muted. "Fine, I guess, up until that last one. The doctor wanted to know what kind of bird I'd like to be if I could be a bird."

"Are you serious?"

"Mm hmm. He really wanted to know what kind of bird I'd be. I guess it's supposed to tell him something about what kind of person I am."

Benjamin was worried about Phinney. Phinney was listless, and he'd never been like that before. And now Benjamin was worried about himself, too, worried and nervous. He'd never thought, not for an instant, about what kind of bird he'd want to be. The question had never crossed his mind. Things like that never did—he didn't have the imagination for it—and he wondered what the doctors were trying to get at.

"What did you tell him?"

"I don't know. I said a sea gull because a sea gull can soar to great heights, effortlessly. Up in the clouds." Phinney didn't look embarrassed, and he folded his hands on his lap. His posture was rigid. "And sea gulls are attractive on the outside, but strong and fearless. You know, junk like that."

Phinney wasn't Phinney anymore. It was as if when their mother died, she took her favorite part of Phinney with her to heaven.

"Well, a sea gull sounds like a good answer," Benjamin said to comfort him, and it did sound like a good answer. Only now Benjamin couldn't use it. Now he had to think up one for himself, so he sat silently. Phinney did the same.

It was the longest time before Benjamin could think of any birds at all, let alone ones he'd want to be, and when he did think of one he couldn't think of any way to connect it to himself. He was going to say a dove, but that didn't sound masculine enough. They'd definitely think there was something wrong with him if he said a dove. Then he was going to say an eagle, but that was too obvious. Everyone said eagle, probably. Then he was going to say penguin because they're supposed to be very intelligent, but then they can't fly, so how smart can they be? Maybe they're not even birds in the first place, he started thinking. Maybe they're mammals. No, he remembered, that's whales. Finally he decided to say a hawk, and he'd make up something about how solid they are, and light at the same time. They didn't weigh much at all. Two or three pounds at most.

A doctor came out and led Phinney down the hall and away from Benjamin, and Benjamin didn't say anything to his brother when he left, he just watched him walk away and turn the corner. Another doctor came and stood before Benjamin. He was a man in his forties, wearing a navy-blue sports jacket beneath his white smock.

"Benjamin?" he said.

"Yes."

"Benjamin, I'm Dr. Regis. Why don't you come with me. I promise this won't hurt," and he smiled and led Benjamin to his office.

The doctor took a seat at his desk, and Benjamin sat across from him. There were framed degrees on the wall and color photographs of a family Benjamin assumed was the doctor's. There were boys and girls cooking hamburgers in one photograph, throwing a red ball in another, sitting at a picnic table in another, and there was one of a brown-haired woman holding a cake with pink frosting. The doctor wasn't in any of the photographs. He probably worked the camera, Benjamin thought.

"How are you, Benjamin?"

"Okay." Benjamin crossed his arms.

"You're feeling okay?"

"Mm hmm."

The doctor was writing on a yellow pad.

"Let me ask you something, Benjamin. Do you feel any differently now than you did a couple of weeks ago?" He didn't look up at Benjamin.

"Sure," Benjamin said, and he did. How could he not? His parents had both died, he and Phinney had moved into Mrs. Magruder's house, he'd met Mary Jude. Life was happening with such reckless speed that he hadn't had time to sort out how he felt. He just knew it was different.

"Well, Benjamin, what feels different?"

"I don't know. Everything."

"What do you mean, everything?"

"Everything. I don't know how to explain it."

The doctor wrote more on his pad. He pulled his eyeglasses from the breast pocket of his smock and pushed them on.

"You have a girlfriend, don't you, Benjamin?"

"Sort of. Mary Jude." Benjamin didn't know how to answer that. She was his friend, she was someone he could talk to, but he hadn't kissed her. What's more, she still had a boyfriend, the boy who met her at the pool every afternoon.

"Tell me about her."

"Well, I just met her a couple of weeks ago, so there's not much I can tell you. She's nice, and she's pretty."

"Where did you meet her?"

"I met her at the swimming pool. She's a lifeguard there."

* * *

"Are you a lifeguard, too?

"No, I work at a bookstore." He corrected himself. "I used to work at a bookstore."

"So, tell me, do you talk to Mary about your parents?"

"Mary Jude?"

"Yes, Mary Jude."

"No."

The doctor's hand swept across his pad, scribbling passionately, and Benjamin knew what the doctor would ask next. He would ask what he thought about what his father had done, and Benjamin wished that he'd ask about the birds instead, but he didn't.

On the drive back to Bluefield, Phinney was as quiet as a stone. He held the dog again.

"I wish I was as good a person as Cupcake," was all he said in more than an hour.

Six days later, firemen had to talk him down from the roof.

CHAPTER 8
THE MAN WITH THE STAR

IN BLUEFIELD, when Benjamin was a boy, he knew a man who was missing three-quarters of his left arm. Earl Van Devere was his name, built like a truck. He had a massive keg of a chest, massive legs, and a single, massive arm, twenty inches around at the bicep, Benjamin had guessed. His hair was the color of soap. It was full and wavy and parted on the side, and it reminded Benjamin of Mark Twain.

Earl lived in a room over the Park Laundromat. He had no friends or family, he was nasty to everyone in town, and he frightened children by making noises like monsters and ghosts. But he was like that even before the accident, the one that took his arm.

"What?" he said whenever someone pulled into the Texaco station, which most people on the road had to do since it was the only one in town and the last chance to gas up before Elmira, twenty miles away. His work shirt was always worn, its collar frayed around his thick neck, the star on his breast pocket bleached pink, and his manner was rough. "What?" He looked at cars as if they were beasts, each fill-up a test of his mettle. The station was across the street from the Laundromat and his room a half a mile from Mrs. Magruder's.

No one knew much about Earl's accident. It had happened when Benjamin and Phinney were small, but they'd heard enough about it. Everyone had. There was whispering about Earl, in precisely the same tone as the whispers about the Sackses. There were plenty of rumors about Earl, some wild, some not. Nothing was for certain. Some said he was drunk and lying there. Some said he threw himself in front of the car on purpose. Only Benjamin knew for sure. Not that Earl ever told him what happened, but Benjamin knew.

It was September, late, no more than two months after Benjamin had moved into Mrs. Magruder's. It was the night that five inches of rain fell in Bluefield—a record—that Benjamin thought he was going to hear the story from Earl, which would've been a neat trick since Earl rarely spoke to anyone, and then only about cars. And when he spoke of cars, it was always how much he despised them, those heaps.

It was the night Benjamin was trapped in the Laundromat without an umbrella, without his rain slicker and without a thing to eat. He hadn't heard a word about the rain. No one at school had mentioned it, no one at the bookstore had said anything, and there'd been nothing on the radio.

Benjamin sat on the washer, reading a *Time* magazine he'd borrowed from the bookstore. His clothes were turning in one machine, Mrs. Magruder's in the next. There were no clothes for Phinney; he was already gone.

Benjamin had first heard of the rain from Mrs. Hardenbrook as she took her baskets out to her station wagon. Mrs. Hardenbrook lived across the street and four doors down. She was one of the women Mrs. Magruder played bridge with on Thursday evenings.

"It's going to come down cats and dogs," she said, to no one in particular. She and Benjamin were alone in the Laundromat. She took a basket out to the car, then came in for another, and Benjamin looked out the window. The night was bathed in the autumn moonlight, chill and pale.

"Is that right?" Benjamin asked.

She seemed surprised, as if she hadn't seen Benjamin there. "Sure is."

"It wasn't on the radio or anything."

"You wouldn't have heard it on the radio. It wasn't in the papers, and it wasn't on the radio either." She hugged her laundry basket to her hip and swung the door open. "I just have a fifth sense about these things."

Mrs. Hardenbrook grasped her skirt as she slid into the car, then drove off, and Benjamin moved the clothes from washers to dryers. Mrs. Magruder's wet clothes felt strange to his hands, partly because they were a woman's, but mostly because they were hers. One minute she was their next-door neighbor, the next she was the closest thing Benjamin and Phinney had to a mother, and now he was wringing her underwear and smoothing the plaid dresses she wore at the luncheonette counter.

Benjamin finished the magazine. Then there was nothing else to do. He closed his eyes and listened to the dryers churning, and when they came to a stop he shook himself awake and folded their clothes on the counter. He kept his eyes on the wall while he folded Mrs. Magruder's, out of a sense of propriety.

The rain came while he was folding. It started suddenly and loudly, so loudly that Benjamin could hear the water slapping against the pavement through the closed Laundromat doors. It thumped vehemently. Thumpthumpthump, like children's fists. Benjamin pushed the doors open and stood with his hands on his hips, watching, waiting for it to let up. The water rushed down the street like a tiny shallow river, and the drops were so large that Benjamin could follow them as they passed in front of the illuminated Texaco sign. Every so often a car pulled into the station with its headlights on and its windshield wipers batting furiously, but Earl never came out to help. The driver would hit his horn, wait, hit it again, wait a little longer, then leave. Five or six cars went through like this, maybe more, and Benjamin recognized two: Mr. Mayer's jeep and Mr. Wall's Buick. None of them got any gas.

Mrs. Magruder's blouses were on hangers and the rest of their laundry was folded in the basket. Benjamin was getting hungry. He pushed up his shirt sleeve and looked at his father's wristwatch. It was nine-thirty. He'd been there for close to two hours.

The rain thumpthumpthumped in the street and against the windows of the Laundromat.

Benjamin checked his watch again. He didn't care if he got soaked or if the laundry did. He could always bring it back the next day, he thought, so he tucked the detergent box into the basket, put the basket on his head, balancing it with one hand, and clutched the hangers in the other. He pushed the door open and raced into the street like a halfback. Before he'd even made it as far as the gas station, he turned back. He was already wet to the skin, his shoes were damp and pliable, and his socks were soggy as washcloths. But that wasn't what sent him back inside. The water had made a noise against his skin. A sad, unrecognizable sound.

"What are you, an imbecile or something?"

Benjamin stuck his head out the doorway and looked up, then ducked back into the Laundromat. It was Earl Van Devere calling down from his room. Benjamin was surprised. It was a good night to be out spooking children, he thought.

"No," he called back. "I'm just not in the mood to spend the whole night here."

"Should have brought an umbrella." Benjamin could imagine the look on Earl Van Devere's face. He sounded amused.

"I guess so." There was a long silence, and Benjamin guessed that Earl had shut his window and gone back inside to laugh to himself. Benjamin stood in the doorway, watching the moon behind the storm, listening to the rain slapping.

"Well, Sacks," Earl Van Devere finally said, "I'll tell you what. You can stay down there all night or you could come up here if you keep your god-damn mouth shut." Whenever he was around Earl, Benjamin was always reminded of something his mother had often said. "God's last name isn't Damn," she'd say, and Phinney would nod his head.

It was a tough choice whether to go upstairs or stay there. Benjamin hesitated. "I'll come up," he answered. He thought Earl might have a television, or a telephone so he could call Mary Jude and have her come get him and the laundry.

* * *

Earl had been calling him Sacks for as long as Benjamin could remember, which Benjamin took to mean that Earl liked him more than he liked most people in town. He'd never heard him call anyone else by name, at least not by their given names, and Benjamin he called by his last name. What was odd about that was that Benjamin's nametag at Kitchener's, the bookstore, said Benjamin on it, nothing more.

That's how Benjamin knew Earl Van Devere. He'd come in to buy books about cars, everything from their maintenance to their history. He never bought any other kind of book, and it didn't take long for Benjamin to catch on to the pattern. Sometimes they'd have the book he was looking for on the shelf, or he'd find one there that interested him, but usually Benjamin had to call up to Baltimore to order a copy. That would take anywhere from a week to three weeks, depending upon inventory, and Earl would come in every afternoon to check, cussing if his book hadn't arrived. Once in a while, if Benjamin was in the mood for a walk, he'd take the book over to the Texaco station as soon as it came in. He was hoping that Earl would pull him aside and say, "Sacks, let me tell you why I buy so many of these goddamn car books," but Earl usually just handed Benjamin the money—his hand always black from the oily tires—and walked back to his chair, tucking the book beneath what was left of his left arm, turning his back to Benjamin.

The only times Benjamin had ever had anything approaching a conversation with Earl was when Benjamin filled up his father's gas tank or when he offered Earl a ride if he passed him walking. He never got in, not once. He'd say, "Don't need a ride," and just walk on, and Benjamin wondered at how powerful his thighs must be. All that walking. He was always walking, when he wasn't at the station, and never it seemed with any direction.

Only a week before the rainstorm, on his way to Baltimore to visit Phinney, Benjamin passed Earl eight miles up Route 22, just outside Elmira.

"Don't stop," Mrs. Magruder said. "Don't slow down, just keep on going," and Mary Jude said nothing.

Benjamin pulled the car beside Earl and when he called out to ask if Earl needed a lift, Earl acted as if he hadn't heard him, but Benjamin knew he had. Mrs. Magruder said, "I told you not to do that, Benjamin. You ought to listen to me sometime. The man's dangerous. Everyone says so."

Driving home later that same day, they passed him again, still walking on the shoulder, a good twelve miles from the Texaco now, more than half the way to Elmira, four miles short of Long Branch Lake, the only spot farther along of any interest. Benjamin didn't stop that time and felt horrible for it, but Earl was always walking.

Benjamin left the clothes in the Laundromat, on top of one of the dryers, and ran outside to the doorway that led to Earl's room. There were no lights in the stairwell, and Benjamin hung onto the rail with one hand, stepping as carefully as he would in a fun house. The door to the apartment was closed and locked, and Benjamin pounded on it.

"What?"

"Earl, it's me. Sacks."

"What do you want?" It was as if they hadn't spoken.

The door rattled when Benjamin rapped on it again, rattling from the cheap old wood and the poor fit. The doorknob clicked three or four times before the door opened. The first thing Benjamin noticed was the books.

The books were everywhere. On bookshelves. On the kitchen counters. Stacked in piles two feet high on the floor. On the arms of chairs, on the window sills, on the tables, under the lamps. Everywhere. It was a library. It had the same smell about it, the same aura of studied serenity, despite the shabbiness. The books overwhelmed the shabbiness. There was grime, there was tattered fabric, there was Earl, but mostly there were books.

"Thanks," Benjamin said after a moment, standing in the center of the room. Rocking on his heels, he waited for Earl to gesture for him to sit. But Earl didn't, he just went back to the kitchen sink along the far wall of the room. Benjamin sat anyway, pulling a book off one of the chairs spontaneously, as if he'd be bare and conspicuous without one. He fingered its binding: *Assembly Line Techniques.* Absently, Benjamin leafed through. There were fewer pictures than he'd expected, and the text was dense and complex, the print fine. There were numbers everywhere, floating through the prose like flies.

"You understand this?" Benjamin asked, holding the book up above his head.

Earl turned and squinted. "Which one is that?"

Benjamin read him the title.

"Would I have the goddamn book if I didn't?" He could have said that about any of the books in the room, Benjamin thought, he didn't need to know its name, and Earl turned to the sink again. "Are you going to keep talking?"

"Sorry, Earl," Benjamin answered. "I hadn't meant to be such a chatterbox." That had been one of his mother's words, chatterbox.

Earl walked over to a chair in the corner, carrying a cup of coffee. He set the cup down on the arm of the chair, picked up a book from the floor, his bicep big as a billiard ball, and sat. He flipped the book open indiscriminately and began reading. It was a thick navy-blue volume called *The Henry Ford Years,* and Earl started about two-thirds of the way in. Every now and then he sipped his coffee, slurping it like a child. Sometimes he looked over at Benjamin, but said nothing. He was a quick reader. That, or he was skimming. The pages turned with a frenzied regularity, faster even than Phinney could turn them, and Earl's huge chest bounced with his breath.

Benjamin put his book down, went to the window, and pulled back the shade. It was coming down as hard as ever. Mrs. Hardenbrook's fifth sense hadn't failed her; it was still cats and dogs.

The rain knocked against the window.

"Earl?"

He smirked behind his book.

Benjamin pointed to Earl's cup. "Mind if I get some while I'm up?" Earl returned to his reading, and Benjamin went over to the stove, took a cup off the shelf, and filled it. He couldn't find any spoons or sugar and didn't ask. He took a seat by one of the bookshelves. He leaned forward to browse. *Report of the State Highway Commission: 1960. Auto Aerodynamics. Repair Manual for Buick Engines. The Kings of Funny Cars. Cars! Cars! Cars! Approaching the Speed of Sound. Customizing.* Some Benjamin recognized, having ordered them for Earl. Most were obscure or old.

Benjamin swallowed some coffee and looked around the room. *Cars! Cars! Cars!* was on his lap. It was difficult to see the furniture for all the books. There was a small wooden dresser along one wall. There were six chairs, most of them worn, scattered about. There was a cot, folded and tucked away in one corner. There were three small tables with lamps. Earl sat beside the largest of the tables, with the lamp on. There was no television and no phone. Benjamin returned to the book.

Cars! Cars! Cars! It was light reading, simple and childish, with full-page photographs of dragsters and race cars. Every sentence seemed to end in an exclamation point. Benjamin worked through two or three pages before he heard a horn outside, then he replaced the book on the shelf and went to the window. He pulled back the shade. Mr. Carlisle's tan Dodge Dart had pulled into the Texaco station.

"Earl," he said.

"What?"

"Mr. Carlisle's car's down at the station," Benjamin said this with a certain urgency. Earl didn't seem to care whose car it was, and he made a point of not looking up from his book.

"If you want my opinion," he said plainly, "on a night like this, Carlisle ought to go straight to hell."

Benjamin released the shade, and the breeze snapped it back against the window. He looked around the room for Earl's keys, on the stacks of books, on the tables. They were on his dresser, and Benjamin grabbed them, ran out the door, down the stairs, and out onto the street. The water was up to his ankles, pulling at him as he ran, and he had to keep a hand at his forehead to see. He made it to the car and stood there, hunched, tucking his hands in his armpits as Mr. Carlisle cracked open his window.

"Earning a little extra dough, huh Ben?"

Benjamin only asked him how much gas he wanted. The Texaco sign was enormous from where he was standing, the only light in the sky, dwarfing the moon, a speck.

"Top it off," Mr. Carlisle said, then closed his window in a hurry.

Benjamin unlocked the pump, unscrewed Mr. Carlisle's gas cap, and held the nozzle, squeezing it. He read the black letters on the base of the pump: TRUST THE MAN WITH THE STAR. He wiped his forehead with his shirt sleeve, but the sleeve was already soaked. There was the sound of thumping water on the ground and against the car, and the sad sound the rain made as it struck Benjamin was the same sound it made when it struck a hollow log, Benjamin thought.

When the nozzle clicked off, it startled Benjamin, and he looked at the meter: less than three gallons. He put the cap back, then the nozzle, and went over to the driver's door.

"You didn't even need three gallons," he told Mr. Carlisle.

Mr. Carlisle nodded and cracked a one-sided smile. He didn't feel guilty about dragging me out in this mess, Benjamin thought. "Just wanted to make sure I had a full tank for tomorrow. Big day, tomorrow. Going up to Baltimore." He'd probably expected Earl.

Mr. Carlisle handed Benjamin some coins and said, "Glad to see you're handling this better than your brother," grinned too widely, waved, and drove off. Benjamin didn't run back to Earl's. There was no sense in it. He couldn't have been any wetter. He walked back, deliberately, sloshing through the street, looking at his soaked reflection in the Laundromat window. The gray spot on the side of his head shone like a star on the glass.

He took the steps upstairs slowly, too, stamping his feet outside Earl's door. A large puddle formed where he stood, then trickled down the steps. Benjamin found the key to the room on Earl's chain and opened the door.

Earl was still in his chair, reading *The Henry Ford Years,* and Benjamin put the keys and money on the dresser. He waited for Earl to say something.

"Earl, a towel?"

"Bathroom." He waved his hand toward the second of two thin doors beyond the bookcases. Before Benjamin reached the bathroom, he heard Earl say something about Benjamin's father.

"What?" Benjamin said.

"I just said that you're crazy, just like your father, Sacks."

"My father wasn't crazy," Benjamin protested, but he did so weakly. At first, when people had started saying things about his father, when the whispers began, Benjamin was vehement in his defense. Now, he answered with little confidence.

"He was crazy to do what he did. Don't tell me he wasn't. And your brother, too. Crazy as a lark."

"Phinney?"

"Jesus, I don't know what his name is, I just know he's crazy, too. I heard they had to get a fire truck to get him down from the roof. Word is that they had to put him in a loony bin."

"He's in a hospital," Benjamin said quietly, and he went into the bathroom, "seeing doctors." He closed the door and wished Mary Jude were with him. He wished he could wrap his fingers around her wrists and clutch them to him.

In September, before school started, the fire truck had had to come get Phinney from the roof of their old house. He couldn't hurt himself there—he'd been only fifteen feet above the yard—but he wouldn't get down. He'd been standing by the chimney, and when he saw Benjamin and Mrs. Magruder in the front yard, looking up at him, Phinney had called, "Come with me, Benjamin," and waved his arms. "Come on."

"Where are you going?"

"To tell God to kiss my ass." Phinney began swinging his arms, singing to the sky, "Kiss my ass! Kiss my ass! Kiss my big fat ass!"

Benjamin had never heard his brother curse before, and Mrs. Magruder clasped a hand over her mouth for an instant, then demanded, "Get down here right *now*, and I mean it." When he didn't budge, she said to Benjamin, "Do something, Benjamin."

"I don't know what to do. He's the smart one."

"Well, how am I supposed to know what to do?"

The whir of the fire truck sounded down the street, drowning out Phinney's voice, and Benjamin stood beneath the roof, his arms outstretched to catch Phinney if he jumped, though Benjamin knew he wasn't strong enough to hold his brother. Phinney was too big. Benjamin just wanted to touch him before he fell into the shrubbery, before they took him away, but the firemen led him down the ladder, and Benjamin didn't touch his brother again for three days, when they let him into the hospital room.

It was an hour's drive to the Baltimore Mental Health Center, an hour each way. He drove his father's car, the Chevy Bel Air, sliding the seat up so he could see over the dashboard. The car had a rounded front, like a bullet, Benjamin thought, and a curved wraparound windshield. His father had looked like a spaceman behind it when he first brought the car home, steering it into the driveway and honking the horn.

Mary Jude played the radio while Benjamin drove. She didn't say much at all, and Mrs. Magruder watched the traffic like a foreigner, intrigued.

"You don't really notice the cars when you're driving yourself," she said.

He knew Phinney wasn't the same anymore. It was as if their mother's death had left Phinney with a hole right in the middle of him. But Benjamin didn't believe it when Mrs. Magruder said that the doctors wanted to keep Phinney in the hospital, that it wasn't safe to let him go home. The hole couldn't be that big.

Benjamin smoked cigarettes while he sat in the waiting room between Mary Jude and Mrs. Magruder, each of them reading a magazine. Then a nurse took him down a series of great, long corridors.

"Piss!" he heard a boy yell in one room.

"Boogers!" another shouted.

The nurse ignored the screams. She walked as if she were in a church.

"Piss!"

"Goddamnit!"

"Stinking asshole!"

"Mommy!"

"Sucker!"

Benjamin stayed behind the nurse, and she stopped in front of one of the doors. She didn't open it.

"No cigarettes allowed," she said.

"What?" Benjamin was concentrating on the maze of white tiled corridors.

"Piss!" he heard.

"Piss and boogers!"

"You can't take cigarettes in there," the nurse said. She'd said it a thousand times, he could tell. "I'm sorry."

"He doesn't smoke. I'm the one who smokes."

"I'm sorry," she said, "it's the policy," and Benjamin stubbed his cigarette out against the wall. It left a black smudge on the tile like a tire track. He handed the cigarette butt to the woman, and she pinched it in her fingers; he pulled the pack from his pocket and put it in her other hand. She opened the door and disappeared, leaving him alone in the small room. There was only a table and two chairs, and they were bolted to the floor. There were bars on the window. Thick black steel. And when another nurse led Phinney in, he was wearing a white dressing gown, his legs bare from the thigh down. His head was shaved, the stubble covering it as thin as a grown man's five-o'clock shadow.

"God, Phinney, what is it?"

And his brother answered, "I don't know. If I knew what it was, I'd be cured."

If they said more, it was only instinct that made them talk. There just seemed to be silence there. Benjamin held his brother to him, saying nothing he could remember, pulling Phinney's chest against him until another nurse came in to lead Benjamin back to the waiting room.

"Jesus Christ!"

"Mommy!"

"Dick!"

"Boogers!"

"Stinking asshole!"

And his cigarettes were there with Mary Jude and Mrs. Magruder.

"Did he say anything?" Mary Jude asked. "Did he say how he's doing?"

"There's not much to say," Benjamin answered.

On the drive home, Mrs. Magruder fell asleep. Her lips made a fluttering noise when she exhaled.

Mary Jude comforted Benjamin. "Benjamin," she said, "sweetheart, these are the things that make us bigger and stronger, things like this. You're going to learn from all of this, from all of the horrible stuff you've had to go through this summer. You're going to be the biggest person in the world because of this."

But how do you stop from getting too big? Benjamin wondered. How do you keep yourself from collapsing beneath it all?

Later that week, when Benjamin had to fill out forms about Phinney at the hospital, he had the odd, fleeting sensation that he'd given birth to Phinney, that Phinney was his responsibility.

Again, on that drive home, he passed Earl and didn't stop. The momentum was too great to stop.

Earl's bathroom was small, just a shower stall, toilet, and sink pressed tightly together. A fifty-watt bulb burned over the sink. Everyone thought Benjamin's father and Phinney were crazy, everyone except Benjamin and Mary Jude. People said so, and if they didn't say so, it was clear that's what they thought. Benjamin could see it in the pity and fear on their faces.

Benjamin pulled one of the bath towels off the shower rod, mussing up his hair until it was nearly dry. Wiping off his face and neck and hands. He took off his ruined shoes and set them in the stall, then his socks, wringing them out over the toilet before stuffing them into his shoes. He took off his shirt and hung it on a hook, and stood in front of the medicine-cabinet mirror, combing his hair with his fingers. That was when he noticed the photograph on the basin, framed in wood and propped up against the soap dish.

It was a small black-and-white one of a girl in her teens, standing on a dock, nothing behind her except water. She was wearing a golfing cap, a loose blouse that may well have been one of her father's discarded shirts, Bermuda shorts and white boat shoes. Her skin was white, too, like linen, and it was hard to tell if she was bored or sick, or both. A fish hung neatly from a string the girl pinched between the thumb and index finger of her right hand, and somehow it seemed as if she were holding the fish more than an arm's length away. It was an odd pose, odd and charming.

Benjamin opened the bathroom door and took a step into the room, still in his undershirt. He cupped the picture in his palm. It frightened Benjamin. He wanted to ask Earl about it, but he wasn't sure what he wanted to know. He wanted to know everything.

"That looks like a bass," he finally said. Bass were all he knew. They were the only fish he could think of, and he wasn't sure if they lived in fresh or salt water.

Earl looked over his book. Oh, the expression on his face, Benjamin thought.

"It is," Earl answered. "A largemouth."

For an instant he ceased to be Earl Van Devere, or maybe for an instant, he became Earl Van Devere, curious and exposed. His chest heaved. His star bobbed, and suddenly everything seemed to hang heavily on him. His chest, his arm, his chin, his legs. Everything except the piece of his left arm. There was a lightness about that.

Earl closed his book and leaned forward in his chair. "I wouldn't figure you'd know much about fishing, Sacks. You don't strike me as much of an outdoorsman." He couldn't fool Benjamin. Benjamin knew he wasn't thinking about fish.

Benjamin nodded noncommittally.

They stayed silent for several minutes, their glances catching then darting away. Benjamin felt like Earl's friend. Finally, he asked, "Who's the girl?"

Earl didn't tell him who the girl was. Benjamin thought he might. He looked as if he would, but somehow he regained himself. He flipped his book open again, this time no more than a quarter of the way in, and Benjamin sat and held the picture, not wanting to return it to the sink. Earl's pages turned with a certain slowness, but he looked the same as always, hard and massive. Only now Benjamin saw the heaviness, too. It hung from him. It was in his fingers when he touched his face. It was in his throat and in his hair.

Earl wasn't reading. He was thinking, and so was Benjamin. Something had happened. Benjamin thought of cars—what else would he think of in that room?—and he thought of car wrecks, of Earl driving too fast through an intersection, of Earl not stopping at a light, of Earl taking his eyes off the road to look at the girl with the linen skin. He looked so heavy. Benjamin looked at the picture again. This time he imagined the girl on the dock, the sleeve of her blouse loose and flapping like a flag, empty, the fish and the string hanging there in space, unfettered.

Earl had jumped in front of the car on purpose. Benjamin knew that.

Two minutes on a page. Three minutes on a page. Then two and a half on the next. A car honked at the station, and neither Earl nor Benjamin jerked. There were more, but Benjamin didn't count. The rain continued well into the night before Benjamin thought of borrowing one of Earl's coats, and after he'd thought of it, he waited an hour or so before asking, watching Earl read, only halfway into Henry Ford's life and yet at the same time almost through.

He watched Earl. How much does it weigh? Benjamin wanted to say as he slipped into Earl's topcoat, one sleeve worn and comfortable, the other stiff as new. How much does it weigh? But Earl might have thought he meant the book or the fish.

CHAPTER 9
HELLO, I'M JAPANESE

THREE-FIFTEEN IN THE MORNING, and the motel walls are shaking. They shake as if someone were punching them, time after time.

Kim groans. "What's that noise?" she says in her sleepy voice. She and Benjamin are entwined on the floor, her head in the crook where his arm and chest meet, his legs curled around hers.

"God," Benjamin says, "I don't know," and he squeezes his eyelids tighter as if that would block out the sound. He's too tired to move. His body seems disconnected.

More pounding on the walls.

"Cut it out!" Kim shouts, finally. "We've got a child in here trying to sleep!"

"That's what I'm here for," a woman says, loudly but pleasantly, from the other side of the door. "I'm here to pick up Tommy." It's the woman from the pool, the boy's mother.

"Oh, God!" Kim struggles to free herself from Benjamin. "What was I thinking!" She hurries to the door to unlock it.

Benjamin keeps his eyes shut tight.

"Sally," Kim breathes. "Geez."

"I'm sorry we're so late," the woman responds. "We lost track of time. You know how it is. You think it's midnight, and then you look at your watch and it's like, 'Oh my *God*, it's two in the morning.'"

"I fell asleep," Kim tells her, "or I would've opened the door right away. I'm sorry."

"No, don't *you* apologize. You're a real sweetheart for taking care of him for us."

"Did you say you had a good time?"

"Terrific."

Benjamin can hear small footsteps as the women move to the bed.

"I hope he wasn't any trouble," the woman says.

"Not at all. He was great. He's a cutie." Benjamin hears the woman rattle her son awake.

"What?" the boy mumbles.

"It's me. It's Mommy."

"Hi, Mommy."

"Mommy's going to take you back to our room now, okay?"

"I'm too tired."

"Mommy knows you're tired. Mommy will carry you."

"I'm sleeping."

"You're talking, you can't be sleeping. Now, come on, Mommy will carry you."

The bed squeaks as the woman lifts the boy from it.

"Thanks again," the woman says, and the door closes behind her.

Benjamin feels Kim moving around the room, and the bedspread drops, covering him from his neck to his ankles.

"You're so handsome when you're sleeping," she says, and she stoops to kiss the top of his head.

She stands again, and Benjamin hears her walk toward the bathroom, he hears the light switch flick, he hears the sound of the glass cosmetic bottles tinkling against the bathroom counter, and he knows what Kim's doing. He knows her shirt is off, and he listens to hear if she's crying, but he doesn't hear a sound.

* * *

Kim runs, and Benjamin dresses and pays for the room while she does. He leaves the door to the room unlocked so they can get back once he's handed over the key.

The man at the front desk is in his early twenties and as tanned as a model. His brilliant white teeth seem too large for his mouth, forcing his lips to protrude peculiarly. He takes Benjamin's credit card.

"Did you and Mrs. Sacks have a nice time?" he asks.

"Until we got divorced," Benjamin answers, and it's only when he says this that he remembers how he'd signed the register: Mr. and Mrs. B. Sacks. "Yes, yes," he corrects himself, "we had a wonderful time. It's a very nice motel you have here."

"I'm glad you enjoyed your stay," the man says, still smiling. He's smiling as if he couldn't stop if he tried, Benjamin thinks.

When Benjamin returns to the room, Kim's already out of the shower and dressed.

"I kept it short today," she says before Benjamin can say anything, "so we can get a move on it."

She helps Benjamin carry their luggage out to the car and stuff it into the trunk. "We have to call Phinney for the rest of the directions, don't we?"

"Mm hmm," Benjamin says, "but we can't do it here. We're already checked out."

Kim grimaces. "We could call from the gas station down there," she says.

Benjamin pumps the gas while Kim calls Phinney, and when Benjamin's through he goes into the store to pay. He can see Kim through the store window. She's standing at the phone booth, one hand over her ear, and every so often she drops this hand to write on Friday's *Sun*. She's been keeping track of the names of all of the gas stations they've passed on the trip, writing them under Tug Macy's name in the margin beside the crossword puzzle: Stop 'N' Go, Pumps 'N' Pantry, Gas 'N' Go, Food 'N' Fuel.

This is a Gas 'N' Grill, with a small cafeteria in the back, and Benjamin takes two Diet Pepsis out of the refrigerator for Kim and puts them on the counter, then hands the cashier his Visa card. When the cashier asks Benjamin for his license plate, he says, "Maryland. H-E-R-S." The Mustang was Mary Jude's. Now she's driving around with the Volvo, in New York, the one with HIS on the license plate. Benjamin suspects she changed the plates long ago.

Kim opens the door.

"I got it," she says, and she taps the newspaper against her hip. "No problem. We'll be there in half an hour. Twenty-nine North to 136 west. That'll take us right to Beatrice." Beatrice is the town where Phinney lives now. She spots the sodas on the counter and thanks Benjamin, putting her hand against the small of his back for a moment, and the cashier asks Benjamin what make of car it is.

Kim tugs at his elbow and cups her hand around his ear. "Tell him it's a Ford Underwearmobile."

Benjamin looks at the cashier and says, "It's a 1978 Ford Mustang," and the man writes that on the slip.

"Chicken," Kim says, and Benjamin can't tell if she's really disappointed. She unscrews the cap of her soda and takes a drink.

He signs the slip and sticks his copy and his Visa card in his wallet, and he follows Kim to the car. She runs her fingers over her underwear, still hanging from the hook.

"Dry?" he asks, starting the engine.

"More or less," but she doesn't take them down. She giggles and puts her fingers to her mouth, holding the open Pepsi between her knees. She slips down in her seat and giggles again.

"What?"

She doesn't answer. The car's already on I-70.

"What? What is it?"

She giggles and points behind Benjamin. He turns toward her and looks over his right shoulder, and when Kim shakes her head, her fingers still over her mouth, he looks over his left. A pair of his boxer shorts droops from the suit hook on the driver's side. It's the red plaid pair.

"Cute. Very cute," he says. He taps the crossword puzzle filled with X's with a finger. "Did you get it?"

"What?"

"Gas 'N' Grill?"

"Yup." She picks up the newspaper and looks over all she's written on it. "They don't just have gas stations anymore," she says. She says this as if she were forty years old, Benjamin thinks. "They all have food now, too. It's like you're supposed to build up an appetite pumping gas or something. And they all have those stupid apostrophe N's." Then she writes BEN 'N' KIM on the newspaper. "See, like this."

Benjamin smiles absently. For an instant he thinks about something Kim had said one of the first times he took her out after work. He'd been late, and when he arrived the waitresses had already split up their tips and Kim was sitting with Yumi at one of the tables. Yumi was talking to another waitress, and Kim was writing on a pad, the one she wrote her orders on. "You be good to my little girl," Yumi said to Benjamin when they left, and Kim dropped the pad in her purse. Later, Benjamin asked what she'd been writing, and she said, "What do you think I was doing? I was practicing writing 'Mrs. Kim Sacks' over and over," and she winked. When he pulled his car in front of her parents' house, she kissed Benjamin and took the pad from her purse to show him. All it said was BUY MAKEUP, SODA, AND BAGELS.

Kim writes in the margin again. "Or like this." He looks up from the road: KIM 'N' BEN.

"Or this." KIM 'N' TUG MACY

"Jesus," he says, shaking his head, "you're not going to start up with this Tug Macy junk again."

"Jealous, are we?"

Benjamin huffs. "Is this the one with the really small waist?"

"Mm hmm," she hums, her lips together.

"The one who borrowed your clothes?"

"He *never* borrowed my clothes. You're the one who said he borrowed my clothes." She points an accusing finger, and Benjamin acts as if he's confused. He bunches his eyebrows.

"I could've sworn you told me that."

"I never said that. You're the who made that up."

"Are you sure?"

"Yes, I'm sure. God, Benjamin, I swear you're impossible."

"Whatever you say," he says, "sweetheart," and the smile she gives him is unmistakable. He keeps his eyes on the road, but he can feel her watching him, watching and smiling crazily, like a bandit. All of her playfulness has distracted him. Her joking has taken his mind off the creek. That's what it is. He was fine when she was joking. But when she's smiling, when she's loving him, it comes back, the creek. It overwhelms him.

"You're staring at me," he says eventually. It's hard to swallow.

"I know."

He lets her stare and smile, and then, to end it, he sings, "Kim and Tug sitting in a tree, K-I-S-S-I-N-G, first comes love, then comes marriage, then comes Kim with a baby carriage, " a song he remembers from the playground, until Kim sits up straight and shoves him.

"Cut it out," she says, embarrassed, and she pinches his arm delicately.

Let's just have fun, he wants to say. Whatever you do, don't make me think seriously about any of this. You'll find out how horrible I am. But he doesn't say this, he just turns on the radio, and Kim dozes like a cat at night, her eyes half-open.

In forty minutes, they're there. They're in Beatrice and driving slowly.

It was early April, and Benjamin unbuttoned his coat as soon as he entered Yumi's, consumed by the warm smell of raw fish and spice. Immediately he headed toward the men's room.

"Hi, Benjamin," each of the women said. Debra. Terri. Tamara. Shannon. Kim. Verna.

Benjamin nodded and said hello. He dipped his shoulder to slip the coat off as he walked, and Yumi came toward him from the kitchen. Her steps were clipped like those Kim had affected. Her eyes were as gray as her hair. Her unwrinkled skin had surprised Benjamin the first time he'd met her. "Yumi the Great," Kim had explained, "stopped aging."

"Hello, Yumi," he said when she was nearly beside him. "*Konnichi wa.*" Hello in Japanese. Kim had taught him.

Yumi smiled. "*Konnichi wa,* Benjamin." The smile was neither friendly nor unfriendly. It was, he thought, the smile that strangers exchange when, for a moment, they believe they recognize one another.

Benjamin continued to the men's room and closed the door behind him. He sat against the sink.

"So, did I tell you the latest about Doug?" Shannon.

"You told me." Kim.

"I know I told *you*, but I didn't tell everyone." Shannon.

"Oh, don't make fun of Doug. I like him. He's so lifelike."

"You don't have to date him." Shannon.

"Is this something crazy again?" Debra.

"His craziest, I think." Shannon. "He's got a whole new scheme to make a million dollars."

"Is this better than the toothpaste with vitamins in it?" Terri.

"Uh huh. This time it's a pair of scissors"—Shannon paused—"That you can run through the house with!"

The women laughed.

"Are you serious?" Verna.

"Yup. It's a great technological advancement, or it will be as soon as he figures out how to make it." Shannon.

"You really found a genius, didn't you?" Tamara.

"You know what they say. Some people are born great, others have to have it thrust into them." Tamara.

"Is that Shakespeare?" Kim.

"Don't you get it?" Tamara. "*Thrust* into them." Benjamin smiled.

"That's not all. Now he's calling up scissor companies trying to get them to give him money." Shannon. "He's even got an ad campaign he thinks will help him double sales: Don't just buy scissors. Buy a *pair* of scissors."

This time the women shrieked, and Benjamin adjusted his position on the sink. The porcelain was never comfortable for long.

"Do you *sleep* with this man?" Terri.

"A lot less since he came up with the scissor idea." Shannon.

"Doesn't he scare you?" Kim.

"Sure, but what's love if you're not scared?" Shannon.

"That's stupid. You should be scared that you might stop loving him. Or you should be scared that he might stop loving you. But you shouldn't be scared that he might cut all your hair off in the middle of the night just to see how his scissors work." Terri.

"Terri's right." Tamara.

"Bill's starting to bore me." Debra.

"We're not talking about Bill." Tamara.

"Well, he's starting to bore me." Debra.

"Again?" Verna.

"Yeah." Debra. "Twice last week he took me to see the same foreign movie at the Charles Theatre. All it was these two guys in love with the same woman, and all three of them sit around and drink wine." Debra.

"I think I've seen that one." Terri.

"How would you know? She just described the plot of every French movie ever made." Verna.

"Well, it was stupid the first time." Debra. "And it was even stupider the second time. I ended up scraping off all of my nail polish just to kill time."

"God, things must be so weird in France." Kim. "I mean, who in their right mind would sit around and drink wine with someone who was in love with his girlfriend or boyfriend or whatever? It just isn't natural not to want to keep someone for yourself."

"Well, why don't you tell us about it?" Tamara.

"About what?" Kim.

"About Ben." Tamara. "You're dating a divorced guy."

"So?" Kim.

"So, it's the exact same thing. He's got you, and he's got his ex-wife. What's she like? Don't you sit around and drink wine with her all the time?"

"With Mary Ann?"

Mary *Jude,* Benjamin thought. Mary *Jude.*

"Yeah. What's this Mary Ann like?" Tamara. "How old is she?"

Thirty-eight, Benjamin thought.

"Forty, I guess," Kim answered.

"Wow, that's almost old enough to be dead." Tamara.

"Listen, girls, respect your elders or your chests will sag." Yumi. "Mark my words. They'll sag like bags of sand."

"So, what's Mary Ann *like*?" Debra. "And be careful how you describe her or your chest will end up on the floor."

"I don't know." Kim.

"Haven't you even met her?" Debra.

"Nope," Kim.

"Well, you've talked to her on the phone. What's she like?" Debra.

"I haven't talked to her on the phone, either. She and Benjamin don't talk to each other at all. I've seen pictures of her. Benjamin's got some pictures in the bottom of his underwear drawer."

"Figures." Terri.

"What's she look like?" Tamara.

"She's gorgeous. Absolutely gorgeous." Kim.

Benjamin closed his eyes.

"He's going to leave you. Mark my words, Sachiko." Yumi.

"Gorgeous?" Tamara.

"Uh huh. Gorgeous. She's got beautiful red hair. It's all wavy, and it just sort of falls down on her shoulders, and she's got freckles here and under here, and these gorgeous lips."

"If she's so beautiful, then why did Benjamin divorce her?" Verna.

"She divorced him." Kim.

"Why?" Terri.

"God, I don't know. I mean, we don't talk about it." Kim.

"I'll tell you why she divorced him." Shannon. "She divorced him because he spends so much goddamn time in the bathroom!"

There was a roar of laughter. Benjamin rose and turned. He twisted the faucet on and looked in the mirror and rinsed his hands under the cold water. The crack in the mirror looked like a crack in Benjamin's face.

"No, I don't know why she left him." Kim.

"Why don't you ask him?" Tamara.

"No." Kim.

"Why?" Tamara.

"Because he doesn't want to talk about it." Kim. "If he wants to talk about it, we'll talk about it."

"He doesn't want to talk about it because he's still in love with Mary Ann, that's why." Tamara.

Some nights, Benjamin thought, I like the shibby talk less than others. No one understands. He dried his hands with a paper towel. He ran the towel over his face to make sure the crack was the mirror's, not his own.

Nebraska license plates have setting suns on them. Or rising suns. Benjamin can't tell which. The suns are divided in half by a red line of the land. Many of the cars have stickers that read GO HUSKERS or UNIVERSITY OF NEBRASKA or LEWIS AND CLARK LAND.

Kim pulls on her running shoes and sits upright in her seat. She reads Benjamin the directions from the newspaper, straining to understand her own handwriting. The town, Beatrice, is one long strip. It's not like Baltimore, where the buildings seem to lean against one another for comfort and support. Here, they're separated by long flat tracts of land and gravel roads.

Benjamin looks in his rearview mirror at the dust behind them, swirling, and soon they're on Phinney's road.

"This is it," Kim says, and there's excitement in her voice. "Right here." She points, and Benjamin steers the car into the driveway.

Phinney is atop the ranch house when Benjamin and Kim pull in. His chest is bare, and he's lying on a beach towel with a book and a transistor radio in front of him, a thin cord running from the radio to his ear. He doesn't hear their car approach, and Benjamin and Kim step out. Benjamin reaches in through the open car window to press the horn. He presses it once, and Phinney doesn't move. Again, and Phinney sits up and pulls the earphone from his ear.

"Benjamin!" he shouts, standing. He is, Benjamin knows, a man always capable of falling. But he keeps his balance gracefully, and he closes his book. He lifts the towel and slings it over his shoulder like a sash.

"What are you doing up there?"

"Tanning. I'm getting a tan." He extends his arms at his sides and turns a slow circle on the roof. "See?" He smiles. "See?"

"On the roof?" Benjamin asks, and Phinney says. "It's closer to the sun."

"Phinney"—Benjamin swallows—"the sun's a million miles away. You're only fifteen feet closer than you'd be if you were on the ground."

"Sometimes fifteen feet makes all the difference in the world," Phinney says, "when you're trying to get a tan," and his skin is brown, in fact. It's nearly the color of cashews, a shade darker than Kim.

Benjamin places his hand on Kim's shoulder, finding her without looking from his brother. "Phinney, this is Kim."

Phinney nods, smiling. "It's good to finally see you."

"Konnichi wa," Kim says, and Phinney cracks a smile.

"I thought you weren't working at the restaurant anymore," he says.

"I'm not. At least not until fall."

"Well, let me come down and say hi in the flesh, person to person," and

Phinney pulls open a small window and disappears into the house.

"And that's Phinney," Benjamin says to Kim.

"Mm hmm. He's bigger than I expected."

"What does that mean?"

"Nothing. I just thought he'd be about the same size as you." She looks at Benjamin, then opens her eyes wide. "It doesn't *mean* anything. I just thought you'd be the same size, okay?"

When he comes out the front door, Phinney's size surprises Benjamin, too. Benjamin last saw his brother nearly three years ago when Benjamin and Mary Jude flew out to Nebraska for Thanksgiving dinner, and the years between show on Phinney's frame. Fuller. Rounder. As if he'd finally grown into himself. His belly bulges over the waistband of his bathing suit. His hands are as big as country hams. In his left he's holding a paperback romance. The book is two, perhaps three fingers wide at its spine, and the title is in pink Gothic letters: *Passion's Burning Flame*. A man and a woman embrace on the cover, the woman's shoulders bared.

He sees Benjamin glance at the book. "I'm not going to read something serious up on the roof," he says. "You can't read Emily Bronte while you're getting a tan. It's sacrilegious."

Awkwardly, holding the book, Phinney bends to hug Benjamin, and Benjamin squeezes him in return. They separate, and each takes a step back, inspecting each other while pretending not to. Phinney is raccoon-eyed and balding. He's jug-eared, as always, and jowly. His face is odd yet engaging, taking on its full measure of appeal when he smiles, which he does when he takes Kim's hand in his own and says hello. He's retained some of his aura of youthfulness, Benjamin thinks, despite the added weight.

"This is your place?" Kim asks.

"For the rest of the summer, it is. Nice little place, isn't it? My boss and his wife live here, but they're in England for the summer, so I'm—what's the word I'm looking for?"

"Housesitting?" Benjamin says.

"Housesitting," Phinney says. His voice pops. "There's plenty of room, see? Nothing to worry about."

Phinney looks at the car. He spots Benjamin's boxer shorts drooping in the window but says nothing.

"I forgot what you do," Kim says to Phinney. "For a living, I mean."

Phinney turns from the car. "I paint houses. Nothing too important."

He leads them inside, where it's cool and air-conditioned.

"This is it," he says, "the palace," and his arms open wide like a carnival barker's. "This is it." He walks through the living room to the dining room, then to the kitchen, and Benjamin and Kim trail behind him. A dog on the kitchen floor, a black one, rests his head on his paws in front of the cabinets.

"And this is Alphonse," Phinney says, "my cat."

"It's a dog," Kim responds.

"Oh," Phinney smiles.

"Oh," Kim says, embarrassed. "I didn't think you knew."

"Alphonse," Phinney says to the dog, "this is Benjamin and this is Kim. Benjamin's the one with the ugly legs."

Kim crouches to pet the dog, and as he does Phinney opens the freezer and takes out a tray of ice cubes. "He loves this," he says, then to the dog, "Want an ice cube, Alphonse?"

The dog scurries to the refrigerator and opens its mouth, and Phinney drops in a cube. The ice crackles between the dog's teeth.

"Want to see my car?" Phinney asks, and when Benjamin says yes, Phinney leads them through another door. There's an olive-green station wagon in the garage, and the dog circles it like a shark.

"How do you like it?" Phinney asks.

"A station wagon?" A family car. Benjamin bends to look in one of the windows on the passenger side. The car has plaid seats, like an old dinette set.

"My parents have one of these," Kim says. "Only it's a different color. And it's a different kind."

"It's a beaut, isn't it?" Phinney squats and taps the side. "Wood paneling, Benjamin. Honest-to-God wood paneling. Women *love* wood paneling," and Kim giggles.

"It's nice," Benjamin says.

Phinney stands. "How many bags of groceries can you get into your car?"

"What, the one—the one outside?"

Phinney nods.

"God, I don't know."

"Guess."

"I don't know. Ten? Twelve?"

"Ha! I can get eighteen in mine. Twenty-four if I put the backseat down." Phinney twists his eyebrows. "I'm just kidding around. Women *hate* wood paneling, and I don't know how many bags of groceries I can fit in here. It's great for work, though. You know, for putting paint cans and ladders and things in the back. It's great for that. It's very practical."

Kim sits on the top rail of the fence between Phinney's land and his neighbors'. Holding her skirt, she kicks one leg over and then the other, then hops down. Weeds run as high as her knees, and she pulls her legs up stiffly as she runs, stomping her feet and swinging her arms.

Benjamin and Phinney lie lazily in garden chairs, stretching their legs out, their feet spread, Phinney holding Alphonse and strumming the dog's belly like he's playing a guitar, both brothers watching Kim move through the field. She runs with her arms extended at her sides, catching the wind like a child pretending to be an airplane, and when she calls his name twice and whistles, Alphonse jerks free from Phinney's arms. He yelps as he gallops toward her, then crawls beneath the bottom rail of the fence on his belly, his head low like a soldier. He dances at Kim's feet once he reaches her. All the while Phinney hasn't moved. He doesn't chase after Alphonse, and his face is expressionless as he watches Kim and the dog run among the cattle, trying to herd them, Kim's skirt flapping behind her.

"She's a beautiful girl," Phinney says to Benjamin, "that Kim."

Benjamin clicks his tongue against the roof of his mouth. His head is still tipped back. If he looks up, he can see the night sky, the stars specks. If he looks down his nose, he can see Kim in the field. He can see them both without moving his head, just his eyes.

"Yes, beautiful," he says and thinks how odd it is that Phinney should call her a girl and not a woman, though she is a woman, of course. What's odd about it is that sometimes when she talks, Benjamin thinks he can hear a little girl in her voice, and it's as if he can see her as she was then, on the kitchen floor of her parents' home in a T-shirt and shorts, barefoot and sitting Indian-style, her dog on her lap and licking her face, and Kim laughing and laughing that uncontrolled, chesty laugh that sounds like bells at noon.

"Whoop, whoop!" she shouts, and both Benjamin and Phinney hear her, shifting their eyes to her. She's swinging an arm above her head now in grand circles, as if she were twirling a lasso. "C'mon little doggies. It's time for the big roundup."

The cows move, but slowly and in no single direction. Kim slaps her palm against the rear ends of a few to no effect, and she thumps her hand against her own hip as if she were prodding a horse. "I met a friend of yours a couple of days ago," she calls to one of the cows. "She was very pretty. Maybe you know her. Her name's C18. Does that ring a bell?"

Abruptly, Kim begins to run among the cows again, weaving, her arms extended once more, flying, buzzing the field, and Alphonse trails her, copying her wild aimless path. "Go get that one, Alphonse," she commands, pointing at a dark cow, the color of soot, grazing beyond the rough circle of cows. "Go get that one and tell her to get over here or else she's out of the club."

Alphonse darts toward the cow. His yelps and Kim's whoops carry to Phinney's house and well past, ringing like laughter.

"What's wrong?" Phinney says to Benjamin, neither of them moving.

"I don't know how to explain it. There are things that go on inside of you that you couldn't explain if you tried. It's like Dad, Phinney. There were things that were going on inside of him that you could tell he couldn't put a finger on. Do you know what I mean? If you can't put a finger on it yourself, then no one else can because they don't have all the information that's inside your head. They don't have all the information that makes up the thing that's wrong."

He knows Phinney's thinking about their father now, and he wishes he hadn't put the thought in his head. Phinney's tone changes, if only slightly. "It's not the age thing, is it?" he asks. "I mean, it doesn't look like the age thing bothers her."

"No, it's not age," Benjamin says. "It's not the age so much as it's the humidity," he laughs, and he isn't sure if what he's said means anything.

Before Phinney can question him, Kim calls from the field. "They don't eat these cows, do they, Phinney? They don't kill them for meat, right? They just milk them, right?"

Phinney cups his hands around his mouth. "They just milk them," he calls. "Promise."

"Good," Kim shouts back, "they're a very pleasant group of cows," and she climbs over the fence. Alphonse slides beneath it. They walk slowly toward Benjamin and Phinney. Kim stops to pull her running shoes off, slappng their soles together to clean them. Benjamin looks down at her, then up at the night, then down at her again as she moves closer and closer. When she reaches the patio, she sits on Benjamin's lap, playfully, but he's not looking at her any longer, he's looking at the night, feeling small beneath the universe.

CHAPTER 10
TELL GOD I'M HERE

BENJAMIN TAKES THE POT OF COFFEE off the back burner and pours himself a cup, then takes a sip, standing at the kitchen counter in nothing but a pair of gym shorts. The coffee is too hot. Alphonse sits at Benjamin's feet and stares up at him, hoping for food, but Benjamin offers him nothing. He looks out the window at Phinney, standing among the cows in his neighbor's field. The cows ignore him as though he were a tree.

Benjamin leaves the cup on the counter and heads out the back door and down the hill, his bare feet pricked by the tall grass, his gait deliberate. He climbs over the short fence and walks to Phinney's side. He stands with his weight on one leg, his head coming to just above Phinney's shoulder.

"You know I didn't mean anything, Phinney," he says.

"You didn't mean what?"

"Anything. That's what I'm saying. I didn't mean anything at all. I shouldn't have mentioned Dad at all. I mean, that's all over. It's in the past." There's a tickle in his throat, and Benjamin coughs. "The past is all over."

"I know, Benjamin. Don't apologize. I was just a kid." He continues, "He was stupid and he was a liar." The thought seems to emerge of its own accord. "Our father, who art in heaven," Phinney says, his head tipped toward the sky, "was stupid and a liar."

"Dad wasn't a liar," Benjamin responds.

"So, are you agreeing that he was stupid, then?"

"No, I'm just saying that he didn't lie."

"Yes he did. All the time. All those stories."

"There's a difference," Benjamin says, "between telling a story and telling a lie."

"And what's the difference?"

"I don't know. A lie comes from your heart, I think. Dad's never come from his heart. He was just trying to have fun, to entertain us."

There's a silence, a natural one, Benjamin thinks, for brothers and sisters. Benjamin just runs his eyes along the field, counting cows and hills. On nights when they were alone in the house waiting for their father to return from the hospital, Benjamin and Phinney had rarely spoken, yet there had been an understanding of what the other was thinking. They'd been thinking about being alone.

"I'm just thinking," Phinney says suddenly. "Are you happy, Benjamin?"

"That's a silly question. Life's too complex to be happy for more than a moment here or there."

Phinney smirks. "You know what I mean. Are you happy ...generally?"

Benjamin catches his breath. "Miserable. Divorce leaves a hole inside you."

"I'm miserable, too, if that's any consolation," Phinney says, and his laugh is sad. "But you have Kim at least."

"No, not really."

Phinney doesn't turn toward his brother. He keeps his eyes on the cows. "No?"

Benjamin wants to tell him about the scar, about the creek. Instead he says, "How do I say this without being crude? Would it be enough to tell you that she sleeps on the couch?"

Phinney's mouth is twisted. "You mean you don't sleep with her? You're living with a beautiful girl, and you don't sleep with her?"

"Phinney," Benjamin says, "you saw us." He'd slept on the couch in the living room and Kim in the guest room. She'd even locked her door. In the middle of the night, Benjamin had heard the knob click again, he had heard her creeping in the hallway and thought she was coming to him, but instead she went to the bathroom, and he'd known what she was doing in there. "I slept in the living room."

"That's not what I mean."

"If you mean do I make love to her, the answer to that is no, too."

"Never?"

Benjamin shakes his head, neither proud nor ashamed. "Not once."

"Is she afraid or something?"

Benjamin snorts, "No," and he puts his hands to his hips. "I'm the one who doesn't want to, if you can believe it."

"Well, do you love her? I mean, in particular?"

"Maybe. I don't know. When I'm with her, I feel something. I'm never quite sure what, but I'm always feeling it. We go shopping and I see things that I want to buy for her, so maybe I do love her."

"As much as M. J.?"

"God, Phinney, I don't know. I haven't known her all that long."

"And you don't sleep with her?"

Benjamin shakes his head. "I told you I didn't."

"Because of M. J., right?"

"At first, because of Mary Jude." Now, because of the creek, he thinks. The creek is keeping us apart.

The cows aren't moving at all, none of them, and the field looks like a photograph to Benjamin. It's funny how he gets that backwards, how photographs are supposed to represent life, and how often he sees life as conveying photographs.

"Are you still in love with M. J.?"

"I don't know."

"You must know."

Benjamin starts his sentence twice. "It's like this," he says. "How do I explain this?" he says. "It's funny, but sometimes I feel like I'm in the middle of a Dickens novel or something and I'm going to love her forever.

I love M. J. so innocently, the same way I loved her when I first met her, you know, the way a boy feels about a girl, and I keep thinking that someday, when we're both old, we'll be together again, that some trick of circumstance will bring us together like, well—what's the Dickens novel I'm thinking of?"

"*Tale of Two Cities.*"

"Mm hmm, *Tale of Two Cities.*"

"Well, M. J.'s gone. She's married to what's-his-name, and she's gone. And besides, the guy in *Tale of Two Cities* ends up dying."

"Hallyday," Benjamin says, and for the first time he says that name scornfully. "I know she's married to him, I'm not stupid. It's just that my brain knows that and my heart doesn't." Benjamin pulls a weed from the ground and begins to tear it into tiny pieces. He remembers what Mary Jude said at their wedding. "Benjamin," she said, "promise me you won't ever take your wedding ring off," and Benjamin said, "Cross my heart."

Benjamin tears at the weed. He tries to sound casual when he asks, "So, how was the wedding?"

"Fine, I guess."

"Well, are you going to tell me about it or not?"

"There's not much to say. I mean, it was just a bunch of old people eating chicken. Old aunts and uncles and parents. Her parents were there, you know."

Benjamin hadn't seen Mary Jude's parents since he and Mary Jude had separated. For a time he'd thought about calling them, or writing to apologize for making their daughter so sad, but he thought the better of it and kept his apology to himself.

"I figured they'd be there," Benjamin says. "Did they ask about me? Did anyone ask about me?"

"Just M. J. She wanted to know if you were coming or not. You should have come, you know."

"Yeah, I know," Benjamin answers. "Kim was working, though," he lies.

"Well, you didn't miss much. But you still should have been there."

"I know. I know. How did she look?"

"The same as always."

"Pretty?"

"Pretty." She looked pretty at our wedding, too, Benjamin thinks, and in the wedding picture in the bottom of his underwear drawer. Mary Jude in an ivory satin dress, looking the way he'd thought angels must look back when he thought about angels.

After a long pause Benjamin asks, "Do you date, Phinney? I mean, at all?"

"No," Phinney says. "Who wants to date someone like me? I'm too much of a burden." He taps his forehead. "I'm not all here, Benjamin. You know that. I'm missing a couple of marbles."

"Don't say that."

"Well, I *am* missing a few marbles. Emmies, not elephants, so it's not like I'm dangerous. I'm depressed all the time—even with the pills—and who's going to put up with that. I keep waiting to feel better. Every night I think, Tomorrow I'll start feeling better. Then tomorrow. Then tomorrow, and it just doesn't happen. Every day I get up and look in the mirror and think, damn it, I'm still me. I'm just not all here anymore."

Benjamin doesn't contradict him.

"You know, they say it runs in families," Phinney continues. "Doctors say that."

"What? Sadness?"

"No, this killing yourself business. It runs in families," Phinney says, "like a disease. Like baldness."

Benjamin tears another weed free from the ground. A ball of dirt hangs from the roots.

"Every job I apply for—every application asks if anyone in your family's ever had heart disease or cancer or other things of that sort, and they always ask if anyone's ever committed suicide. You have to check a box that says yes or no," Phinney says. "Now, they can't be asking that just because they're curious. See, Benjamin, they're asking because there's a correlation."

"Have you asked your doctor?"

"He says they ask it because they're concerned and they want to be able to help you."

"So?"

"So, that sounds like a lot of baloney to me. They do it, they *must* do it, because they think you're a risk to do it yourself. And it makes plenty of sense if you just think about it, if you think good and hard. What I think happens is that someone in your family does it—kills himself—and it plants a seed in your subconscious so that it's always there in your mind, so that you're always thinking that if things get bad enough you can just do whatever the other guy did; you can just get away from it all by killing yourself. It's like you always hear about people killing themselves, but it's not real until it's someone you know, and then you realize it's not that bad. It's not that bad."

"Please don't talk about this," Benjamin says, and he finishes counting the cows. There are forty-three.

"But you know what it means, don't you? It means it's in us, Benjamin. It means it's in there, and we can't get it out, and maybe it'll happen, and maybe it won't, but it'll always be in there, and we won't be able to stop it if it decides it's time."

"It won't happen."

"It could."

"But it won't."

More silence passes through the moist Nebraska air.

"Do you know anyone who isn't miserable?" Phinney asks. "I mean, anyone our age?"

Benjamin doesn't hesitate, "Frank Babisch," he says. "I work with him." He pauses and his eyebrows sink. "I think you've met Babisch."

"And he's happy, legitimately happy? He's not faking it?"

"No, he's happy," Benjamin says. "Terrific wife, gorgeous house, the whole nine yards. He even likes his job."

"That's sick. That's absolutely sick." Phinney shakes his bowed head and paws at the ground with his foot. "How tall is he?"

"Who?"

"This guy you're telling me about."

"Babisch?"

"How tall is he?"

"What do you mean?"

"I mean, how tall?" Phinney holds his hand before him and moves it up and down.

"Geez, I don't know. Five ten or five eleven."

Phinney holds his palm in front of his eyebrows. "Here?"

"About."

"I could've guessed that. I could've *guessed* that," Phinney says. "Did you ever think, did you ever think that maybe all of life is the distance you are from five eleven? That everyone's always trying to figure out why it is some people are happy and some people aren't, and maybe it's something as simple as your height?"

"No."

"Well, how tall are you?" and when Benjamin doesn't answer, Phinney says, "*See?* It's just the distance from five eleven."

Benjamin rubs his brother's hair. He can't tell Phinney about the creek. Phinney can't help him anymore. It's not like it was when they were boys, and it's not the way he'd planned when he left Baltimore.

"I have to get to work," Phinney says. "It's a big world, and there's a lot left to be painted." As they walk to the house, they hear Kim in the kitchen.

"Want an ice cube, Alphonse?" she's saying. "Want an ice cube?"

The notes were all different, and when Phinney and Benjamin found them in their father's shirt drawer, two weeks after their mother had fallen in the well, two weeks during which she hadn't regained consciousness, when they found the slips of white paper that read "From the Desk of Eugene Sacks" in the upper left-hand corner, they knew that their father was practicing his last words, that he would make himself meet his maker before their mother met hers, that he was taking his time choosing the proper words to leave behind.

One said:

BENJAMIN, TAKE CARE OF PHINNEY. PHINNEY, TAKE CARE OF BEN.

Another:

I CAN'T WATCH YOUR MOTHER COLLAPSE LIKE THIS. I LOVE HER TOO MUCH TO WATCH, AND THEN WHAT DO I DO WHEN SHE'S GONE?

The rest:

I WANT YOU BOTH TO GO TO COLLEGE. EVEN IF YOU DON'T WANT TO, DO IT FOR YOUR OLD MAN. DO I HAVE A DEAL?

YOUR MOTHER WAS A BEAUTIFUL WOMAN. SHE WAS EVERYTHING.

FORGIVE ME FOR LEAVING YOU ALONE. PLEASE FORGIVE ME. IF YOU KNEW WHAT I FELT LIKE INSIDE, YOU WOULD UNDERSTAND. DON'T HATE ME.

I HAVE TO BE VERY PLAIN ABOUT THIS, BOYS. YOUR MOTHER IS GOING TO DIE. I DON'T WANT TO BE AROUND AFTER SHE'S GONE. AS MUCH AS I LOVE AND CHERISH YOU TWO, YOU ARE ABOUT TO HAVE YOUR OWN LIVES. IT'S BETTER THAT I GO BEFORE HER BECAUSE THE WAY SHE IS NOW, SHE'LL NEVER KNOW. NEITHER ONE OF US WILL HAVE TO SUFFER WITHOUT THE OTHER. DOES THIS MAKE SENSE?

BEN, PHINNEY, I'M SORRY. YOU KNOW WHERE THE BANK ACCOUNTS

ARE. THE HOUSE AND THE CAR AND EVERYTHING ELSE WE OWN ARE YOURS. PLEASE HAVE HAPPY LIVES. I'LL WAIT FOR YOU IN HEAVEN. I'LL TELL GOD WHERE YOU ARE.

Benjamin and Phinney put the notes back where they'd found them, trying to duplicate their original disorder. They went to the garage and took their bicycles out, riding beneath the light of the streetlamps and a three-quarter moon until they found their father's car driving down a side street. There he was: their father, looking like a spaceman behind the car's wraparound windshield.

"Are we supposed to tell him that we know?" Benjamin had asked Phinney.

"No, don't say anything. God will take good care of him."

They just put their bicycles in the backseat of the car and drove home with him.

Every night, after their father returned from work and from the hospital, he'd leave again, to drive until the small hours of the morning, and Benjamin and Phinney would look on the counters and the beds to see if he'd chosen his words, believing that only then, when they found a note intended for them, would they have enough evidence to figure out how to stop him.

"He won't do it," Phinney said. "God won't let him."

If he did leave a note, Phinney would explain to their father that God was going to take care of their mother, that she'd be fine, and then Benjamin would act cheerful, as if he believed his brother, as if he hadn't seen precisely what his father had in the hospital bed: his mother in an oxygen tent, like a sleepy soldier.

They would listen for the sound of the garage door, Benjamin and Phinney lying on the bed they shared. The day they came down to the kitchen and found a note taped to the refrigerator door that said PLEASE START DINNER, they couldn't have known that that would be it.

Phinney went to the bakery. It was Benjamin's day off from the bookstore, and the news of his father came to Benjamin at the pool over his small transistor radio, the news from Elmira of a man standing on the hospital roof, four floors above the street and without a net to fall in. The announcer said the man was a lunatic, but Benjamin knew better, he knew the man was in love, and he raced to get his bike from the rack, leaving his shirt and shoes and towel in a heap beside the pool.

He didn't get there in time to see the jump as others had. He never came close to seeing it, he was still on his bicycle and two miles out of Bluefield when the news came over the transistor, but there was blood on the sidewalk and a picture in the paper. In the picture, his father's feet were not on the roof, but several inches above it, looking as if he were levitating above the building, as if he'd overcome gravity eternally, but the caption below made it plain that there was no levitation here: BLUEFIELD MAN LEAPS TO GRUESOME DEATH.

That was the first night Benjamin and Phinney spent at Mrs. Magruder's, sleeping in her guest room. Phinney thumbtacked the newspaper clipping to the wall over their bed—BLUEFIELD MAN LEAPS TO GRUE-SOME DEATH—so it looked as if their father would fall on them.

Benjamin made the sign of the cross as he lay on his back. He touched his thumb to his forehead, his sternum, then his shoulders, his left before his right. His eyes were still open. Please, he thought, tell God I'm here, in Bluefield.

Two weeks later, in their mother's hospital room, Benjamin and Phinney held their mother's hands. They were like tiny crooked teacups. The calluses from the digging were gone.

She'd been unconscious all along, but she opened her eyes briefly. She looked at them and said, "I love you. I love you. It really has been fun." Her eyes swelled as if to say, I may just surprise you yet.

And she did surprise Phinney, by dying.

CHAPTER 11
GOING DOWN DRAINS

September 12, 1963
Dear Ben,

It's me, Phinney. I wanted to write and let you know that I'm sorry for everything that happened, but they wouldn't let me have a pen and paper until today. I know I embarrassed you and Mrs. Magruder, and I wanted to write a formal apology. So, here it is, Benjamin: I'm sorry. You know I love you.

I'm glad they let you in to see me two or three days ago. I just wish I'd been more awake so we could've talked more. More coherent. It's just that I don't know what to think anymore. Have you ever had that feeling, that your mind's working and you wish it wouldn't because it doesn't know what it's doing anymore, it doesn't know what it *wants* to think?

I feel very relieved being here, almost. This is the place where they put you so you don't have to think anymore. I could use that for a while. I just don't feel like *thinking*. There's too much to think about now.

Do you think I'm crazy? Really, Ben, be straight with me.

They're coming to get me so we can talk some more. How can you talk if you can't think? It's just mush if you're not thinking. So

I have to end this so they can put it out in the mail.

Again, I'm sorry. I'm sorry, I'm sorry, I'm sorry, I'm sorry. Give yourself a hug for me, and give Mrs. Magruder one for me, too. And tell her I'm sorry, too.

Love,

Phinney

September 16, 1963

Phinney—

No, I don't think you're crazy. Stop saying that. I think you're just sort of depressed or lonely or something. Confused is a good word. But you're not crazy, and you shouldn't say that because then they'll keep you there for a long time. Tell them what they want to hear, and I'll get you out of there as soon as I can figure out how. I promise. Just hang tight.

School starts tomorrow. God, it's going to be so weird walking there without you. One year to go. I think I can make it.

You know, I didn't mention it to you, but I talked to Earl Van Devere. No kidding. I was even in his apartment. You were right about him. It wasn't like he was evil or anything, just a little strange. I also figured out how he lost his arm, if you're interested. He did it himself. Really. There was this picture of this girl in his bathroom, and it was spooky. It just sort of hit me that something had happened to the girl and that Earl jumped in front of Carlson's car. He knew I figured it out, too. You could tell.

Living with Mrs. Magruder isn't that bad. You know what I was thinking was that when you come home we can maybe paint our room there. We can make it look just like our old room. I hate the color of it now. That's the ugliest color green I've ever seen, and the whole place still smells like the perfume counter at Mill-hauser's. Some smells you can't get rid of unless you start from scratch, I think, which means we'll have to paint it.

Look, Phinney, I've got to get to work. (I'm working at Kitchener's again, starting two days ago.) I'll get you out, I promise.

I miss you. I can't believe I can miss someone this much, but I do.

—Benjamin

September 13, 1963
Dear Ben,

That was a rotten letter I sent you yesterday, so I'm sorry. I wasn't in the greatest of moods. I'm not in the greatest of moods right now either, for that matter, but at least I know that last letter was a rotten one.

When does school start?

Will you do me a favor? When you come this week, will you *please* bring me something to read, something good? Maybe bring the new *Boy's Life* if it's come in the mail. They'll probably check them at the door to see which are okay, which ones are *safe* for me to read, so bring a few. I haven't read a thing since I've been here, and it's driving me up a wall. But if I'm going to be driven up a wall, I guess there's no better place for it to happen than here. (That was supposed to make you laugh.)

My doctor told me that you brought an older lady and a girl with you when you came. I figured out that the older lady was Mrs. Magruder. That one wasn't too hard. I guess the girl was Mary Jude Glover, am I right? I like Mary Jude very much. She's really turned out to be quite pretty, hasn't she? She used to be plain-looking, but I don't think she is anymore. That's always nice when someone plain-looking grows into someone nice-looking. They still *act* like a plain-looking person. (That last sentence wasn't grammatically correct. Don't tell anyone.) Mary Jude's always been very pleasant to me. Did you know that that's her grandmother's name, Mary Jude? She told me that in grammar school when I told her that I thought it was an unusual name. It's her grandmother's name exactly: Mary Jude Glover. She has a bit of a problem hearing sometimes, too, and she usually has to sit in front of the classroom, so be nice to her about it, okay? Please say hello to her for me.

I don't know what to tell you about this place. I'm not really scared to be here, so don't worry about me. Everyone's very businesslike, and the other people here, the other ones like me, they're not dangerous or anything like that. Mostly they're just sad, I think. No one here seems happy. You always think of crazy people, *disturbed* people, as walking around with dopey smiles on their faces, but it's not like that at all. Disturbed people look just like you and me. The funny thing is that if you just came here to visit thinking that the people with dopey smiles were the crazy ones, you'd think the nurses and the orderlies were the crazy ones. They always smile when they talk to you, like you're too dumb to realize that they smile for *everyone* and not just for you. Actually, I do find that sort of scary. If you keep smiling when you're not happy, then what do you do when you're happy? I guess being a nurse isn't the greatest job in the world, emotionally.

Don't forget to bring me some books, okay? And if you get a chance, please write. Like I said, I have nothing whatsoever to read.

Take care of yourself, Ben.

Love,

Phinney

Their letters were crossing in the mail. It was impossible for them to keep current, as if time were moving at different rates for each of them, Benjamin thought. It jerked, and it stopped, and it moved backwards three days at once.

Phinney would be three or four days behind, the time it took for the mail to travel. Yet, at the same time, Benjamin knew that he was three or four days behind, too.

Time had a mind of its own.

September 16, 1963
Dear Benjamin,

Thanks for writing. And thank Mary Jude for her letter, too. I'll write her back tomorrow if I can think of anything to tell her.

Benjamin, I think you're missing the *scope* of all of this. I can't just tell them what they want to hear. It's funny, but I think that the only way I'll be released, the only way they'll say I'm sane is if I say that Dad was *in*sane. I know it's too early to tell what it is they want me to think or do, but they just keep asking, "So, what do you think about what your father did?" like I'll have a different opinion of it each day. It's like my sanity is related to *his*. If I say he was right to do what he did, then I'm crazy. And if I say he was crazy to do what he did, then I'm sane. They just won't let us be *separate*.

Will you bring me some pajamas? I don't know if they'll let me wear them or not—no one else has them—but it has to be worth a try. If they won't let me keep them, then you can just take them back home with you.

I'm tired. Have a good night.

Wish you were here.

Love,

Phinney

* * *

September 17, 1963
Phinney—

I'll be by tomorrow, so this will be a short letter.

I'm not going to take any more French classes. I'm taking Introductory Spanish this marking period instead. You know, the basic stuff. *¿Estás Susana en casa?* That means, "Is Susan in the house?" in case you've forgotten.

How's the food there? How are they treating you? If they're not treating you well, let me know, and I'll take care of it. Me and Mrs. Magruder.

I heard a strange story in school today. It seems there was this four-year-old boy, and he woke up one day and started speaking Russian. Very spooky. But it happened in Moscow, so I guess it's really not that big a deal. (Mrs. Byrne said that in Biology today, and only a couple people laughed. I nearly laughed my head off.)

—Benjamin

September 17, 1963
Dear Ben,

There's nothing much new. I'm the same.

There's a boy here named William. He's in the second grade, and he doesn't speak. See, he was born without arms—I met him and can confirm this condition—he just has one tiny hand at the shoulder. It's the size of a baby's, and it doesn't function. It's just sort of like a Christmas decoration he carries with him. Among his fears is that he'll go down drains. This isn't funny because you can hear him scream at the flush of a toilet. I'm serious. He screams like he's dying. Fifty times a day he's dying. So, what I want to know is, who made him this way? God? He must be the number one suspect, right?

Say hello to everyone for me. Ask Mary Jude what people in our class are saying about me, will you?

Love,
Phinney

Phinney—

It was good to see you yesterday. Really, it was. You look good. You'll be home in no time. I don't see why they don't let you come home right now.

I'm writing this in math class, by the way. We're learning about vectors today. Or should I say *they're* learning about vectors today. I'm not paying attention. If someone ever comes up to me on the street and says, "Hey, can you tell me what a vector is?" I guess I'll be pretty embarrassed. But what are the odds of that happening? Three to one? Four to one?

It's strange, Phinney, but I've been in a funny mood lately. I'm either really happy or really sad, one or the other. Do you know what I mean? I never know which it's going to be, either. And it's never in between. Today I'm in a good mood, and God knows why. M. J. and I held hands last night while we were walking. Nothing else. We just held hands. We're just friends. But is it possible that something dopey like that could put you in a good mood, just holding hands? Maybe. Maybe not. Maybe the whole thing has something to do with vectors *and now I'll never understand!*

Class is over. I can tell—everyone's leaving. I have to go, too. I'll see you next week. Take care. Be happy.

Love,
Ben

* * *

September 21, 1963

Dear Benjamin,

It's ¿*Esta Susana en casa?* Not *Estas*. There isn't an *s* at the end.
Estas is the second-person-personal form of the verb. *Esta* is the
third-person. It's pretty confusing at first, but you'll catch on.

Now that that's done, let's get down to the meat and potatoes
of this letter, as we like to say in the meat-and-potato business. I
don't think Dad was crazy. I really don't. I know I told you I was
going to try not to think while I'm here, but I've been thinking a
lot. I've been thinking that, sure, Dad was different. He was *eccen-
tric*, but big deal. He wasn't crazy. You know why he killed himself
just as well as I do, and it wasn't because he was crazy. So, if he's
not crazy, then it follows as a consequence that I am. We really
should have said something to him, about the letters. I'm sorry I
told you not to say anything to him. But I'm crazy, remember.

Benjamin, do you miss them, Mom and Dad? Sometimes I can't
tell if you don't miss them or if you're just acting like you don't. So,
tell me, do you miss them? Everyone wants to know how I feel all the
time, but I want to know how it is you feel. You know, how do you
feel about everything that happened? Do you think we're responsible? Everyone here keeps saying, "Phineas, you're not responsible
for what happened. Things like that always happen." I know what I
think, but I want to know what you think. Are we responsible?

That boy William is screaming again, but it's not just him anymore. Now, whenever he screams, five or six other boys do. I don't
know if he's talked to them, or maybe they've all figured it out for
themselves. Maybe they all think they're going down drains. I wish
I could think of something to do. I wish I could just explain to
William that he's too big to go down drains. But, being the way he
is, without arms, I'm not so sure.

Love,

Phinney

September 23, 1963
Phinney—

How are you feeling today? Nothing much is new really. There's a pep rally Friday, and there are banners in the gym that say WHAT DOES YOUR FIGHT SONG MEAN TO YOU? And BEAT THE REBELS! That's pretty much it.

I just got your letter asking for pajamas yesterday, so I'll bring them next time we come. Do you want the blue ones or the striped ones? I'll tell you what, I'll bring them both and you let me know which ones you want and I'll take the others back.

I'm having my weird moods still, and I think it is Mary Jude. She's dating that guy Costello in my class. You know him. I guess he's okay.

Mrs. Magruder says she wants to see you next time we come, provided it's okay with you. Is it okay? If it's not, I'll tell her the doctors said no, and she won't know a thing about it. I don't want to hurt her feelings.

Take care. Be happy.
—Benjamin

September 25, 1963
Phinney—

I'm crying as I write this. I just got your letter.

Phinney, you're not responsible.

I'm responsible.

Now come home already.

Love,
Benjamin

* * *

September 28, 1963
Dear Benjamin,

I'm responsible. That's all I have to say today.
    I hear screaming.
    Phinney

October 2, 1963
Dear Phinney,

Phinney, how can you be responsible? If anyone's responsible, I am. I'm the older brother. Phinney, I know you're thinking that it's you fault for saying that we shouldn't say anything to Dad about finding the notes, but that's wrong. It's my fault. I'm older than you. I'm not as intelligent as you, but I'm *supposed* to be. I was supposed to say, "No, Phinney, we have to tell Dad or we have to tell the police or a doctor or someone." I'm stupid, though. Everyone thinks I'm smart—not smart like you, but smart still—and they don't know what they're talking about. I'm not smart enough to watch out for anyone. Bad things happen to people I care about—Mom, Dad, you—because I'm stupid, and now bad things are going to happen to Mary Jude and Mrs. Magruder because I'm starting to care about them.

    Phinney, it's not our fault. It's mine *entirely*. Now, tell your doctors that and pack up your stuff and come home. If you don't want to talk to me anymore, that's okay, but come home.
    Love,
    Benjamin

October 5, 1963
Benjamin—

It's my fault, and we don't *have* a home. They're not going to let me out of here anyway.
—Phinney

P.S. Remember Grant.
    Remember Lee.
    The heck with them.
    Remember me.

    It was great being your brother.

CHAPTER 12
THE TRUTH ABOUT FATNESS

BENJAMIN WATCHES from the living-room window while Kim stretches against the car, and when she begins her trot down the street he moves into the kitchen. Phinney's gone to work. It's just Benjamin and Alphonse in the house until Kim returns from her run.

He moves from room to room. There's nothing in the kitchen he wants to eat, no place in the living room is comfortable.

There's nothing to do and plenty of time to do it, and the feeling Benjamin has is that of being nowhere. Nowhere, and it wasn't even marked on Kim's atlas, but here it is, a place without any dimension or shape but his own. It's the feeling of being, nothing more.

The television, the furniture, the pictures on the wall, Alphonse, the food in the cupboards and in the refrigerator—none of these has any meaning. They have no bearing on my life, Benjamin realizes. It's just me and my thoughts in here, and that's worse than being in the recliner back home. He'd always felt the recliner was in possession of a special sort of sympathy.

She wouldn't take her shirt off, and it was June already. Benjamin was bare-chested, in just his boxer shorts, and Kim was in her underpants and a black-and-white Bruce Springsteen T-shirt.

Benjamin climbed into the bed after her. The comforter was folded at the foot of the bed, and she'd pushed the top sheet down, too. The window was open, and small breezes and the sound of the cars below drifted in.

"How was dinner?" she asked. She'd cooked. She'd fried catfish.

"Fine. I've never had catfish before."

"Never?"

"Never." He was sure he'd had catfish sometime, probably at Mrs. Magruder's, but he couldn't remember when. Fish was fish to him, the particulars didn't matter.

"But you liked it?"

"Uh huh. Best I ever had."

"But you just said you'd never had it."

"Then there's no question whatso*ever* that it's the best I've ever had, is there?"

He hovered above her and smiled cleverly. His hands were on the bed at her shoulders, his feet at hers, his body above hers like an awning, and he swooped his head down to kiss her, then brought it up again. His face was six inches from hers. He looked into her eyes. They seemed fresher now that it was summer.

"I'll get a job soon," she said. It was two weeks since she'd left Yumi's. "I'll start looking again on Monday. I promise. Cross my heart."

"Don't worry about it. Take your time. Wait until you feel better."

He swooped down to kiss her again.

"Well, I promise I will. And I feel fine." He could tell she wasn't being honest. "Everyone loses their job every now and then. Not that I *lost* my job, I just sort of got laid off. Yumi will have me back there soon. But it's a fact of life. Sometimes you get laid off, you know. It's a part of life's rich pageant."

Benjamin chuckled.

"I've never heard you say that before."

"Say what before?"

"Life's rich pageant."

"Yeah, well, it's my father's expression. He says it all the time. Like if his car breaks down, he'll say, 'It's no big deal. Having your car break down is a part of life's rich pageant.' Or if someone burned some brownies in the kitchen and there was smoke everywhere, he'd say, 'No need to get all upset. It's just a part of life's rich pageant.'"

Benjamin bobbed his head to kiss her.

"And if his daughter wants to move in with an old man," Benjamin said, "then that's just a part of life's rich pageant?"

"Well," Kim said, "those weren't his *exact* words," and she laughed and wriggled beneath Benjamin.

Benjamin let his elbows collapse until his body was on top of hers. Her body supported his entirely, and he opened his mouth to kiss her.

They kissed, and the numbers on the digital clock turned. Seven-fifteen. Seven-twenty. Seven-thirty. Seven-forty. Seven-fifty-five. The sweat from his chest mixed with the sweat on her T-shirt, soaking Bruce Springsteen's face. Her hands were on Benjamin's shoulders, then his back, then his buttocks. They moved along his body until they were between his legs, and his hands were in her hair. He brushed her breasts through the T-shirt with the palms of his hands next, then along her stomach. He could feel her ribs—she was so thin—and he moved a hand down to her legs. Soon her underpants were on the floor.

He moved a hand back and forth between her legs, then moved his other hand under her T-shirt. She squirmed.

"No," she whispered. "Keep doing what you're doing."

But in minutes, he had worked his hand up under her shirt again, and again she whispered, "No, no."

He continued kissing her, and she hooked her legs around the small of his back, trapping his hand between her legs. A third time, he put a hand under her T-shirt.

"No!"

She pushed him off and slid to one side of the bed. She reached for the comforter, then pulled it up to cover her lower body.

"Please don't yell," he asked.

"I'm not yelling," Kim said, "I'm just speaking distinctly. Just don't touch me there."

"Why not?"

"Just *don't*,"

"I'm sorry. I don't understand," and he didn't. "I was just being spontaneous."

"Well, don't be."

Benjamin rolled onto his back.

"You think I'm stupid, don't you?" she said. "You don't think I have a mind of my own. Well, I do, and I'm not stupid."

"I never said you were, and I don't think you are." He didn't know what this had to do with her breasts or her T-shirts.

"Yes, you do. I can tell." She paused. "Tell me you're sorry and I won't say another word about it."

"I'm sorry."

"No you're not."

She balled her right hand up into a fist and socked him on the shoulder, hitting the bone. In the morning, a patch of his skin would be blue and sore.

"No you're not," she repeated.

He moves to the den. It's strange how so much of what happened makes sense now, now that the creek's been revealed, and how, at the same time, it still makes no sense at all. She wore the T-shirts—she wears the T-shirts—to cover the scar. That much is simple. Little else is, including his own feelings. He doesn't understand himself. He doesn't understand his own reaction to the creek.

Benjamin stands before the bookcase. They're not Phinney's books. They're his boss's and his boss's wife's. *The Truth about Fatness. Forty Days to a Slimmer You. Eat All You Want—And Lose, Lose, Lose!*

He turns the television on and flips through the stations, images of people flashing by like matches being struck, then shuts it off. He moves into the kitchen and picks up a pencil, then thumps it against the countertop. Thumpthumpthump like a bored drummer.

He thinks of Kim running.

He thinks of Kim sleeping in a ball on his couch.

He thinks of Kim at Yumi's. "My breasts get bigger when I'm on the pill," she'd told the other waitresses. He'd heard her say that and he hadn't understood why she was talking about the pill.

Benjamin taps the pencil against the counter, and he sees the Yellow Pages on top of the refrigerator. He takes it down. It's already open to PHYSICIANS-PLASTIC SURGEONS, and Benjamin picks a name at random and dials the number beside it.

A woman answers, and Benjamin asks for Dr. Sparrow.

"What is this in reference to?" the woman asks.

"I just had a question for him." Benjamin doesn't know what he's going to say. Alphonse is sitting on his haunches.

"She's a she."

"What?"

"Dr. Sparrow is a woman."

Benjamin apologizes and says, "I just have a question for her."

"She's very busy right now. Is it something I can answer?"

"I don't think so. It's a medical question. Could you see if she has a second? I promise it won't take long."

The phone clicks as the woman puts Benjamin on hold. A tinny version of "Tie a Yellow Ribbon 'Round the Old Oak Tree" plays in his ear while he waits, and Alphonse circles the room, his tongue out. Benjamin rises from his seat and, stretching the telephone cord as far as it will go, moves to the refrigerator. The cord just reaches, all its curlicues pulled straight, and Benjamin opens the freezer compartment. He turns the ice tray upside down to get a cube. Alphonse sits in front of the refrigerator and, pointing his nose to the ceiling, opens his mouth. Benjamin drops the cube in. The dog cracks it in his teeth, and Benjamin shuts the refrigerator and sits again. He takes the pills from his pocket and puts one on his tongue, then washes it down with a mouthful of coffee. He's not sure whose cup he drinks from. Three were on the kitchen table, none empty. He'd taken the closest.

It's five minutes before "Yes, this is Dr. Sparrow," comes through the telephone, startling Benjamin.

"Yes," Benjamin says, sitting upright. "Yes, Dr. Sparrow, thank you for your time. I just had a quick question to ask you."

"Are you a patient?"

"Well, no, but I might be. Or a friend might be. What I wanted to know is, can you do plastic surgery on a creek?"

"What?"

Benjamin repeats himself slowly, "Can you do plastic surgery on a creek?" and when he realizes that he'd said "creek," he apologizes and begins again. "What I mean is, can you do plastic surgery on a scar someone has from open-heart surgery?"

"How big is your scar?"

"This isn't about me," he says, "this is about someone else." He doesn't want to say the scar is his girlfriend's, so he says, "It's my wife's."

"How big is her scar?"

"Geez, I don't know. I guess it's about eight or nine inches long and maybe half an inch wide."

"I'd have to take a look at it to know for sure. Do you want to bring your wife by?"

"Actually, I'd just sort of like to get an estimate."

The doctor laughs briefly. "I'm not a mechanic," she says pleasantly, "Mr.—" and she pauses for Benjamin to fill in his name.

He hesitates. "Babisch," he says.

"I'm not a mechanic, Mr. Babisch. Now, without seeing it, I'd have to say there's not much we could do about it. We could probably make it a little thinner, but not much. Now, if it were for you, we could probably come pretty close to getting rid of it entirely, but you probably wouldn't want to do anything because your chest hair would likely conceal the scar. It's different for women, though."

"Why can't you do anything for a woman? What difference does it make if it's a man or a woman? I don't understand."

"You see," she says, matter-of-factly, "when we do plastic surgery, what we do is we cut away the scar and pull the skin tighter, stretching it, and then we try to redirect the skin so that we can hide the scar. For instance, if you have a scar on your forehead, we can slice away some of the scar tissue and try to tuck what remains under your hairline. But with a scar on a woman's chest, we can slice away a little bit of the scar tissue, but if we try to slice away too much or if we stretch the skin wrong, it'll probably move the nipples to a different position on the breasts. And we wouldn't even try to tuck the scar somewhere because there's no place to tuck it."

Benjamin nods to himself.

The doctor continues. "Like I said, though, I'd have to see it to know for sure. Is there a time when you could both come by?"

"I don't think so," Benjamin answers, "she works." He thanks her and hangs up the phone.

So the creek is permanent. You can't hide it. You can't make it disappear, you can't make it smaller, and you can't hide it. She has to live with it, or not live with it, and Alphonse is at Benjamin's feet, panting for ice.

"Come on, boy," Benjamin says, walking to the refrigerator, the dog rubbing against his leg. Benjamin opens the door and shakes the ice tray, letting a dozen cubes fall to the floor. "Have yourself a field day," and Alphonse's tail beats like a wild metronome as he pushes the cubes across the kitchen floor, against the cabinets, against the chair legs, and against the refrigerator.

The spring after Benjamin moved into her house, Mrs. Magruder's dog Cupcake died. Benjamin buried it in the forest behind the house, dragging the carcass in a sack and digging a shallow grave beneath the oaks as Mrs. Magruder fluttered her fingers on her chest. It was a cool May morning, and Mary Jude stood beside Benjamin, chewing her nails as Mrs. Magruder hung over the grave. The children from the house next door, the house where Benjamin's family had lived, sang as they went off to school. They sang the theme to the Popeye cartoon, with new words: "I'm Popeye the sailor man, I live in a garbage can, I eat all the worms and spit out the germs, I'm Popeye the sailor man." Their laughter carried to the forest.

Mrs. Magruder was dressed in her beige-and-white work dress, a long apron looped around her neck and tied at the waist, and she squatted to arrange small rocks at the top of the grave.

"Thank you, both of you, for helping with this," she said. Mary Jude crouched beside her and threw her arm around Mrs. Magruder's shoulder, and Mrs. Magruder leaned into her for a moment, then circled the grave alone, inspecting it.

"He was a good dog," Mrs. Magruder said. She'd found the dog lying by the refrigerator and thought it was sleeping. "He was the best dog a person could ask for."

Mary Jude plucked at Benjamin's elbow. "The woman," she said, "can't see the forest for her Cupcake."

Benjamin knew that Mary Jude hadn't meant to be funny, and he didn't laugh. What she meant was that Mrs. Magruder doted on her dog, which was true enough. There was a picture of Cupcake in the den within three feet of Mrs. Magruder's wedding picture, black-and-white but yellowing fast, Mrs. Magruder and her husband standing as stiff as dolls.

After school, before he went to work at Kitchener's, Benjamin walked to the luncheonette to see Mrs. Magruder. She wasn't at the counter. There were only a handful of people there, two women and three men, each separated by a seat. Both women had black beehive hairdos.

The men were talking about fishing.

"When I was a boy," one said, "I knew a man named Sugarboots. Now, Sugarboots, he didn't have a fishing pole. So, what he did is he took a string and tied a Goo-Goo Cluster to it, and in five minutes he caught a fish that was *bigger* than the Goo-Goo Cluster."

"Well, of course it was bigger than the Goo-Goo Cluster," the other man said. "If it was smaller, it couldn't rightly get the Goo-Goo Cluster in its mouth."

"Technically, it could."

"No, it couldn't."

"The chocolate on the outside of the Goo-Goo Cluster would melt in the salt water, see, so the whole thing would shrink."

The only waitress Benjamin could see was Julie, a girl in her early twenties, blond and chubby. Her lips were pillowy, and she bit them when she wasn't talking to make them seem thinner. She bit into them so deeply that a line of blood sometimes appeared.

When she saw Benjamin, she waved. "Hi, Benjamin."

"Hi, Julie. How are you?"

"Fine. Nothing new." Her voice was thin and birdlike. She set a plastic menu in front of Benjamin, with MILLHAUSER'S in script on the front. She had a phone number written in black ink on the back of her hand. "There's never anything doing around here," she said, "you know that."

Benjamin nodded and opened his menu. "Is Mrs. Magruder here? I don't see her."

"She's in the back," Julie said, and she tipped her head toward the door behind the counter. The sign on the door read EMPLOYEES ONLY. "She's not having a very good day, is she?"

"Nope," Benjamin said. "Can you tell her I'm here?"

"Sure thing," and she scraped her front teeth across her bitten lower lip.

Benjamin read the menu. He'd nearly memorized it—hamburgers, hot dogs, grilled cheese, Millie's breakfast special, malteds, the three-piece chicken dinner—he'd eaten there often after he moved into Mrs. Magruder's house. She got an employee's discount, twenty percent off.

"Benjamin, what are you doing here?" Mrs. Magruder said when she saw him. "You're supposed to be at work." She reached behind herself to retie her apron as she spoke. She strapped it tightly around her waist, as if to keep her insides from spilling out, and Benjamin thought he heard her groan slightly.

"I'll be a little late, I guess. I just wanted to make sure that you're okay."

"I'm okay, I'm okay. Now get out of here and get to work before Mr. Kitchener fires you."

"He's not going to fire me. Can I get something while I'm here?"

"Only if you're sure you're not going to get in any trouble."

"Coffee?" Benjamin said. "Cold?"

"Benjamin, we don't have cold coffee."

"Then I'll let it go cold," he answered.

"Anything in it?" she asked, and when he didn't respond she turned and looked at him, then said, "Nothing in it. I wasn't thinking."

When she brought him the cup, he pushed it to the side and let it sit.

"Have you taken your medication today?" she asked.

"God, don't worry about me. I came here because I'm worried about you."

"That's sweet." She bowed her head. Then, as if she'd been startled, she said, "Holy moly, I've got to wait on my other customers. I'll be right back."

In a minute, Mrs. Magruder returned with two hamburger platters. The hamburgers were on large green leaves of lettuce, and a mound of fries spilled over the side of each plate. She set them down in front of the two men.

"So," she said, "where was I?" She tapped a finger against her forehead. "We're two poor souls, aren't we?" Her apron was so tight around her that she nearly winced when she moved.

"I think you're right about that," Benjamin answered, and he slurped down his coffee and walked to Kitchener's.

That night Benjamin and Mary Jude drove out to the cemetery. They searched for the headstones with a flashlight. Two men in their late twenties sat at the grave directly beside his parents'. They had long hair, almost covering their ears, and they drank from brown beer bottles.

Benjamin stood in front of his parents' graves while the men whooped and sang, their words slurred from the alcohol. EUGENE ALEXANDER SACKS, DEVOTED HUSBAND AND FATHER, 1910–1963. CATHERINE AURORA SACKS, DEVOTED WIFE AND MOTHER, 1912–1963. They'd been separated by two years, just as Benjamin and Mary Jude were. Mary Jude hooked her arm in Benjamin's.

"I was thinking," he said.

"You always are," Mary Jude answered. "You ought to give that brain of yours a rest every now and then," and she tapped a fingernail against his scalp.

"I was thinking that I don't want you dating Costello anymore. I was thinking that I'd like you to break up with him because I was thinking that you and I really should be dating."

"Benjamin, you're my best friend."

Benjamin cracked a tiny smile. "You're my best friend, too. It's just sometimes I get this feeling inside me, and I don't know what it is. Or I didn't know what it was until I figured out that it was you, that I'd get this feeling inside me, this heartache, whenever you were with Costello. And I don't want you to be with him anymore."

Usually, he got the feeling that he was in love with her, and that he didn't just love her, when they were alone at night. The movies or out walking. Or when they were dancing. Sometimes she would show up at Mrs. Magruder's to watch "The Buddy Deane Show" with him. They'd watch other teenagers dancing to hit songs, the girls in tight skirts, their hair piled high, the boys in short dark pants. They did strange dances on television. The Mouse. The Roach. The Mashed Potato. The Bug. And Mary Jude watched, entranced. "Let's do the Bug," Mary Jude would say, "come on," pulling Benjamin from the couch. "The trick," she explained, "is don't let your feet leave your legs."

She would try to pile her hair up like the girls on TV, but it would fall inevitably back upon her shoulders. She and Benjamin would twist in the living room under the picture of Mr. Magruder. "Now, the Caterpillar!" she'd call, and they'd switch their steps. "The Mouse!" "The Sprinkler!" It was then that he was sure he was in love.

"Benjamin, he's good to me. Steven's very good to me," Mary Jude offered. She was trying to be polite, he could tell. He'd made a mistake telling her how he felt, but there was no going back.

"I know he's good to you. I wouldn't expect you to date anyone who wasn't good to you. I just think that you and I should see each other. Haven't you ever thought about what it would be like to be with me?"

"Yes."

"Well, what did you think?"

"I don't know. It just seems so different from everything else. It's like, here's life without you, she put her hands together to her left, "and here's life with you," then she moved both hands to the right. "They're different."

"Well, are you happy when you're with me, when you're thinking about what it would be like to date me?"

"Mm hmm."

"So?"

"I don't know, Benjamin. It just seems so scary. I never want to lose you. I don't even know why you like me so much. It's not like I'm interesting. I don't know why you think I'm interesting. I couldn't be interesting if I tried. I'm *boring*." She pointed at him. "You're the interesting one."

She was confusing being sad with being interesting, he knew. He was sad. He was always chewing on the past, on what happened to his parents, and to Phinney, and to himself. He couldn't help it.

"You *are* interesting," he told her. "You're wonderful," he said.

"You're biased." She tipped her head back to look at the sky. "We haven't even known each other a year yet, and I already know that I never, ever, want to lose you. You make me feel fulfilled and helpful, and you're my best friend. I just don't want to lose you. I want to know you the rest of my life."

"You will." Benjamin paused. "Will you think about it?"

"Uh huh," she said, and she kissed him on the cheek. "You're a sweetheart, you know."

Beside them, the men stood. They collided and fell to earth, then stood again, balanced against each other for support. They took their beer bottles and turned them so the beer spilled to the ground a foot from the headstone, where their friend's mouth would be, as if they were sharing a drink with him.

"Bye, bye, Jimmy," one said, his voice taking on a distinctly southern quality now. "Bye, bye," and Benjamin was offended until he saw the men's eyes. It was the same look Mrs. Magruder had had. The sadness seeped from their eyes like the cold air from the Maryland earth.

Kim opens the front door, and she's perspiring. Her hair's matted with sweat, and her legs glisten.

"God," she huffs, "I feel like I'm dehydrated. I'd sit down," she says, "if I didn't think I'd ruin their beautiful furniture."

She stands in the corridor, dripping and catching her breath, and Alphonse licks her ankles.

"Hi, there, Alphonse," she says.

Benjamin's on the couch. His shoes are off, his feet up on the coffee table, and he's reading *The Truth about Fatness,* plucked from the shelf.

"Hi, Benjamin."

He looks up from the book. "Did you have a good run?"

"I feel like I lost fifty pounds," she answers, then says, "I'm going to take a shower."

She heads down the hallway to the bathroom, and Benjamin hears the bathroom door click shut. Kim starts humming, then the shower goes on. Alphonse sits in front of the bathroom door, staring.

Benjamin doesn't move from the couch. He's entranced by the book. Page after page of diets. Grapefruit diets. Water diets. Diets that limit calorie intake. Diets that keep track of carbohydrates and proteins. Some emphasize roughage. Some, vegetables. There are photographs of thin, handsome people directly beside those of their heavier selves.

"Inside every heavy person," he reads, "is a skinny, dynamic person just waiting to burst out!"

The water in the bathroom shuts off, and Benjamin continues flipping pages. There's a fruit diet. There's a tropical diet. There's one that even lets you eat desserts. There's a woman who lost 175 pounds.

"Emma Callahan was two people, but not anymore!" the book proclaims.

It's then that he hears Kim scream his name, over and over again: "Benjamin! Benjamin! Please, Benjamin!"

Alphonse rises to his hind legs and scratches at the door, barking wildly, his paws scraping the doorknob, and Benjamin leaps from the couch.

"Kim?" he shouts as he runs down the hall in his bare feet. "Kim, what's the matter? Are you hurt?" He imagines her on the floor, her ankle broken, but he hadn't heard a fall. He hadn't heard any noise at all.

As he reaches the door, all he hears is her crying. He brushes the dog away, then pushes open the door.

"Kim, are you okay?" he asks. Kim is kneeling on the bathroom floor, on the bath mat, a towel in her hair and another wrapped around her. The cabinet under the sink is open, and a sea of magazines surrounds her.

"Look," she says. She can barely talk, she inhales over and over. "Look what I found."

Magazines are stacked in the cabinet of the bathroom, under the basin, and there are a dozen or more spread out on the floor, opened to pictures of women, nude. There are pictures of women with their mouths open and their eyes closed, as if they're dreaming. There are pictures of women with their fingers on their breasts, or their thighs. There are pictures of women bent at the waist, with men standing behind them, and now the men's eyes are closed, as if they're dreaming. There are pictures of women in negligees, see-through. There are pictures of women with other women, pictures of women with men hovering above them, pictures of women pouting, pictures of women who look to be in pain, pictures of women falling off beds. On the bathroom floor are pictures of dozens of women in all of these poses. And their skin is perfect.

"It's disgusting," she says. Her hands are clasped over her heart, and Benjamin can see the very tip of her scar rising from beneath her towel. "It's horrible." He helps her to her feet, though her eyes remain glued to the photographs.

"I know," he says, "sweetheart. Let me help you lie down."

She puts her weight on him, then as she calms down some, she looks into his eyes. "Phinney's?"

"No, no. They're not Phinney's. I'm sure of that. They must belong to his boss."

"Are you sure?"

"Kim, I know my brother."

"Then his boss is a pig." Benjamin leads her out of the bathroom. He returns and picks the magazines from the floor, closing them, then placing them back on the pile in the cabinet.

"Ben," Phinney says when he returns from work and hears what's happened, "I'm sorry. You know they're not mine."

"I know. I didn't think for a second that they were yours. I don't even know if there's anything wrong with your boss having them, it's just that it bothered Kim a lot. Some women get upset by things like that—"

"Ben, I get upset by things like that."

"—and some don't. It's just that there's something about Kim. I mean, I think it bothers her on one level because they're offensive, but it bothers her on another."

"What?"

"Nothing. It's nothing worth talking about."

"Then we'll throw them out," Phinney says. "I don't want her to be uncomfortable, and I certainly don't want them to be in here."

He brings a green trash bag into the bathroom. Benjamin holds the bag open, and Phinney dumps them in, seven or eight at a time. When they're done, the bag must weigh thirty pounds. Thirty pounds of nude women, Benjamin thinks.

* * *

She comes to him that night, shaking him by the shoulder.

"Ben?" Kim breathes. "Ben?" She pushes him again, gently. "Ben, I didn't want to sleep alone," and he slides against the back of the couch, and, running his hand along the cushions, he gestures for her to lie next to him which she does. Her back is to him, and his arm flops down about her waist. The cotton of her T-shirt against the inside of his forearm brings an odd serenity to Benjamin.

"I thought you only hated to sleep alone in Baltimore," he mumbles, and his eyes are still closed.

"But, Benjamin," she says, "I dreamt I was in Baltimore."

And when Benjamin falls asleep, that's where he dreams he is, too. Baltimore.

He's in the apartment, in the dream. He's sitting on the edge of the recliner, wearing only his checkered pajama bottoms, pulling on a pair of dark socks. He hears the sound of water running and looks to the door of the apartment. Water is trickling into the room through the crevice at the bottom of the door.

Benjamin walks to the door, soaking his socks and the bottom of his pajama legs in the puddle that's quickly forming. He twists and tugs at the doorknob to see where the water is flowing from, but even after he's turned all of the locks the door won't open.

Water begins spurting from objects around the room. It spills out of the refrigerator. It shoots out of the lamps like little geysers. It bursts out of pictures and out of the oven and drips from between the mattress and the box spring. Wherever he looks water is spilling out, and the level rises quickly to his knees.

After rolling up the legs of his pajamas, he heads to the window and tries to pry it open, but it remains sealed. Then water begins to leak in from the base of the window. The water level is at Benjamin's crotch.

Benjamin makes his way to the bathroom and grabs an armload of towels and facecloths. He presses several against the bottom of the living-room window to stop the water, but it pours from the top now. The water is at his waist. He climbs up on the top of the coffee table to escape it, to sort things out. Above him he can hear a piano playing. It's Duke Monroe, the piano player from the Blue Cloud. He's singing "The Battle Hymn of the Republic" and playing "Blueberry Hill."

"Duke," Benjamin yells, "it's me Benjamin Sacks. I need help." The piano continues. "Duke, you've got to help me. It's me. It's Benjamin Sacks!"

The water showers into the room from the overhead fixtures now, and, with Benjamin still atop the coffee table, the water climbs to his chest, then his chin. He begins to tread water, kicking furiously, but there is nowhere to go and nothing to do but float upward with the tide. Soon his head presses against the ceiling, and the water level creeps from his chin to his lower lip. He tips his head back to stare at the ceiling, to gulp more air, to buy more time, but the water finds his lips once again. Finally, Benjamin takes a tremendous breath, filling his lungs with as much air as they can possess, and dives underwater.

Suddenly, Mary Jude's there. She's wearing snorkeling gear: a wet suit that hugs her figure, flippers, a mask, and an oxygen tank.

Benjamin tries to pull his way toward her through the water, the air in his mouth and lungs vanishing. He's within a yard of her. Then less than a yard. Then several inches away, and Benjamin begins to feel relief. I'm going to be fine, just fine, he thinks. And as he reaches for her, for the mouthpiece of the oxygen hose, she darts away from him like a small fish through the hole of a fisherman's net. She retreats to the bathroom and pushes the door closed.

Benjamin turns. Duke Monroe is still singing "The Battle Hymn of the Republic." Benjamin looks to the living-room window, and Kim's standing on the ledge outside, eating an apple. Benjamin starts to call her name, and his mouth, his throat, his stomach, his lungs all fill with water.

* * *

In the morning, the living room is as quiet as a fishbowl, and Benjamin's hand is on Kim's hip.

"Shhh," she says. "Listen. It's like the world's stopped," and Benjamin kisses the back of her neck. She squeezes his fingers in her own, the hand that's at her hip, and when she hears Phinney open the kitchen door, she says, "Uh oh, the world's starting up again," and Alphonse scurries across the kitchen floor to meet Phinney. The sound Alphonse makes is a yelp, the sound of tire rubber on pavement.

CHAPTER 13

STRAWBERRY PILLS

BENJAMIN WAS WEARING HIS NAVY-BLUE bathing trunks, the ones with the elastic waistband and the snap pocket on the back. Smelling of the lotion he'd rubbed on and of the mustard that had dripped from his sandwich onto his chest. The combination of the two smelled like the cologne that Mrs. Westphal was wearing, two seats down, though hers might have been heavier on the mustard. That wasn't true at all Benjamin knew. He'd just thought that because he didn't like the way she and the rest of the adults in town treated him, like he was a priest.

Mrs. Fitch put her bag down next to the chair at Benjamin's left, between Benjamin and Mrs. Westphal. Benjamin nodded and grinned, acknowledging her. Both Mrs. Fitch and Mrs. Westphal were friendly with Mrs. Magruder, in a distant way, and Benjamin was still living in Mrs. Magruder's guest room.

Two years after his father's death, and here he was, at the same pool where he'd heard the news, the same pool where he'd met Mary Jude. Two years, and Phinney was still in the hospital. Two years, and now Mary Jude was his, heart and soul, as she said. "I'm yours, heart and soul."

"It's nice to see you, Benjamin," Mrs. Fitch said as she pulled off her robe. She was wearing a one-piece bathing suit with tiger stripes on it.

"You, too," Benjamin said.

That morning, on the way over, Benjamin had picked up a pack of cigarettes and a copy of the new *Life* magazine at Snell's Drugstore. He lit a
cigarette and snapped the magazine open in front of him so Mrs. Fitch
would know better than to try to start a conversation about her daughter.
She didn't say anything. The cigarette drooped from his lips, and he turned
the pages to an article on Tuesday Weld, the actress: "Tuesday Weld—A
Star Learns to Be as Young as She Really Is." She was on the cover, too,
wearing a sleeveless pink blouse over her bathing suit, her hair parted on
the left and pushed over her left ear.

Tuesday. Benjamin found it interesting that she'd been named after a
chunk of time, a day. He envied her. She'd stopped time. She was always
Tuesday.

The article was more interesting than Benjamin had expected. It
wasn't just about how precocious she was. It was a very sweet little article,
about her and her nieces, with black-and-white photographs. Tuesday on
a Ferris wheel with her nieces, all three peeking over their shoulders at the
camera. Tuesday and one niece playing a boardwalk game with water pis-
tols. Tuesday and her nieces on the Staten Island Ferry. Tuesday wagging
hand puppets. A large one of Tuesday with her sunglasses up in her hair.

Benjamin thought that Tuesday sounded charming in an old-fashioned sort of way. Gentle, unassuming. She sounded like the kind of
person Benjamin could sit down with over a meal and talk to. She didn't
sound a thing like the people in Bluefield—except Mary Jude—and Benjamin was glad that he hadn't picked up *Newsweek* instead.

When Benjamin was halfway through both the cigarette and the
article, he dug his watch out of his gym bag to see how long it'd been since
he'd finished his sandwich. Ham and provolone cheese on rye, with mustard. He was supposed to wait thirty minutes after a meal, and it'd been
close to thirty-five, so Benjamin stubbed out his cigarette and walked to
the water fountain between the men's and women's rest rooms, passing
Mrs. Fitch and Mrs. Westphal. They'd been talking about Mrs. Skinner,
whispering, before Benjamin rose, and they stopped their conversation

while he passed.

The pills were in Benjamin's back pocket, and he undid the snap, took out the plastic vial, unscrewed the lid, and snapped a fingernail against the vial until one of the pills dropped onto his palm. He placed it on his tongue and held it there, shutting his mouth and eyes. It tasted like strawberry jam. Eventually Benjamin bent over the fountain to wash the pill down with a swish of warm water, but he had no idea how long he stood there, tasting the pill. Sometimes he did it for five minutes or more, until the pill disintegrated, swallowing the chalky residue without any water. This time there was still something left to wash down, so it couldn't have been that long.

Benjamin walked over to his chair, nodding again at the women, and readjusted the back so he could lie on his stomach, letting his shoulders get some sun while he finished the article. Mrs. Fitch and Mrs. Westphal were talking about something Mrs. Skinner had said during bridge, and Benjamin placed the magazine on the cement and slid up in the chair, hanging his head over the edge so he could read. He was up to the part where Tuesday left New York City for Hollywood when a shadow covered the magazine. He turned on his side to see who it was. It was Walt Mountford and Jim Jefferson.

"Hello, Mr. Sacks," they both said, more or less in unison. The two boys were always together, and Benjamin hadn't seen them in nearly three weeks.

"Hello, Walt. Hello, Jim," Benjamin said in answer. "Are you enjoying the pool today?"

"Yes, sir," Walt said, and Jim scowled and contradicted him. "We haven't even been in yet. We just got here." Their bathing suits were dry.

The boys stood there awkwardly for a moment, rocking, their arms hanging at their sides, and Benjamin nodded his head and grinned for lack of something better to do. Finally, Jim said, "Mr. Sacks, we had something we wanted to ask you," and Benjamin gestured for them to go ahead. He noticed how pale his chest was in comparison to theirs. "We wanted to know if you could tell us what our grades were for last marking period."

"Now, Jim, you know I can't do that," Benjamin said, sounding like the teacher he'd become, which was more and more maddening each day. "Besides, report cards will be in the mail by the end of next week."

Jim and Walt were in one of Benjamin's classes. He taught mathematics at Eisenhower School, fifth grade. Mr. McMahon, the principal, had come in to the bookstore one day in October and offered Benjamin the job. He explained that one of the teachers had left to look after her sick mother, the school year had already started, and there wasn't time to search for a new teacher. "It's yours if you want it," Mr. McMahon had said. Benjamin accepted immediately.

He'd taught four classes in all last year, thirty children in each, and Jim Jefferson was the worst of the lot. Walt Mountford wasn't much better. He'd given Jim a D and Walt a C-minus, and he felt horrible about it. They were good boys. They reminded him of Phinney when he was a boy: creative, sensitive, not very good with numbers. Benjamin ate six donuts in the teacher's lounge before he handed in his final grades to Mr. McMahon's secretary, and he must have taken just as many pills—six— fretting over them. He changed their grades three or four times each before settling on the original ones, reasoning that it wouldn't be fair to the other students if he raised Jim's and Walt's grades. At least that's what Mr. Santello, sixth grade Social Studies, convinced him, and Benjamin thought he was probably right. Still, once the report cards are mailed, Benjamin had thought, I don't plan to come within ten blocks of the pool. I don't want to have to face them, and I don't want to face their parents, either.

The boys said good-bye, and Benjamin said something about it having been a pleasure to have them in his class. He was still smiling, and he felt like a traitor. The boys walked away, and Benjamin watched them sit by the ladder and kick off their sneakers, then jump into the pool, rolled up like balls, holding their ankles. He turned back onto his stomach and searched for his place in the article, tracing the paragraphs with his finger. He didn't read, though. He tried, but he couldn't get anywhere. He stared at Tuesday Weld's dimples, as large as caverns, and got lost in their darkness.

"Blah blah blah trumps blah blah she'll get what she deserves blah blah blah blah blah blah blah blah that Bridget Skinner," Mrs. Fitch was saying.

Benjamin was thinking of Phinney.

"Blah blah blah blah she didn't show up for the bake sale either blah blah bridge blah blah blah blah," said Mrs. Westphal.

He was thinking of the time he had to keep John Belew in from recess because he cursed in class. He said "shit."

"Blah blah blah blah."

"Blah blah Skinner."

He was thinking about how John Belew had cried and said he was sorry and that it had just slipped out, and how he'd wanted to hug him and tell him that he understood, that it happened to everyone, then send him outside to play, but didn't. He was thinking about what he'd wanted to say. He'd wanted to say, "You don't understand how rotten people are. If they see you crying, they'll remind you of it forever," but he hadn't said anything at all other than to tell him to wash the blackboard and clap the erasers. Instead, Benjamin had just graded papers, and he didn't look up from them until the bell rang. He pretended he was underwater, a thousand feet down, deaf.

He was thinking about the people in the grocery store, whispering about Eugene and Phinney Sacks as if they were celebrities, their eyes darting to see if Benjamin or Mrs. Magruder had overheard.

He was thinking about Phinney praying. He thought he had a special relationship with God, Phinney did. When the skies were clear and the ground dry, he would pray for rain, and when it came, six or seven days later sometimes, Phinney would race through the house shouting, "Look what I've done. Look what God and I have done."

He was thinking about the time he saw Jim Jefferson looking onto Sheila Danyon's test paper. He was thinking about the doughy women working in the cafeteria, their hair in nets, their mouths short gashes. He was thinking about the look on Mrs. Mennon's face when her daughter forgot her lines in the winter pageant.

He was thinking about Phinney eating apples. Core, seeds, and all.

"Blah blah who does she think blah blah blah."

He was thinking about Phinney, sitting in the tree behind the garage, reading *Boy's Life,* his hair short and sleek, his skin browned, his face sad and beautiful like those boys in the movies.

"Blah, blah."

"Yes, blah blah blah."

"Blah."

"Blah blah blah Skinner."

He was thinking of the time he saw Debbie Howser's mother drag her by the arm through the post office. He was thinking of Scott Worth, on the ground by the jungle gym, gravel in his knee. He was thinking of Cal Kostner, standing before the class, explaining how to figure out how many cows there were at Arcidi's Farm by counting the legs and dividing by four.

"Blah blah witch blah."

He was thinking of Phinney playing Little League baseball, sitting Indian-style on the grass in left field, reading Bazooka Joe comics while his coach yelled, "Phinney! Phinney! Stand up! Stand *up!*"

Once Phinney had slipped out of the tree in the backyard, falling like a branch and landing just as solidly, slicing his forehead, blood on his cheeks and on the pages of his book. Their mother had been in the kitchen making tomato sauce on the stove, and when she saw him fall past the window she ran out and held her apron, stained with tomato sauce, against Phinney's head. The blood and sauce became inseparable.

He was thinking of Mary Jude, in Ocean City for the weekend with her family. It was where he'd always gone with his family. Now it seemed part of another country entirely.

He was thinking of Phinney picking blueberries behind the church. He was thinking of strawberries.

Benjamin sat up in a hurry and put his sneakers on, stuffed the magazine and lotion into the gym bag, zipped it, and stood to leave. He was in a rush. He didn't put a shirt on, and he didn't say anything to the two women. From the corner of his eye he saw them shake their heads from side to side when he passed. As he walked, he pulled the vial out of his bathing trunks. There were two pills left, and Benjamin put one on his tongue and sucked on it as he walked back to Mrs. Magruder's house. He walked as fast as he could, lurching forward, trying not to break into a trot, fearing that he'd erupt if he did. He sucked on the pill so hard that he could hear the saliva gurgling at the back of his mouth.

He thought of Phinney while he walked. He thought of Phinney, six years old, maybe seven, stopping at the Texaco station to wish Earl Van Devere a happy Easter, and how their father called Phinney back and told him to stay away from Earl, and how Earl didn't chase Phinney away that time.

He thought of Phinney running into the kitchen to tell them all that he'd seen God in the clouds, how he'd seen a cloud in the shape of a G, then one in the shape of an o, then, right behind it, a cloud in the shape of a b. Their mother caught her laugh in her apron and explained that that spelled Gob, and Phinney stayed outside the rest of the day, and three days more after that, lying on his back and looking at the sky for a d. There weren't many clouds, and what clouds there were looked like farm animals and profiles of presidents.

He thought of the time he came back from the movies, moaning and touching his belly with the flat of his hand, trying to find Phinney. He went up to their bedroom and fell onto the bed, loosening his belt and the button of his slacks, then drawing his knees up to his chest. Phinney had been at church, but when he returned, in his good navy suit and loafers, he knelt beside Benjamin and said, "Please, Lord, help Benjamin. He's foundered on Goobers." And when Benjamin's pain disappeared later in the night, all Phinney said was, "Yes, yes, I know," before he was asleep again.

And when Benjamin reached the house, Mrs. Magruder's, and saw the house next door, the house that had been theirs, and the tree over the garage, he thought of when their mother was in the hospital, silent and unconscious, and how Phinney could do nothing then. Phinney kept his hand on his mother's chest, over her heart. "Heal this woman's heart," he would say. "I beseech you to heal this woman's heart." Benjamin had seen that Phinney was confident she'd recover, and he'd seen at the same time that she wouldn't, just as their father had seen it, seen it in her complexion, in her weakness. Everything was changing. They were all changing.

"Benjamin, can I talk to you?" the psychologist had said. It was Dr. Regis, one of the psychologists he'd talked to right after their parents died.

"About Phinney?" Benjamin had just left his brother and was headed back to Mary Jude and the waiting room.

"No, about you."

"No. I'd really like to get home. Besides, there's nothing wrong with me. It's Phinney who's all messed up."

"Can we talk anyway?"

"I'd rather not. I have to go home."

"Is there some reason you don't want to talk?"

"No."

"Then let's talk. It won't take long. You have my word."

"Fine," Benjamin had sighed, and he'd followed the doctor to his office. The doctor had closed his door, and both he and Benjamin had sat, nearly at the same time, in seats across from each other.

"How are you feeling?" Dr. Regis had asked.

"Fine."

"*Really*, how are you feeling?"

Benjamin had stood to leave. He was becoming more and more impulsive every day, he felt, though he wasn't sure that impulsive was the right word for it.

"Did I say something wrong?"

"I just don't want to go through this again. It was enough to have to go through all the questions once."

"Please sit, Benjamin. I can't do you or your brother any good if you don't cooperate."

"Is Phinney *cooperating?* He looks like a war prisoner or something the way you keep him in here, with the shaved head and the gown. God knows what you're doing to him."

"Benjamin, do you want to look at his records? Is that what you want, to look at his records? All the medication we give him, all the treatment, every little discussion we have is on a chart. Do you want to take a look at the chart? Would that make you feel better?"

"Look, I'm not accusing you of anything, but if you were doing something horrible to him, I doubt you'd write it on a chart."

"We're not doing anything horrible to him, as you say. Benjamin, what can I tell you? He's not stable yet. The boy thinks it's his fault that both of his parents—both of your parents, excuse me—are dead. Now, we're treating that the best way we can, the best way we know how, and I'm confident that he'll be better soon."

"It's not his fault that they're dead."

"I know that, and you know that. Now we have to treat him so he'll know that."

"Are you using electricity?"

"What?"

"Are you using electricity, electrical shocks? I read that they use electrical shocks sometimes."

"Benjamin, I know you used to have a speech problem, when you were little."

"So?"

"Well, we—"

"How did you know that? I never said anything about it."

"Your brother did."

"Is that right?"

"He said that you had a speech problem, that you used to go to speech classes in school because there were certain sounds you couldn't pronounce."

That was true. He couldn't speak right when he was a boy. Strange sounds came from his mouth when he tried to say certain words, sounds he'd never intended, and when the other children in his class had been studying English, a woman would come and take Benjamin and five other children down the hall to a small room the size of a bathroom next to the gymnasium. The room had white cinder-block walls, and the sound of basketballs and volleyballs bouncing filled it. Benjamin would watch the other children, their faces contorted and stretched as they'd tried to say "oh" and "ay" perfectly. Their attempts would miss the mark and reverberate off the walls like the sound of the balls on the other side: "Oh." "Ay." Bam! Bam! "Oh." Bam! "Ay." Bam! It had frightened Benjamin at first. They'd been noises people weren't supposed to make, and the slam of the balls was always unexpected.

"So?" Benjamin had said. "There were other people in the class, too. It's not like it was just me. And it's better now. I don't see what it has to do with the price of tea in China."

"Do you lack self-confidence?" Dr. Regis had asked. "Do you know what I mean, self-confidence?"

"I know what you mean, and I don't lack self-confidence any more than anyone else." But he did, and he knew it.

"Do you feel self-conscious, like people are watching you?"

"Where are you getting this from? I don't want to talk about this. I don't want to talk at all, and if I did I'd want to talk about Phinney."

"Well, Phinney's concerned about you."

Benjamin had remained quiet.

"He's worried about you."

Softly, Benjamin had said, "There's nothing for him to worry about."

"I understand that he's been writing you."

"Yes."

"And what do you write to each other?"

"I don't want to talk about it. It's very personal, just between me and him."

"Benjamin, I want to give you a prescription."

"Me?"

"A prescription. They're for pills—imipramine. You only have to take them twice a day."

"What?"

"They're antidepressants."

"What?"

"Benjamin, stop saying, 'What?' We read your letters, Benjamin. You know that. When they come in, we read yours, and we read his when they go out."

"What?"

"Will you stop saying that? Benjamin, you're a smart boy. You're out of high school. You're teaching, so you're not stupid, I know that. You must understand that we have to screen everything that your brother sends out to be sure that he's progressing the way we think he is. We don't want to think everything's progressing and then find out that he's sending letters to people that prove otherwise. And, by the same token, we don't want our progress to be hindered by something someone else says, something that comes in the mail and undoes all of our stitches."

"Are you saying that I'm hurting Phinney? By writing to him I'm hurting him?"

"I'm saying Phinney's worried about you."

"Isn't that good? Isn't that normal for a brother to worry about his brother? I worry about him. Is there something wrong with that? We're brothers."

"Benjamin, you wrote him—"

"You have no right to read what I write him."

"—you wrote him that something rotten happens to everything you touch, something drastic."

"So?"

"It's the same thing I'm—we're—trying to work out with him, that if he thinks that, then of course horrible things are going to happen. You wrote him about how you're afraid to get too close to the girl in the waiting room because you think she'll die if you do. You think Mary Jean will die if you spend time with her?"

"It's Mary Jude, and I can't believe you read that."

"Is it true? Do you think something bad will happen to her?"

"Maybe."

"Because of you? Something bad's going to happen to her because of you? You have that kind of effect on people?"

"What?"

"You have that kind of effect on people, that you can make horrible things happen to them? You can control who's going to live and who's going to die? You controlled what happened to your parents?"

"I don't make things happen. They happen. They happen to me. Whenever they happen, it's really happening to me. It's to hurt me that they happen because I can't stop them from happening."

"That's the way your brother thinks, too."

"Well, we must obviously think differently because I'm wearing my own clothes and you've got him wearing a dress."

"Let's keep you wearing your own clothes, and maybe we can get him back to his own clothes, too."

"Meaning?"

"Meaning I want to help you, Benjamin. I want you to take this medication. They're just pills, Benjamin, twice a day. And whenever you come by to see Phinney, if you could just take thirty minutes out to talk to me, Benjamin."

Benjamin, Benjamin. Benjamin.

"Thirty minutes?"

"That's it, that's all I'm asking. Benjamin, I know what you've been through."

And I don't think it's done yet, Benjamin had thought, but he'd kept that to himself.

Now Benjamin was nearly panting, exhausted as he reached the door. Mrs. Magruder was out, and Benjamin had to search for his keys in the gym bag. He pushed everything around, wrinkling his *Life* and knocking the cap off his suntan lotion. The lotion ran onto his sports shirt and onto the magazine. The pill was gone, dissolved.

Benjamin found the keys, sticky now with lotion, opened the door, put the gym bag down on the kitchen table, and laid the magazine flat to dry. It was folded open to the picture of Tuesday. There was suntan lotion all over her. The cigarettes couldn't be saved, and he put them in the trash basket under the kitchen sink.

He went to the living room and picked up the phone, then pulled that into the kitchen, setting it down on the table. The phone book wasn't in the kitchen. He looked in all the kitchen drawers, flinging them open, leaving them open. He looked in the cabinets. He looked under the living-room coffee table and in the magazine rack. It wasn't in the bathroom. He moved into the guest room and threw open the closet doors. He got on his knees and pushed his way through his shoes. The phone book was under his brown loafers, the ones he'd ruined that night at Earl Van Devere's, the ones he only used for yard work now. He pulled the phone book out and raced to the kitchen, working backwards through the book until he got to the *H*'s.

His breath was heavy, as if it had its own mass to it now. He took a seat at the table, still wearing just his trunks and sneakers, and stuck the remaining pill on his tongue. It was the last one for two weeks. That's how long the prescription was supposed to last, and he wouldn't be able to get it filled again until then. He didn't know how he'd get by. He didn't remember what he was like without the pills, just that one of the psychologists had prescribed them and he'd been taking them every day for close to two years. He was afraid that without them he'd become like Phinney, and he didn't want to think about that. It was bad enough driving up to Baltimore twice a week to see his brother.

Benjamin closed his eyes and threw his head back for five minutes. It felt like seconds.

The principal's secretary's name was Hanson or Henson, something like that. Maybe Mason. Benjamin didn't know her first name, and he didn't know what town she lived in, just that it wasn't Bluefield. He was going to call every Hanson and Henson and Mason in the book until he got through to her. When I do, he thought, I'll tell her that I made a mistake with the grades, that something went wrong with my multiplication, that I double-checked them all and Jim Jefferson and Walt Mountford both had C-pluses for the last marking period. C-pluses, not a D and a C-minus. He must have multiplied wrong. He'd apologize for calling her at home and on a weekend.

He dialed the first Hanson.

"Is this the Hanson from Eisenhower School?" he asked, and when the woman said no, Benjamin hung up. He didn't apologize. She didn't know who he was.

He called the next, and it wasn't her. And the next, and the next, and the next and the next. There were dozens of them. None of them was her. Most were men. His head was beating and the pills were gone. For some reason, Larson suddenly sounded right now. He didn't know what to do. He went to the refrigerator. The jar of jam was on the door, behind the mustard. He twisted off the cap and took a scoop with his fingers and slapped jam on his tongue until he couldn't breathe for the smell of it.

The phone was on the hook. Benjamin's arms were folded on the table, his head resting on them, his mouth full and shut. He was looking at the soiled picture of Tuesday, falling into her dimples again. Tuesday was ruined. He was thinking of the snow train they used to form when he and Phinney were boys, riding down the hill in a line on their sleds, their father first, Phinney next, holding their father's ankles, Benjamin last, holding Phinney's. His hands were always too small to hold their father's ankles.

He was thinking of Phinney at the funerals, the way he swayed from side to side as if keeping time to different hymns.

He was thinking of Phinney on the roof of their house, refusing to come down.

Benjamin found his watch in the gym bag. It was three o'clock. He was running out of jam, and the market didn't open again for another fifteen hours.

It was three hours before Mrs. Magruder came home with two grilled-cheese sandwiches from Millhauser's, the smell of the burned cheese moving through the house like a specter, and she and Benjamin each ate one, sitting at the kitchen table, washing the sandwiches down with orange juice. Afterwards, she shared her cigarettes with Benjamin, then he went up to his room and sat on the bed, his father suspended above him. The photograph was still there where Phinney had left it. He couldn't tell Mrs. Magruder that he was out of pills again. They'd want to put him in the hospital, too, if they knew what he was thinking.

At midnight, Benjamin left his room and Mrs. Magruder's house. There was a cigarette machine outside the grocery, and he bought a pack. Smoking, he walked across town to the YMCA. He hadn't swum in years. With his thumb and middle finger, he flicked the cigarette butt away. He dangled one foot over the edge of the pool, balancing on the other, and he dipped his toes into the pool. It was as warm as dishwater, though there were goose bumps on his chest and arms when he peeled his shirt off, over his head. He tossed the shirt toward one of the lounge chairs. It hit the chair and fell to the concrete, and Benjamin sat at the edge of the pool.

He shivered in the night air.

Benjamin placed the soles of his feet flat against the side of the pool and arched his back as he lowered himself in, slowly, his fingers tight as they gripped the concrete lip of the pool, his body warmed by the water inch by inch. When his feet were at the bottom, he released his grip and stood. The water was to his navel. It was as if the water divided him in half, everything above it chilled and dazed, everything beneath warm and sleepy.

Keeping his arms at his sides, his palms grazing the surface, Benjamin walked to the center of the shallow end. He let his legs collapse beneath

him until his torso was soaked with the pool water. He didn't let his head
go under.

There was no place to go but down. If he stood, his chest would be
even colder than before, so he inhaled deeply, puffing his cheeks with air.
He pinched his nostrils closed with the fingers of one hand. The other
hand he held directly over his head, as if he were volunteering an answer.

Then he went under. He could hear nothing. Before, he'd thought how
quiet the night was, but *this* was quiet. The sounds that he was missing he
couldn't discern. It was as though the earth produced its own noises, of its
own accord. They weren't the noises of birds or bells or cars, but something else that filled the air, and when he went under water they disappeared. He heard nothing at all, and his movements were those of a ballet
dancer, slow and precise.

He sprang up, and the cool air bit at his chest and face. Again, he
shook, then he lowered himself so the water was to his neck. His legs bent,
he walked like a rooster deeper into the pool. He walked down the incline,
and soon he was on tiptoe to keep his head above water. His head was tilted
back, his chin pointing to the moon.

He pushed off the bottom with his toes, and he waved his arms
through the water, treading at the surface. The water held him like a swing.
This is what Mary Jude feels like when she swims, he thought. She feels
light. He stopped waving and brought his arms to his side, letting himself
fall under completely. The noises of the earth disappeared again the
instant his head was beneath the surface.

When he waved his arms and kicked his legs together, like a frog, he
returned to the surface. And, again, the noises were there, but he couldn't
figure out exactly what each was.

He waded. He swam.

And, unnoticeably at first, he sank. The water moved from his shoulders to his neck, from his neck to his chin, from his chin to his lips. He
wasn't strong enough to keep himself above the water.

His arms flailed like birds' wings now. He kicked his legs. Water slipped between his lips, and he spit it out. It tasted like seltzer. He went under. The pool water rushed into his mouth and nostrils, and he kicked himself to the surface, though he didn't know how. He coughed. He went under again, the water tugging at his ankles like heavy chains.

What is the sound that fear makes? Nothing.

He heard nothing.

The coughing had taken him over. He couldn't scream for the coughing, the gurgling in the back of his throat, and there was no one around to help him anyway. He didn't even try to scream, he'd be too embarrassed to be found: the teacher who wailed like a baby when he couldn't float anymore. And he was afraid words wouldn't come out of his mouth. He was afraid that the sound he'd once made in speech class would.

He bobbed up again, coughed, and dropped beneath the surface. The bubbles of his breath raced to the top, but he couldn't follow them. They weren't a part of him anymore. He dropped farther down, and the water was dreamy now. It was cloudy, and he floated upward, but he had no idea where he was. How close he was to the surface. How far from the bottom. How close to the sides. All he knew was that he was surrounded by this water. It cushioned him. The chlorine stung his eyes gently, but he couldn't close them. They were pinned open enough to look about the pool. Enough to see the markings about the sides: 4 FT, 5 FT, 6 FT, 8 FT, 10 FT. Enough to see the metal grate at the bottom. There were popsicle sticks wedged between the bars. There was a wristwatch, face up, too, its band snapped. He kept his eyes open enough to see the underside of the diving board through the surface. Enough to see the lifeguard stand form a twisted angel. Enough to see his own arms and legs, motionless beneath him. Enough to see an arm lock around his neck and pluck him from the water like an apple.

A single arm, and the man slung Benjamin over his shoulder and carried him back to Mrs. Magruder's house. Benjamin rested his head against the man's chest while he walked. He heard the sound of the wind and of the dogs. All he could see was a pink Texaco star on the man's shirt pocket.

That was when Earl first spoke to Mrs. Magruder, other than outside the gas station.

CHAPTER 14

TWINS

BENJAMIN WALKS OUT OF THE BATHROOM, dressed and scrubbing his hair dry with a towel. Kim and Phinney are talking in the kitchen. It's Friday. The suitcases are already packed and in the living room.

"*Konnichi wa,*" Kim's saying, "means 'hello.' *Konnichi wa.*"

"*Konnichi wa,*" Phinney repeats, and this is what he says when Benjamin enters the room. He says, "*Konnichi wa,* Ben."

"*Konnichi wa,* Phinney," and Benjamin takes a seat at the table.

"Try this one," Kim says. "*Dozo yoroshiku.*"

Phinney struggles to repeat the words.

"Close," Kim tells him. "Very close. You just have to put the words closer to each other like real Japanese people do, like this: *dozo yoroshiku.*" She says it as if it were one simple word.

"What does it mean?"

"It means 'Pleased to meet you.'"

Her skin is brown now, reddish brown beneath her eyes and on her neck. "I need a tan," she'd said earlier in the week, "I look like Casper the Friendly Ghost," and when Benjamin had driven into town to fill the gas tank, he'd returned to find her on a towel on the roof, painting her toenails blue. "Look," she'd called, "Kim on the roof," and she'd pretended she was losing her balance, like a poor tightrope walker. All the while her T-shirt was tucked into the waistband of her bikini bottoms.

Phinney sips at his coffee. "Let's try another word," he says.

"*Toy-ray wa dokko dess ka?*"

"Come on," Phinney says, "give me a break," and Kim helps him, one syllable at a time.

"It means 'Where's the bathroom?' We get that one a lot at the restaurant. People are always asking where the bathroom is. It's the sort of question that needs an immediate answer, if you know what I mean."

She teaches him more Japanese as they eat breakfast. She teaches him "I would like another beer" and "The bill, please" and "Do you have any Alka Seltzer?" and "A watermelon has broken my leg."

"I only use that last one with people who don't know Japanese," Kim explains.

They eat, and Phinney gives Benjamin a sheepish look.

"Ben?" he says.

"What?"

"Ben, I'm going to miss you."

Benjamin tries to avoid his brother's eyes. "Me, too," he says. "It's been nice."

"If I asked you if I could come home, would you let me?"

"What do you mean?"

"I mean," he says, "I've been thinking the past couple of days, since you and Kim got here, and I'd like to come home. Back to Baltimore."

In two days they're in Baltimore, Benjamin and Kim in Benjamin's Mustang, Phinney and Alphonse following in the station wagon, the dog buckled into the front seat and the rear of the car loaded with crates and suitcases.

They pull into parking spaces two blocks from the apartment building, and as Benjamin unbuckles his seat belt, Kim turns in her seat. "Benjamin," she says, "do you want to break up?"

"No," he says. "Why are you asking?"

"I don't know. I thought you might want to," and she gets out of the car.

Kim's birthday was in January. January 6. It was a Tuesday, her day off, and Benjamin drove to her parents' house to pick her up. He had two boxes with him, each wrapped in red-and-white striped paper. Kim was in the living room when he arrived. Her mother didn't come out of the kitchen, but Benjamin could hear her in there, the lids of the pots clanging.

He handed Kim her presents when he entered and gave her a quick kiss on the cheek. "Happy birthday," he said, and she didn't take his coat. She took the presents and sat with them quickly.

They sat across from each other, Benjamin in a stiff chair, Kim on the couch. The *Sun* was spread in front of her, opened to the comics page.

"I'm a Capricorn," she said. "Want to hear my horoscope?"

"Sure."

"They have special ones on your birthday, just for your birthday," she said, and she leaned forward to read. "'If January 6 is your birthday, current cycle highlights change in connection with completion of major projects, family, property, home, could include interior decorating, possible purchase of art object or repainting. Domestic adjustment may occur. Beware of heavy lifting. You have unusual presence, sense of drama, could teach, act, write, or instruct others in connection with self-expression. Taurus—'"

She looked up from the paper to Benjamin. "What sign of the zodiac are you?"

"Virgo."

"Oh," and she went back to reading her horoscope. "'Taurus, Libra, Scorpio persons play important roles in your life. August will be profitable, memorable for you this year.'"

She folded the paper and set it down on the coffee table. "I don't think I have a sense of drama, do you?"

Benjamin said he wasn't sure.

"Can I open my presents?" she asked.

He nodded yes.

"Let's see," she said, taking the smaller gift, "what's the most dramatic way to open this?"

Kim peeled the paper off and rolled it into a ball, stuffing the ball between the cushions of the couch. She opened the box and pulled the watch out, a gold Lomax watch with a thin gold strap.

"It's beautiful," she said, and she grinned as she put it on, making a fist and holding her arm out for Benjamin to fix the clasp.

"I always look at giving watches metaphorically," he said. He'd given Mary Jude one on their first anniversary, before he'd started work at Lomax. "It's like you're saying, 'Here, I'm giving you time.'"

"Well, I love it." She made a pinched face. "No," she said, "I can do it more dramatically than that. Let me try it again," and she clasped her hands together and pulled them to her chest. "I love-love-love it!"

"Perfect," Benjamin said. "Very dramatic."

Kim picked up the larger box, and Benjamin told her that it was nothing special. In it was a blue T-shirt.

"You said you like T-shirts," he said, "to go running in."

She smiled broadly and said, "I *live* in T-shirts," and shook the shirt open until it hung flat from her hands. White letters spelled LOMAX TIME-PIECES...BECAUSE EVERYONE NEEDS TIME. "I'm going to go put it on," and she left the room with the shirt, leaving Benjamin to himself.

When she returned to the room, she was still wearing a sweater.

"Where's the T-shirt?" he asked.

"Underneath."

Benjamin and Kim drove downtown for dinner.

"So, what are we going to do?" Kim asked after they'd eaten.

"I thought we could go see a movie."

"Maybe we could just go for a walk," she suggested. "I really don't like movies all that much."

"No?"

"No. They're just a bit too, I don't know, *graphic* for me, I guess."

"They don't make them like they used to." He wished he hadn't said that. It made him feel old. It called attention to his age.

"Well, I get embarrassed just talking about things that are sexy. I blush. Do you know what I mean?"

Benjamin nodded.

"The way me and Christie were brought up, you didn't talk about people's body parts. So I won't say"—she moved her hands in front of her breasts—"*B*'s, at least not normally."

Benjamin smiled at her. "So, no movie then?"

"If that's okay with you."

"It's fine," he said. "Fine."

"You know, we were talking about movies the other day at work, and Shannon said something really smart about them, so it's not like this is my original idea, it's Shannon's. Anyway, she says movies aren't real enough."

Benjamin arched his eyebrows.

"Really, they're not. There's always one piece missing that keeps them from being real."

"What's that?"

"Well, did you ever realize that in a Robert Redford movie, Robert Redford can refer to whatever he wants, but he can never refer to Robert Redford. He can never say, 'Hey, who do you think you are, *Robert Redford?*' See, he can never say the words 'Robert Redford.'"

Benjamin bobbed his head.

"So," she said, "it takes some of the reality out of it when you know there are certain things that someone can't say." She held her thumb and index finger half an inch apart. "As long as there's a tiny little piece missing, it's not reality." She took a sip of her drink. "Did I ever tell you about the time my father took me and Christie to see *Barbarella?*"

Benjamin shook his head.

"Well, he did. It was Christie's birthday, and I think he thought it was *Cinderella.* I mean, I guess he got them confused or something. I loved it anyway. I mean"—she leaned forward and spoke in a hushed voice—"did you see Jane Fonda's breasts? No one has breasts like those."

Her face turned ruddy.

"What's the matter?" Benjamin asked. "Is everything okay?"

"Oh brother," she said, "did you just hear me? I just said *B*'s," and she put her hands in front of her chest again. She moved her eyes across the room, looking at the other tables. "Do you think anyone else heard me?"

"No," Benjamin said, "I don't think anyone did."

Benjamin paid the bill and guided Kim out of the restaurant, across the traffic, and to the waterline. She clung to him, pressing against him while they walked. They stopped in front of a statue of Christopher Columbus.

"This is where Columbus landed," Kim said.

"No it isn't."

"I know, I know. It's just that I can't figure out what it's doing here."

Along the base of the statue were the names of Columbus's ships. The *Niña,* the *Pinta,* and the *Santa Maria.* Standing in front of the monument, Kim brought her face close to Benjamin's and shut her eyes.

"Thanks for the presents," she said, and she kissed him, once quickly, and then a long one as Benjamin wrapped his arms around her. Beyond them, cars passed quietly, like canoes.

"Want to hear something dramatic?" she said. "I think I made a discovery here," she pointed to the statue, "right where Columbus discovered America."

"Columbus didn't *land* here," Benjamin answered, and he held her and swung his hips slightly, and he did the same thing when they went back to his apartment. He put a Frank Sinatra album on. He played "In the Wee Small Hours of the Morning," and he held Kim, one hand in hers, the other at her waist. She danced like a woman who didn't know she could. She was all elbows and feet at first, bumping, but soon she began moving with something approaching grace.

She was a woman, he thought, always approaching grace.

He helped her remove her sweater, pulling it over her head and tossing it onto the recliner as they continued dancing. Her arms moved with his, the watch sliding from her wrist, slippng and spinning to her forearm like a mosquito circling her perfect skin, then returning to her wrist when Benjamin lowered their hands. He looked at her shirt, LOMAX TIMEPIECES ...BECAUSE EVERYONE NEEDS TIME curving around the swell of her breasts, and he smiled.

He looked at her bare arms. There were small bluish bruises on each.

"What happened?" he whispered, and he fingered the bruises.

"I'll bet you didn't know that waitresssing was a contact sport."

"I didn't."

"I've got one on my left knee from bumping into a table"—she pulled her knee up awkwardly, like a performer in a war dance—"and one on my right thigh from falling in the kitchen."

"I'm sorry," Benjamin said.

Kim grinned. "It's okay. It's hard work sometimes, but it burns calories. At least I think it does." She paused, then gestured with her chin toward the bruise on her left forearm. "And this one is from bumping into the bar. I wasn't watching where I was going."

Swaying still, Benjamin pulled her arm to his lips and kissed her there. He nearly kissed the watch.

"I'm sorry," he repeated.

"It's not your fault," she said.

Kim presses her fingers against the couch cushions, then releases them. The cushions spring back.

"It's very comfortable," she tells Phinney, "to sleep on."

"It doesn't matter." The couch is where Phinney slept when Benjamin and Mary Jude brought him home from the hospital. Not this couch, but another one, and Phinney used it for two months before he said it was time to leave, time to get away from Maryland. He went to Oregon at first, then settled in Nebraska.

"Yes, it does matter. It's important for you to be comfortable, and it really is. Comfortable, I mean. I'm not lying. You'll sleep like a baby."

Her magazines are in a stack on the coffee table. *Rolling Stone, Glamour.* Benjamin's are at the other end. *U.S. News and World Report, Life.* Her clothes are still scattered about the room, twenty T-shirts or more stacked beside the recliner, her underwear beneath the coffee table, her socks rolled into balls the size of baseballs and piled in the corner.

"What's all this?" Phinney asked when they opened the door.

"My life," she answered.

Now she says, "Let me get all this junk out of your way," and she scoops them up, the T-shirts first, and shuffles into the bedroom, making trip after trip until the living room is cleaned of her clothes and replaced with Phinney's hung over the chairs and tables as if a wild, wild wind had raced through the apartment.

There's mail on his desk and on his chair when Benjamin returns to his office, and his clock has stopped dead at eight-seventeen. He doesn't know when it stopped. Monday? Tuesday? Wednesday even? Eight-seventeen A.M. or P.M.?

Benjamin pulls the mail from his chair and adds it to the stack on his desk. It's mostly manila envelopes—shipping orders—only a few legal-size envelopes there.

He twists the wand of the Venetian blinds to let some sunlight in, then picks the clock from the desk and sits, clutching the clock in his left hand, winding it with the thumb and index finger of his right until the wheels won't wind any more. One by one, he peels open the manila envelopes, glances over the shipping orders and builds a new stack.

When his secretary arrives, she peeks into his office. Her bag is still slung over her shoulder. She's wearing white sneakers, holding a pair of shoes by their heels.

"Hello, Mr. Sacks," she says. "Have a nice vacation?"

"Sure did, Cecily," he says, and he places his palm flat upon the growing stack of shipping orders. "Looks like it's over, though, doesn't it?"

She bobs her head and steps on the heel of one of her sneakers, twisting it off. She removes the other, drops them both into her shoulder bag, then bends to put her shoes on.

She asks if he'd like some coffee, and when he answers yes, she says, "I've been saving some for you all week. It's nice and cold. You'll love it."

He isn't sure if she's kidding or not. If the coffee isn't a week old, it tastes as if it is. It's stale and sticky.

Benjamin's still opening his mail when Babisch shows up, knocking on the door although it's already open.

"Benjamin," he says cheerfully, "Benjamin, Benjamin, Benjamin, Benjamin. How are you? How was Hawaii?"

"Hawaii?"

"Sure," Babisch says, "wasn't that where you went? Hawaii?"

Benjamin smirks. "It was Nebraska, Babisch. Don't pretend you didn't know it was Nebraska."

"Nebraska. Hawaii. I get them confused." Babisch pushed the door shut. It slams. "So, how was Nebraska? Did you bring us back a pineapple?"

"No," Benjamin answers, "I forgot to pick up a pineapple for you. We just brought back a couple of coconuts." He hadn't thought about what he'd tell Babisch. "If you really want to know, the trip was just fine." He pauses. "Phinney came home with us."

"Really? That's great. How is he?"

"Good," Benjamin says. "Good. He's doing good."

"I'm glad. That's great. How long is he here for?"

"I don't know. For good, I guess. I mean, he's moved back. He packed up everything and moved back. He's going to stay with me and Kim until he gets a job and his own place and all that."

"Really?" Babisch says again. "And he's doing all right?"

"Babisch, I know what you mean, and I'm worried abut him too, but I think he's fine. We had a good time together. We got to talk some."

Babisch moves to the window. He twirls the wand of the Venetian blinds, closing them all the way, opening them all the way.

"And Kim?"

Benjamin continues to open envelopes. "What about her?"

"How are things with you and Kim?"

"There's nothing wrong with me and Kim."

"Oh," and Babisch raises his eyebrows. "Well, if there ever *is* and you want to talk about it…" His voice fades.

"We had a nice trip. It was a nice drive, we got to see a lot of interesting things. We stopped at that frozen custard place you told us about. Really," he says, "we had a nice time."

"Good."

"Did you get our postcard?"

"Saturday," Babisch says. "Hawaii really looks beautiful."

No one's home when Benjamin arrives. Kim and Phinney are out, maybe together, maybe not, maybe grocery shopping, and Benjamin drapes his suit jacket over the arm of the recliner. Alphonse leaps from the couch and dances at Benjamin's feet.

The leash is hanging from the doorknob, and Benjamin hooks it to the steel loop on Alphonse's collar. They ride down in the elevator, and Benjamin walks him to Howard Street, then four blocks up.

"Come on," he says, "you'll like Baltimore. You're a good dog," but the dog seems confused by the new surroundings. He stops and starts for no reason. He turns his head at odd angles, frightened by the traffic. He pulls free from his collar and sprints across the street, barking. He leaves Benjamin holding the leash, the empty collar attached.

"Alphonse, come here!" Benjamin calls. "Sit! Sit!" Benjamin waits for the traffic to halt at the light, then begins to chase the dog. The dog has a large lead though, and Benjamin can't close the gap. He hopes Alphonse will stop on his own, but he continues shouting, "Sit! Sit!" nonetheless.

He finally reaches the dog five blocks later. Benjamin holds his stomach. He's breathing hard, and the dog isn't. Between breaths, Benjamin says, "sit, sit," but Alphonse is playing in a bag of garbage. He's ripped the side of the plastic bag open, and he's gnawing at an orange-juice container.

Benjamin plucks the container from Alphonse's mouth and sets it down on the top of the pile. He kneels and forces the collar over the dog's snout and past its eyes. It pulls its ears back as if in a sturdy wind, and Benjamin soon has the collar around the dog's neck again.

"Come on," Benjamin says, "let's go home. That's enough exercise for the year."

Benjamin has to stop a moment to get his bearings, and then he leads the dog home. There's juice and sauce on Alphonse's sides, and Benjamin thinks there must have been some bleach in the trash because the dog's hair has been stained white in small quarter-sized spots.

He takes the dog up in the elevator, and he doesn't unclip the leash once they're inside the apartment. He leads the dog to the bathroom and into the shower. He runs a weak stream of water over the dog's back, and Alphonse doesn't seem to mind. He wipes the dog dry with a towel, but the spots of white remain.

"You're not gong to like this," Benjamin says, and he sits on the bathroom tiles, holding the dog on his lap. "But that'll make us even for the day, won't it?"

He opens the cabinet and stretches to reach the Lady Clairol. He looks at the label.

"There's nothing here about dogs," he says, and Alphonse grunts while Benjamin smooths the haircoloring onto his hide.

"Don't worry," Benjamin says. "Only your hairdresser will know for sure. I won't tell a soul."

For fifteen minutes, he rubs the dog's head. He washes the dog off in the shower, and, when he's done, the hair is precisely the same color.

"Look," Benjamin says. "Twins."

* * *

Benjamin was drinking a cup of coffee before going to Kitchener's when Mrs. Magruder came in through the front door with Mrs. Bender. She waved for him to follow her outside. She looked distracted, and Benjamin left the table and pushed the door open to see a group of neighbors gathered in the road: Mrs. Kilkenny, Mrs. Hardenbrook, Mrs. Dewhurst, Mrs. Bender, Mr. Crawford, and Mrs. Kleinfelt. Two of the children who'd moved in next door, into Benjamin's old house, were circling the group on their bicycles, making loud noises like Indians and monsters.

"Benjamin, you have to come out," Mrs. Magruder said.

"Yes, hurry," Mrs. Bender said, and they took Benjamin by the elbows and led him down the driveway, in his socks, to the group. There was a large green trash bag at their feet, and it looked heavy and solid.

"Mrs. Reaver's dog is dead," Mrs. Magruder said. "Someone has to tell Mrs. Reaver."

"Muffin?" Benjamin asked.

Mrs. Kleinfelt dropped her head. "No, Crumpet."

"Are you sure he's dead?"

"Yes," Mrs. Magruder answered. "That's exactly what my dog looked like when he died. Cupcake."

"She's sure," Mrs. Bender said, nodding toward Mrs. Magruder.

All the neighbors looked at Benjamin, and he knew what they wanted. They wanted him to volunteer.

The children were still riding their bicycles around the group, starting out in a large circle, then winding closer and closer, like a whirlpool, until they brushed against skirts and jackets. They were so young that Benjamin couldn't guess their ages. He didn't know much about children, and he hadn't learned their names when they'd moved in.

"I don't know how she's going to take it," Mrs. Bender said. "Poor Margaret, the dear."

"She's such a loving woman," Mrs. Hardenbrook added. "She loved that dog like it was her own."

"I'd do it," Mrs. Dewhurst said. "I'd tell her myself if I weren't so afraid

I'd say something wrong. Saying something wrong at a time like this could be very traumatic."

Mrs. Bender said, "It's a delicate matter. It always is."

Finally Benjamin told them that he'd do it, and they looked relieved. He grabbed the bag and lifted it from the ground. It was as heavy as he'd thought, and to his weak arms it felt like five hundred pounds. He struggled with the bag, taking a few small steps, but the bag began to twist and jump in his hands until he couldn't hold it any longer. It fell to the road and Mrs. Reaver's dog leaped out, sniffing, confused. It chased one of the boys on the bicycles, then raced across Mrs. Magruder's front yard, across Mrs. Bender's, and toward the forest behind. The dog disappeared, but they could still hear the barking.

All of the neighbors were angry, and some drew away from Mrs. Magruder.

"Next time we're not going to listen to her," Mrs. Bender said, meaning Mrs. Magruder. "Next time we'll get a doctor's opinion."

The neighbors dispersed, each headed back to his or her own house, leaving the empty trash bag in the road, lying there like a stain. Benjamin headed toward Mrs. Magruder's house to put on his shoes for work, and he walked on the grass beside the driveway so he wouldn't get his socks any dirtier than they already were. He didn't like doing the laundry.

Before he reached the door, though, he heard what sounded like crying, and he turned to see who it was. Mrs. Magruder was sitting on a rock beside her mailbox, her elbows resting on her knees and the heels of her palms pushed into her eyes.

Benjamin walked back and crouched beside her, like a catcher. He asked what was the matter.

"Maybe my dog wasn't dead," she said.

When she was back in the house, Benjamin left to get Earl.

CHAPTER 15
MRS. SACKS

A MAN WITHOUT ARMS can't open his arms to hold his wife or his children against his body. A man without legs can't use his legs to dance with his wife or children. A man without arms and legs can't use his arms and legs to hold his wife and his children against his body and dance with them. A man without eyes can't use his eyes to watch the faces and movements of his wife or his children. A man without.

A man without someone to love wouldn't miss the human body.

This is what Benjamin thought as he helped Earl dress.

Earl's neck was thicker than Benjamin had imagined. It wasn't until he actually touched it that he realized just how large it was, as large and as solid as a club, and Benjamin had to stretch to loop the tie around, very nearly climbing up Earl to do it. He folded the tie around itself and slid a Windsor knot to Earl's throat, then arranged the tie against Earl's shirt. Earl wore a navy-blue suit, the left sleeve tucked like a mannequin's into the coat pocket, and his shirt was white and pressed.

They were in Mrs. Magruder's guest room, Benjamin's room, and Earl stood before the mirror on the bureau. He held his hand to the center of his broad chest.

"What?" he said when he noticed Benjamin, seated at the desk, considering him, "What?"

"Nothing," Benjamin answered. "It's just that you look sharp. Sharp as a tack," and Benjamin made an O with his thumb and index finger.

Earl's wedding day was the first time Benjamin had seen Earl in anything but a Texaco shirt. But the Texaco shirts had changed, too, in the short time since Earl had carried him up Mrs. Magruder's front steps. They weren't the tattered gray shirts with the bleached pink stars anymore. Mrs. Magruder had bought Earl new shirts, dark gray ones—battleship gray, the man at the store had said—and she'd cut red stars from felt and sewed them onto the breast pockets of each. She never spoke much about Earl. She just walked about the house, applying lipstick, blotting it with a tissue, then applying more. Sitting at the kitchen table with her sewing basket, her lips the color of tomatoes, she stitched MR. EARL VAN DEVERE I script on the pockets, above the star. "For respect," she told Benjamin, and she closed the left sleeve of each shirt with thread as well. The sleeves no longer flapped.

Earl was different, too. He was as brusque as ever, but as he stood before the mirror, the lightness about him couldn't be denied. As long as his shirt sleeve was folded into a pocket or sewn shut, Benjamin thought, he would always carry some weight with him, the weight of the past, but the weight was not as much of a burden now. It was as if he'd shed some of the weight of the past and retained what he needed.

Benjamin and Earl walked down the stairs to the living room, Earl's new shoes clacking on the steps. Women filled the room. Mrs. Reaver. Mrs. Bender. Mrs. Turnbull. Mrs. Carreker. Mrs. Dewhurst. Mrs. Kleinfelt. Mrs. Dixon. Mrs. Crawford. Mrs. Peller.

Earl hadn't asked anyone to attend, but Mrs. Magruder had invited twenty of her friends. Not all had shown. Many of them—most—didn't like Earl. They'd stopped coming by to visit, and Benjamin had heard Mrs. Magruder on the phone: "I know he doesn't talk...he talks to *me*...I'm almost fifty-three years old by now, and if I don't know what's good for me by now, I guess I never will now will I?...there are things you don't have to tell a person...I will *not* listen to this, I'm going to pretend you're talking in a foreign language." She'd invited them all still, and Mary Jude, who stood in a small circle of women by the fireplace, wearing the clothes and countenance of a woman twenty years older. She wore a peach dress and black high heels.

Mrs. Magruder was in a fruit-red dress, her shoes black, and she went to the bottom of the stairs and hooked an arm in Earl's, leading him to the living room.

"I'm sorry some of your friends decided not to come," he said.

"But, honey," she said, "my friends *are* here. Look."

When Earl and Mrs. Magruder stopped in front of the couch, the women took their seats on cue, scattering around the room as if the music had just stopped in a game of musical chairs. Some sat on the arms of a chair, some on the window sills, and the justice of the peace patted the air to quiet them down. Benjamin hadn't noticed him until then. The justice began the ceremony, Benjamin at Earl's left side, brushing the empty sleeve with his shoulder, clutching the wedding band. Mrs. Bender stood next to Mrs. Magruder and held a small bouquet.

The justice began, his voice blasting, and when he asked, "Olympia Magruder, do you take Earl Van Devere to be your lawfully wedded husband?" she said, "I do," and several of the women applauded. It was, as far as Benjamin could recall, the first time he had heard anyone say Mrs. Magruder's full name. He'd seen it on her mail, but he'd never heard it before, and he thought of how difficult it would be for him to start calling her Mrs. Van Devere now, Mrs. Van Devere as if Mrs. Magruder no longer existed.

The justice asked Earl, "Do you take Olympia Magruder to be your lawfully wedded wife?" Benjamin was afraid that Earl would say "What?" and send Mrs. Magruder off sobbing, but Earl said, "I do," and reached for the wedding band in Benjamin's hand. Earl's hand felt rough in Benjamin's, just as Benjamin's own father's had, rough and warm, and Earl took the ring and pinched it between his thumb and middle finger, bearishly. A wedding ring is meant to sit on the left hand, and he slid it onto Mrs. Magruder's left. But she didn't have a choice. She pushed Earl's ring onto the wrong hand—the right one—and grinned.

Mrs. Van Devere.

Mrs. Magruder vanished, and Benjamin considered both of their faces. Mr. and Mrs. Van Devere.

No, Earl didn't weigh as much anymore.

Earl followed his wife out to her car, and they left for the Poconos. They'd made reservations at a hotel there, and Mrs. Magruder had shown Benjamin the brochure. "Look," she'd said, "a heart-shaped bed."

The women helped Benjamin and Mary Jude clean up, piling dishes and glasses in the sink, and when they all left, Benjamin led Mary Jude out of the house and down the street. They passed Kitchener's. They passed Millhauser's. They passed Adair's Pub.

"Where are we going?" she asked, time after time, and he wouldn't answer. He just led her into town, her high heels clickety-clicking on the pavement.

"Just trust me," he said, and when they were there, at the church, she gave him a puzzled look.

Benjamin opened the heavy oak door for her, and she stood still. "Come on," he said. "Get in," and he followed her inside.

"Are we supposed to be here?" she whispered.

"Of course. It's a church," and he braided his fingers in hers and walked her down the aisle. His heart quickened.

"What are we doing here?" she asked, but Benjamin continued down the aisle with her, passing the empty pews, only the candles upon the altar casting any light into the room.

"Benjamin, we're going to get in trouble."

He told her they wouldn't, and when they reached the altar he clutched her elbow. Candles cast giant shadows upon the wall.

"What are we doing?" She giggled.

"Just sit, will you? I swear, sometimes you drive me up a wall."

"Benjamin."

She held the hem of her dress in her fingers, and he stood before her, cocking his hip slightly, rubbing his palms together. "Mary Jude, I know you'll think this is corny, but I wanted to do this here in case you said no, I'll always be able to say that I got this far."

"What are you *doing?*"

"Mary Jude, please. You're not supposed to talk now. I've got it all worked out what I'm supposed to say, and it's a monologue. If you ask questions, then it becomes a dialogue, and it's supposed to be a monologue. At least this part is."

"Okay." She held back a smile and pressed her hands together, squeezing them between her knees. "I'll be a good girl. Promise."

"What I was going to say before you interrupted so rudely"—he grinned to let her know he was teasing—"was that I care about you."

"Benjamin," she breathed.

"You're doing it again!"

"Benjamin. You're bananas."

"Cut it out!"

Mary Jude bowed her head, suppressing a laugh, and Benjamin pushed his hand into his back pocket and pulled out his medicine vial. When he flipped the cap off and tilted the vial, a ring fell onto the palm and sat there like a nut.

"Mary Jude, this is my mom's engagement ring. I know you didn't know her, but you would've loved her. And, I know she would've absolutely loved you. So I want you to have this, and I want you to have the same name as her, too: Mrs. Sacks."

"Benjamin," Mary Jude said. She looked embarrassed, Benjamin thought, and happy. "Benjamin, you're not just doing this because Mrs. M. and Earl got married, are you?"

"No. I'm doing it because more than anything in the world, I want you to be my wife, and I want to be your husband, and I just want to be with you forever."

"It's too good to be true," she mumbled. "That's what I always think, that you're too good to be true. You're so wonderful to me, that it just can't be true."

"It's too good not to be true, that's the way I look at it. I mean, I love you, Mary Jude Glover." He said her full name, her grandmother's name exactly. That always pleased her. "You know that, don't you?"

She bobbed her head. "I know that."

"Do you know how much I love you? I love you tons."

"What?" she said and grinned. She fingered her earlobe. "I didn't hear you," and Benjamin repeated himself without minding.

"I love you, too, Benjamin. You have my heart," she said, "completely." She held her hand out, and Benjamin pushed the ring on. It was too big. To keep it from slipping, she had to clench her fist.

"It can be fixed," she said, and Benjamin said, "Aren't we supposed to say hip-hip-hooray now or something?"

He helped her up. They kissed quickly, on the lips, and they walked back to Mrs. Magruder's house.

"Do you think we'll be able to get Phinney out so he can come to the wedding?" Mary Jude said.

"We'll figure out some way. I'll throw my weight around," and he led her up the stairs to his room. She didn't say a word. She wasn't nervous and didn't pretend to be, and he opened the door.

"This is my room," he said, and she followed him in.

"I know." She kicked off her high heels and closed the door.

He touched his desktop. "This is my desk."

"Benjamin."

He moved to his closet. "This is my closet."

"Benjamin."

He pointed to the floor. "This is my baseball mitt, there."

"Benjamin."

He moved to his bookshelf and put a hand on it. "This is my bookshelf."

"And this is your bed," she interrupted, "right?" and she gave him a smile, then sat on the edge of the bed. "Come here."

Benjamin sat beside her.

"What do you want to do?" she asked.

"I want to kiss you on the lips," he said, and he kissed her on the lips. Her eyes closed as they always did when he kissed her.

"I *melt* when you kiss me," she sighed, "do you know that?" and he began kissing her again and again, their mouths open.

"I want to kiss you on the ears," he said, and he did.

"And I want to kiss you on the neck," and he did.

"And I want to kiss you here," and he undid the top two buttons of her dress. He pressed his lips to her faint freckles.

"And here."

"And here."

"And here."

"And here."

"And here."

"And here," he said. "Mrs. Sacks."

CHAPTER 16
THE ADVANTAGE OF LOVE

WORKING WORKS WONDERS, Benjamin thinks. Both Phinney and Kim are working again, and both seem light and invigorated. They bound through the apartment on their toes like dancers unchained.

Phinney answered an ad in the *Sun* to clean a house in Roland Park three times a week, just as Mary Jude had done once years before.

"You don't mind?" Benjamin had asked.

"What, giving up the prestige of being unemployed?"

He attacks the job with pleasure, marching off to battle the house at eight o'clock, a plastic bucket filled with cleansers, window spray and sponges in his hand. There are mops and brooms in the rear of his station wagon. Work and Baltimore had done it. Little by little, his spirit was returning to him, filling him like honey in a jar, drop by drop.

Benjamin had walked into the bathroom one Sunday morning to find Phinney in his gray suit—his only suit—choking a tie around his neck.

He smiled at Benjamin. "I need to go to church," he said, almost embarrassed; then tugging at the waistband of his slacks, he added, "and to aerobics."

Kim has her job back at Yumi's, six nights a week. She called Benjamin at work and said, "Brace yourself. You're talking to an employed woman."

"Who is this?" Benjamin asked, attempting to sound angry. He cradled the receiver between his shoulder and ear. "I don't know anyone who fits that description. Is this a crank call?"

"Very funny. It's me. I've got my job back, can you believe it? At Yumi's."

At Yumi's, where she belonged.

It's only been two weeks since she returned—she had her kimono dry-cleaned and bought new makeup—but she seems different already; she seems the same again. She seems more like Kim in the same way that Phinney seems more like Phinney. In Benjamin's mind.

Kim's stretching on the living-room floor.

"Why don't you wait for the rain to let up?" Phinney says from the kitchen.

"Don't worry," she answers, "I know how to run between the drops." She pulls at her foot.

"Isn't it too cold to run?"

"Phinney, sweetie, it's only October. You have to be able to run year-round."

Her legs form a wide V, and she bends sharply to grab the toes of her running shoes. She has gardening gloves on and a kerchief in her hair, bandaging her ears, and she's wearing the running pants she bought in the mall in Towson. The pants are black with stirrups and have a think green racing stripe along each leg. They cling to Kim as tightly as Saran wrap, except at the calves. There she's put safety pins through the material.

The material is thin and slick to the touch, shiny like plastic. Lycra, the boy at the store had said.

"I never realized I had such small calves," Kim said when she emerged from the dressing room wearing the pants. The material sagged at her ankles.

"Uh huh," Benjamin answered, and they both stood before the mirror.

"Why didn't you tell me?"

"It never came up," Benjamin said. "What was I supposed to say? 'I really enjoyed dinner, and, by the way, you have no calves to speak of.'"

Kim put her hands on her hips and twisted to look at the pants from different angles. "They make me feel sexy," she said, and she looked at her bottom in the mirror, then paid for the pants. "They make me feel aerodynamic. Sometimes I think I can be the fastest woman in the world—in a manner of speaking."

When she's through stretching on the floor, she jumps to her feet and makes circles with her extended arms, moving them with the cautious speed of a second hand.

"See you in seven miles," she announces, and Benjamin says, "Time. Time. Tell me in minutes," but she just winks and cracks the door open, squeezing through so Alphonse won't get out.

"I need to know in time," Benjamin says to Phinney while they're stirring pots on the stove.

"Why does everything have to be in time for you?" Phinney asks.

There's tomato sauce bubbling in a pot on the back burner, lasagna noodles cooking on the front. The kitchen smells vaguely as their kitchen did when they were boys.

"I don't know. That's just the way it is." Benjamin unties his apron and says, "Can you take care of this for a while?"

"How long?" Phinney laughs.

"Fifteen, twenty minutes." When Phinney doesn't answer, Benjamin adds, "I have to take care of my hair before Kim gets back," and he flicks his fingers through it.

"Sure, no problem."

Benjamin walks to the bathroom and closes the door. First he takes the vial from the medicine cabinet and swallows one of his pills, savoring its flavor. Then he kneels and pushed his way through the cleaners and sponges stored under the bathroom cabinet. DON'T LEAVE THE HAIR COLOR ON TOO LONG!

His hair's going gray, and not just in the spot where Phinney hit him with a stone either, but everywhere. Everywhere strands of gray poke through like weeds. On the top. On the sides. On his sideburns. He can't see the back, but he's sure they're there, too.

Benjamin pulls the Lady Clairol Home Coloring Treatment Kit out and turns the faucet on.

"I'd hate to be you in the rain," he says to himself, and soon he's sitting on the cover of the toilet, reading the ingredients on the side panel of the box.

Benjamin was in the recliner with *Franny and Zooey* in front of him when Mary Jude returned from the grocery store. She unlocked the door and swung it open with her hip, two brown grocery bags in her arms.

"Can I help?" Benjamin asked. He closed the book, his index finger marking the page, and began to rise before Mary Jude said, "No, this is it."

She carried the bags to the kitchen, then called to him from there. "I got something for you, Benjamin."

"Fig Newtons?"

"Yes," she answered, distracted, "I didn't forget the Fig Newtons. I got something else, though."

He was back in his recliner, reading. "What's that?"

"I'll show you as soon as I finish putting everything away," and in five minutes she was standing in front of him, a naughty smile on her face, her hands behind her back.

"What is it?" he asked.

"Voilà," she said, and she jerked the Lady Clairol Home Coloring Treatment Kit in front of her.

It was a moment before Benjamin realized what it was, "Oh, geez, I like it the way it is," he told her. "I really do," and Mary Jude climbed on top of him, kneeling on his lap, and walked her fingers through his hair.

"No you don't" she said. She gestured toward the bathroom with a snap of her head. "Come on, let's go play beauty parlor," and she slid off his lap, grabbed Benjamin by the wrists, and led him to the bathroom.

"Come on, come on, come on."

Mary Jude left Benjamin in the bathroom while she ran to the living room to get a chair, and he looked into the mirror, turning to inspect the gray spot Phinney had left. He was so used to it that he sometimes forgot that it hadn't always been that way, that his hair was supposed to be black all the way around.

Mary Jude pulled the chair into the bathroom and set it in front of the counter, the back of the chair to the basin. She unbuttoned Benjamin's shirt and helped him pull it off, hanging it on the hook beside the shower, then guided him into the chair.

"Mary Jude," he whined.

"Don't be a baby," she said, and she draped a towel over his shoulders and patted her fingers under his chin so he would tip his head back into the basin. The hot water ran through his hair and into his ears, and her voice warbled through the water as she spoke.

"See," she said, "it hasn't hurt yet, has it?"

"Mary Jude."

"Hush." She read the instructions on the back of the box, a finger at her lips.

"Have you done this before?"

"Nope. Now will you hush already?"

She turned the faucet off, and Benjamin sat upright, the water from his hair dripping onto the towel and onto his T-shirt. Mary Jude lifted the towel from his shoulders and covered his head with it, twisting it in all directions, Benjamin's head moving with it, then she returned the damp towel to his shoulders and opened the box. She emptied its contents and set them on the counter. Then she began to unfasten the buttons of her blouse.

"What are you doing?" Benjamin asked. "You're going to do this in the nude?"

"Don't you wish. I just don't want to ruin my clothes doing this," and she pulled off her blouse, then her skirt. She hung them from the doorknob, and, in her underpants and camisole, she unscrewed the cap of the haircoloring.

Benjamin closed his eyes tightly, and soon he could feel Mary Jude's fingers at his scalp, working the lotion into his hair. The lotion made a sound like swishswishswish, but it was an unpleasant swishing. Next, he felt her pull the plastic cap onto his head.

"It's okay," she said. "That's it. You can open your eyes."

"Thanks," Benjamin replied, and Mary Jude scratched at her ankle, leaving a thin black streak.

"Think nothing of it."

There were black streaks on her arms, too, and polka dots on her legs. Her palms were black.

"We just have to wait now to let it work," she said, and she turned on the water to clean her hands. No matter how much soap she used, they remained gray.

"Damn," she said when she found the plastic gloves on the counter. She held them up. "I forgot to put these on. We'll save them for next time."

"Next time?"

"Sure, you've got to do it every couple of weeks."

"Great."

Benjamin folded his hands on his lap, the cap pinching his brow, and Mary Jude stood in front of the sink, scrubbing the black marks on her arms and legs. She scrubbed at the beauty mark on her calf for a moment before she remembered that it was a part of her and not the haircoloring. When she was done, she toweled herself dry. Her skin was pocked with gray spots now, and she hoisted herself up onto the counter.

"What's in this stuff?" he asked.

"What?"

"The haircoloring. What's in it?"

Mary Jude picked up the box and read from the side panel. "Water," she read.

Benjamin said nothing.

"Oleic acid. Isopropyl alcohol. Octoxynol-1. Ethoxyiglycol," she said. "I could be pronouncing that wrong. Propylene glycol. Nonoxydol-4. Ammonium hydroxide. Resorcinol and Hershey's chocolate."

"What?"

"Just seeing if you were paying attention," she said, squeezing his shoulder, once then twice. When fifteen minutes had passed, she hopped down from the counter, lifted the cap from Benjamin's head and rinsed the color out. When his hair dried, it was as if Phinney had never hit him with the stone.

"What happens when it rains?" Benjamin asked.

"When it rains, it pours," she said elusively, then she dropped an eyebrow. "Who said that? Churchill?"

"I think it was the Morton Salt girl," Benjamin said, and she nodded, smiling. There were black specks on her camisole, nearly invisible they were so small, like tiny termite holes over her chest and stomach.

"But really," he said, "what happens when it rains?" and Mary Jude shrugged and wiped the countertop clean with a sponge.

"God knows," she answered.

Benjamin shelters his face from the showerhead with his small cupped hands, and he splashes the gray water about with his feet, kicking at it. Soon the water is clear and he turns off the shower and steps out onto the bath mat. He dresses again, putting on the same clothes save for a fresh pair of boxer shorts. He hides the empty Lady Clairol box in the cabinet beneath the sink, then returns to the kitchen. He fluffs his hair with his fingers like he's shooing flies. Phinney is still working at the stove.

"How's it coming?" Benjamin asks.

"No problem. We've got company," and Phinney jerks his head toward the living room. There's a boy sitting on the couch, watching television. He's in his early twenties, and he's wearing a football jacket, the kind high-school boys wear, red felt with shiny gray sleeves. The sleeve nearest the kitchen has the letters TE sewn on it in red, the number 88 secured beneath.

"Who is he?" Benjamin whispers.

"I didn't catch his name. He said he was looking for Kim."

Benjamin wipes his hands on Phinney's apron, thinking there might still be some haircoloring on his fingers—there isn't.

"Excuse me," Benjamin says, and the boy stands and offers his hand.

"Mr. Sacks?" the boy says, and Benjamin bobs his head slightly. He doesn't recognize the boy and has the odd sensation he isn't supposed to.

"Mr. Sacks," the boy says, "I got your address from Mrs. Cassella, Kimmie's mom. She said Kimmie was living down here now."

"That's right."

"Well, I was hoping I could talk to her."

"She's out right now." Benjamin's confused. "I'm sorry if we've met before, but I don't remember you."

"I'm Kevin," the boy says, and he waits for Benjamin to comment. He shifts his weight from one leg to the other, then back again. The boy's tall and thin and handsome, his hair a salad of curls. He looks vaguely like a question mark standing on Benjamin's carpet. "Kevin Purcell," he says.

Still, Benjamin says nothing. The name sounds familiar.

In the silence, Benjamin hears the woman on the television. "I won't sleep with anyone until I'm married," she's saying.

"Will you call me when you're married then?" the man on the television answers, and the laughter pours out of the set and into the living room.

Benjamin's still considering the boy in front of him.

"God, this is difficult. I figured I'd just say my name and you'd throw me out of here. I'm Kevin Purcell, Kimmie's boyfriend. Or, I used to be her boyfriend when we were in high school." He points north, in the direction of their school. "I just wanted to talk to her."

Benjamin doesn't know what to do. He moves about uneasily, walking two steps to the left, then back again.

"She'll be back in a minute. Can I get you a beer or a soda?"

"A beer sounds good," the boy says.

Benjamin gestures for him to have a seat, then goes to the kitchen to get a beer. Alphonse follows him in, and Benjamin opens the freezer, plucks an ice cube from the tray, and drops it into the dog's gaping mouth.

"I know. I didn't want to be the one to tell you," Phinney says under his breath, and Alphonse chews with the sound of glass breaking. "How tall do you figure he is?"

"What are you talking about?"

"The guy out there." Phinney ducks his head to gesture toward the living room. "How tall?"

"I don't know. What do you want me to do, go out there and say, 'It's very nice to meet you. Why don't you take your coat off. And, say, by the way, how tall are you?'"

"Really, Ben. Take a guess."

He can feel the jealousy bubbling inside him. "I don't *know*. Five ten? Five eleven?"

"See, it's what I told you. He's probably very happy."

"What are you talking about?"

"My theory about height and happiness, how it's how far way you are from five eleven that determines how happy you are, remember?"

"Uh huh."

"And he's five eleven on the nose. On the button."

"Great."

"He's a football player," Phinney says.

Benjamin nods. "I know. I saw his jacket.

"And he's in college."

"Well, I guess we've got ourselves a little Renaissance man here, then, haven't we."

"Ben," Phinney says, "don't be that way. It's not very becoming," and Benjamin moves back to the living room with a can of Miller Lite.

When Kim returns, Alphonse dashes to her. She bends to pet him and pulls off her gloves.

"I just had—" and when she sees Kevin she reached for the doorknob and turns around, then turns back. It's an unusual motion, frightened. It's the sort of movement people only make in bad dreams. It's a movement that reassures Benjamin.

"What's he doing here?" she asks Benjamin. She doesn't address Kevin.

"Your mother told him you were down here."

Hesitating, the boy moves toward her. He doesn't lift his feet from the floor.

"But what's he *doing* here?"

"Kimmie," Kevin says, "I wanted to talk to you. There are some things I wanted to get straight, and when I went to see you your mom said you were living down here now and that you'd want to talk."

"My mother says things she shouldn't say. I don't want to talk to you."

"Kimmie."

Kim drops her gardening gloves to the floor, and Alphonse sniffs them. "What?" She shakes her head and doesn't look at him. Her expression is pained. "What do you have to say?"

"I think it'd be better if we talked in private. It'd be more comfortable. I don't know exactly what I want to say, the words, only I feel uncomfortable with Mr. Sacks here."

Benjamin pulls himself out of the recliner and walks to the kitchen, standing there with Phinney. He can't hear what Kim and Kevin are saying, he can only hear the flow of voices like at Yumi's, but soon Kim screams his name—Benjamin's—so loudly that it seems to hang in the air. It seems to float in the apartment like a leaf: "Benjamin!"

Benjamin rushes to the living room to find Kim standing in front of the television. Her arms are folded and Alphonse stands in front of her like a bodyguard, his tail flapping against Kim's running pants. It makes a noise like wet paint. Kevin's in the recliner, sitting upright.

"Look, I'm sorry," Kevin says.

"So. Big deal."

"So. So all I'm asking is for you to forgive me. Geez, God will forgive me."

"I guess God and I are two completely different people then. I'm not about to forgive you." She turns to Benjamin. "Get this guy out of here," she says. "Get him out of here now. Pick him up and toss him out if you have to," and she walks toward the bedroom. "I have to get dressed for work," she says. "I don't have time for this crap."

Benjamin couldn't move the boy if he tried. He's too large. But Kevin stands and leaves before Benjamin says a word. He takes his beer with him.

It's drizzling at eleven-fifteen when Benjamin puts his overcoat on. He takes the umbrella and walks to Yumi's.

He leans against the sink in the men's room at Yumi's again. He doesn't look in the mirror—the crack's still there—and the shabby talk wafts into the room through the heating duct like warm air.

"Does anyone know anything about dreams?" he hears. It's Verna.

"You mean like Freud and psychology?" Debra.

"Uh huh. Interpreting dreams."

"I know a little. Everything means something else." Debra.

"Okay, then. I had this dream the other night that I was having sex." Verna. "I think it means that I want to fly a plane. What do you think, doctor?"

The women hoot. Several voices are going at once, like car engines revving, making it difficult for Benjamin to make sense of them.

"Don't dream about having sex before you come to work." Yumi.

"Why?" Benjamin doesn't know who asked this.

"If you dream about sex, then you won't pay attention to your work, then—"

"Then what?" Tamara.

"Then your eyes will become very weak." Yumi. "Mark my words."

After a short silence Tamara says, "Do you want to hear the craziest thing?"

Several of the other waitresses say yes.

"This doesn't have anything to do with anything. You know my friend Janet, the one who's the hostess at the Rusty Scupper?"

"Janet *Marie* Price, the girl so nice they named her thrice?" Shannon.

"Yes, her."

"What a stupid thing to do, using three names." Shannon. "Like two's not enough. Like there are fifty other Janet Prices in Baltimore, and they've got to use their middle names so they don't get confused."

"She's such a bad dresser, too." Verna.

"She went to Duke University, you know." Tamara.

"Well, she obviously didn't go to Benetton." Shannon.

"Well, listen to *this*. She's been dating this guy Mark who's a doctor at Union Memorial Hospital, right, for about six or seven months now. So, Mark says, 'Listen, Janet Marie—'"

"*No*, he doesn't call her by all her names, does he?" Debra.

"I don't know. Maybe he does, maybe he doesn't. Anyway, he says to her, 'Listen, Janet Marie, I'm going down to North Carolina to visit my parents. Why don't you come along?' Janet says sure, but she's all nervous about what his parents are going to think of her, so get this: she calls in sick at work, and she goes down to Washington and checks into a really fancy hotel down there for two days."

"Did she stay in the Mayflower?" Terri. "I heard that one's really nice." Tamara says, "I don't know."

"I heard the Four Seasons is great." Shannon.

"I don't know where she stayed," Tamara answers. "The point is she stayed in a really fancy hotel for two days. The first day that she's there, she goes shopping and buys all new clothes for the trip. Underwear, dresses, skirts, blouses, everything. She spends a fortune. Then, the next day, she goes to the beauty parlor and gets a brand new hairdo and manicure." Tamara pauses dramatically. "And then she got a full body wax."

The sound of the women screaming floods the men's room and doesn't let up for a minute or more. It runs on and on, until Verna says, "A full body wax? Just to meet his parents?"

"A full body wax," Tamara says, dryly, and the screaming begins again.

"Including her stomach?" Kim.

Tamara must have nodded, because there are more screams.

"Like what are his parents going to do," Verna says, "ask her to lift up her sweater?"

One of the women imitates a man's voice: "Son, that's a mighty nice little filly you've got yourself there, and I especially like that hairless belly of hers. Keep up the good work."

"God, you couldn't pay me enough to get a fully body wax to meet Bill's parents." Debra.

"Kim, would you do it to meet Mr. Bathroom's parents?" Verna.

"Mr. Bathroom doesn't have parents. They're dead," Kim answers.

"Oh, yeah. They'd probably be about two hundred if they were alive today." Tamara.

"Shannon, would you do it to meet Doug's parents?" Terri.

"I've already met Doug's parents, and they're just as weird as he is. They'd probably like me better if I had *more* hair on my stomach."

"I thought they liked you." Terri.

"Nah. I don't think he told them that I'm Japanese."

"You're Japanese?" Verna shouts, sounding surprised, and the women scream.

"Shannon's Japanese! Get away! Don't *touch* me!" Debra.

"Oh, ick!" Tamara.

"Quick, somebody call a doctor!" Verna.

"We're going to have to be disinfected!" Terri.

"We're going to have to get tetanus shots!" Debra.

"They'll make us shave our heads!" Tamara.

"They'll make us get full body waxes!" Debra.

"Shannon's Japanese! How could you trick us like this! What a cruel charade!" Verna.

When their laughter trails off, Benjamin comes out of the men's room, and only then does he realize how little Kim had said. Her back against the wall, she wears a thin, uncomfortable smile, and on the walk home, he asks if she's okay.

"Fine," she says, "I don't like them making fun of themselves. It's very," she says, "counterproductive."

Benjamin pretends he doesn't know what she' talking about, and Kim explains that while he'd been in the men's room, the waitresses had been teasing one another about being Japanese.

She hooks her arm in Benjamin's, and pushes against him, but the umbrella isn't large enough for two. Her right shoulder and his left are exposed to the rain.

"Are you okay about the guy who came by today—Purcell?"

"Sure," she says.

"Really?"

"Really. It was no big deal. It's just that it was unexpected. Now, if I'd expected it, things would've been different. Things are always different if you can plan them out."

"What would you have done?"

"I'd have ignored him entirely, like he wasn't even there. That, or I'd have punched his lights out. I'm not sure which."

Phinney's watching television when they return to the apartment, and Benjamin follows Kim to the bedroom. She unties her kimono and drops it on the floor by the bed. She's wearing the royal blue T-shirt that says LOMAX TIMEPIECES...BECAUSE EVERYONE NEEDS TIME, and underwear that cuts up high on her hip.

"Will you tell me?" he says.

"Tell you what?"

"Everything."

"Benjamin, don't. We've been through all this before. I don't like talking about it and you don't like listening, so the perfect solution for both of us is to not talk about it. See, it's easy. It's perfect, so let's just go to sleep."

"Please," he says, "sweetheart," and she flops onto the bed.

"I love it when you call me that." She picks *To Kill a Mockingbird* from the nightstand and flips the pages. She started reading it a week before, and she hasn't said a word yet about the note in it, the note about Hallyday that Benjamin had written at the beach. Benjamin's certain that she's read the note, though. He can tell by her eyes, the way they seem more sympathetic than usual, and by her voice. She speaks to him with care, like someone walking on frozen ground.

"When something happens to you," she says, "and you talk about it later, it becomes part of a new moment. It's part of the moment when it happens, and then it's part of the moment when you talk about it. It becomes a whole new event."

"You can tell me, sweetheart. I promise it'll be okay."

She stretches to put the book back on the nightstand and lies on her side, pulling one of the pillows from the top of the bed and tucking it beneath her head. Her skin is peachy pale. She speaks, and her voice is mild. She looks straight up.

"I was trying out for the softball team at high school, okay—this was about a thousand years ago—and you know how they make you take a physical before they let you play any sport. So there I am with everyone else who's trying out, and I get to the doctor, and he puts the thing of the stethoscope on my chest, the icy metal part, and then he does it a second time, and then he asks me to stand off to the side by myself for a minute. So I stand there in just my panties for about five minutes while he checks everyone else, and then he puts the stethoscope on me again. God, what was his name? Dr. Donigliaro or Dr. Campagna or something like that. No matter, he wasn't the one who did the operation. Anyway, I ask him what's the problem because I'm starting to get sort of nervous, and it's freezing besides. I don't think they heat nurses' offices. And he says, 'It's probably nothing, honey, but I'd like to be sure,' so my mother and I had to go to his office. So we go to his office, and he does the same thing with the stethoscope, and he's squeezing my, you know, he's checking me out, and the next thing you know he wants us to go to Union Memorial Hospital. He says, 'It's probably nothing,' *again*, and my mom was just about hysterical. That's the way she is. She can't deal with things. She can't—what's the word I'm looking for?—*compensate*. So, she's just talking nonstop, and we go to the hospital and all I'm thinking is, 'what's this doctor's deal.' I mean, I just want to play softball."

Kim's on her stomach. She flops her legs like a fish out of water.

Benjamin's sitting against the bureau.

"But that's where they found it, when they X-rayed me. You could see it plain as day, this hole right through my heart about the size of a marble. So then I had to see a heart doctor. Dr. Plessy, he's the one who did the oper-ation. At first he didn't think it was going to be a big deal. He didn't even think I'd need surgery because he said it wasn't life-threatening. It just meant that when I got to be forty or something I wouldn't be able to do too much, I'd get tired out real easy. But then he took an X-ray from another angle, and it was worse than he thought, and he said they might have to operate to close it, you know, to close up the hole. So I had to stop doing physical things, and I couldn't go to gym and I couldn't play softball, and everyone was treating me real strange. Then one day I get all tired and dizzy just walking down the hall, and the next thing I know I'm in the principal's office, lying there on his couch, and there's a police car outside, and the principal, Mr. Wendell, tells me that they have to get me to the hospital right away, that the doctor, Dr. Plessy, called, and they had to do the opera-tion right away because something could be the matter. So they take me to the hospital in the police car, and I get there and they give me an injection of anesthesia, and Benjamin, it felt just like wine, whatever it was that they gave me. And the nurse and I sang, 'Michael, Row Your Boat Ashore' until I was mumbling and laughing and getting the words all wrong, and when I wake up, there I am, wrapped up like a samwich or something."

She turns on her side.

Benjamin opens the box of Fig Newtons on the bureau and puts a cookie in his mouth. It's curious, he thinks, how her tenses shift, how sometimes she talks about the past in the past tense, and sometimes in the present. And sometimes it's a combination of the two, as if the events haven't yet become the past but are on their way.

"You know, I didn't even think of it for a couple days, but I could've died right there. I mean, I could've been in geometry class one minute—that was my next class—and the next thing you know, I'm dead, and my parents and Christie are crying, and everyone at school is talking about how Kimberly Cassella got taken away from the school in a police car and then dies at the hospital, and then in a couple of months it'd be like I was never alive in the first place. It's not like I've ever *done* anything here for people to remember me. I mean, they didn't even give me a chance to think. It all happened so fast that I didn't even get a chance to say good-bye to everyone in case I did die."

Kim rolls off the bed and stands by the window.

"They should've given me a chance, and what's worse is that that's what you think when you're in the intensive-care ward afterwards. All the time that's what you think about. Every day they'd wheel someone else out, another one who died. They were dying like pancakes in there, I swear, and you just figure that maybe you're next. And you kind of hope that the next one who goes will be someone else. It's horrible to think like that, isn't it? I mean, I'm horrible, aren't I?"

Benjamin and Kim are standing toe to toe now, in front of the bureau and the mirror, and Benjamin isn't sure how they got there. He doesn't know who moved toward who, he doesn't remember standing up or Kim getting off the bed, and when he touches her face, her skin has an odd tacky feel to it. Her tears have dried already, dried like blood.

"Don't cry, sweetheart," he says, and Kim responds, "I'm not crying. It's just my eyes."

Benjamin looks into them. Sometimes he forgets how stunning they are, the grapes.

He thinks they should kiss, but they don't.

Kim sits on the bed again.

"Well, what happened afterwards was worse for me. First, the scar got all infected, so it kept getting wider and wider. The other thing, it's weird. This is very philosophical, but I keep losing people ever since it happened, and I don't know where to go. It's like when I had the hole in me, people could pass through me. But now I think, at least then they could get inside me for a while. Now, they can't even get in for that long. Like my family. I love them. Half the time I want to murder them, but I still love them. But what happened with Christie was really weird. It's like, well, I don't know how to describe it, it just happened. I mean, when were kids, we used to do everything together. Is Phinney your older—no, that's right, Phinney's younger than you. That doesn't make sense then what I was going to say then. Anyway, I remember she was very protective of me. Once, when I was about five or six, I was playing outside in the cardboard box. See, I'd made this little house out of a big old box, and I drew windows and curtains on it. So, I was playing in the playhouse with my stuffed animals, and these two boys came into the playhouse. They were ten years old maybe—maybe they were older—and they were scrunched down because the box was so short, and both of them had those plastic machine guns. You've seen them. The plastic ones. So they had these plastic machine guns, and they told me to pull my shorts down. They kept saying, "Pull your shorts down or we're gonna kill you dead." And I just started crying and screaming because I didn't want to pull my shorts down, and the two of them started touching me, and I guess Christie heard me or something because all of a sudden she was there, and she was punching both of them until they ran away. But after my operation, it wasn't the same anymore. Sometimes I just think that it's because we were both a lot older, but sometimes I think that it was something else."

Kim pauses to wet her lips, and Benjamin says, "What about this kid who showed up tonight, Purcell? What kind of person is he?"

"What kind of person is he? Rotten, rotten, rotten, rotten, rotten. I don't really understand what happened with him, the jerk. He just sort of dropped me like a hot rock. For a long time I really hated him. I'd see him at school and wish he was a hundred miles away and in excruciating pain. Do you know what I mean? Have you ever felt that way? But the way I look at it now, we were only high school kids, and he just didn't know any better. He was just acting like a high school boy. Not that I know that I would've acted any differently if I were him, but the way he acted just didn't make any sense. I mean, he said he loved me. He used to call me his sweetie-bo-beetie. If he loved me half as much as he said he did, half as much, then the way he acted just doesn't make any sense, and you start thinking, maybe he didn't love me. Maybe he didn't have any idea what he was talking about, or maybe he just wanted to fool around and stuff. I mean, this is going to sound corny, but sometimes I think that the advantage of love is that you can tell anyone that you love them, even if you don't. The disadvantage is that everyone knows what the advantage is. Or, if they're like me, they find out soon enough. I just sort of thought it was going to be like in the movies, that he was going to hold my hand and kiss me on the forehead and tell me that everything was going to be okay. Do you know what I mean, like he'd be there, and he'd sleep in the chair next to my bed, and when I woke up he'd be sitting right there and just smile, and then I'd know everything was okay. But, God, it was nothing like that. I didn't see him at all before the operation, which was sad, but I understood that. He was in school and everything, and he probably couldn't get out of classes even if he tried. Then he had football practice, and they don't let you out of football practice unless your arm gets ripped out of the socket. But, afterwards, there was no *excuse* for not coming to see me. You know what it is, it's that all guys want to do is touch you there, on the breasts, and he must've figured, Well, forget her now. I guess that's what everyone thought, the guys I mean. I can't explain why the girls acted the way they did. Maybe they were scared and thought, Stay away from Kimberly Cassella or we might *catch* it."

Kim's hair is up in her fingers.

The light from the liquor store sign shines in the window.

"Yumi was different from everyone else. Yumi was the only good thing that happened. I just sort of moped around for a couple of years after graduation. God, what am I saying? It was almost five years. Anyway, I was downtown shopping and for no good reason whatsoever I walked in there one day, into Yumi's, and it was like the whole world just opened up and changed. I don't know if it was the lighting or the temperature or everything together, but I just had the feeling something good was going to happen. Have you ever had that feeling, where you think something good might happen, you just don't know what it is, and then it happens? Maybe it happens by itself and you just predicted it, or maybe you made it happen because you wanted it to happen. But, anyway, it ends up happening, and that's all that matters. That's what it was like at Yumi's. Like I said, I was just looking in shop windows and killing time at Harborplace, and somehow I ended inside Yumi's. Shannon was at the hostess stand and she was really nice. And then Tamara was nice. She waited on me. I said something to her about what a great job it was, and she said, 'If you're looking for work, you might want to stick around. Yumi will be by this afternoon.' So, just out of curiosity, I stuck around, and the first thing Yumi said was, 'You're not Japanese,' and I said, 'I know, but I can fake it.' I really was excited about working there, and I kept saying, 'Come on, give me a chance. I mean, fire me if I stink, but give me a chance.' So eventually she said okay, and I was so happy. I mean, just about a stupid waitressing job, if you can believe it. But it was strange because I could be sad all day, but when I'd walk into the restaurant—bam!—I was happy again. Here are all these tiny Japanese women acting all deferential and everything, but when the restaurant closes, forget it. They're not the least bit deferential anymore. They're the greatest, funniest women in the world. It's like they all dress the same and talk the same when the restaurant's going, but all of the time they've got someone else inside them, and you can only see the someone else when it's dark out and the customers are gone and they're just women, not Japanese women. See? Does that make sense?"

Benjamin nods, but Kim isn't looking at him. She's lying on her back. Both hands are on her stomach.

"So then it becomes funny to watch them be deferential, because you know it's only an act. I mean, here's Tamara, for instance, bowing and saying, 'Yes, sir,' and 'No, sir,' and 'Was the meal to your liking, sir?' and then, not an hour later, there she is with the rest of us and the shibby talk. Like last night she says something like, 'Did you see the guy who left me a ten-percent tip? I'm having my period for God's sake, and he leaves me ten percent! Jesus, there should be a rule or something, Yumi. Fifteen percent minimum and twenty percent if your waitress is having her period.' Isn't that great? You'd like Tamara if you knew her better."

"I like Tamara," Benjamin says, and he does.

"So anyway, I couldn't talk to my mom or my dad or Christie about how I felt—my dad never thinks anything should bother you—and, well, I don't know why but one night I just decided to stick around and talk to Yumi about it. You know, I just sort of hung around. 'Yumi, can I give you a hand locking up or something?' And she said she didn't need any help, and then I said that I wanted to talk. So she said, 'Is this about your boyfriend?' and I said, 'Yumi, I don't have a boyfriend.' Then we sat down, and I told her everything about my heart and the scar. She just listened. She just let me talk, and when I was done she said, 'Sachiko, you don't understand that the best things in life fall from the highest shelf,' or something like that. And I figured out what she meant. It's like how you keep your best china up on the top shelf, and sometimes they fall and break on the floor, but the only reason they fell so far in the first place was because they were so special, because they meant so much. You know? So Yumi started making me believe that I was special and that that wouldn't have happened to me, to my heart, if I weren't special in the first place. But then I started feeling like she's the only one who thinks that. My parents don't, and Christie doesn't, and Kevin didn't, and, well, it was just Yumi. And then she had to let me go for the summer, and what was I supposed to do? I mean, I understand why she had to let me go, but I needed Yumi. Do you know how miserable I'd be if she hadn't given me my job back? I think I might have killed myself."

Benjamin says, "Don't talk like that." He's leaning against the window sill.

"I really don't want to talk about it anymore. I've said enough already," she says. "I mean, Benjamin, a heart is something special. And I don't mean in a corny sort of way like Valentine's Day cards. Or maybe I do, but only peripherally. The things you feel for people are inside you. Do you know what I mean? They're inside you, and there's something wrong with my insides. Somebody's hands were fiddling around with my insides."

"But they fixed it," Benjamin interrupts.

"They didn't fix it. They patched it up. There's a big difference. Every day I've got to look in the mirror and look it right in the eye. Sometimes I put my bra on with my eyes closed because I don't want to look, and sometimes I take a shower with my shirt on. Really. Can you believe it? Am I crazy or what? An adult taking a shower with her clothes on because she can't stand to look at herself. Every time I do it's a reminder that there's something wrong with me inside. God, I feel like I've been beaten up. It's a reminder that I don't function right, and that I can't hold onto someone and love someone the way a normal person can, and that no one can love me the right way. God, Benjamin, I can't love you forever. I don't work right. And you can't love me either. If Phinney weren't here, I might still be sleeping on the couch."

"You're so insecure," Benjamin says. "When I first met you I never would've thought—" But that wasn't true. He had known there was something wrong. He'd seen it. "There's no reason for you to be insecure."

"Don't tell me not to be insecure," she says, not harshly. "It's a way of life. I try and I try and I try and I try, but that's the way I am. I can't just stop because I want to. It's not like going on a diet. It's not like"—she snaps her fingers—"poof, I'm not insecure anymore."

Before long Benjamin's beside her on the bed, his shirt on the floor in a heap with her kimono. He kisses her, and she returns his kisses.

"You know," Kim says, "in my dreams I don't have a scar."

"Really?"

"Mm hmm. But then, in my dreams I also know how to speak French." She laughs at herself, and Benjamin smiles.

"You don't know how to speak French?" He knows she doesn't, but he's just making romantic talk now, the tone more important than the content, and his voice is as sweet as summer pudding.

"Unh uh. The only French I know is Yoplait," and again Benjamin smiles. "That's the name of yogurt," she says, and Benjamin tells her he knew that.

"In my dreams, everything's perfect," Kim says. "I'm perfect. It makes waking up pretty rotten."

Benjamin rolls onto his side and runs his foot along her calf.

"Your feet are cold," he says, and Kim answers, "I know. My hands and feet get cold because they don't get much circulation. That's why I have to run, to keep them warm."

"I'm sorry. You told me that. I forgot," and he kisses her neck. She twists her head, and Benjamin tugs at her T-shirt, pulling the bottom from her shorts.

"Ben, please," Kim says. She holds her head to the side and shuts her eyes. "Please."

Benjamin pushes the T-shirt farther up, revealing more of the white skin of her belly. He touches her there, and it's warm, like toast.

"Please what?" he says. "Please stop, or please go on?" and he bends to press his lips to her stomach.

"I don't know," she squirms. "God, Benjamin, you'll hate me if you see it."

He pushes the T-shirt farther, and she arches her back to let him. The southernmost part of the scar shows beneath her brassiere.

"Please," she says.

He whispers, "Please what?" and Kim turns her head to look up at him. She lifts her head suddenly from the bed. Her hair dangles, touching the pillow, and she opens her mouth to kiss him.

"Please," she says, into his mouth, her eyes an inch or so from his. "Please don't hate me. Please don't break my heart."

"Don't think that," he says, and she stretches her arms above her head.

Benjamin lifts her T-shirt. He tugs it over her head. Her shoulders are bony and white, and her eyes are closed again. He kisses her lips, then the bridge of her nose, and she sighs as loudly as he's ever heard someone sigh. It's a sigh that sounds like a scream.

Unfamiliar with the hook of the brassiere, Benjamin fidgets with it, twisting the strap, crooking his neck to look over Kim's shoulders and at his own hands. When the brassiere comes undone, Kim holds her arms outstretched before her to allow Benjamin to slip it off.

"Please, God," he hears her whisper.

"Relax, sweetheart," he says, and, exposed, she hugs him to her tightly. He looks at the headboard of the bed. When she releases him she falls back onto the bed, her head to the pillow, and Benjamin slides down. He hovers above the creek, considering it. It's as long and as thick as he'd remembered, pinkish gray and winding, and he takes his eyes from it to look at Kim's face for a moment. Her eyelids are shut, closed tight the way children do in fear, and Benjamin dips his head toward the creek, bringing his lips to its southern tip, moving upstream deliberately, between her breasts. Her heart trembles beneath him.

He kisses the scar, and her skin is sensitive there. Kim giggles and squirms again, trying to shake him off, but he continues making his way up the scar, little by little, one kiss after another until it ends. Then he kisses her neck and is at her mouth again.

"Make love to me," she says. Her eyes remain closed, but not as securely as before. They're closed in a comfortable way.

"Are you sure?"

"Yes," she says.

Her underpants are still on, and Benjamin kneels on the bed to remove them. Her arms are crossed over her breasts.

"I love you, Benjamin," she says. "I really do," and, with one hand, she finds his zipper and eases it down.

Benjamin shifts on the bed to remove his pants, tossing them onto the pile with his shirt and her kimono, and Kim slips her fingers in the waistband of his boxer shorts and eases them down his buttocks. He pushes them the rest of the way, catching at his knees and again at his ankles, and, when they're hooked at his ankles, he kicks them off. He stretches to turn off the lamp.

Again, Kim takes her arms from her breasts, baring the scar. She moves her hand between Benjamin's legs and holds him there, in her fist. She squeezes him and she pulls him toward her, opening her legs wider beneath him.

"No," he says, "first let me—" but she interrupts him.

"There's no time," Kim says, "sweetheart," and she pulls him inside of her, and she twists beneath his weight. Opening her mouth wide, she kisses him. She breathes into his mouth. It's as if she's reviving him with the strength of her breath.

She turns as he bounces on top of her, her hands on his buttocks, his head beside her shoulder. The springs of the mattress moan below them, like a tiny ghost awakened. It's a sound Benjamin hasn't heard since Mary Jude left. Benjamin thinks about their skin particles mixing in there—his, Mary Jude's and Kim's—and he dives to kiss Kim's breasts. He kisses the creek.

The image of Mary Jude flashes beneath him. Mary Jude, with her legs locked around the small of his back and her fingers at his neck. "Push," she would say, "Push."

Kim twists, and she rolls, and she smiles, and her head tips, and she utters small, wordless noises. Afterwards, with part of Benjamin still inside her and shrinking, all she says, is, "I understand if you hate me."

Benjamin clears her hair from her forehead. "How can you say that?" he says. "How could anyone ever hate you? How could *I*?"

He looks down at her, into her eyes, but in the dark her eyes don't look green. They look black.

The lights should have been on.

* * *

The heaviness about Benjamin is as great as ever, though he's determined to ignore it. The divorce papers are in his desk, but he doesn't look at them. He knows what they say. Mary Jude's picture's in his underwear drawer, but he doesn't look at that, either. He struggles to act normal, to act like someone else.

It's when Babisch says, at lunch, "Get out your handkerchiefs," that Benjamin realizes how evident it is.

"What do you mean?"

"I mean, I know you, Ben. Something's wrong. Something's always wrong. I can tell by looking at you." He points at Benjamin, somewhere between his forehead and nose. "You've got that my-dog-just-died look on your face."

"I don't want to talk about it."

"Is it Mary Jude again?"

"No, not really. Not specifically," he lies. "Maybe Mary Jude impacts on it, but it's not her in particular."

"Kim?"

"Mm hmm."

"I knew something was up. I could tell," Babisch says, "before you went to Hawaii."

"Nebraska."

"I could tell before you went to Nebraska. What is it?"

"It's something different than it was then," Benjamin says. "I don't want to be rude. It's the sort of thing it would be rude to talk about. Impolite."

"Sex?"

Benjamin nods and says, "Yes. I mean, I'm not a prude, I'm just not the kind of guy who goes around saying, 'Hey, check out the ass on that one. Boy would I love to give her a lube job.'"

Babisch swallows and coughs. "A lube job?" he says.

"I was just trying to find some sort of euphemism."

"Well, lube job's a very good one," Babisch says, congratulating him as if he were speaking to a child.

"Don't give me a hard time."

"So, what is it?"

"We've been, you know, fooling around the last couple of nights."

"So?"

"So, we hadn't been."

"What's the big deal?"

"For us, it's a big deal. I just don't know what I'm supposed to do."

"You forget?"

"No, no. You're not listening, Babisch. I just don't know what to do with her now. I don't know if this is getting serious, or if it's already serious, or if I want it to be serious."

"Ben, she's been living with you for nearly a year. I think we can safely say that it's serious." Babisch puts the last of his sandwich in his mouth. After he swallows, he says, "Let me tell you how it is with Julie. See, when you're a boy and you see a girl you like, all you want to do is kiss her. But then you get older, you get into high school, and everything gets distorted. You see a girl you like and"—Babisch makes a fist, and Benjamin doesn't know if he does this purposely—"and all you want to do is give her a lube job, as you so eloquently described it. But then, I saw Julie, and all I wanted to do was kiss her. Do you see what I'm saying? The be-all and end-all was just being with her, and the sex wasn't the point of it."

Babisch is being vague and honest at once.

Benjamin doesn't answer.

"It all comes down to what you feel, Benjamin. What you want," Babisch says. "What do you want from her?"

"Kim?"

"Yes."

"I don't know what I want. Sometimes I want to do one thing, and the next day I'll want to do something else."

"So, make up your mind. You're too old to be so wishy-washy. Figure out what you want to do, then do it. And don't be half-assed about it. Do it full-assed. It's important," Babisch says, "to use all of your ass."

"I'll try," Benjamin says. "Making up my mind is always the hardest part."

As he finishes his sandwich, he thinks of Kim. He thinks of the creek.

He thinks of Mary Jude. Under her clothes, nothing. Nothing but Mary Jude.

CHAPTER 17
THE NIGHT IT RAINED FOREVER

KIM'S IN THE SHOWER. Benjamin listens to the sound of water rushing over her while he dresses, the door to the bedroom open. Shoopshoopshoop over her. If she's wearing a T-shirt, Benjamin can't tell.

Phinney's not in the apartment, he's out walking Alphonse. The water runs in the bathroom, and the radio beside the bed is on. There's a love song playing, though the words are drowned out by the shower. He knows it's a love song, though, and he takes his gray slacks from the hanger and steps into them. He's already showered, and he tucks his T-shirt in and buttons the slacks.

Kim had walked into the bathroom after he'd stepped out of the shower, and he rubbed a circle in the condensation on the mirror so he could see his face. His cheeks seemed to bulge.

"Do you think," he said, "that I'm getting fat?" He fingered his face, pressing with his fingertips.

"What?"

"Do you think my face is getting fat?" He looked again. "It's like my cheeks are consuming my face, slowly but surely."

"You look the same as always," she said. "Cute. Sort of like a chipmunk."

"That's great for someone my age."

"You look like an old chipmunk, then. Is that better?" and she locked her arms around his waist.

Benjamin shrugged. "Great."

"It's not that bad. Winter's coming."

"So?"

"So, you could store food in them," and she squeezed him with her forearms. "I'm teasing," she said. "You look fine," and she crinkled her nose and kissed him beside the ear.

Benjamin zips his pants, the shower water stops suddenly, the words to the song are audible now: "Everybody wants to be my baby but my baby." He's heard Kim sing it before, when it's come on the car radio.

She always sings along with love songs. Once, on her night off, they went to a club in Washington, one Kim had read about in the paper. It was just a small dark room with a bar on one wall and a small stage at the front. There couldn't have been more than twenty people there. At midnight, a thin girl took a seat on a stool onstage. Her eyes were large and round, and she held a guitar on her lap.

Into the microphone, the girl said, "You know, a lot of folk singers get up on stage and tell you all about their wretched childhoods and how that made them so sensitive and artistic. I won't tell you about my wretched childhood," she said, "because my parents are here tonight." She gestured with her head toward the rear of the room. "That's them back there."

The girl strummed her guitar, striking the strings softly, and sang, "If I gave my heart to you, then I'd have none and you'd have two."

Kim sipped her soda, and when the girl came to the chorus again, Kim mouthed the words. Since then, he's caught her singing the song. He's caught her while she was reading *Airport*. He's caught her while she was working on the crossword puzzle in the *Sun*. He's caught her while she's dressed for work, wearing her kimono, rubbing rouge into her cheeks, singing, "If I gave my heart to you, then I'd have none and you'd have two."

"Benjamin?" Kim calls through the closed bathroom door.

"Yes?"

"What should I wear?" They're going to drive to Bluefield with Phinney to visit Earl and Mrs. Van Devere. Though she's spoken on the phone with each of them, Kim's never met either one, and she's been acting peculiar about it. She's been acting fidgety, as she might if she were meeting Benjamin's parents.

"Wear whatever you want," he answers.

"But what should I wear? I mean, what does Mrs. Van Devere wear?"

"Why?"

"I don't know. So I can wear something compatible, I guess."

"She usually wears support hose and orthopedic shoes. Should I run out and get you some?"

"Benjamin, you're not being any help. This is important."

"Really," he says, "whatever you wear will be okay."

"Then I guess it'd be okay with you if I wear my pink go-go boots and a pair of hot pants."

She catches him off guard, and he laughs, but he doesn't let her know he's laughing. She walks into the bedroom with a red towel turned around her head. She's wearing a blue John Hopkins Lacrosse T-shirt and a pair of black gym shorts. Since Phinney moved in, she doesn't walk through the apartment in her underpants anymore.

"I was only joking," she says. Her skin is still pink from the shower. "I don't even own go-go boots," and she opens the closet door.

Benjamin pulls on a plaid shirt, then stuffs the bottom into his slacks.

"I should tell you that Earl's missing an arm," he says.

"Why?"

"Why am I telling you?"

Kim nods.

"I don't know. I didn't want it to surprise you. I didn't know if you'd be surprised or upset by it or what. A lot of people are upset by things like that."

"I'm not. Are you? I mean, everyone's missing something."

"No," Benjamin says, "it doesn't upset me anymore."

"I knew a girl in grade school—Michelle Lesko—who was missing a finger. This one," she says, and she points to the ring finger of her left hand. "She was a very attractive girl except for that. But you know what's funny about it is that she told some people that it happened when she stuck her finger in a fan—you know, in the fan blades—and she told other people that a chicken bit it off."

"A chicken?"

"Mm hmm."

"So, what was it? Was it a fan or a chicken?"

"God, I don't know." Kim pulls off her shorts. When they fall to the floor, she sweeps them into the closet with a kick of her foot. "I never even thought of asking her." She takes a black paisley skirt from the closet and drops it over her shoulders, then cocks her hip to help the skirt down to her waist. She moves to the bureau and opens a drawer, pulls a red wool sweater out, and tosses it onto the bed. She unwraps the towel from her hair—the towel's nearly the same shade as her sweater—then throws the towel toward the closet. Her hair is still damp, and it smells sweet, like strawberries, as it always does. Her shampoo comes in a pink bottle.

"So," she says, trying to keep the conversation going. "Earl's missing an arm."

"As long as I've known him."

"How did it happen?"

"A chicken bit it off," Benjamin says, and Kim laughs as she pulls on her sweater.

"No," she says, "really. Do you know?"

"It was an accident," he tells her. "A car accident." He doesn't tell her that Earl did it on purpose.

He'd told Mary Jude once. He'd told her on one of the drives to Baltimore to visit Phinney in the hospital. He'd told her before Mrs. Magruder had met Earl.

"On purpose?" was how Mary Jude had reacted. "A man throws himself in front of a car on purpose?"

"It had to do with a girl," Benjamin said. "There was a picture of her in his bathroom."

"What about this girl? Did he tell you who she is?"

"No. I really don't know who she is. Maybe it was his girlfriend or his sister or someone."

Mary Jude was puzzled. "But you know he did it on purpose?"

"I'm almost positive he did. The way I figure it—and I could be wrong, but I don't think I am—something horrible happened to the girl in the picture, and Earl felt guilty about it."

"It's that simple?"

"I think so."

"Do you think he was trying to kill himself?"

"No, no, no, you're missing the point. I don't know if he was trying to kill himself, it's that he felt so guilty that he would do it on purpose. It's that it wasn't an accident is what matters, see?" But he could tell that Mary Jude didn't see. It was like his father. He'd done it, he'd jumped on purpose, and that was what mattered. The intent, not the conclusion.

Benjamin and Kim both sit on the bed until Phinney returns with the dog. They leave Alphonse to the apartment, the television on. They walk two blocks to the car.

Kim sits in the front seat with Benjamin, easing her seat forward so Phinney will have room for his legs.

"I saw the funniest thing on TV yesterday," she says. "This guy and this girl had just gotten married, right, and they were opening up their wedding presents. One of the presents is this ugly sculpture or something"—she moves her hand as if she were sculpting—"and they couldn't figure out what it was, so the guy says, 'This is horrible.' Then the girl goes, 'Honey, it's the thought that counts,' and he says, 'Well, I wish they'd thought of something else.'"

Benjamin laughs and hears Phinney do the same.

"It was a good show," she adds. "Very amusing."

They're on Howard Street already, one of the north-south roads, and Kim continues, her words racing. "I guess you're just supposed to thank people for presents even if you don't like them. The presents, that is. I guess," she says, "that's the courteous thing to do."

The traffic is light for a Sunday. There's usually traffic backed up, headed to Harborplace or the aquarium, but today the streets are quiet, several cars and people carrying newspapers on the sidewalks.

Benjamin cuts across to Charles Street and heads north, and Kim's still talking. "That's probably what Miss Manners would say. You know Miss Manners?"

Benjamin says, "Uh huh." Phinney has a section of the Sunday *Sun* folded open on his lap.

"Did you ever think what the odds were of that?" Kim asks.

"Of what?" Benjamin says. They pass a stationery store with a large yellow pencil sticking out the front of the building, like a plane that had crashed.

"Miss Manners," Kim says. "I mean, her name is Miss *Manners,* and that's what she writes about: manners."

Benjamin smiles, but not too broadly. Kim's nervous and she's trying to be funny to fight it off.

"I mean," she adds, "what are the odds that your name and what you do are the same thing? It's like that baseball game we went to last summer, Benjamin, the Orioles game. You see, Phinney"—she twists in her seat, kneeling to face Phinney—"there was a guy in an Orioles uniform, and on the back it said BATBOY. And guess what—that's what he was, the batboy."

She settles down, watching the road, only talking to help Phinney work the crossword puzzle as Benjamin drives.

"Dakota capital," he says, and Kim answers "Fargo" without a moment's pause.

"Specially fitted."

"How many letters?"

"Eight. The third one's *I.*"

"Tailored," she says. "T-A-I-L-O-R-E-D."

"The Feast of Lots."

"Purim. It's a Hebrew word."

"Are you sure?"

"Yes, I'm sure. I've had that one before. They always use that one."

"Mark time."

"How many *letters*? You've got to tell me how many letters."

"Sorry," Phinney says. "Five. The second one's *W*."

"Await. A-W-A-I-T."

They call out the clues and answers, and when they reach Bluefield, the puzzle nearly done, Benjamin drives slowly through the center of town. Kitchener's Bookstore is gone. It's a video store now. There are large posters taped to the windows and a bright yellow electric sign above the door.

"That's where I worked," Benjamin tells Kim. "Back when they sold books there."

The Bluefield Quality Bakery is still there, but it's twice the size it used to be.

"And that's where Phinney worked."

The laundromat is called Rick's Super-Fast Laundromat now. Adair's Pub is still there, and Shelmeyer's Grocery, too. The Texaco station is still there, but it looks different. There's a convenience store where the garage used to be, with signs advertising COKE and HOT DOGS in the window, and there's a black overhang above the pumps. The overhang says TEXACO, with a star surrounding the *T*.

"And that's where Earl works," Benjamin says, though he can't imagine Earl doing anything but working the pumps and doing tune-ups. He can't imagine Earl selling hot dogs or working an electronic cash register.

Benjamin continues driving toward their old house. There are fewer trees than there used to be and more houses. He parks the car in front of their old house and gets out. Phinney and Kim do, too, but Kim stays by the car.

"Do I look okay?" she asks. "I should have asked before we left home."

"You look wonderful," Benjamin answers. "Stop worrying."

He and Phinney stand in the yard before their old house, next to Earl and Mrs. Van Devere's. Their house is blue now, the shutters white, the tree over the garage a giant with arms above the telephone wires. The fall wind is capricious. It blows at their hair one moment, then vanishes the next. It muscles the tree branches, and crisp red leaves sprinkle down on the lawn and the street.

Each time he's returned, Benjamin's thought the house seemed smaller than he'd remembered. He remembers the house as it was when he was a boy, not as it was the last time he'd viewed it. His childhood is his reference point.

Kim is sitting in the car, fixing her hair in the rearview mirror. When she's done, she joins Benjamin and Phinney on the lawn.

"Is this their house?" she asks, and Benjamin tells her no, that it was theirs.

The three of them stand in the yard inspecting the house. The front screen door swings open. A man in his twenties is holding it, still standing inside. He pokes his head out. His hair is pushed back, and he's wearing two sweaters, one over his chest, the other tied around his shoulders.

"Can I help you with something?" he calls.

"This is where we grew up," Phinney says. "This house" and he points to it.

"We're here to visit the Van Deveres," Benjamin adds.

"That's next door," the man says. "Right there," and Benjamin says, "I know. We know."

Their father called up from the bottom of the stairs. "If you get in bed I'll tell you a story," he said. They could hear his footsteps on the stairs, light for a man so large.

"We are in bed," Phinney answered.

"Both of you?"

"Yes. Look."

"Oh, is that Benjamin next to you? I thought it was a sack of potatoes," and their father tickled Benjamin's sides until he laughed and wriggled. "That *is* Benjamin."

"What story are you going to tell us?" Phinney asked.

"Do you want to hear one about Mr. and Mrs. Magruder?"

"There is no Mr. Magruder."

"There used to be, when you were little."

"What's the story about?"

"It's about the night it kept raining," their father told them. "It's about the night it rained forever. Do you want to hear it?"

"Mm hmm."

"Ben?"

Benjamin nodded in the dark.

"Okay, well, when there was a Mr. Magruder, he and Mrs. Magruder were afraid of the rain. Well, not really afraid, but worried about it. Worried, that's the word. Anyway, what Mr. and Mrs. Magruder did was they arranged all the furniture in their home so that they could get out of any room and out of the house itself without ever having to touch the floor— by walking on the furniture, by crossing bureaus and tables and desks and chests, by stepping on couches and chairs and bouncing off beds, by swinging from hanging plants and chandeliers like Tarzan. See, they didn't have to touch the floor at all. Everything was linked like the cars of a train so they could leave any room without walking on the floor."

"Mr. and Mrs. Magruder walked on their furniture?"

"No, they didn't walk on their furniture. That would have been barbaric. It's just that they placed the pieces of furniture in each room in a manner that would allow them to leave without touching the floor. They could walk on the furniture if they wanted to."

"Why?"

"In case the floor was on fire. In case the carpet was unbearably filthy. In case the room was flooded with water knee-deep or higher. So Mr. and Mrs. Magruder thought they were very smart people. But one night it rained a great deal, more than it had ever rained before and probably more than it ever will again. Mr. and Mrs. Magruder were both sleeping, and they were awakened by the sound of water in their bedroom, water that must have been knee-deep or higher by the time they heard it. So, in their pajamas, they went from the bed to the nightstand," and their father walked onto the bed, shaking it with his weight, then stepped onto the night table, "then from the nightstand to the dresser," and he stepped up onto the dresser, stretching his legs to reach, then, crouching atop, "then from the dresser to the desk," and he did this, "then the desk to the second shelf of the bookshelf and out into the hall."

Their father was in the doorway now. He continued. He walked to the linen cabinet. "Here they crawled onto the cabinet, hopped onto a small table, slid down the banister." His voice grew more and more distant. He was downstairs now, calling to Benjamin and Phinney. "Next, they climbed onto the table where their telephone was, then into the living room, and all the while it was still raining. By the time they got to the kitchen," he shouted, "and they got to the kitchen easily, the kitchen table was submerged in water and so were all the kitchen chairs. They tried to get back to the living room, but all the furniture was floating in the center of the room now. It wasn't where they'd put it. They couldn't move anywhere. See, they'd never planned on it raining *that* much."

Their father was down in the kitchen with their mother now, and when he said nothing more they knew the story was over.

"Do you believe it?" Phinney asked, and Benjamin said no, that the Magruders never would've gone downstairs if it was raining that much. They'd have stayed upstairs.

Benjamin is at the door. He rings the doorbell. Kim and Phinney have returned to the car to get the pie Kim baked. She'd started early in the morning, spooning apple chunks into a piecrust she'd made from scratch. Her baking had surprised him. He'd never seen Kim bake a pie before.

Mrs. Van Devere gasps when she opens the door.

"Benjamin!" and she puts a hand to her mouth.

Benjamin bends to kiss her on the cheek. "You knew we were coming," and he gives her a suspicious smile.

"Does that mean I can't get excited?" She calls out to Phinney and stands on her tiptoes, waving. "Phinney! Oh, Phinney!"

Phinney kisses her, too, and Benjamin introduces Mrs. Van Devere to Kim.

"Come here, sweetheart," Mrs. Van Devere says, "you get one, too," and she kisses Kim beside her nose, then holds her by the elbow and leads her inside.

CHAPTER 18
DID SHE JUMP OR WAS SHE PUSHED

IT'S SNOWING, THOUGH IT'S ONLY November, but the seasons have never pulled much weight in Baltimore. In Baltimore there's no telling when the sun will go cold.

"If you don't like the weather," Babisch will say, "just wait a minute," and he was right about this one. The morning sky had been clear and deep blue, and Benjamin hadn't brought an umbrella or a hat. But now the sky is as gray as Benjamin's coat. He hustles home from work, his chin tucked to his chest, snow soaking him as he tries to dodge it. When he reaches the apartment building, he shakes his arms and legs in the hallway to knock the snow from his clothes. He wipes the top of his head with his palm. He takes the elevator, removing his coat on the way. There's a note taped to the apartment door: MR. VAN D. CALLED. SAYS MRS. VAN D'S IN THE HOSPITAL IN NEW YORK. I'M AT YUMI'S. WILL FILL YOU IN IF YOU WANT—K.

The note weakens Benjamin. For a moment, he stands still, his mind racing, his fingers on the doorknob but the keys still in his pocket. He doesn't know whether to call Yumi's or walk there himself.

Finally, Benjamin yanks his coat back on, and he takes the elevator back down, then jogs to Yumi's. The air is moist and bitter against his skin, but he ignores it, and when he reaches the restaurant, Debra is at the hostess stand.

"Hi, Ben," she says, and he says hello, his breath heavy, and asks where Kim is. Debra turns and stands on tiptoe to look around the restaurant, then answers, "In the kitchen, I guess."

"Is it okay if I go back there?"

"Sure."

There are only a few people in the restaurant, and Benjamin walks to the kitchen and swings the door open. The room smells of raw fish, and Kim is in the back, wearing her kimono, stacking plates with Tamara and Verna.

"Kim, what happened?" He moves through the kitchen, winding his way past counters and crates. One crate holds fish heads: a hundred eyes staring at the ceiling, a hundred at the ground.

Benjamin moves until he's beside Kim.

"Stay calm," she says. "Earl called." She finishes stacking the plates while she talks. She wipes her hands dry on her kimono. With all the rouge on, it's hard to tell if she's been crying, but Benjamin thinks she has. Red streaks run through the whites of her eyes.

"Tell me what happened," he says.

"Mrs. Van Devere had a heart attack." She stops to pat Benjamin's arm. "Not a bad one, but a mild one. It happened when they were getting ready for bed. They were at some hotel."

"What did Earl say?"

"Well, like I said, it's not a bad one, but they're going to keep her in the hospital for a week or so. He says she'll be fine, Benjamin. He said for you to please not worry."

"Did Phinney talk to him?"

"No. He's off somewhere. I don't know where he went. I should've left a note for him, too. Oh, God, I can't believe I didn't do that." She inhales. "and the dog. I was so, you know, wound up, I forgot to walk Alphonse before I left. There's going to be pee everywhere when we get home."

Benjamin feels himself breathing. It's as if he's been holding his breath since he reached the apartment and saw the note. "Listen, honey, I'm going to go up there to see her."

"Benjamin, Earl says she'll be fine."

"Yeah, I know," Benjamin says, "but I don't want to take any chances." He nearly tells her, "That's how my mother died, heart attack." He hasn't told her yet. He's afraid that she'll overreact, though he isn't sure how. He's afraid of the implications, so he says nothing. He stretches his neck to kiss Kim on the cheek, and she wipes her hands again on her kimono before she squeezed his elbows. In a strange way, he knows that's meant to comfort him.

"How are you going to get there? Don't drive. You're too tired to drive, and you know the way your car is." The car hardly runs anymore. It makes clunking noises, like bowling pins falling.

Benjamin says, "I'll take the train. I'll call you later, okay?"

"Okay. Please give her my best." She rubs her eyes with the back of her hand and begins to stack plates again. She calls, "Tell her everything will be all right" as the kitchen door swings closed, and only then does it occur to Benjamin that she knows what she's talking about.

Benjamin says good-bye to Debra on the way out, and he walks to Howard Street to wait for the bus. The bus to the train, the train to New York, and a cab to the hospital.

There are a half-dozen other people at the bus stop, all wrapped up against the cold, all having done a better job of it than Benjamin. He shivers.

At the curb a man in a camel's hair coat and gray fedora holds the *Wall Street Journal* in front of him, the paper folded in thirds like a letter. To Benjamin, he has the look of an advertising executive. Clean, sharp, smooth, and scary, all at once. The fedora makes him look dated. Warm, though.

Behind the advertising executive, two teenage girls stand in the gutter, knapsacks slung over their shoulders, each smoking a cigarette, each trying so hard to make the act look natural that it looks unnatural, Benjamin thinks. The smoke seems to stick to their lips like candy.

"I can't believe she's dead," one of the girls says. "There's no way she did it herself. If you want my opinion, someone killed her. Murder."

"Who are you, Nancy Drew?" the other girl says. "How do you know what happened?"

"Intuition," the first one answers. "She was a terrific actress, you know. I saw her on TV a couple of weeks ago, and she looked older than she used to." The girl blows a puff of smoke.

Benjamin reaches into the back pocket of his slacks for his cigarettes. Mrs. Van Devere. He only thinks about her name. He taps the pack against the heel of his palm until the brownish tip of a single cigarette slides out, brings that to his mouth, and drags the cigarette from the pack with his lips. He returns the pack to his pocket, draws his lighter from his front pocket, and lights the cigarette. The top button of his coat comes undone, and he winces, anticipating the cold. He rebuttons it and puts the lighter back in his pocket.

He puffs on the cigarette, exhales, and draws the smoke up into his nostrils. He looks down the street just as the bus comes into view. The bus doesn't seem to be moving fast enough.

Everyone moves closer to the curb. The bus is nearly empty when Benjamin climbs on, kicking his shoes against the metal steps to free the snow. He drops a dollar bill into the coin slot beside the driver and slides into a seat beside the window. The air in the bus is stale and warm, and Benjamin wipes condensation from the window with his coat sleeve, watching the other people climb on.

The driver asks the two girls to put out their cigarettes. They protest, "Hey, what about that guy?" and try to locate Benjamin. Before they do, he crushes the cigarette against the armrest. There's still half an inch of tobacco left, and he lets it drop to the floor.

As the bus pulls onto Charles Street, people run along the sidewalks, pulling their knees up high as they slosh through the mess of gray snow. A group of young girls, most dressed in down jackets, two or three in thick sweaters, dash from awning to awning, along the same route as the bus, shielding their heads from the light snow with their purses or their hands. They file into a pizza parlor, shaking themselves dry in the doorway, and, as the bus leaves them behind, Benjamin tries to decide how old they are. He can only place them between fifteen and twenty-two. He can't imagine them being as old as Kim. He thinks he should sigh, but he doesn't.

The bus stops every two blocks to take on more passengers, all carrying umbrellas it seems, and Benjamin's surprised at the short time it takes for the bus to fill with riders. He can smell the dampness of their clothes, the sharp, warm smell of wet burlap, and the smell of their body heat, the perspiration from their armpits and collars.

He's trying not to worry. Earl told him not to.

Benjamin is the first off the bus at the train station. There's a large green-and-red wreath around the clock at the top of the building and a line of yellow taxis out front. Their exhaust pipes cough out puffs like Indian smoke signals.

Benjamin walks to the main doors, then directly to the ticket counter. The next train to New York doesn't pull out until seven o'clock. Benjamin stuffs his ticket in the pocket of his overcoat, then moves to the newsstand. *Newsweek, Sports Illustrated. Glamour.* Beneath the magazines, on a small shelf, are the newspapers. The *Sun.* The *Evening Sun.* The *New York Times,* The *Washington Post.* The *New York Daily News.* The *New York Post. USA Today.* The last three all have the same photograph on the front page: the photograph of the actress found dead in Manhattan

Benjamin takes the *Evening Sun* to the counter and pays for it. He moves to the row of phones at the far end of the station. He doesn't know where he's going to stay in New York—or how to get to the hospital—and he wonders whether he should call Mary Jude. He wonders what she'd say, and he pulls out his wallet. Tucked behind his credit card are two slips from his bank machine. One has the message he'd written to Kim: I'LL BE AT J. C. M ARTIN'S, HAPPY CHILD, GETTING A DRINK. I'D LOVE IT IF YOU STOPPED BY. BY THE WAY, MY NAME IS BEN. BENJAMIN SACKS. The other reads MARY JUDE PHONE. Below that is the number.

He drops a quarter into the phone and tells the operator that he'd like to charge the call to his home phone. The phone buzzes in his ear, it doesn't ring like the extensions in Baltimore do, and Benjamin's stomach tightens.

"Mary Jude, it's me, Benjamin."

"Benjamin." She sounds startled herself. "Is everything okay?"

"No, not really. I was wondering if you could pick me up at Penn Station and give me a lift to NYU Hospital tonight."

"Benjamin, what's the matter?"

"It's not me. It's Mrs. Van Devere. She's in the hospital." Before Mary Jude can interrupt, he says, "She's *okay*, Mary Jude, I just have to see her. My train gets in at ten-forty-five."

"I'll be there," she says, and, after neither speaks, she says, "I'll be there."

Benjamin walks into the main lobby of the station and takes a seat on one of the wooden benches. One of the janitors is polishing them with a gray rag, and Benjamin reads the paper, trying not to worry, trying to keep his mind busy. Again he thinks of Mrs. Van Devere's name.

Olympia Van Devere. It's a name that's too strong to be ill or hurt.

When the train is called, he tucks the paper under his arm and walks down to the platform with a large mass of people.

On the train, a heavy man in a navy trench coat drops into the seat next to Benjamin, both of their seats jumping when he does. Benjamin turns up the corners of his mouth and nods to acknowledge the man, then leans forward to try to pull his cigarettes out of his front pocket without standing. When he finally wriggles the pack out from beneath his overcoat, he spots the NO SMOKING sign at the front of the car. He writhes in his seat again as he pushes the pack back into his pocket.

The heavy man frowns and pulls a copy of the *New York Daily News* from his coat, throwing the paper open in front of him. Before the man turns to the horoscopes, Benjamin catches the headline on the front page again: "Did She Jump or Was She Pushed?"

It's peculiar, but he can't picture Mrs. Van Devere. He can't picture her at all, not with him, not with Earl. He remembers her doing things. Making chocolate icebox cakes. Working at Millhauser's. Kissing Earl's lips. But he can't see her doing them, and it's this that frightens him most: Mrs. Van Devere, slipping away.

The train rumbles as it pulls away from the platform. It rumbles as it approaches and leaves every platform they pass. Everything's connected when you view it from a train, Benjamin thinks. The world's connected. This state to that, this event to that. It gives the world a sense of continuity.

In Wilmington, Delaware, an old woman with crazy white hair, her face sympathetic and neatly round, takes the seat across the aisle. She puts a bag between her feet and unbuttons her coat. With navy yarn, she knits what looks to be a scarf. Another the same color is turned twice around her own neck. A grandmother, Benjamin guesses, Mrs. Van Devere's age if not older, and he watches her hands working the long needles. He can't remember ever owning a scarf. No, there had been a scarf, a plaid one. Mary Jude had given it to him one Christmas. He'd lost it at work.

Benjamin opens his newspaper, folding it in half. He read most of it in the train station, and now he finds the crossword puzzle. When he's done what he can, he fills in the remaining squares with X's, then leans back and closes his eyes, the paper on his lap.

As he travels in the dark, he thinks of Mary Jude and what they had lived through together in Baltimore, passing through time.

Phinney, in the hospital, then out of it.

The first man on the moon.

"The Buddy Deane Show" going off the air.

Three Orioles' world championships.

Nixon and Reagan.

Five years of night classes each at the University of Maryland.

Slow parties at Babisch and Julie's.

The building of Harborplace out of the docks.

Rosa.

His moods.

The Colts leaving town in the middle of the night, in Mayflower moving vans.

Spiro Agnew and Marvin Mandel.

The talk about having a baby.

He thinks and he dozes. He only wakes when the heavy man rises to exit. The man adjusts his coat, and he leaves the *Daily News,* open to the television listings, on his seat.

Benjamin looks out the window, and a faded sign on the wall reads PENNSYLVANIA STATION. The old woman is gone already. She may have gotten off in New Jersey, Benjamin thinks. There aren't many people left on the train. Still Benjamin waits, letting other riders through the aisle, and he looks through the *Daily News.* He pushes up his coat sleeve to see his watch. Ten-thirty.

Off the train, Benjamin drops both newspapers in the trash can, pausing first to examine the front page, "Did She Jump or Was She Pushed?" a head-and-torso photograph of a light-haired woman, face down, her neck twisted, a shiny gray ocean surrounding her.

Benjamin shakes his head in an exaggerated way. He's hungry, and he orders a hamburger and a grape soda at one of the shops on the main concourse. He knows that he shouldn't, that he'll wind up with an upset stomach from the grease. He soaks the hamburger in ketchup and eats it standing, then hurries to wash the taste from his mouth with the soda.

Benjamin follows the signs in the station out to Seventh Avenue, buttoning his coat. There are people everywhere, too many to count. Passing the newsstand in the foyer, he looks over the collection of newspapers. The *New York Times.* The *New York Post.* The *Wall Street Journal. Newsday.* At the end, spread out like playing cards, The *New York Daily News.* Did. Did She. Did She Jump. Did She Jump or. Did She Jump or Was. Did She Jump or Was She. Did She Jump or Was She Pushed? Did She Jump or Was She

Pushed? Did She Jump or Was She Pushed? Did She Jump or Was She Pushed? A dozen women with twisted necks.

This is, Benjamin thinks, the kind of day that people only have in books. Mrs. Van Devere having a heart attack, like my mother. Did She Jump or Was She Pushed? Like my father's jump. It's the kind of day when everything comes together in one moment, when the pieces of the past fit together like a jigsaw puzzle to make sense of the present, when a character makes some grand discovery about his life; "Oh, so *this* is what my life means!" Only nothing is coming to mind now. Everything that's happened is connected, but only by time, it seems. It doesn't amount to anything.

He leaves the building and stands in the damp air for a moment to get his bearings. He hasn't been to New York in five years, not since a convention with Babisch. He looks left then right down the avenue. He checks his watch. Ten-fifty and no sign of Mary Jude.

Benjamin waits in the cold for five minutes, smoking, searching for Mary Jude's Volvo, before he returns to the building and takes a seat on one of the benches in the foyer. He checks his cigarettes. Three left, and he shakes one out of the pack and lights it.

When it's down to the filter, he stubs out the cigarette on the sole of one of his shoes and looks out into the foyer. There she is, Mary Jude, all red hair and shapely, walking past the doorway, not looking in. She seems a little heavier, especially about the face. Benjamin lets her pass, no more than ten yards from him. He's thinking of her in the kitchen, baking cookies and tossing salads. At the kitchen table late at night, her work spread in front of her, tapping at the keys of her calculator. On the floor next to the television, reading in one of his wool sweaters, the sleeves pushed to her elbows. He's thinking of her in the bedroom. He's thinking of how he put her hair in his mouth, how she said, "Let's make a baby, honey. Something half me and half you."

Mary Jude. Two weeks before she packed her bags to leave, he'd walked into the bedroom to find her sitting on the edge of the bed, facing the window. She hadn't noticed him. She was holding a bottle of his cologne, the cap off, just sniffing it.

"Benjamin," she calls, approaching him. She smiles thinly.

He stands and slips an arm around her, and he kisses her on the neck. "It's good to see you."

She nods. Her overcoat isn't the coat he'd bought her for their anniversary, but a new one, dark red. It's an attractive, feminine coat. She's wearing a black-and-gray patterned blouse beneath it. The blouse has a high collar and no buttons on the front, and she smells perfumed and sweet. She smells just like Mary Jude, he thinks. She smells the way the apartment used to smell: the sheets, the towels, her clothes, and me.

"How's Mrs. Van Devere?" Her eyes are large and concerned.

"Fine. At least I think so. I really don't know much at all. Earl called and left a message at our place."

"Well, what is it? Do they know?"

"Heart attack. A minor one. A minor heart attack."

"Oh, God, Benjamin, I'm so sorry. This must be impossible for you." She places her hand on her chest for a moment, then gestures toward Benjamin's coat. "I remember that coat. I recognize it."

"Yeah, it's Phinney's."

"I know." She looks at him. "God," she says, "a heart attack." Then she leads him out of the building to her car. It's parked in the towaway zone with the taillights blinking on and off. Benjamin walks a step behind her, and he watches her hips as they walk. He hopes that she won't catch him looking. At the car, he notices the license plate. It's a New York State plate: LMR-653. HIS is gone.

Mary Jude starts the car, the engine turning over immediately. She flicks off the blinkers and dips her head to look for a break in the traffic.

"So," she says, "how have you been? I mean, besides what's happened today, how are things?"

"Same as always," he answers, and he sneaks another look at her as she pulls the car into the traffic. "Same job. Still working with Babisch. Still living in the same apartment. Phinney's home, though. Did I mention that?"

Mary Jude shakes her head.

"Phinney's home."

"Terrific. How is he?"

"Good. We talked him into coming out from Nebraska. He isn't working yet"—he doesn't want to tell her that Phinney's housekeeping, though he knows Phinney wouldn't hesitate to tell her—"but he's home."

"I hope it does him some good."

"How have you been?" Benjamin asks, though he isn't sure he wants her to answer. He wants to know about her and Hallyday, but he doesn't want to hear it.

"Nothing new. We've just been working on the apartment."

Benjamin turns the vents up so the hot air blows on his face, and Mary Jude turns onto Thirtieth Street.

"Do you have any plans for tonight?" he asks.

"I was meaning to talk to you about that." She looks at him briefly, then back to the road. "Benjamin, honey, you called so late, and I already had plans. I have to go back."

"I understand." Benjamin tries not to sound disappointed, and since she doesn't look back at him, he guesses that he's succeeded.

"Well, of course, you should stay at our place. There's an extra bedroom, so you can sleep there. And don't say no because it wouldn't make sense for you to stay at a hotel here. It'd be hard enough finding a place this late, and then you'll pay an arm and a leg. Okay?"

Benjamin agrees, reluctantly, and Mary Jude says, "Good. Good. There's an extra set of keys to the apartment in my purse. You know where we are now, don't you?"

Benjamin shakes his head, no, as he opens the purse. Mary Jude tells him the address, Seventy-third and Broadway, and he finds a set of keys beneath an assortment of cosmetics.

Mary Jude makes a turn onto First Avenue and pulls the car in front of NYU Hospital. Looking up at the building, pretending to take note of its size, Benjamin tries to find something to say.

"Look," he says, "I really do appreciate this, and I'm glad we'll have a chance to talk maybe."

"Listen," she says, embarrassed and apologetic, "I might not be in until late."

"Of course."

"But make yourself at home, okay?"

Benjamin waves a hand toward the building. "You're not going to come up?"

"I really don't have time to." She looks at her wristwatch, and Benjamin notices her wedding and engagement rings. They nearly sparkle with newness. "But please let her know I'm thinking of her and that I'll call tomorrow. Please. And say hello to Earl for me."

"I will." He digs his hands into the overcoat pockets. "It was good to see you, Mary Jude," he tells her.

Benjamin closes the door with a swing of his hip, then walks into the hospital. He doesn't look back at her car. He steps up to the reception desk and says, "I need to get a visitor's pass."

The woman behind the desk tells him that visiting hours have passed, and Benjamin tells her that he's here to see his mother.

"Please," he says, "I won't stay long. I just found out and took a train up from Baltimore. Here," he says, "I'll show you my ticket," and he searches for the stub of his train ticket.

The woman holds a hand out to stop him.

"It's all right," she says. "I believe you. What's your mother's name?"

"Thank you," Benjamin says. "Magruder," and the woman behind the desk flips through her rotary file.

"I'm sorry," she says, "but there's no Magruder here."

It's a moment before Benjamin shakes his head and says, "I mean Van Devere. She got remarried." The woman turns the file, then gives him a yellow cardboard pass that reads ROOM 1513.

He heads to the elevator, and the woman calls out to him. "She's probably sleeping," she says.

"That's all right," Benjamin tells her, "I just want to watch her for a while, if that's okay."

The elevator doors slide apart, and Benjamin gets on, pushes a button, then steps off on the fifteenth floor, all without thought. Room 1513 is the seventh one down on the left side of the hall, and Benjamin pushes the door open and pokes his head in the room. "Mrs. M.?"

There's no answer. He'd expected to see Mrs. Van Devere in an oxygen tent, as his mother had been, but instead she's sleeping in one of the room's two beds, and Earl is asleep in the chair next to her.

He's in the chair like Benjamin's father was for his mother. Like Kevin Purcell should have been for Kim.

Benjamin closes the door behind him. All the lights in the room are on, and the Rangers game is on the television, the sound off. Benjamin switches off the lights and moves to Mrs. Van Devere's bed. Immediately he recognizes her. This is what she looks like, he remembers, and he knows she isn't slipping away. He kisses her on the forehead, then takes a seat on the edge of the other bed.

The *Daily News* is on the nightstand between the two beds, folded in half, twisted neck facing down. By the light of the television, Benjamin reads the article, "Did She Jump or Was She Pushed?" The woman, an actress he'd never heard of, was found dead at four in the morning by a neighbor walking his dog. An open window on the eighteenth floor. No note. Her apartment door locked, the furniture in place, seemingly nothing missing. No scream. No witnesses. And the police were looking for her boyfriend, though they said he wasn't considered to be a suspect at this time.

Benjamin folds the paper again and returns it to the nightstand, trying to forget the picture and the story that sits within a foot of him. The Rangers skate back and forth, back and forth across the screen. He isn't sure who they're playing, but, despite the chill of the rink, the players look warm in their navy and red sweaters. And Mrs. Van Devere, her blankets pulled tight to her armpits, looks warm. And Earl, still wearing a leather jacket, the left sleeve tucked in one pocket, his right hand in the other, looks warm. Very warm. And Mary Jude had looked warm, too, hadn't she, though already he can't remember what she'd been wearing.

Benjamin turns sideways and pulls his legs onto the bed and sleeps that way, the wool overcoat rolled beneath his head, "Did She Jump or Was She Pushed?" on the nightstand.

Benjamin had spent last Thanksgiving at the Van Devere's. He drove out at eleven in the morning and stopped at the Bluefield Quality Bakery to get a cheesecake. While he waited for the girl to tie a string around the box he thought of Phinney in Nebraska, half a country away from Bluefield and the bakery where he'd worked that summer that everything happened. The girl let Benjamin have the cake for half-price because it was nearly closing time.

Benjamin and Earl were the only men at the table, sitting at opposite ends, the women between them. Mrs. Van Devere—next to Earl—Mrs. Kleinfelt, Mrs. Hardenbrook, Mrs. Bender, and Mrs. Dewhurst. They were all dressed in their Sunday clothes, their cotton gloves set beside their places. Benjamin was wearing corduroy slacks and an old sweater; Earl, a pressed Texaco shirt and gray slacks.

The women carried the food in from the kitchen, like the cars of a train circling the table, and when Mrs. Van Devere brought the turkey out, she set it in front of Benjamin and not Earl. When she handed him the fork and knife Benjamin realized why, and he plunged the fork in deep and strained to carve the turkey, slicing the meat to the bone.

"You know," Mrs. Dewhurst said, resting after she cleared her plate, "I've never been very fond of Thanksgiving. It always seems to me that you get up early in the morning, baste and stuff the turkey or whatever else you do, and then it's all over. Wham, bam, thank you ma'am"—she slapped her hands together and Benjamin suppressed a laugh—"everyone's eaten everything, and they don't appreciate it for a moment. It's like it was *nothing* to make Thanksgiving dinner. Nothing. They just go watch television and leave you to the dishes."

Mrs. Bender nodded. "Football."

"Stanley never watched football on Thanksgiving," Mrs. Hardenbrook said, "at least not while he was alive. He'd spend the whole day with me and the children, help me with the dishes, then take me out for a walk in the woods."

"My foot he spent the whole day with you," Mrs. Bender said.

"My foot, too," Mrs. Dewhurst added. "Your Stanley was over at our house watching football with Hal, so don't try telling me that Stanley wasn't watching football."

Mrs. Kleinfelt, at Benjamin's left, patted his hand approvingly. "I'll bet Ben wasn't like our husbands. I'll bet he never got up from the table to watch football."

Benjamin told them that yes, he had. He felt as he used to in the recliner, the same mood that had kept him there until the late hours while Mary Jude was in bed alone, the one that had come when he realized that Mary Jude didn't depend on him, that she could do just fine by herself, that he wasn't in control of both of their lives—and not even his own. Mrs. Kleinfelt had used the same tone as she did to discuss the women's late husbands. For Mary Jude, he thought, I'm as good as dead, two hundred miles away and out of her mind.

"Benjamin, did I say something?" Mrs. Kleinfelt asked.

Benjamin knew what he looked like. He'd caught this expression before, peering into shop windows, and he'd thought someone else was looking back. It was as though all the muscles in his face had given out at once, that expression like his face had collapsed under its weight. He'd been startled at how little he could look like himself at times.

"It's Mary Jude," Mrs. Van Devere whispered to Mrs. Kleinfelt. "It hasn't even been a year yet."

Now they were speaking as if Mary Jude was the one who'd died.

"Benjamin, I'm sorry," Mrs. Kleinfelt said. "I wasn't thinking. Can we talk about something else? I'd very much like to hear about your work.

Wouldn't everyone like to hear about Benjamin's work?"

"Let's talk about Benjamin's work," Mrs. Hardenbrook said. "I'm very interested in time."

Mrs. Van Devere stopped them. "Ben, can I tell you something? Now, stop me if I get out of line, but it's always seemed to me that the one thing in life we have to overcome is our own despair. Do you know what I mean? You have to *overcome* Mary Jude, if you don't mind me saying that. If we could all overcome our own despair, well, wouldn't it be wonderful if we could all overcome our despair?"

Benjamin didn't respond. This was the third time Mrs. Van Devere had told him to overcome Mary Jude, and he wasn't sure if she'd forgotten that she'd said so before or if she was merely being persistent. If I wanted to overcome Mary Jude, he thought, I wouldn't be the way I am. I don't want to overcome Mary Jude. I want to overcome myself. Then she can come back home.

"Take Henry Patchett, for instance," Mrs. Van Devere continued. "*Mr.* Patchett. He lost two wives and three dogs. *He* knew despair. Henry *Patchett* knew despair, but he overcame it. Do you know how many dogs he owns now?"

"Four?" Mrs. Bender asked.

Mrs. Van Devere nodded. "Four."

Mrs. Kleinfelt patted Benjamin's hand again. "Have you ever thought of getting a dog? Maybe a nice Labrador? That's what I have. They're beautiful dogs, and they're hardly any trouble at all."

There were three candied sweet potatoes left in a bowl on the table, all wrapped in tinfoil, and Mrs. Van Devere rose from her seat, carrying the bowl, and put one on his plate.

"I remembered how much you used to love these when you were a boy," she said, and she peeled back the foil. It looked like a flower opening, a silver flower.

"Olympia's right," Mrs. Bender said. "I mean, Mrs. Van Devere is. For every thing, its time and place, Benjamin. That's what I say."

Mrs. Van Devere placed a pat of butter on Benjamin's potato, and he ate it slowly, keeping his mouth full because he had nothing he wanted to say. For every thing, its time and place, he thought, and after dinner he carried the dishes out to the porch with Earl. Benjamin held the dishes, and Earl washed them off with the garden hose, the scraps dropping to the wet ground. Benjamin looked over at the house next door, the house that had been theirs. Now there was a family playing football in the backyard, the father throwing the ball to the children, the children shrieking with each toss.

"Ack! Ack!" the children screamed.

The symphony of barking filled the neighborhood like a fog rolling in.

"Earl, what am I supposed to do?"

"Well, I wouldn't rush out to get a dog if I were you."

Benjamin stacked the plates and wondered what would become of all the dogs when the women were gone. He imagined them dashing down the road with the speed of racehorses, and Mary Jude watching them run. "To New York, dogs," he imagined her saying, swinging her arms. "Come on all you dogs, come with me to New York," and her face was as ruddy and happy as a baby's.

Earl and Benjamin carried the wet dishes back into the house, leaving them in stacks on the kitchen counter. The Macy's Thanksgiving Day Parade was on television, and a high-school band was playing a cheery song. Benjamin knew he'd heard it before and couldn't think of its name. He sank back in a chair and listened to it with his eyelids at half-mast.

He dreamed he was happy.

Four days later he went to Yumi's for the first time.

In the middle of the night, Benjamin wakes, disoriented. He feels warm puffs of breath against his cheek, and he lifts his head cautiously. Then he remembers he's in New York in the hospital room. Her arm is around his waist. Her chest is pressed to his back.

"I always knew we'd be lying in the same bed again someday," Mary Jude says.

CHAPTER 19
BASKETBALL

"I'M BACK. I wanted to see how she is," Mary Jude whispers, "Benjamin."

Benjamin whispers, too. "I think she's going to be all right," and he doesn't pull away. Instead, he drops his head back upon his folded coat and lies there in her arms, protected.

"How did you get up here?" he asks. "How did you get up to the room?"

"I told them that I'm her daughter."

"Great. I hope no one walks in and sees us like this."

"Why?"

"Because I told them that I'm her son."

Mary Jude giggles and rubs her cheek against Benjamin's. She shifts more of her weight onto him. Her leg is on top of his, her shoes off.

"I don't think this bed's supposed to seat two," she says later, and that's where they are in the morning, when the nurse pushes Benjamin's shoulder roughly. They're in bed together, her arms about him.

Mrs. Van Devere is still asleep, but Earl isn't.

"When did you get here?" Earl asks. He stands. He has a wrestler's crouch, and he moves closer to Mrs. Van Devere's bed.

"Last night. I came as soon as I heard. I didn't want to wake you."

Earl looks at Mrs. Van Devere. He holds the bedrail firmly, as if to maintain his balance. Mary Jude slides on the bed until she is sitting beside him. She hooks her shoes with her stockinged feet and drags them closer to the bed.

"Come on," Benjamin says to Earl, "let's go get something to eat," and they stand in the corridor while Mary Jude adjusts her slip and slides her shoes on.

"She's going to be fine," Benjamin says. "I can tell."

Earl doesn't respond. Instead, he says, "Which one of the commandments is the adultery one? I always forget. It might be the seventh. Or is that the one about coveting thy neighbor's property? No, I think it's the eighth."

"Why are you thinking about that? I thought you were an atheist," Benjamin says, and then it occurs to Benjamin that Earl saw him in bed with Mary Jude. "It's the eighth, I think," and Mary Jude walks out of the hospital room closing her coat and fixing her scarf.

Mary Jude stays between Benjamin and Earl in the elevator as they descend. She walks between them once they get off, setting the pace.

They pass a small boy in a wheelchair. The boy's black-haired, like Benjamin.

"Am I going to die?" they hear the boy ask the woman beside him.

"No, no, sweetie, it's just your tonsils," the woman says, and Mary Jude suppresses a smile.

Mary Jude leads Benjamin and Earl up to Third and Thirty-seventh, to the Bagel Nosh. After they order and pay, they take their trays to a table by the window. Mary Jude nibbles one of her bagels—she ordered three—sitting beside Earl in the booth and across from Benjamin, her back to the window, her hair the sun against a gray sky. Their coats are stacked at Benjamin's side, and he sips at his coffee, which is still too hot.

"She's a strong old gal," Earl says. "She'll be fine," and Benjamin wonders if he's talking to himself or to them. "She liked the Empire State Building, by the way. She likes things like that. The oldest something-or-other, the biggest this-or-that. She likes things like that."

"Did you?" Mary Jude asks.

"Nah, you know me. It's just an old building to me. It's not enough that something's old. It's got to be interesting on top of being old." Earl chews. He doesn't seem to be looking anywhere in particular.

"Earl, there's nothing to worry about. If the doctors say she'll be fine, she'll be fine," Benjamin says. He's conscious of how often he's said "fine." He can't help himself.

"It's one of the best hospitals in New York," Mary Jude adds. She puts her arm around Earl's neck, and Earl manages a smile. Mary Jude takes her arm back.

Though Benjamin tries not to, he looks at Mary Jude. Her eyes aren't like Kim's. They're not beautiful by themselves, they're beautiful in their history. They have, Benjamin thinks, sentimental value. He makes himself look elsewhere, out the window at the traffic, at Earl, at the sugar container, but each time, in seconds, his eyes are drawn to hers. She looks left, she looks in his eyes, she looks right, she looks in his eyes, she looks up, down, everywhere, and their eyes catch, inevitably.

No one talks, they eat. Benjamin and Mary Jude staring into each other like they'd done on their honeymoon in South Caroline, when they'd felt inseparable, and though she doesn't say it, Benjamin knows that she misses him. The look on her face tells him as much. It's a look she couldn't hide if she tried.

Earl is the one who puts an end to the silence. "It's good to see you two are still talking to each other," he says to them, and neither answers.

Hallyday. Where the hell is Hallyday? Benjamin thinks, but he doesn't ask. Instead, he pulls a handkerchief from his pocket. He turns his head to blow his nose, and his ears squeak.

Earl finishes his breakfast first, and he gestures toward Benjamin's cup. "Are you ready to head back yet?" he says, and Benjamin tells him no, that his coffee hasn't even gone cold yet.

"I can't touch it until it's cold," Benjamin says.

Mary Jude grins as if she'd forgotten that. She grins recognizing the past, and, and there are tiny cracks at the corners of her eyes and mouth when she does.

"I want to be there when she wakes up," Earl says, "so I'm going to head back. You two head back when you're ready."

"We will," Mary Jude says. "We'll be right behind you. Remember how to get back?" and Earl nods.

"I've walked places before," he says. He slips his coat on without effort. "When you go back, you just do the same thing in reverse."

"We'll be there in a minute," Benjamin says.

"Take your time," and Earl leaves.

The steam is still rising from Benjamin's coffee. He lifts the cup to his mouth, purses his lips to blow into it, then slurps. It burns his tongue, and he shakes his head. "Too hot."

"They can't make it cold," Mary Jude says. It's the way she'd always responded when Benjamin had said her coffee was too hot: "I can't make it cold, sweetheart." Sometimes he'd pour ice water in if he were in a hurry, but that spoiled the taste. It always tasted muddier then.

Benjamin looks at her hand, her left one. The diamond in the engagement ring is nearly twice the size of the one in his mother's ring—the ring that had been Mary Jude's, too. The wedding band is gold with tiny diamonds embedded all the way around.

When Mary Jude returned his mother's rings, Benjamin hadn't known what to do with them. He'd thought about putting them in a bank vault, but he'd never see them if he did that. He told Mary Jude that he wanted her to keep them but she said that wasn't a good idea, they meant too much to him, so he wrapped both rings in a tissue and put them in one of the orange vials for his pills. Then he pulled off his own wedding ring. He knew it was crazy, but he could feel where the ring used to be. But rather than the finger feeling lighter without the ring, it was as if the rest of him became heavier. He wrapped his ring in a separate tissue and placed it in the vial as well. He clicked the cap in place, then put the vial in the bottom of his underwear drawer, on top of Mary Jude's note, YOU'RE OUT OF CLEAN UNDERWEAR, SO DO THE WASH ALREADY! They stayed there for a week, until the drawer was empty except for the vial and the note, and then he took the rings out of the vial and set them in the bottom of one of her drawers, empty since she'd left. The rings had stayed there until Kim moved in, and then he moved them back to his underwear drawer.

"What are you thinking?" Mary Jude says.

"Nothing."

"Benjamin, I can tell you're thinking something."

"Nothing I want to talk about."

They sit and say nothing, just looking at each other, and Mary Jude reaches across the table and grabs his wrist. She grabs it with her right hand.

"Everything will be fine," she says, and she releases his wrist and runs her hand back and forth over the back of his hand. "Whatever you're thinking about will be fine. Are you thinking about Mrs. Van Devere?"

Benjamin lies. He tells her that he is when he's really thinking about her and about Kim. He's thinking about both of them. Mary Jude and Kim, at once. He's picturing them in the same room, standing back to back like schoolgirls, trying to determine which is taller. "I'm tired of people leaving," he says. "You know, the way people just come and go and never give any reason for doing either. It's just, 'Good-bye. Take it easy.'"

"Oh, honey."

"Sometimes you meet them and they're already half gone."

"Benjamin, she's not half gone. She's going to be fine. If the doctors say so, then it's true." She's talking about Mrs. Van Devere. "They have to be careful what they say, you know. They know that if they say someone's going to be fine and they're not, they'll open themselves up to a huge lawsuit. So they only say someone's fine when they're fine."

"I'm so scared of losing people," he says, and she squeezes his fingers and stands, pulling him up with her. Mary Jude, the lifeguard. Standing next to the table, she hugs him. He tips his head onto her shoulder, and she tips her head onto his, and they stand there, tipping slightly, side to side.

"I know what you mean," she says, "losing someone you love. It's like losing a part of yourself. You lose a part of yourself, and someone else you love," she says, "never replaces that loss."

Benjamin kisses her on the cheek, and, slowly, Mary Jude breaks their embrace. "Grab your coffee," she says. "If it's not cold by the time we get back to the hospital, it'll never get cold. Not ever."

Benjamin and Mary Jude had only been in Baltimore for five months when they started taking night classes at the University of Maryland. Benjamin was at Lomax from nine o'clock until six most days, and Mary Jude had taken a job cleaning houses three days a week.

"I'm good at cleaning," she said. I'm very methodical," and she was, but the first day she'd come home complaining.

"I nearly fainted at the mess," she'd said. "Empty diaper boxes in the living room, piles everywhere—Band-Aids, magazines, neckties, books, baby shoes, food packages, coasters, slippers. I'm amazed that people can live like that." She'd dropped onto the couch. "The only good thing is that they told me to eat whatever I want, and the kitchen is jam-packed. I think that's what they call an employment benefit."

After work, she and Benjamin would eat dinner at the apartment, then walk to the university.

"Today, it was Neopolitan ice cream," she would tell him—or crackers, or a sandwich, or donuts, or whatever she'd taken from the kitchen at work.

It was usually eleven o'clock before their days were done. But Benjamin enjoyed it, and Mary Jude said she did. There was no reason to believe she didn't, and, on the walk home, they would stop off at the Blue Cloud to get a drink, to dance, to sing with Duke Monroe and listen to his stories.

Most of the other students in their class were businessmen. One sold linens. Another owned a restaurant that served lobster and crab. Two sold men's clothing. One sold toilets and sinks. Five or six sold used cars, and one sold them new.

On Saturdays, some of the men from the class gathered at the gym to play basketball. They played in the school's intramural league, against students in their late teens mostly, and, though he'd hardly ever played before, Benjamin agreed to be part of the team. He would watch them play and think of his father, dribbling the ball with both hands at once.

"Do it," Mary Jude had encouraged him. "It'll be good exercise," and she was right about that. Most Saturdays he would end up winded and perspiring, and Mary Jude would have to take tiny steps as she walked home with him.

"I'm not exactly married to Wilt Chamberlain, am I?" she teased, and Benjamin answered, "Go ahead. Give him a call. If you like him that much, I'd hate to stand in your way."

Mary Jude went to all the games sitting on the gym floor, her back against the cinder-block walls. She would study while they played, a textbook spread on her lap, and cheer whenever Benjamin ran onto the court.

"Go, honey!"

"Pass the ball!"

"That was a good one!"

"No, no, *no!*"

Mostly she remained quiet, though, and Benjamin would look over if he sunk a basket or swiped the ball from the other team. He'd look over to see her smiling.

They lost their games by lopsided margins—they're *kids* we're playing against, Benjamin would think, though they weren't much younger than he—and it wasn't until one of the last games of the season that they had a chance to win. In the third quarter, the referee blew his whistle and pulled Benjamin aside.

"You've got to take that off," the referee said. He wasn't more than twenty. There were blemishes on his nose and around the rim of his mouth.

"Take what off?"

"The ring. You have to take it off."

"What?" Benjamin protested.

"I'm sorry, mister, but you can't wear jewelry. It's the rules. People can get hurt."

"That's a stupid rule."

"I'm sorry," the boy said.

Benjamin looked over at Mary Jude and said, "Then I'm not playing."

He marched off the court and sat beside Mary Jude, his sweaty T-shirt clinging to the cinder blocks, and he wiped his forehead with a towel.

"Benjamin," one of the men called, one of the used-car salesmen.

"Come on, Benjamin, don't be a child about this."

"I won't take my wedding ring off," he explained, and another man from his class, the restaurant owner, took Benjamin's place on the court.

In five minutes, though, Benjamin stood and wrenched the ring off, and he put it in Mary Jude's hand, forcing her fingers closed around it.

"Here," he said, "hold onto this for me. I'm going to go win the game." He ran onto the court to the sound of Mary Jude not cheering, and afterwards, he wished he hadn't taken the ring off. He'd promised her he wouldn't, but he had, for a basketball game, and when he slipped it back on, it didn't feel the same. The gold felt cold, and they'd lost by twelve points.

The doctor's a young man, much younger than Benjamin, perhaps thirty, with wire-rimmed glasses and a wide forehead. His eyebrows are like thick black spiders crawling toward each other.

He tells them that Mrs. Van Devere will be all right, that she'll need rest, that the heart is the size of a fist and very delicate still, that a heart attack feels like an elephant sitting on your chest, that today eighty-five percent of those who have heart attacks will survive, that Mrs. Van Devere's was a minor one, that she'll need some morphine for the pain, that she has to stop smoking, that she has to control her diet and should exercise, that she should take aspirin, that she might experience a depression when she leaves the hospital, a depression like she's been left floating with no one to care for her, that she may be afraid that every little twinge may be a new heart attack, that she should take walks in the morning and in the afternoon, that she should increase the time of her walks each week. While the doctor tells them this, Earl seizes his wife's face in his hand, the heel against her chin, the palm along her jawbone, the fingers fingering the very bottom of the lobe of her ear.

And, for a moment, Benjamin imagines the other hand, the invisible one, along the other side of her face making the same delicate movements.

"So, she'll be okay?" Earl asks.

"The answer's the same as every other time you've asked," the doctor says, a slight grin forming. "She's going to be just fine. She'll be as good as new—better—if she follows my instructions."

Benjamin moves closer to the bed. He looks down at Mrs. Van Devere. He kisses her forehead. It's a paternal kiss, he thinks.

"You're going to be just fine. You're in good hands," he says.

And Earl corrects him. "Hand," he says.

Benjamin walks out to the sidewalk with Mary Jude.

"Want me to get a cab?" he asks, and the bitter wind rushes up his wrinkled pants leg.

Mary Jude tells him no. "I drove," she says, and she points to a parking garage across the street. "My car's there."

In the garage, Benjamin holds the stairwell door open for her. They walk up to the third level of the garage. It's marked by a large gray door with a black number three.

Mary Jude unlocks the passenger door first, and Benjamin gets in and reaches across to push open her door. She guides the car down the ramps and hands the attendant a twenty-dollar bill, then rolls her window up.

"*Twenty?*" Benjamin asks.

"Twenty," she nods, with the pride of a native New Yorker.

The radio plays as they drive uptown, and before long they're in her apartment.

"I have to get changed," Mary Jude says. "I feel like I've lived half my life in this outfit."

"Mm hmm," Benjamin answers, and he studies the apartment. It's a large one, large and extravagantly decorated. There's a strong sense of order. There are paintings and sculptures throughout the living room and oversized books on the coffee table. The vases on the end tables match the lamps. The drapes are tied back, with tassels hanging from the cords. Much of the furniture Benjamin recognizes from Hallyday's apartment in Baltimore. It may be antique. The wood of the tables and on the arms and legs of the chairs is polished, but in the halfhearted way that antiques are. It shines, but not too much.

Mary Jude turns her back to Benjamin and bends a knee. She sweeps her hair over one shoulder and unbuttons the back of her blouse, past her brassiere strap. Her skin is still dark there, and Benjamin wonders whether this is the remains of a summer tan or whether she and Hallyday were on a vacation somewhere. Maybe she even goes to one of those tanning salons.

Mary Jude pulls the bottom of her blouse free from her skirt. It hangs from her, and she twists the material to the side so she can undo the rest of the buttons. She shakes her head to let her hair fall and cover her back and puts one foot behind the other and steps out of her shoes. She draws her skirt up to her thighs and, with one hand, pulls at the waistband of her pantyhose. She pulls the right side down to her thigh, then tugs at the left side, pulls the right side, then the left, then the right again until the pantyhose are above her calves. She lets her skirt fall to cover her knees again, then, with both hands, pushes the pantyhose to her feet. Only when she does is the birthmark on her leg revealed. She pulls the pantyhose off, then bends to pick her shoes from the floor.

"I'll be right back," she says. "Grab something to drink from the refrigerator."

She walks to the bedroom, her blouse unbuttoned and hanging from her shoulders. "Benjamin, I'm having trouble with my skirt," she used to say, and he'd walk into the bedroom and find her naked except for a skirt, jerking at the zipper. "I can't get it," she'd say, but the zipper would move smoothly along the grooves when Benjamin would try. "Thank you," she'd say. "I don't know what I'd do without you," and she'd push him onto the bed. Or he'd push her, one or the other.

Now, while she undresses, Benjamin walks to the kitchen. There's a six-pack of red, white, and blue Diet Pepsi cans on the top shelf of the refrigerator. He calls to her, "So, you're drinking diet soda now, too?"

"I thought everyone was," she shouts back.

He pulls out a can and walks back to the living room, sitting on the couch, not expecting her to call him about trouble with her zipper, but not sure she won't, and soon Mary Jude returns, wearing a wool sweater, the sleeves pushed to the elbows like she'd always worn them, and a pair of Levi's. She looks comfortable in them. She looks safe. Safe in her clothes, safe in her apartment and safe in her marriage.

She sits at the edge of the cushion and turns so she can see him fully.

"I'm sorry," she says, "I forgot your girlfriend's name."

"Kimberly. Kim."

"Kim?"

"Kim."

"*Kim?*"

"Kim." He says.

"Julie said you were living with someone, last time I talked to her. Kim doesn't sound right, though. I thought she said something else. Kathy, I thought she said."

"No, I'm sure she must've said Kim."

"Can I ask you how things are?"

"Sure. Everything's all right, no problems."

"What's she like? Is she like me?"

Benjamin doesn't respond at first. "No," he says. "I don't know. Maybe.

It's hard to answer that. Sometimes I try to figure that out myself, so you'd think I'd be able to give you a straight simple answer, but I can't. Sometimes I think you two are as different as night and day, and sometimes I think that's impossible. On the surface maybe you're different—you look different, you sound different, you're different ages—"

"I heard she's very young."

"She's twenty-three, she'll be twenty-four in a couple of weeks. The beginning of January. So, on the surface, you're different, but then I think that inside you have to be a lot alike. For both of you to like me—"

"Love."

"—you'd have to have a lot of the same qualities inside. So, you must share a lot, it's just that I'm not smart enough to get beneath the surface and figure out exactly what those qualities are that make you both like—love—me."

"Reggie's a lot like you."

"Hallyday's nothing like me," Benjamin protests.

"That's not true at all. It's just like me and Kim, probably. I don't know her, so I can't say for sure, but it's probably the same thing you just described. You're not Reggie and he's not you, not physically, not emotionally, not in any way that you'd notice outright, but there's something else that makes you similar."

"Maybe."

"Are you in love with her?"

"Mary *Jude*," Benjamin looks at a painting across the room. Men and women sit on beach chairs looking at the ocean. They're wearing bathing suits—and the women wear bathing caps—but the sky is as gray as a mean winter storm. It's haunting.

"What?" Mary Jude says.

"It's not fair of you to ask that."

"Why not?"

"Because I don't think you take it seriously. I don't think it's fair of you to ask that when you're married again. I think that maybe you think it's funny or something how I *have* to date a girl in her twenties like I'm some dirty old man or something and all I care about is screwing around with her."

"Benjamin, I don't think that at all. I just want to know."

"I don't know if I can tell you how I feel. It's strange, because if someone else asks me if I'm in love with her, if Babisch asks, I can say yes or no, and it won't have any consequences. There aren't any implications. I don't have to think about what I say, I can say yes or no, whichever comes out of my mouth, and it won't make an ounce of difference. But if I tell you, it has consequences."

"I don't understand."

"It's like this. If I tell you, 'Yes, I love her,' then I have to act on it. It's like the game's up. I love her, and that's it. And if I tell you, 'No, I don't love her,' then there's no reason to keep living with her or dating her or any of that. Then it becomes a joke, sort of."

"Why is it different with me?"

"I don't know. It just is. If I tell you, I have to stick by my answer."

"Do I love her? My answer is my answer permanently."

"So, think about it for a second, then tell me. Do you love her?"

"It's more complicated than that. It's…" Benjamin says, "it's more complicated. You wouldn't understand." Benjamin realizes it's Mary Jude he's wanted to talk to about the creek, that Mary Jude's the only one who can help him.

"*Talk* to me, Benjamin. I miss talking to you."

Benjamin doesn't know how to begin, and he crosses his hands over his chest. "I haven't talked to anyone about this," he says.

"About what?"

"I feel so stupid because I can't think of any way to tell you that doesn't make it sound trivial. Kim has this scar on her chest"—he runs the fingers of his left hand over his own chest, from his throat to his ribs—"it goes from here to here, and it's about half an inch wide."

"God, that's horrible," she says. "Is she okay?"

"I think so."

"What happened?"

"To Kim? She had open-heart surgery when she was a teenager. I don't know much about it. She tried to tell me, and I didn't listen to her, I was so wrapped up in how ugly it was. Then after that I started thinking what a horrible person I am for thinking that it's ugly. Horrible. A good person wouldn't even think about that, but I did until I realized that I wasn't all that concerned about the way it looked, but about her heart itself. It's like I'm afraid that it doesn't work right."

Benjamin talks on and on about Kim's heart until Mary Jude is brushing his hair with her fingers.

"Are you afraid that you're going to lose her, that she's going to die?" Mary Jude asks.

"I'd say yes, only that makes it all sound so simple."

"Benjamin, Benjamin," she says. "Benjamin, Benjamin, Benjamin, Benjamin," her voice becoming softer and softer. She moves back on the couch until she's beside him, and she wraps her arms around him. He puts his arms around her waist, and he holds her tightly, not knowing if he's doing it because he's missed her or because he's finally talked about the creek.

"You're the best friend I ever had," he tells her.

"Me, too," she says.

Twenty minutes later Mary Jude says, "We have to cut this out. We have to go," and they break their embrace. She drives Benjamin back to Pennsylvania Station, and there, quickly, she kisses him good-bye. And though neither's lips part, the kiss has the familiar aimlessness of lovers' kisses. The familiar linger. It is a kiss, he knows, that they will both have to live with.

"Remember," she says, grazing his hair with her fingertips, "We'll always be related."

CHAPTER 20
BENJAMIN SANK

"BEN," KIM SAYS, poking her head into the bedroom, "it's for you," and she holds the phone out, her palm over the mouthpiece. She's still dressed in her kimono, but she's wiped the makeup off with a washcloth. "It's Mary Jude," she mouths, and Benjamin takes the phone.

It's two days since Benjamin's return from New York, and Kim remains in the doorway while Benjamin brings the phone to his ear. He holds up his index finger, letting her know he'll only be on a minute, then closes the door as much as he can, the curlicue of the phone cord flattened between the door and the frame.

"Mary Jude," he says, quietly, stretching the cord into the room until the curls disappear.

"Benjamin, how are you, honey?"

"Fine, fine. You?"

He feels as if he's about to sweat.

"Fine. That was Kim, wasn't it?"

"Mm hmm," Benjamin answers. He sits on the edge of the bed.

"She sounds very nice."

After a pause he says, "It was good to see you, up in New York."

"Yes, it was, wasn't it?" Mary Jude says. "Have you spoken with Earl again?"

"Uh huh. I spoke to him and I spoke to Mrs. Van Devere for a little bit."

"How does she sound?"

"Chipper, very chipper," he says. "But you know the way she is. She was more concerned that she was a bother to us."

"Oh, the dear."

"They'll be headed home this weekend."

"Good," Mary Jude says, "that's good news." Then, "Benjamin, there's something I wanted to tell you, some more good news."

"What's that?"

He wonders if she's about to say that she's still in love with him, or that she's leaving Hallyday, but instead she says, "Benjamin, we're going to have a baby. Reggie and me. I'm already two months in, and you know how I feel about babies. I would've told you in New York, but I didn't think it was the right time to tell you with Mrs. Van Devere in the hospital and all. You know, the timing was wrong." She coughed.

It was a surprise, more of a surprise than when he learned she was marrying Hallyday. It's funny, Benjamin thought, how I never even considered they might sleep together. It's the way I go through life, assuming that everyone else is a part of my life, and never consider the extent to which everyone else thinks of himself as being in his own life, and how I'm just a part of it.

His mind strays further and further from Mary Jude, like Alphonse set loose from his chain.

I never considered the extent to which Mary Jude had her own life, with her parents in it, and me, and her friends, and Reggie, and now a baby, too. I never considered the extent to which Phinney has his own life, and Kim, and how I'm just a part of it. It's like the world is a book, *My Life*, and everything in it only reflects on me, the central character. No one exists except when I'm with them or when I'm thinking of them. It's like they're in cold storage. Deep freeze. Even now, he thinks, I'm trying to figure out how their baby fits into *MY Life*.

"You know how it is with women my age," Mary Jude continues. "I'm getting up there, in years, and if I didn't have one soon, I'd probably never have one. But my doctor ran tests, and he says I'm doing great, and the baby will be fine. They don't know what it's going to be yet, boy or girl, but I have a feeling it's a boy. Just a hunch."

This is the first time I've thought of anyone else having a life separate from mine, he realizes. This child's. Listening to Mary Jude talk, her voice bright and bouncy like the women in detergent commercials, he realizes what it was Mary Jude was living without during their marriage. Hallyday does love her, he thinks.

Benjamin holds the phone like he's holding her wrist.

"What's it like?" he asks.

"I don't know. I haven't noticed any major changes yet. I must pee fifty times a night now, but that's about it."

"Really? Fifty times?"

"Close. It seems like I spent half my time going to the bathroom now. And I'm getting fat. God, Benjamin, I gobble down anything I can get hold of and shove it in my mouth. I've already gained eight pounds. I can feel the extra weight. But other than that I really don't feel all that different. I feel the same as I always have except that once in a while I just think about how I've got this little baby inside of me."

"Mary Jude," Benjamin says, "I'm happy for you." And he is. Happy for her, not for himself. "Congratulations. Sincerely. Honestly. Truly. And congratulate Hallyday for me."

"I will."

"Good."

Kim has a life, too, separate from mine. I'm just a part of it, a recent part.

"You know what I've been thinking, Benjamin? I've been thinking how we're so far away from each other now, but how the bitterness is gone because of it. It's like God gave it to us so we can stay close."

"We will. I promise," Benjamin tells her. "Will you let me know how you're doing—you know, how the pregnancy's going—and call me when he's born? Or when she's born?

"Mm hmm."

"Promise?"

Mary Jude laughs, "Promise. Cross my heart," then, after a moment, she says, "I love you, Benjamin."

It catches him by surprise.

"I didn't hear that," he says, and she laughs again and repeats herself.

"Me, too. Congratulations." He's known her forever, and even now he feels he has to love her. He has to love Mary Jude, or else.

"Will I see you again?" she asks.

"Soon," he promises.

They say good-bye, and Benjamin opens the door and takes the phone to the living room, dragging the cord back with him. Kim and Phinney are watching television, Phinney sprawled on the couch, Kim in the recliner. Alphonse is on her lap.

"Is everything okay with Mary Jude?" Kim asks, and her concern is real. He can tell from her eyes. It occurs to Benjamin that she's been calling Mary Jude Mary Jude lately.

"She's, well, she's going to have a baby, her and Hallyday."

Phinney just looks at Benjamin, and Kim bows her head.

"Isn't that great?" Benjamin says.

Kim lifts her head. "Are you all right?" she says, and Benjamin nods.

He remembers Mary Jude's voice when she said she had "this little baby" inside of her. Her voice nearly cracked on her words. Her voice was always on the verge of cracking, never more so than when she tried to sing on Benjamin's birthday. "Happy birthday to *you*, happy birth*day* to you," she'd sing, and the words would crumble like cookies.

He'd been at Mrs. Magruder's for more than a year when the dream came to him. It wasn't a daydream. It wasn't the kind he could manipulate and twist until it ended happily, until Mary Jude was in his arms. No, it was his mind at work behind his back.

He was at the pool, and Mary Jude was swimming laps, and the news of his father on the roof of the hospital came in over the transistor radio, just as it really had. Benjamin jumped up and ran to the edge of the pool, and he shouted for Mary Jude to help him. She kept swimming, back and forth, unable to hear. Finally, he jumped into the pool to stop her, but he couldn't. She swam past him, and, when he stood in her path, she seemed to swim through him.

Benjamin climbed out of the pool and ran to his bicycle. He pedaled as fast as he could, his head bouncing. Though Elmira was twenty miles away, he could see the hospital ahead, at the top of a hill. His legs chugged, but the hill became steeper and steeper, almost a mountain, until he fell off the bicycle and onto his back. When he stood, balancing himself against the incline of the hill, the bicycle was gone. He began to run up the hill, and as cars passed he waved for them to stop and called, "Stop! Help me!" but none did.

The hospital didn't get any closer, and he passed a man selling ice-cream cones from a cart. Benjamin stopped and bought a popsicle, but the man took it away and put it back in the wrapper when Benjamin didn't have the money to pay for it.

He ran up the hill, the cars speeding past him, a different ice-cream vendor every twenty yards or so. He passed a park, where it was raining, and there were a thousand umbrellas overturned, catching the rainfall.

He ran up the hill, and there were the children from his speech class singing in a choir. They were all dressed in black robes, standing in a row, each one holding the hands of the children next to him, only there was a gap near one of the ends where two of the students stood, three feet apart, their free hands holding the air where Benjamin should have been. They sang "Rudolph the Red-Nosed Reindeer" but with their speech impediments intact, uncorrected, all W's instead of R's and R's instead of L's. It sounded like gibberish.

"There's Ben-german!" one shouted, spotting him. They began calling his name.

"Ben-german!" another said.

Then, "Bendamin Sacks!"

"B-b-b-b-enjamin!"

"Den!"

"Denjamin Thacks!"

"Benjamin Sank!"

"Ben-german!"

When he finally reached the hospital, there was a figure on top of it the size of a marble. No one paid any attention to the figure. Doctors and nurses walked in and out. Some were eating ice-cream cones, some were driving ambulances and wearing fur coats, some were dancing in the parking lot.

"Benjamin, catch me," said his father, and he jumped from the roof, getting larger and larger as he fell, falling and laughing. Benjamin realized he was wearing his baseball mitt on his left hand. He hustled to position himself beneath his father, but his father seemed to drift as he fell, first left, then right. And, as he fell, he became larger and larger until it seemed that he would crush Benjamin flat.

Benjamin heard screams, and when he woke he didn't recognize immediately that they'd been his own. He thought they sounded like his father's.

He only had that dream once, and Mrs. Magruder was in the room quickly to calm him. But he's thought about it often since. He'd daydream about it and have to go down to Mrs. Magruder's kitchen to get something to eat. Or close the door to his office. Sometimes, sitting in the recliner, considering the past, he's remembered the dream as if it were the past. By doing that, it became the past. Always, it was him, circling beneath the falling figure with his baseball glove.

Sometimes the figure was his father, falling and laughing.

Sometimes it was Phinney.

Sometimes it was their mother.

Sometimes it was Mrs. Magruder.

Sometimes it was Earl.

Occasionally it was Babisch.

Sometimes it was Mary Jude.

And always, the bodies grew larger and larger, to their actual size, then beyond. And Benjamin couldn't catch any of them.

When Benjamin goes to bed, he thinks about the dream, and he imagines Mary Jude falling, only this time she remains the size of a marble. She never grows larger, she just tumbles toward him. He's prepared to catch her in his mitt, but suddenly someone else snatches her. Though he can't see who, Benjamin knows it's Hallyday.

It's my dream, Benjamin thinks, my mind. It's my mind, he thinks, that made Hallyday catch her. He's a better man than I am, and Benjamin shifts his weight in the bed, preparing to go to sleep.

But then there's another figure on the roof. She calls his name.

"Benjamin," she calls. "Here I come," and she leaps, and she, too, grows larger and larger. It's Kim, he knows, but he still doesn't know why she's on the roof.

This is what Benjamin's thinking when Kim kisses him good night. She puts her mouth over his and holds her hair so it won't fall across her face.

"Are you sure you're doing all right?" Kim asks. "I mean, about Mary Jude and the baby. You seam to be breathing differently or something." She puts her hand flat on his chest and lets it rise and fall with his breath.

He lies. "I'm fine. I'm just tired out today. Thanks for asking, though."

"Well," she says, "if you want to talk, you know where I am. I'm just an arm's length away." She's propped up on one elbow now, looking at him. "I've never, you know, had to deal with something like this, but it might help if you talked to someone. Just wake me if I'm sleeping, okay?"

Benjamin doesn't move.

"Okay?" she repeats.

"Okay. I promise."

She kisses him again, on the forehead this time. "Night sweetie," she says, then she falls on her back.

Babisch isn't in. He's at a convention.

"I'm off to Pittsburgh," he'd said Monday morning, "the City of the Angels."

Benjamin said, "That's Los Angeles."

Babisch looked at his airline reservations. "No, no, it's Pittsburgh," and left the office chuckling.

He's still there, in Pittsburgh. There are just photographs of him and Julie, and of him and Benjamin, occupying his office. He's out of town for a week, and Benjamin wishes he wasn't. He wants to talk to him about Mary Jude and her baby.

Benjamin sits in Babisch's office, in his chair. He picks up the phone and dials Babisch's number at home, and when Julie answers she says, "I'm sorry, Benjamin, but Frank's not home."

"I know, I know. I just called to give you some news." And he tells her about Mary Jude and the baby. At first Julie sounds excited, her voice jumping, but soon she asks Benjamin, "Are you all right?"

Benjamin tells her yes, he's fine, but it's the same question Mrs. Van Devere asks when he calls her at the hospital: "Benjamin, are you all right?"

"I'm fine," he tells her, too. "You're the one who's in the hospital. I'm supposed to ask you that."

"So, go ahead."

"Are you all right?" he asks.

"Fine and dandy," she tells him. "I feel great."

"Good," Benjamin says. "Good."

"Your phone bill's going to be enormous if you keep calling."

"Please don't worry about my phone bill when I'm worrying about you."

"Listen," she says, "thanks again for coming up to New York to see me. That was stupid of me."

"What?"

"I don't know, what happened with my heart. It was stupid of me. I'm sorry you had to come all the way up here."

"Don't say that. Of course I was going to come. Wild chickens couldn't have kept me away."

Mrs. Van Devere laughs.

"It was nice of you," she says. "You and Mary Jude."

"She cares, too."

"Well, I'm really glad you were there. Earl said that you two still look very nice together."

Benjamin groans. "Mrs. Van Devere, I already told you she's pregnant."

"I know, but that doesn't change everything. Stranger things have happened in this world." She hesitates. "Anyway, I really am doing fine. I haven't had a single cigarette since it happened. I know that it's only been a couple days, but you know how I am." She says, "Remember when we used to share packs of cigarettes?"

"Uh huh. I remember that."

"Well, not anymore."

"Good," Benjamin says. "I'm glad to hear that. So, is there anything else new?"

He wanted her to talk about Mary Jude again.

"No. Me and Earl are the same as always."

"Listen, is there any chance that you and Earl could make it here for Thanksgiving? Kim and Phinney and I are going to cook, and we'd like to have you here."

"That's nice," she says. "I'm sure I'll be up and around by then. I'll have to ask Earl though, but I'm sure he'll say yes. I have to ask him as a courtesy."

"Frank Babisch," Benjamin says, "and his wife Julie will be here, too. So it'll just be the…one, two, three, four, five, six, seven. It'll just be the seven of us."

"I'll talk to Earl," she says. "Now, Benjamin, your phone bill," and soon she's saying good-bye. She doesn't mention Mary Jude again.

He returns to his office and closes the door to review shipping orders. He leafs through them mindlessly, keeping his hands busy. Then, at ten o'clock, Benjamin calls home. He doesn't remember if Phinney's working or not today. He doesn't remember if Phinney had breakfast with him this morning. He doesn't remember if Kim was there, either. She must have been, he tells himself, or who made the coffee? It was already made when he arrived in the kitchen.

Phinney answers.

"Do you have lunch plans?" Benjamin asks.

"Me? Who would I have lunch plans with?"

"I don't know. I thought maybe the mayor was interviewing new housekeepers. Look," Benjamin says, "why don't you come meet me at my office and I'll take you out to lunch or something."

Phinney says, "Good," and when he shows, he's wearing painter's pants with splashes of red and blue all over them like gashes had been opened in him and paint had run from the cuts. Benjamin introduces him to his secretary, then leads him out of the building.

They walk down St. Paul Street, an odd couple, the tall handyman, the short businessman. Their pace is relaxed as they approach Harborplace, the two green-roofed buildings on the waterfront. There are restaurants and fast-food stands in one building, shops in the other, and Benjamin and Phinney walk into the first building.

They talk about nothing really, until, suddenly, Benjamin says, "I keep waiting, Phinney."

"For what?"

"For everything to make sense. To figure out what my life means. I don't want to be maudlin here and spoil our lunch, but I don't understand what it means. I thought maybe you would know."

Phinney shakes his head from side to side. "It doesn't mean anything, Benjamin."

"It must. It must mean something. There has to be some theme to it."

"Why? Life's just a bundle of incidents. All you can hope to do is to handle them well and to be a good person. Try to be happy. Try to make other people happy."

"Is that what you think?"

"Yeah."

"Really?"

"Really," Phinney answers, "but remember that you're asking a crazy man."

"You're not crazy," Benjamin whispers. "Don't say that anymore."

Phinney lowers his head and says, "Okay. I won't. I'll just think it."

They order fried chicken in one of the fast-food places, and while they wait, Benjamin asks, "Phinney, are you still miserable?"

"Sometimes. Sometimes not."

"Good. At least one of us is making progress," and, when they're finished with their meals, they move into the other building. They look into the shop windows. A running-shoe store. A men's store. A hat store. A game store. A card shop. A puppet shop.

Benjamin looks at the puppets through the window. There's a yellow chicken in the window.

"Hang on a second," Benjamin says and walks into the shop. The puppet's on a wooden peg, and Benjamin takes it down and stuffs his hand into it.

"What do you think?" He pinches his fingers and thumb together to make the chicken's beak flap. "What do you think?" he repeats in a screechy voice, pretending it's coming from the chicken's mouth and not his own.

"For Kim?"

"No," Benjamin says, "for the baby." The baby, the child of a beautiful woman he will never get out of his mind.

CHAPTER 21
WE DON'T NEED A WELL

"THIS IS MY FIRST THANKSGIVING DINNER," Kim says. It's the Sunday before the holiday, ten in the morning, and she's leaning on the handle of the shopping cart, steering it down the cereal aisle. Her steps are small. "The first Thanksgiving dinner I've ever prepared, I mean."

"I know," Benjamin says.

Kim takes a bag of croutons off the shelf. "Stuffing," she announces, and she places the bag in the cart.

"You don't have a list?"

"Nope."

Mary Jude always had a list. She was efficient, even systematic. She had the items grouped by their aisles, and she could steer her cart happily through the store, from the freezer section to the breads and cereals, barely stopping as she filled it.

"Did I tell you what happened last year?" Kim says.

"Unh uh."

"Remember last year there was that scare about spoiled turkeys?"

"Unh uh."

"Well, on the television the guy from Channel 11 news said that there was some brand of turkeys that was spoiled and that if you bought one you were supposed to bring it back to the store and they'd give you a new one.

They'd replace it because it was spoiled and you couldn't eat it. So my mother hadn't heard anything about it, and at dinner, right there at the dinner table, Christie said, 'Mom, this isn't one of those spoiled turkeys, is it?' and, like I said, my mom hadn't heard anything about it. She'd thrown away the plastic that the turkey came in and she couldn't remember what brand it was."

"So, you didn't eat it?"

"Of course we *ate* it, silly. It was Thanksgiving. But when we were done we just sort of sat around the table for three or four hours waiting to get sick."

She pushes the cart up another aisle.

"Of course," she says, "no one really got sick. It was sort of psychosomatic—is that the right word, psychosomatic?—it was sort of psychosomatic the way everyone started thinking that they maybe had a stomachache, but no one really was sick."

She lifts a bag of potatoes from the shelf and puts it on the rack beneath the shopping basket. She zigzags through the store, retracing her steps.

Potatoes.

A turkey. Twenty pounds, prebasted. "Do you think it's safe?" Benjamin asks.

Celery stalks. "For the stuffing," she says, "you'll see."

Lettuce. Tomatoes. Cucumbers. Radishes. Red peppers. She puts all the vegetables in the same plastic bag and twists a red tie around.

Eggs. "For the stuffing, too. Geez, haven't you ever had stuffing before? Are you from Mars?"

Cranberry sauce. "It doesn't matter if no one *eats* it. It's not Thanksgiving unless you have cranberry sauce. You can look it up. Besides, what if Frank says, 'Hey, Benjamin, where's the cranberry sauce?' What'll you do then?"

Rice.

Two bottles of salad dressing, Italian and Thousand Island.

Fig Newtons. "Dessert for you."

Flour. Butter. Apples. Sugar. "Dessert for the normal people."

Pears. Oranges.

"That's it," she says. "Thanksgiving in a basket," and she pushes the cart toward the checkout line.

"No bread?" Benjamin asks.

"Nope. You've got to get that the day before or else it'll go stale."

In the checkout line, there's a black woman ahead of them with a small girl standing in the cart, in the midst of boxes and bottles. The girl looks like a package herself. She's wearing a pink parka and pink corduroy pants, and she looks like the children on television commercials. She has an enormous white smile and eyes as wide as an adult's, only hers seem innocent set in such a small face. It's as if the rest of her hasn't caught up with her eyes.

"Honey, be still," the woman says to the girl. "You'll squash the cookies. You'll squash the…see, you just squashed the cookies. Now all the cookies are broken. See? You better not say a word when I give you broken cookies."

"I won't," the girl says. "That's the way I like them."

Behind Benjamin and Kim are two gray-haired women in their fifties, both white. They're reading the *National Enquirer,* and one woman is telling the other about a palm reader: "And she told me that my husband and I were married in another life. What do you figure the odds are of that? It's got to be a million to one, don't you think?"

Benjamin tries to ignore them so he won't laugh, and he can tell Kim's doing the same. The woman ahead of them moves through the checkout, and her daughter stays in the cart as it fills with brown paper bags.

Benjamin and Kim stack their items on the conveyor belt, and the man at the register rings them up, passing them over the electronic eye. He frowns when he sees the vegetables in a single bag. He undoes the tie and, item by item, weighs the vegetables on the scale. He's wearing a red apron and thick glasses. On the apron it says WE'RE HERE TO SERVE YOU BECAUSE WE CARE. When he's done with the vegetables he puts them back in the plastic bag and twists the tie.

"Forty-eight dollars," he says when all the items have passed, "forty-eight on the nose. You couldn't do that again if you tried," and Kim pulls two twenty-dollar bills and a ten from her purse before Benjamin opens his wallet.

"It's on me. I'm working again, remember?"

The woman behind them says to her friend, "Imagine being married to Walter twice. Now I feel like I've been cheated out of one entire lifetime."

Kim helps Benjamin load the brown paper bags into the backseat of the car, holding the passenger seat forward for him. They reach the apartment building just as Phinney does. He's returning from church, walking, wearing his gray suit and his old Burberry overcoat, the one Benjamin's been wearing for nearly a year now.

Kim's cradling the turkey in her arms like a new mother. "So," she says to Phinney as he approaches, "did you enjoy yourself?" and Phinney grins. He seems almost embarrassed, unable to stop smiling, and he reaches to take one of the grocery bags from Benjamin.

"It was great," he answers. He opens the door to the apartment building, then holds it open with his leg so Benjamin and Kim can pass.

"What happened?" Benjamin asks.

"Nothing special. It was just a good, quiet, honest-to-God mass. I'm beginning to feel very comfortable there. I recognize some of the people. I know the priests' names. I'm just feeling," he smiles, "comfortable."

Kim smiles at him, a huge, wide smile, and she gets up on tiptoe to kiss his cheek, the turkey between them. She continues to cradle the turkey on the elevator.

"Rockabye, Tom Turkey," she says once they're in the apartment, and she leaves it on the kitchen counter while she dresses for work.

Their last Thanksgiving together, Benjamin and Mary Jude flew to Nebraska to see Phinney. In September they'd booked their flight out of Baltimore-Washington International, and the day before Thanksgiving they arrived at the airport four hours before takeoff. We're being orderly, Benjamin thought, and Babisch and Julie drove them to the airport, leaving them at the curb.

They didn't carry much luggage with them, only one suitcase each, enough clothes for three days. Clothes and food. Mary Jude had packed a Virginia ham at the bottom of her suitcase for Thanksgiving dinner.

"It's a special treat," she said when Benjamin had caught her packing it. "Phinney will *love* it."

They went to the ticket counter to get their seat assignments, and they didn't check their luggage.

"We'll carry it on," Benjamin told the woman at the counter, "to save time," but the alarm at the metal detector rang when they passed through. Mary Jude had set the alarm off. She passed through the metal detector twice more, then handed one of the guards her bag. The ham showed up on the X-ray machine as an oblong metal box, and she said, "It's just a ham," but security guards popped open the suitcase and piled its contents on the counter. Her brassieres, her underpants, her blouses, her slacks, her shoes, her pantyhose, and a ham tin.

"It's just a Virginia ham," she objected. "It's a ham for God's sake."

"Jesus, it's just a ham," Benjamin repeated, but one of the guards held his hand up to quiet them.

The other guard, the taller of the two, held the tin at arm's length, trying to read the label.

"See, it's a ham," Mary Jude continued. "It's from Virginia. That's where they grow hams."

"I'm sorry, ma'am, but there could be something dangerous inside."

"It's a ham," Benjamin said. "What's she going to do, threaten to clog up someone's arteries with it? It's a *ham*," but the guard took it to a small room behind the metal detector, then returned the tin to her after nearly thirty minutes. He returned it to her opened.

"Just a precaution," he said, and Mary Jude said, "How am I supposed to carry it now?"

She put it in a plastic shopping bag and carried it separately. The plane smelled of the ham for three hours, and, though it was fine when they ate it in Phinney's apartment, Mary Jude was inconsolable. She wouldn't eat any of it. She pouted. She just ate potatoes and corn and hardly spoke.

"They messed with our holiday," she said. "They ruined it," and she spent most of the day sullen and sad, cleaning Phinney's apartment for him. She dusted his tables. She wet-mopped the floors.

Benjamin drops his coat on the recliner when he and Kim return from Yumi's. It's nearly midnight, and Kim goes directly to the bathroom to get out of her kimono.

"Someone has to do the laundry," she calls from behind the closed bathroom door. "I vote for you," she tells Benjamin, and he passes the door on his way to the bedroom.

"I vote for you," he says.

"Then it's a tie again. I guess we'll do it together."

Benjamin sits on the edge of the bed, a tiny squeak emerging from the mattress, and he bends to take off his shoes.

Kim walks from the bathroom to the bedroom. Her hair is out of its ponytail. It hangs loosely, like town lace across her forehead and upon the back of her neck. She's wiping her face dry with a washcloth, sweeping off her makeup, and when she's done she turns to toss the washcloth down the hall and into the bathroom. It lands on the floor. Her T-shirt reads I'M A BIG SISTER.

Benjamin stares at the T-shirt.

"I was thinking," Kim says, and she sees the expression on Benjamin's face. She looks down at her chest, then back at him. "I found it under the kitchen sink with some other rags," she says, and she grasps the bottom of the T-shirt in one hand, wagging it. "I figured it was Mary Jude's or something," she says.

He starts to correct her, to say, "It's Mary Jude," before he realizes that's what she said.

"Is it okay if I wear it?"

"Sure," he says, though it isn't, and he doesn't know why. Kim in the Big Sister shirt. She's so much younger than Mary Jude. She's younger than her own sister, Christie. She's older than Rosa, Mary Jude's Little Sister, but even so, not by much. Rosa, Benjamin thinks, must be fifteen or sixteen by now.

"I was thinking," Kim says, "that maybe we should get some nuts or something for Thanksgiving dinner. You know, mixed nuts still in their shells. We'll just put them out in a bowl with a nutcracker or something. That's what my mom always does."

"That sounds like a good idea," Benjamin says, and as Kim sleeps he lies half-awake and on his back. He dreams that he's in the front yard of the house in Bluefield. His parents', not Mrs. Magruder's. He's clipping the hedges. His back is to the street, and when he slides around to shear the other side of the hedge he sees dozens of tanks headed up the road. They're army tanks like the ones in the movies, but they're all painted yellow, a brilliant Day-Glo yellow.

He ducks behind one of the bushes to see where the tanks are going. They stop in front of the house, and some men pop their heads out and begin speaking to one another. Benjamin's too far away to hear what language it is.

He looks to the sky, and it's filled with paratroopers, thousands of them. They're dressed in bright yellow, their parachutes the same color, all of this making the sky look like the board in a children's game. One by one they drop onto the lawn. Thousands of them, and they land only on the Sackses' lawn, not on any of the neighbors'.

Benjamin puts his hands on the top of his head to protect himself and runs to the backyard. Men in red uniforms stand by the well, drinking from its bucket, laying out maps on the ground, loading rifles. Their uniforms are as bright as those of the men in front. They all look like toy soldiers who've just come out of their boxes.

"Here, Benjamin," one of the men says, only what he says isn't "here, Benjamin," it's "Hee-wa, Ben-german."

None of the men in the red uniforms speak correctly.

"Take thith," another man says, and he pushes a rifle toward Benjamin. Benjamin grabs it instinctively. He's never held a rifle before. It feels heavy and uncomfortable.

"Who are we fighting?" Benjamin asks.

"The men in the wewwow wuniforms."

"But who are the men in the yellow uniforms?"

There's a crackling sound around them, and Benjamin's frightened. His eyes jump to see what's happening. The men in red drop to the lawn, each grabbing his head or his chest or his belly. Their mouths open, and nothing comes out.

Benjamin runs to the porch and pulls open the screen door. He goes into the house. From the kitchen he watches as every last one of the men in red falls to the ground and the well explodes. The yellow men flow into the backyard from both sides of the house and inspect the bodies. Then one of the men points to the house and says something to the others. Benjamin can't hear him, but because the man is yelling it's easy to read his lips: "Benjamin Sacks must be in the house!" and the men charge to the porch.

There's a row of cabinets under the stove, four doors that open up to a storage space of about two feet by eight feet. It's where the pots and pans were kept, and Benjamin opens the two middle doors and sweeps all of the pots and pans to the floor. He crawls in, still hugging the rifle, and pulls the doors closed.

Lying under the stove in the blackness, careful not to make a noise, Benjamin closes his eyes tight and listens to the soldiers in the house.

"He's not in the bathroom."

"I checked the bedrooms."

"Ollie ollie oxen free."

They speak perfectly.

"Come out, Benjamin. We're taking you to the hospital. You can be with Phinney there."

"Find him."

"Are you sure he's here? He's not in the den."

Benjamin begins to grow confident. They're not going to find me, he thinks. They're not going to find me!

But then, "Have you checked under the stove?" It's a woman's voice, strong and girlish still. "Benjamin, will you tie the trash bags tighter so Mrs. Magruder's dog won't get at it. Phinney, finish your dinner. Boys, it's dinnertime. Eugene, we don't need a well."

It's his mother's voice. She's the one who betrays him.

Benjamin wakes.

He stares at the ceiling.

He stares at the window.

He stares at the back of Kim's head, then rolls off the bed and walks to the bathroom. He opens the medicine cabinet and puts three of his pills on his tongue. He sucks on them like he's sucking on candy.

Someday, he fears, I'm going to become immune to the taste of strawberries, and then what?

He shuts off the bathroom light and moves to the living room. Quietly, he lifts the phone from an end table and takes it into the hallway so he won't wake Phinney, asleep on the couch. He sits on the floor, holding the phone on his lap, and dials. He dials Babisch's number and lets it ring ten times before hanging up. He doesn't know where they are. They're always home, Babisch and Julie. They're always there, but they aren't now. He dials their number again five minutes later. No answer, and he lets it ring twelve times. Again he calls, and again, every five minutes or so. He lets it ring. He isn't just dialing the phone, he knows that. He isn't waiting for Babisch and Julie to answer. No, he's sending out a signal.

Eight rings.

Eleven rings.

Eight rings.

Fifteen rings.

Six rings.

Ten rings.

He's sending out an SOS.

He was in the first grade and seven years old, his hair still black all the way around, and there were few letters of the alphabet he was able to say correctly. It was as if he had a language all his own, and an ugly one at that, made up of tripping consonants. He rolled his *R*'s, his *S*'s came with spit, his *TR*'s sounded as *FR*'s. His parents could understand the language, but his classmates and teachers couldn't, and Phinney prayed for him at night, placing his fingertips against Benjamin's lips.

"Heal this mouth," Phinney would command.

Benjamin's mother was patient and gentle about it. Every night she took her son to the kitchen table and practiced with him, the two of them laughing, Benjamin on her lap. "You can't speak like Benjamin anymore," she'd said. "You have to speak like us. You have to speak like the rest of the world."

His mother would set an object on the table, and Benjamin would name it. She would set a truck down, and he would work until he could say it, until he could say "truck," the word a chick from its eggshell. And when he was done with one, they would move on to the next.

*Screw*driver.

High *heels*.

*Pow*der.

Fork.

Arti*ch*oke.

Cere*al*.

*Bl*ouse.

Envel*ope*.

They came slowly, but they came, until there was one left, one more sound that would end the lessons, one more sound that would pull him from his mother's arms once he'd perfected it. His mother went to the cabinet and returned with a yellow-and-red box of cookies. She set the box down on the table.

"Go ahead, have one," she said, and Benjamin opened the box and pulled a cookie out. He bit into it and tore it in half. The cookie was both gritty and sweet.

"Now, Benjamin, say it. You can do it," she said. "What are you eating? Say it, sweetheart. Say Fig *Newton*."

And he would say, "Fig Nubon," night after night, until she carried him to bed, until he was already in the fifth grade, through boxes of cookies and missed television shows.

But she was patient with him. "Good night, Fig Nubon," she would say as she lowered him into his bed.

He was eleven before he could say it right.

His father had been patient, too, with both him and Phinney. It was he who'd taught them how to write. He'd taught them at the beach, a little each trip.

When they went to Ocean City, Benjamin and Phinney walked along the beach behind their parents, trying to step in their footprints. Their mother packed a basket with fruit and drinks, and the four of them would lay a blanket on the sand, beneath the sun until it disappeared.

Their father would take them close to the water, where the sand was damp from the tide and the salt from the breaking waves blew in the wind. Dragging the heel of his foot, he would write the alphabet in the sand, first in lowercase letters

abcdefghijklmnopqrstuvwxyz

then in upper

ABCDEFGHIJKLMNOPQRSTUVWXYZ.

The alphabet stretched for fifty yards or more, around the blankets and umbrellas and sandcastles of other bathers. Later, he would teach them how to write their names in the sand.

He would write EUGENE SACKS in letters four feet tall.

He would write CATHERINE SACKS.

He would write BENJAMIN SACKS.

He would write PHINEAS SACKS.

That was how Benjamin and Phinney learned how to write their names. They would copy their father's movements, drawing their names with their feet, and sometimes their father would write messages in the sand.

"It's for the planes passing by," he said. "There'll be jumbo jets going right over this piece of land, and hundreds of people will look down and read our messages."

He wrote LONG LIVE THE SACKSES!

He wrote THE AMAZING SACKS FLYING CIRCUS.

He wrote HAPPY BIRTHDAY, CATHERINE SACKS.

Phinney wrote HELLO GOD.

Benjamin wrote DO YOU LIKE THE ORIOLES?

Their father also played football with them on the beach. Phinney and Benjamin would put their hands on their knees before him, and they'd listen exquisitely as he designed plays in the sand, marking their paths with his toes.

He made a dent.

"This is you," he said, "Phinney."

"Oh."

He pressed his big toe in the sand again, leaving another pock, six inches from the first. "Benjamin, this one's you."

Benjamin nodded solemnly.

"Now, this is me," and their father ground his toe into the sand between the two dents. "Me, the quarterback."

"Are you Johnny Unitas?" Phinney asked. Johnny Unitas, the Colts quarterback, a crew-cutted hero.

"Mm hmm, I'm Johnny Unitas," he answered, then he pointed to Phinney. "Now, listen closely. When I say, 'Hike,' I want you to do this," he made a line from Phinney's mark to a point ten inches away, "then do this," and he made a right angle in the sand.

Phinney clapped his hands like a real football player.

"Now, Benjamin. Benjamin, are you listening?" Benjamin turned his attention from the sound of the waves to his father. His father stuck a finger out and held it there. "You do *this*," and, moving his toe from the mark, he made a capital *L*, the mirror image of Phinney's path. "Got it, Big Ben?"

Benjamin bobbed his head.

"I like this play," Phinney said. "It's very *symmetrical*."

Their father looked down at the marks in the sand. "That's a letter, isn't it?"

"An *L*," Phinney said, and their father shushed him.

"Benjamin, what letter is that? Come on. You can say it. We're your family. Your friends you can pick, but your family you're stuck with. Now, you can say it, can't you?"

Benjamin crossed his arms on his chest and said, "El," and his father winked and said, "Attaboy. That's my boy."

The three stood in a line—Benjamin, their father and Phinney in a row—and their father scooped the football from the sand.

"Ready?"

"We're not supposed to talk anymore," Phinney said, "once we get out of the huddle."

Their father called, "Hike!" and the boys ran, sand kicking up at their heels. They ran at nearly the same speed, and when they finished their *L*'s, they waved their arms.

"I'm open, Johnny," Phinney called. "I'm wide open."

Something about the ocean brought Benjamin back every summer after their parents were gone. It wasn't just habit, either. There was something about the ocean, he thought, how you could stand so close to something that scared you and enjoy its beauty at the same time. It was love and fear and the way they were forever entwined.

When Benjamin took Mary Jude to Ocean City, he did the same thing his father had done, writing messages in the sand with the heel of his foot to amuse her.

One year, he wrote 4 EVER 2 GETHER.

Another year, it was TE QUIERO. "I love you" in Spanish, and she'd said, "What? You know I don't understand Spanish."

Another, MARY JUDE SAYS, "FLY THE FRIENDLY SKIES."

Another year, she was quiet and dour on the drive out. She was wearing her rainbow-striped clam-digger pants, the ones that reached the midpoint of her calves, and she hardly spoke. She just read in her beach chair, turning the pages of *The World According to Garp,* and when she wasn't reading she was hugging herself as if she were cold, her knees pulled up to her chest, her feet on the edge of the seat, and her arms locked around her legs at the ankles.

Benjamin asked what the matter was, and she forced a smile and said, "I don't know. Maybe I'm going through menopause now. You'll thank me later. In about thirty years."

She was thinking of children and watching the ones playing in the surf. He could tell that was what she was thinking.

"No, really," she said, "I'll be fine. I'm just having one of those days. I just need some time to sit and think."

She tried to smile but failed, and Benjamin pushed his lips to her forehead.

"Where do you think Rosa is?" she asked. "My Little Sister?"

"Probably having fun with her family somewhere. Probably at the beach or eating ice cream somewhere."

"Probably."

"Look, sweetheart," Benjamin said, "what's the matter?"

"Nothing. Or everything." She rubbed at her ankle. "It's the everything taken as a whole."

"You're being obscure," he said, and he smiled and mussed her hair. "Mary Jude, the Obscure."

"Cute," she said, sarcastically. "That's very cute."

He apologized and put a serious look on his face. "I just don't know what you mean."

"I don't know anymore."

"Is this about the baby?" They'd come to speak about it as if it already existed. The baby. "If it's about the baby, there are a lot of women today who have fulfilling lives and don't have babies."

"You're imposing their values on me, Benjamin. You're imposing your values on me," she said. "Besides, it's not just the baby."

"It's you," she said.

"It's me," she said.

"It's the both of us," she said. "Everything would be different if things hadn't stayed the same."

The waves pounding on the shore made the noise of airplanes taking off. Benjamin rose, patted Mary Jude's hand and began to dig his heels into the sand. In four separate rows, running from Mary Jude's chair to the surf, he wrote

I CAN'T LOVE YOU
ANY MORE
THAN I
ALREADY DO.

Mary Jude pitched her head to the side and slanted her eyes to read it. She gave him a weak, crooked smile, and Benjamin sat beside her, holding her hand to his chest. She scratched at the hairs and went back to her reading, taking her hand back the first time she needed to turn the page. By four o'clock, the tide came further up the beach, and the message read

I CAN'T LOVE YOU
ANY MORE
THAN I

By four-thirty, it said

I CAN'T LOVE YOU

ANY MORE

By five-ten,

I CAN'T LOVE YOU

And by five-thirty, there was nothing. It was as if they'd never been there. Benjamin, who couldn't speak right, and Mary Jude, who couldn't hear. The ocean water had reached their chairs. It had poured in like a slow divorce.

Alphonse is darker than the night. Benjamin can see him, black all around, asleep by the window, his chin on his paw, when Benjamin drags the phone back to the living room. He had let the phone ring on and off for hours, and no one answered.

He returns to the bedroom, opening the door slowly and quietly, and he dresses in the dark.

He has to get out of the apartment. He has to go for a drive. He doesn't know where he'll go. He has to go *somewhere,* and he doesn't know how long he'll be gone. He'll come back when it's right to.

There's a certain absolute logic to it.

It's five in the morning, and the light from the liquor store sends thin rays into the room, stripes that cross the bed. Kim's back is to Benjamin. Her knees are pulled to her chest as she sleeps, tiny like a ball in the Big Sister T-shirt, the comforter at her ankles, and Benjamin pulls his pants on and leaves the comforter where it is. She might wake if he moved it.

Benjamin pays little attention to what he's wearing, and he picks up his shoes, steps over Kim's kimono and shoes, and moves to the living room, waiting until he's there to zip his pants. Phinney's sleeping on the couch, the blanket pulled up over his eyes, his legs bare and bent, hanging over the end like sausages.

Benjamin sits at the edge of the recliner and crosses his legs to pull his socks on, then he bends to slip his shoes on, using his index finger as a shoehorn. He ties the laces and pulls the wool overcoat from the closet, buttoning it to the neck as he leaves the apartment, closing the door without looking back. Herky-jerky, the elevator bounces toward the first floor. The old metal moans.

As he descends, he remembers what he'd heard in the men's room at Yumi's two nights before. Benjamin was leaning against the sink when he heard Terry ask Kim, "So, are you going to marry Mr. Bathroom?"

"Kimberly Bathroom," Shannon said. "It has a pleasant ring to it. Mrs. Kimberly Bathroom."

"*So?*" Terri said. "Yes or no?"

"I don't know what we're going to do," Kim said.

The elevator doors crawl open, and Benjamin leaves the apartment building with a certain immediacy in his step. It doesn't last long. It had snowed during the night, no more than a quarter inch, and the whiteness of the streets surprises Benjamin. The snow slows him down. He has to take the steps of the apartment building gingerly, and he walks down Eager Street to find his car, the snow crushed beneath his shoes. There's a milky moon still hanging in the sky. The wind pushes at his hair.

Puffs of breath leak from Benjamin's mouth like cigarette smoke, and he stuffs his hands in his pockets while he walks, his chin dug into his chest. A thin layer of snow covers all of the cars, so he looks for the license plate. He looks for HERS, and he finds the car parked across from the church, behind a blue van with HEY CULLIGAN MAN painted on the rear doors.

Benjamin pulls his bare hands from his pockets and haphazardly sweeps the snow from the windows. The snow leaves ice blotches on the windshield and a stinging feeling in Benjamin's fingers. He unlocks the door, straps on his seat belt, and turns the key in the ignition. The engine stutters. It doesn't turn over the first time, he has to depress and release the gas pedal over and over, pumping it like an organ pedal. The radio comes on when the engine finally turns over.

"Brrr. It's a cold one out there, all you Baltimorons," the man on the radio bellows, and Benjamin switches the radio off. When the engine is warm enough, he flicks the windshield wipers on to clear his view. He steers the car toward Charles Street. It jerks forward with the same abrupt movement as an ancient elevator, like the one in their apartment building. The car stops and starts. It chugs beneath Benjamin. It doesn't want to go, but it does.

The needle of the gas gauge still points to full.

Benjamin doesn't know if he's headed toward New York or Bluefield or someplace else, someplace new. Benjamin's out of the question—Benjamin, Indiana. It's too far and too familiar. He doesn't know if he's going to see Mrs. Van Devere, or Earl, or Mary Jude, or no one at all. He'll go where his mind takes him, where it wants him to be, and stop for gas when he needs to. Please, God, he thinks, take care of me. Please, he thinks, help me do something right.

And he feels the creek, pulling at him.

The traffic light's yellow when he reaches the intersection of Eager and Howard. Benjamin pulls the car to a stop and waits patiently, though there's no traffic on Howard. He waits at the intersection, two blocks from Charles, and thinks about how different Baltimore looks at this time of morning, dark and covered with snow. It's a city that contradicts itself. It looks old and new at the same moment, full and empty.

He thinks of Mary Jude in the bathroom, coloring his hair.

He thinks of holding Mary Jude in the hospital bed in New York.

He thinks of how Kim hates to sleep alone in Baltimore.

He thinks of Kim on his birthday. Not the evening, when he discovered the creek, but the morning, a box wrapped in silver foil on the recliner as he put his suit jacket on for work.

"Can I open it now?" he asked.

"Later," she said, "after dinner."

"What is it?"

"Shh," she said, and she put a finger to his lips. "Don't be so curious. Remember, curiosity killed the bat."

"*Cat*," Benjamin said. "Curiosity killed the *cat*."

She put a hand over her chest and looked horrified. "It killed the cat, too?" She knew. She always knew, and when he opened the box, and tried on the blue jeans that were inside, they fit perfectly. She'd measured him in the night, she explained, while he was sleeping.

The creek is pulling at him. It's running high.

He thinks of Kim on the drive to Nebraska. "It's like the sun's always following us," she said, and he'd thought it was more like they were racing the sun, trying to stay ahead of it and losing each day. Each day it caught up with them.

He thinks of the comforter lying like a dog at Kim's feet.

The light changes to green, and Benjamin continues to Charles Street and makes his turn there, headed north. There's only a single pair of tire tracks on the road, and Benjamin follows them, passing the Rite Aid drugstore where he has his prescription filled, driving twenty-five miles per hour, his car slipping as he does. Most of the traffic lights turn yellow as he approaches them. He can't avoid the yellow lights. Between them and the snow, it's a slow trip past the train station and the Chesapeake Restaurant, the Charles Theatre, the Little Tavern hamburger stand, Johns Hopkins University, then Loyola College, then streets lined with white trees and houses until at last he reaches Route 695.

When he pulls the car onto the highway, the road is black. It winds through the snow, turning like a ribbon of black molasses.

Benjamin drives off the exit ramp five miles down the road, in Lutherville. Trucks storm past him on the highway, rumbling. He directs the car over the overpass and back onto the highway, headed in the opposite direction.

He heads home, and when he returns, he parks the car in the same space in front of the church. There's a black rectangle of pavement there where his car had been.

I'm ashamed of myself, he thinks, and of my selfishness.

Leaving is a selfish thing to do, he thinks, to leave her alone. I have to help her. She needs me to help her.

He climbs the stairs outside the apartment building, stepping heavily, as if her were stomping on a paper cup, to free the snow from his shoes, then rides the elevator to their floor. He turns his key in the lock as slowly as he can so the click is nearly soundless.

Alphonse is awake and crawling on his belly like a worm. He stops at Benjamin's feet, and Benjamin crouches to pat him. With a dog, it's more like a home now.

Benjamin steps out of his shoes and leaves them by the door to dry, and he drapes his coat over the recliner. In his stocking feet, he passes his brother and walks back to the bedroom.

And now I want to help her.

I need her to help me, too.

Kim's asleep in the same position, a ball, and Benjamin climbs into bed on his knees, still dressed. She rubs her face and mumbles something when the mattress bounces slightly under Benjamin's weight, though Benjamin doesn't know what she's said.

The creek tugs at him.

He reaches down to pull the comforter up, covering both of them, and he slips closer to her, inching his way until his hand is at her hip. He listens to her breathe in and out through her mouth. When she turns toward him, she stretches her legs flat beneath the covers and puts her arm around his shoulder, mindlessly.

Again she mutters something. In her sleep, she mutters, "Mmmm, go to sleep, honey. I love you."

Benjamin turns his head and rests it on Kim's chest. His ear is pressed against the cotton of her T-shirt and he listens to her breathe, he listens to the beating of her heart beneath the shirt. He listens to it as if it were a voice, telling him everything there is to know about her.

The creek pulls at him, and he feels himself go under three times, but only comes up twice. Without flailing, he submits, the creek rushing over him, engulfing him, and when he's under completely, he continues to sink, dropping slowly, a speed slower than gravity, falling farther and farther into Kim, feeling warmer by the second, and it isn't until this moment that he sees how deep the creek is, deep enough to hold him forever.

The thumping of her heart sounds in Benjamin's ear, and he shuts his eyes to return to sleep, keeping his heard upon her chest.

He imagines himself on the beach with Kim. She's wearing a one-piece bathing suit and sitting in a lounge chair. The scar sneaks through the top of the bathing suit. She's holding a small blond girl on her lap, and the girl's in a bathing suit, too. Kim passes the girl with his hands about her tiny waist, and the girl laughs just as Kim does. They both laugh Kim's hiccup of a laugh.

She's going to be my wife someday, Benjamin thinks, Mrs. Kimberly Bathroom, and the snow starts up again, though he can't see it. It falls like ticker tape past their window, landing without a sound.

Tomorrow, everything begins again, he thinks.

Tomorrow, we get rid of the Maybelline.

Tomorrow, I start to give her time.

At seven o'clock, when the alarm buzzes, Kim's already out of bed and in the kitchen. Benjamin can hear her voice, and Phinney's, and he walks to join them, still dressed in his shirt and slacks. They're only slightly wrinkled, creased at odd angles on his thighs and his shirt-sleeves.

Benjamin smiles at Kim and pulls a chair out to sit across from her. There's snow dropping outside the kitchen window and a steaming cup of coffee in front of his chair already.

"I thought it'd cool down by the time you got here, sweetie," she says, and Benjamin feels himself smile again, as if the corners of his mouth were being pulled by tiny guy wires. He stares down at the cup, straight through the table, down to the kitchen floor. He thinks he can see their feet touching there.

And when he lifts his head to look at her again, a ray of sunlight slips through the dotted sky and into the kitchen. It turns her face to gold.